Peter Wells, born in Auckland in 1950, is a prize-winning author and film-maker. His memoir, *Long Loop Home*, won the 2002 Montana New Zealand Book Award for Biography. He conceived and set about writing *Iridescence* as the Inaugural Randell Cottage Writer in Residence in Wellington.

Iridescence
Peter Wells

V
VINTAGE

The assistance of Creative New Zealand is
gratefully acknowledged by the publishers.

National Library of New Zealand Cataloguing-in-Publication Data

Wells, Peter, 1950-
Iridescence / Peter Wells.
ISBN 1-86941-583-3
NZ823.2—dc 21

A VINTAGE BOOK
published by
Random House New Zealand
18 Poland Road, Glenfield, Auckland, New Zealand
www.randomhouse.co.nz

First published 2003

© 2003 Peter Wells

ISBN 1 86941 583 3

The moral rights of the author have been asserted.
Cover: original photograph by Adrienne Martyn.
Vienna Bon-Bon, a dress designed by Peggy Wilson.
Courtesy of the Collection of the Hawke's Bay Cultural Trust.
Cover design: Adam Sheffield
Text design: Elin Termannsen and Janet Hunt
Author photo: Amanda Dorcil
Steel engraving of Boulton and Park on page 458 — Mansell Collection, Timepix
Printed in Australia by Griffin Press

Contents

To Sally, who was an inspiration.

Book One

'I must take you back to the scene of the fire, and try to make you understand how delightful it was.'

Station Amusements, Lady Barker

A Poetic
Promenade

*H*e listened.

There was a creak. Then a souring laugh, which could have been the wind between the wafer-thin walls, or a draught lifting the shingles on the roof.

He listened again, concentrating.

He seemed, in that tiny, darkened bedroom, to be indivisible from shadow, so still as to have melded to the iron bedstead draped in a length of shimmering Japanese silk; or to have fragmented into the green leaves patterned into a bosky trellis all over the papered walls. It was the master bedroom of a worker's cottage. There was a pool of light darkening, deepening what was a mirror. On either side of it, in an elegant arrangement, steel engravings were cut out from a newspaper and pinned to the wall.

One was a view of the proscenium arch of the Strand Theatre, London. A row of smartly dressed people was held rapt by whatever was happening on stage. The stage itself was intimated by sparks of light — as if from a dazzling source. The wording read: *A View of Modern Babylon.*

The other steel engraving was of two actresses, both with seemingly identical heart-shaped faces. They were hugely doe-eyed, with tiny cupid's mouths curved into enigmatic smiles of desire. One — Miss Fanny Clinton — appeared to be blonde, vastly ringletted, with a miniature ship of a hat tossed atop the sea of her coiffure. The other, Mrs Stella Graham, was glossily dark-haired, her eyes possibly even brown. Her hat seemed to end on an apostrophe of absurdity above her slightly monstrous hairdo. Each woman looked down modestly to gloved hands that held a fan on which was written, cursively, her name.

Samuel Barton detached his gaze, heard his own breath emerge, crinkly and crackly in the still air. He could see dust motes. Floating in a scurf of light that dared to come in through a crack in the drapes. He had just put down the bottle. Recklessly, at the last moment, he had needed to sate his thirst.

Or was it quiet his nerves?

He knew she was out there. Waiting.

His eye shifted to the window. Should he pluck aside the heavy brown drapes and slide the window up? The sound of the lead weights beating against dry wood would announce him. Besides, gentlemen — even gentlemen in difficult circumstances — didn't really climb out of windows.

He tried, delicately, to turn the wooden door handle around. It coasted for a second, silently, then struck an impediment. There was a long slow creak, as of a floorboard when someone's weight was shifting. He held still, door handle clasped in his hand. The brandy was enriching his system, warming him, returning him to that familiar state of easy confidence. Then, recklessly, because he could wait no longer, he edged the tongue out of the latch-plate and pulled the door back.

Hetty Haresnape stood there. Looking directly at him.

She said nothing. Even though she had had to train herself *not* to curtsy, *not* to bob, *not* to obey all the old instinctive rules that were still stayed inside her head. Jack's as good as his master here, she told herself, almost fiercely, under her breath.

'Oh, Mrs Haresnape.' Samuel whirled around in the tiny, dirty passageway. Both front and back doors were open, so the passage seemed nothing more than a hole between two mud patches: one with washing blowing in the wind. Hetty was standing there with another load clamped under her arm. She was breathing a little too heavily. Susie hung on the bottom of her heavy tweed skirt, snot growing green out of her nose as she stared up at the strange foreign mister who kept to his room, who seemed at times weirdly out of place — like someone tossed out of a fairy story, come grievously awake.

'Oh dear,' he said, and took a step back. 'I'm sorry.'

'It's a fortnight overdue, Mr Barton.'

'I'm off to check the mail. I'm sure, I'm positive . . .'

Samuel tried to sound convinced.

Hetty sighed.

'Well, sir, I'm afraid I'll have to let the room to other parties if you don't . . . if you can't . . .'

Samuel flushed a painful colour. Hetty looked into his too-thin, ravaged face: he was a young man not even in his thirties. Yet there was something a little too old about him, something subtly cracked as if some great weight had come to fall upon him. He was dressed, she saw, in his second-best: the once-rich blacks growing a little green around the lapels, the battered jacket, the check trousers dirty round the cuffs: the once beautifully white shirt now rumpled, unironed. He no longer wore the garnet studs. He looked as if he had not slept well, his fine brown hair a whirl of self-disgust upon his head.

'I give you my word,' he said, backing away from her, turning into a slim silhouette against the light that blitzed into him, ate into his being.

'I've had your word before, Mr Barton, sir. I'm afraid,' Hetty drew her breath in, 'it's either pay up by three p.m. today or you're *out*.'

He did not listen, tried not to hear as the dirty little cur from two along zigzagged towards him, sniffed around his ankles.

'Good Gertie,' he said to the little bitch, which he knew had pupped only a week or so ago. She was a terrier cross and had anxious, wounded eyes. Her pups had disappeared: drowned. Now she followed behind him, sniffing, smelling, seeking some other smell that sent her away, half crazed.

Samuel Barton was aware he was being watched, judged, weighed and found wanting. His tongue. If he could only pluck out his tongue. Or talk as they did — the Haresnapes and their neighbours. They all shared a medley of accents accrued from the dim and distant parishes of rural England: curlicued and barbed, slurred and sloven. Hardly anyone in that part of Napier had his voice: his sharpened accent, which had obdurately and alone refused to break down in the mud and dust and stink of those unpaved roads.

His London shoes stirred up the dust. He gazed down at them, dreaming of the day they had first been slid onto his feet. Freddie had been there, bored, yawning, attentive, too close. Jingling golden sovereigns in his pockets. Deep dark pockets. Warm. His pale white hands heavily signeted with gold. White cuffs. Brilliant white. Black kid sliding onto Samuel's feet: the most expensive shoes, tight-fitting, narrowing into a cove over his toes, subtly raising him up an inch-high heel so his back was thrown straight, his stomach tautened. *A fine figure of a man*, Freddie had said, not even laughing, though Samuel knew it was a joke.

Now, down the end of his being, at the antipodean pole of his self, his shoes were ruined. The elegant sole had corrugated apart in a gaping hole. There were cuts and slashes on the once mirror-black leather. The laces too had broken, been tied, then retied with a thin brown string of leather. He had tried, arduously, to polish them — he who had never polished shoes. He was astounded at the level of labour. He had grown exhausted, lost heart. He thought: *I don't care any longer*. The shoes fell out of his fingers. He felt suddenly exhausted. Again. That pole-axing exhaustion that had overcome him ever since.

Ever since the ever since.

This was his mental telegraph to himself. He never referred to it as anything else. As if to think of it was to place himself back there. He could not trust. He did not allow. He would not survive.

This now was his existence.

This strolling along, in a broad, too dusty daylight, along 'Carlyle Road'. How confusing it had been when he first arrived. No nameplates on the streets. As if everyone there had a map inside their heads. Inimical to strangers. As if nameplates were an extravagance, one the plain people disdained. They who had lived there for years, it seemed.

'It's down Carlyle,' one had said, pointing a knobbly digit southwards. 'You can't miss it. Follow your nose.'

Crudely laughed.

This was when he had first arrived, with his carpetbag, looking for somewhere to . . . hide?

He had got used to streets that petered out into swamp, or simply ended, exhausted, as if the idea had been too daring. Streets daubed in the names of poets — Spencer, Shakespeare, Tennyson — named by the Reverend William Tye, who had said, sniffily, that he did not want the local convicts naming the streets after themselves.

Poetry raised the tone of things.

Or tried to.

A rush of pigs came towards him. Brindle-haired, obscenely pink, their cunning little eyes flickering up at him. Then ignoring him. A herd of swine was superior to him. A single one, hesitating, swung its snout towards him, saying emphatically, implying: *I have more reality than you. I belong here more than you, Samuel Barton, fallen gent.*

*H*e had earlier taken his second-best shoes out of the wardrobe. He had felt down within them. At the toe-end was a small canvas-wrapped package. How many times had he felt for this? How many times, in scalp-pricking panic, in a maze of drink or near despair, had his fingers probed the shoe and, finding the small package there, felt . . . hope? Some kind of security? That late morning he had — finally — withdrawn the small package. Laid it on his palm. He had inspected the faded scarlet linen threads that held it captive. He had tossed its weight, contemplatively. It felt appreciably heavy.

He had withdrawn his secret, then placed it in the left-hand inside pocket of his jacket. He had patted the bulge, placed his second-best shoes back.

He had made his decision. It was time.

*T*he brandy was leaving his blood. The tot he had taken to get his nerve up. To slip out the door. To try to escape the demon Haresnape.

'Airs and graces is all very fine back in the *old place*,' he'd overheard her mumbling to Susie, 'but *out here* they disappear into *thin* air.'

She despised him — his inactivity, his staying in his room. The unpulled curtains. The way he would not let her in to 'do' the room. She despised his disorder, as well as the daintiness of the pictures on the wall.

She despised everything he stood for. He had come to understand this.

Their very conversation was a clash of accents, with her plain voice riding his down like baying hounds.

He was escaping.

Taking a stroll 'up-town'. Past the undertakers ('Furnished with Greatest Economy & Respectability'), the cabinetmaker helpfully next door, the carpet warehouse ('Brussels, Kidderminster, Linoleum etc'); the bricklayer and mason ('Asphalting done in a workmanlike manner as per'), the NZ Loan and Mercantile ('The Company will Take Risk on Wool, and All Kinds of Merchandise on Land & Sea').

He was escaping the hustle and bustle of signs for the more absolute emptiness of sea. The promise of an empty horizon, on which he could lay his thoughts.

It was a brilliant arc of sunlight now. Ten minutes to eleven, he noted by his watch. Or rather, the workaday watch that had replaced his watch. This was one serviceably run up in distant Birmingham, a stout watch such as ticked in distant jungles, on prairies, in rackety goldmining towns, in noisy city streets that smelt too closely of the abattoir — a resounding ticking sound as if it were the whirring mechanical heart of the Empire.

It was a beautiful freak of a winter's day.

He might have been on the Riviera if . . .

If.

He would not go there.

Samuel placed on his head his straw hat with the Cambridge blue ribbon. He had kept the hat through thick and thin. It had a kind of forlorn yet elemental elegance. Low-crowned, wide-brimmed, a once rich and buttery straw. Now battered. But it shaded him, accompanied him. Protected him.

Or didn't.

He who had tried to escape.

He who had got upon a boat, lost his old self, he believed. He who had tried to exchange a self he could no longer afford. He who had run. He who was chased.

Not by the law, not by any crime — but by memory itself.

*T*his is what had happened.

He had lined up, naked, with the other men. They were labourers, from parishes of ruined villages all around Southern England. They had lines of red along their burly arms. Necks cragged. He was white all over, whiter than a page. They had inspected him, his whiteness, then looked right through him. They were all hungry, those men, those labourers. They were hungry for another way of life, for difference. They wanted change, and this too-white freak among them they could overlook. It was unlikely he could challenge them in terms of labour. They were labourers looking for an escape. He was a gentleman fleeing, unaccountably without money or — stranger than this in the old country — without connections.

He had seen the poster advertising for labourers to come to New Zealand. This was when he was in hiding. He had simply run. Taken flight. Caught a train. Any train. He was drunk. With disaster. He had ended up in Southampton. He had been walking past a railway station. He saw the poster.

He had gone in. Had his medical.

He had been, unaccountably yet gloriously, chosen.

At this lowest moment of his life, he had been given a chance.

The doctor, examining, had spoken to him sparsely. It was a tiring day: long queues of men, an unsubtle smell of desperation.

Samuel had said very little. He knew his voice would betray him. He simply said he needed to go somewhere new.

The doctor listened to his voice, looked at him intently. The doctor said: the work will be hard.

He said: I will work hard.

Without knowing what it meant.

And when he was accepted he had written to his brother.

'You need worry about me no longer. I will disappear.' He did not say 'forever'. There was no need to.

His brother had insisted on a final meeting. He had sent, in an envelope, a single pound note for the journey. Samuel had returned to London.

He could remember that final interview. It had taken place in his brother's trading office in Liverpool Street, after hours. Nobody else was around. His brother had let Samuel in, first of all looking out into the street. As if meeting him were tainting.

Once he, Samuel, had disdained the office with its single row of ledgers, linoleum on the floor, and picture of St Matthew, lamp in hand, hesitating before the door. But now it comforted him. He felt he was back, briefly. But as a visitor.

His brother had said how shocked he was. The family were. His mother. Plunged into grief. She was now an old woman, she who was only fifty-two. Her life ended by the shame. He must go. As far away as possible.

Though pressed with a young family himself, he would help. In whatever way he could. Between him and his mother they would sacrifice. His mother would come and live with him, so a payment would arrive. Once a month.

Five pounds, two shillings and — a pause — *sixpence*.

It was the sixpence that hurt. Its specificity. As if he, Samuel, were some maid or servant being pensioned off, got rid of with the loose change. He had felt a swell of anger. He had wanted to cry out loud: *I won't take it.* He longed to say, in a heated voice, *have you forgotten it was me our mother always loved? You will never be loved, dear brother.* Instead he looked into the chilly greyness of his brother's pupils.

'I'm sorry.' His brother had faltered as he stood up. 'But my dear wife and I ... we can only . . .' There was a faint blush down his features. Samuel thought of his brother's pudgy wife with her mercantile forebears. Her lovely plush income rolling in from the grubby north.

His brother was standing.

Samuel, who was midway through his glass of port, and feeling only at that moment an unthawing, realised he was being asked to leave. Forsaken.

This is the pattern of my life now, he thought to himself subliminally. Being asked to leave. Either politely, as now, or expressly.

He rose to his feet. He wanted to say: I will never see you again. But he saw, too quickly, the relief in his brother's face. He knew his brother would talk to his mother, to his wife, in terms of lost sheep, while letting him disappear to that land of merinos, ewes and rams.

His brother at the last grasped hold of him, pulled him into himself and held him tightly. As if he might like to pull the breath out of him. Samuel remembered, briefly, another brother, an earlier one who had loved him. But now his older, tired brother was pulling himself away, humphing to himself as if congratulating himself that he could still feel.

'Here.' He was feeling in his sovereign case. Samuel watched him slide out three sovereigns, then subtly try to slide one back. His brother was aware that Samuel saw this. But he still slid the third sovereign back.

Samuel did not want to take the gold but he found his hand rising to take it. He felt a terrible blank fear overtake him.

His brother walked him to the door.

When Samuel tried to say something, his brother raised his hand to his own mouth as if to indicate that the situation was so deeply emotional it would be better if nothing more were said.

The door closed behind him.

And that was it.

*S*amuel walked past the draper's window: Towne & Neale ('Men's Boy's Ladies' Wearing Apparel Too Numerous To Mention').

He had once placed his card in the window. 'Pianoforte, voice and song.'

His name looked better in the folderol of print. More real. It took him quite some weeks to understand that the town was overloaded with the needy genteel. Nobody had time to sing, to play the pianoforte. Or at least there were so few of them, the competition for pupils was fierce, even bitter. He had been accosted by a sallow Miss Perrett, who had nodded her bonnet, and asked him, sharply, where he came from. Searching all the time for his antecedents, his family, his connections.

Since his name was no longer his own, he could only prevaricate. She had a triumphant flare in her nostrils as she shook open her umbrella. It was raining hard that day. She was wearing walking boots, stout, mud-encrusted on the sole. She had walked, he saw. While her top half paid homage to gentility. A striped calico dress fussed into a bustle of sorts, red gloves, and something red in the bonnet tipped improbably towards the front of her head. The fashion, he observed, was at least five years out of date.

As if sensing his scrutiny she had hissed at him, 'It is dreadful here, dreadful.'

He understood, via Hetty later, that Miss Perrett had an invalid mother and a brother who drank. Her gentility was floating out to sea, sinking all around her. She needed, depended utterly upon, her few pupils.

This was all conducted in the street, where she had accosted him boldly. She had introduced herself, then drawn him towards a shop window. Their entire conversation was passed, covertly, looking in at a range of boots, above which was ranged an enfilade of enamel pots. To the side, almost armorially placed, tomahawks, and then, in splendid lettering: *Just arrived: 250 head well-bred quiet cattle. 20 Cows and Calves (broken in). No Reserve. Sale at 11.30 a.m. sharp.*

'See!' she almost hissed to him again. He saw she had long, strong teeth, faintly yellow, with a sizeable gap between the two front teeth. She had a rank, fierce sexuality of which she seemed unaware.

'See!' she said, and threw a red-mittened hand towards the window. As if to say, This is the world we find ourselves in now, sir. Not that of dear Mr Schumann or dear Mr Brahms.

She had laughed a little convulsively. Then stared into his white face, looking suddenly thoughtful.

'I hope you understand. It is not maliciously meant. I just want to warn you, sir. Not to get your hopes . . .'

'My hopes!' he said and coughed. She looked a little shocked. She glanced behind her, to two labourers walking along, one wheeling a barrow filled with rude clay. The clay had the smell of ordure in it. Her nose wrinkled up, she trailed her striped calico away. Restlessly she opened and closed her umbrella.

'I would not like you to think . . .' she tailed off.

She noted he was hardly paying attention. His eyes were following the two workmen as they walked away.

'How much are they paid?' he had asked instead.

'Oh,' Miss Perrett coloured. 'You'd be surprised at *their* wages. There's a need, you see, in this place for the ruder skills. If I had understood, before I left . . .' And she sighed. Once more, but as if finally, she allowed her umbrella to rise.

'I would not like you to think us quite without culture, Mr . . . Mr . . .'

'Barton.' Samuel smoothly provided his name.

'We have many . . . many clubs, associations. Oh, there's a need, a terrible need for lacing over our emptiness, stitching in a name here and there. The Napier Artillery

Volunteers, the Napier Inter-club Regatta, the Debating Society, the Dramatic Society of the Working Men's Club and . . . have I mentioned our marvellous Athenaeum?'

Samuel stood waiting. He shook his head slowly, as if caught in the updraught of her wild enthusiasm. He whose only hope was to be alone.

'Sir, I would not like to be thought bold.' She coloured, spoke in a low voice. 'But at the Athenaeum you can find, *free of charge*, any of the latest magazines — *The Pall Mall Gazette*, *The Nineteenth Century*, *The Westminster Review*.'

She looked momentarily triumphant. Then, 'Well, when I say latest, of course, I count the ninety days in between our dear old country and *this* . . .'

She left an appalled silence.

' . . . this dear wee spot,' she finished satirically. She shook her umbrella, as if deciding it was time to set off into the fine gauzy drifts. 'Good day, Mr Barton. I'm sure we'll see each other again.'

There was, about her farewell, the tartness of a threat.

*H*e had arrived in Napier by mistake. He had been driven there, as if by some internal storm. The boat had delivered him to the port of Wellington. He at last felt almost safe. He was walking along a pavemented street, which heaved with the roll of an invisible sea. Then he had heard someone call his name. He had not turned around immediately. He had felt himself go pale, his body seize up. Fear stoked up his nostrils. It is a delusion, he thought. But a hand — yes, a hand — was laid upon his shoulder and he was spun round to face the glinting happiness of — *who*?

'Why it's me, Will Alredy! Surprised to see me here?' the stranger cried. Through his fear, he — 'Samuel' — saw the man in front of him morph back into a younger, more hesitant self. A face, really, at the back of the crowd at The Strand, the person who could always be relied upon to laugh at a joke — and, at inconvenient moments, to pay a rashly run-up bill.

Will was thicker now, coarser, more deeply embedded in himself. Some alchemic change had happened, Samuel saw. A couple with him, a rather diffident man and a woman in an impossible dress, had drawn to the side. Samuel glanced around to see if there was anybody from the ship nearby.

Nobody. He forced himself to rinse away his fear. He could sense, almost feel, Will's eyes sliding down his body, taking in the dimmed state of his elegance. But Will's abrupt, swinging glance seemed to intimate that it no longer mattered.

'*You're — here* !' Will called out, as if it were a magic trick.

'Oh yes, I'm here all right,' Samuel had replied.

'We must meet! Oh, the fun!' Will seemed to be gasping for breath. He began to speak in high theatrical tones:

> I see that you a passion for me foster,
>
> Passion for you? High, Mighty Double Gloucester.
>
> Oh call me Double Gloucester if you please,
>
> So long as I am, in your eyes, the cheese . . .

He burst into laughter at his incomparable wit. His face flushed an unbecoming purple. His hairiness seemed to expand, somehow.

'Simon, Lucinda! Come!'

The diffident couple came nearer.

The woman was wearing, Samuel noted, a pale grey faux-silk edged with an amethyst fringing. The whole effect was too emphatic, too furbeloved. Around them working men and women, children, animals and dogs. A horse nearby, as if sensing something contumely, arched its plumy tail and slithered out a glittering rope of shit.

The lady called Lucinda bridled and tried to turn her back on the mess.

'This is . . . oh this is a *dearest, dearest* chum,' alleged Will Alredy. He effected the introductions. The diffident couple bowed. Samuel bowed. He tried not to see what they were so capably and smoothly overlooking: the dusty state of his dress, his somewhat wrecked looks. Will was, annoyingly, singing his praises to the very skies, as if to cover over. That sharp, intense look from the hard-faced Lucinda. She could smell the stench of poverty.

'Oh, this is a grand place for the man who wants to work,' Will was saying to him idiotically. Running on while he, the man now called Samuel, was waiting for it all to end. This nightmare. So he could back away.

'You knew him from . . . ?' Lucinda was saying, inspecting the tiny pearly buttons on the back of her glove. The stink of ordure was quite powerful now. Perhaps the wind had changed. They were stopping the flow of passers-by on the footpath.

Will had tried to nuzzle them into a shop doorway: it was the rather formal and brassy one of an insurance office. From inside a frock-coated old man looked up at them, then, assessing them, returned to the document he was perusing.

'Oh that would be confessing!' Will too gaily called. Then, 'You'll have to come up! Oh tonight! Tonight! To have a sing-along! And we're having . . .'

Samuel was not listening. He was aware only of the pale grey eyes of Lucinda stealing all over his body, unclasping his new identity, stealing his new-found confidence. Will, he knew, would be easy to elude. Pompous fool.

'. . . pianoforte. A tremendous thumping of the keys, eh?'

'Indeed,' the gentleman called Simon said, leaning out of the doorway and looking at what appeared a more pleasing vista. Elsewhere. The lady called Lucinda swept her skirts slightly to the side.

Will was writing out the address on a card.

'Big wooden place. Up Tinakori Road. Can't miss it. Don't bother with the maid. Just bung the old bell and bowl on in. This is the New World!'

Samuel unclasped himself from Will's fervent grasp. He bowed to the cold couple who returned his bow with a slighter, more formal acknowledgement that they would be pleased never to see him again.

Samuel fled.

He went back to the boat, where his trunk had just been unloaded. He found . . . he found the first boat out. It could have been almost anywhere. But there was a barque leaving for a place he had never heard of. It was leaving within the hour. He could afford the fare. It would only take one night. And so, in a fever of deliverance, a panic attack, a fright, he had arrived in Napier.

*H*e took a right-hand turn at the corner of Carlyle and crossed along Dalton to reach Tennyson Street. This street boasted half a side of wooden footpath. Dusty, of course, and now striated with veranda shade. It was hot in the sun. The antipodean sun had a fierceness, a lack of mercy, even in winter. Samuel's boots echoed on the raised wooden platform.

Down through the slits he sensed something moving: a rat perhaps?

He was beating his way towards a particular shop.

He passed a grand array of upturned cow corpses hung on hooks. Samuel slid his glance away from a hook sunk into a severed neck. The heavy bass stench of blood. Flies.

A horse across the road, tethered to a post, bridled, tried to turn sideways, then returned to stillness.

It was all so still. As if nobody but himself were alive. And that butcher man, one eye-socket empty, who was just turning his other eye to look upon him, cleaver raised in half salute. Samuel nodded quickly.

That moment, that apprehension, that frightening sensation of silence and stillness fractured all around him.

A child rushed along, pushing a clattering iron hoop. First one horsecab, then another, then three horse cabs circled to a halt in front of the post office. The men were calling to each other, joking. Somewhere a hammer took up, and, as if in reply, there was a cacophony of hammers driving nails into wood.

'Oh, begging your pardon, sir.'

He did exist.

It was a man squatting on his haunches on the footpath. He was looking down a crack in the wood.

'I've dropped . . .'

The man had an American accent. He turned a frankly exasperated stare up at Samuel. He was trying to feel down through the cracks, but his rather too large hand couldn't fit.

'I've dropped my eyeglass.'

The man emanated a slight smell of something Samuel could not quite place. His broad back was held in an emphatic plaid jacket. As he leant down, the fob on his watch-chain jingled.

Samuel's fingers, sweating lightly, stole inside his jacket. He felt . . . his world went dark for a moment. It was as if he were viewing the world through a black mirror — but yes, there it was, the precious cargo. It had simply dislodged itself down the side of his pocket.

'Can I help?'

The older man made way. Samuel tried to fit his slimmer hand down the crack. Down there he could see the lens. It was lying, glinting, on a soft bed of clay dust. There was something else down there — a dried corpse of what looked like a sparrow. Small claws upturned. Whitened. He shuddered.

'Give us a go, sir!' They both looked up into the face of a boy, confident yet weasely. 'I'll do it for nothing.' Then, on a more venal note: 'What you lost?'

An elderly woman's skirts came into view, clay-speckled. A pair of workaday boots. Nails worn through, glinting.

His fingers almost —

'Give us a go! Give us a go!' the boy was chanting.

'Young Jimmy McSweeney, I'll give you more than a go unless you have better manners for the gentleman!'

This was the older woman. She put down a basket in which Samuel could see some potatoes — fresh dirt clinging to them, a bottle of liniment and a neatly folded newspaper, dated 4 September 1872.

Samuel got up from his knees, dusted himself down. 'Look, I'm sorry —'

'No, indeed. Many thanks, sir. Perhaps the lad —'

The boy was immediately crouching, face glinting with professional pride as he felt down through the crack.

'I'll get it. I'll be damned if I don't,' the boy said.

As Samuel walked off, he heard behind him a sharp, reproving slap.

*I*nside the shop all was stillness. There was a long counter of wood, and behind it, in cases, a glittering array of rings, brooches, watch chains, watches, necklaces — even, more fancifully, aigrettes.

There was a run of rather dusty carpet along the floor, and in the middle of the ceiling, between two slowly whirling fans, an attempt at a chandelier — metal. Standing by the public side of the counter was a rather awkward young man. He was got up in a high collar with a showy cravat. It was clearly his Sunday best. The cravat, Samuel saw at a glance, had a cat's eye mounted in a braid of silver. The young man had over-exaggerated cuffs, which went with the roll of auburn hair on his head. He turned and glanced at Samuel, who halted.

On a piece of maroon velvet lay a scattering of rather humble rings.

Engagement rings, Samuel thought. The tiniest winkling of semi-precious stone, a dim twinkling of garnet. The young man — possibly a groom or upper servant — held in his hand a ring of amethyst and pearl.

The jeweller was saying in a deep, still voice, 'The young lady herself, sir, perhaps might like to venture an opinion?'

The groom looked thoughtful.

'You said it was five pounds?'

'Exactly sir. Though if that price is inconvenient we could, of course, come to some arrangement. Perhaps . . .?'

At this the jeweller glanced towards Samuel, who was back-lit. Behind him fizzed a brilliant square of light, intruding into the doorwell, burning itself into the knobbly, slightly worn carpet. Samuel realised his advantage. He took his time to look at the jeweller, Mr Linz.

Mr Linz had an intensely watchful face. He was saturnine in colouring and not unhandsome, though he was bald, as if hair had no place on his dome, which was elegantly egg-shaped and so shiny it seemed to have been polished to a point of philosophical brilliance. Yet if he was bald, he also appeared to be hirsute: his cheeks and jaw were closely shaven. His eyes were large, moist and, though heavily hooded, both watchful and sad.

'I will be but one moment, sir,' said the Jew.

Samuel realised that Mr Linz's features could rearrange themselves with great mobility: he now appeared quite happy.

'This is the ring . . . for my Betsy,' the young man said in a swerve towards decision.

He held out the amethyst and pearl. 'I'll bring in my ... my ...' he stumbled.

'Your young lady?'

'My fiancée,' the young man said, as if running the unused words within his mouth, getting them used to his tongue. Samuel felt for the young man, and would have liked to offer him some protection. But knew he had none. Himself.

There was a moment of a pen scratching across paper. The subtle sounds of money being exchanged. Linz's voice was soothing and placating, as if lulling the young man into a sense of peace: until finally the money, or whatever part of it was being handed over, passed into Mr Linz's clasp. At which point it seemed to disappear like magic.

The young man, now overcome with gratitude, was embossing a showy farewell, all bows, thanks and repeated thanks.

Mr Linz walked him towards the door, shook his hand, and finally the sound of the young man's boots faded across wood.

*S*amuel's hand placed his package down on the scarlet velvet. Mr Linz, magician-like, had first flickered the velvet in the air, removing any errant specks of dust. His supple brown hands, completely without rings, smoothed the cloth. Now, with a decorous gesture, he indicated that Samuel himself should undo his parcel.

Mr Linz, shokhet for the nineteen Jews who lived in Napier, knew how to disassemble a body with a minimum of waste. He knew a good cut at a glance, and knew how to drain away blood so it left a minimum of mess. In a larger town these religious duties might have sufficed — would have sufficed. But in a smaller place like Napier all men, all women, had to turn their hands to anything that could keep them afloat. From a watch repairman, he had become a jeweller — one of three in the small town.

He watched, without expression, the not-so-young man unpick the threads. He could tell that the package had been long and securely tied. There was dirt, grease and a scumbled layer of usage on the canvas. The young man's hands were trembling. They were a gentleman's hands, Linz could see at a glance. The nails were overlong, which he did not like. Gothic-narrow. Flesh as white as cooked flounder.

Finally the thread was undone. The canvas was pulled back and —

His first instinct was to look towards the door. The light was burning there still, upon the carpet. He found himself walking towards the door, saying in as peaceful a voice as he could — he who was used to slaughtering animals, who knew how best to judge the moment — 'I will close the door for one moment.'

He felt in his breast that impacted breath all humans feel before a great discovery.

He had locked the door, driven the bolt home, and switched over the sign, to read 'Closed'.

It was midday, it was true — or to be exact it was ten minutes past twelve and thirty-seven seconds, as twenty-two chattering clocks agreed in Linz's Jewellers — as Solomon Linz walked back towards what he would for ever after describe as the discovery of his greatest treasure.

There was a pause, a long pause now as he drove his gaze upwards, towards the young man. Almost languorously, as if some sexual swoon had overtaken him, Solomon Linz looked at the man. He noted the eyes, a little too close together, yet staring at him with a furious intensity. The small weak mouth, possibly petulant; the broad forehead, too broad perhaps as if in his dome beat storms. There was a prettiness about his features, a delicacy, yet an ugliness too — a strange unsettling masculinity amid the fairness. The man's eyes were neither blue nor grey but some fusion of the two.

He was tense, Linz could see that. Of course this was some ultimate moment. Was he a thief? It was entirely possible. Linz wondered then if he had been too hasty in locking the door. Perhaps his only safety lay in someone walking in. But no, he sensed — and at this moment he had only his senses to rely upon: the same instinct that told him when it was best to stun the waiting animal, to kill it with least fright: this instinct drove him now to murmur to the young man, lazily, as one lover might to another, after awakening from a night of passion — 'It is yours, of course?'

The young man seemed taken aback. He looked — was it frightened? Or was it affronted? He was suddenly breathing too quickly. He was raising a hand, that pale dirty hand, to his forehead.

'It is . . . mine. Of course. What else . . . ?'

The young man seemed out of breath. His voice was unusually high. It came from the top part of his throat, and Linz, specialist in this, smelt fear.

Instinctively, and without seeming to do so, Linz took in the young man's clothes: their shabbiness, yet also the fact that they were, or had once been, quality clothes. He understood. Or thought he did.

His eyes returned to the jewel.

He did not want to touch it yet. He wanted to enjoy the sensation of simply looking at a first-class piece of jewellery such as he had never seen in his life before. He recognised, frankly, his amateur status before this object of superlative beauty. He felt his lips making a small, almost silent smacking sound, and he heard his own breathing rising up his throat, which was suddenly dry, just as he felt the rustling storm of air running down his nostrils. His skin. He felt the surface of his skin all over. And he thought — he knew — at that moment: *I will always remember this.*

He reached down, but the young man seemed to panic and reached out, as quickly, and withdrew the jewel. He closed it in his hand and Linz felt a terrible pain — of deprivation, of loss.

'Please,' Linz said, and he found himself saying it in the voice he knew so well, his swoonly slaying voice, the one he used on the calves as he got them between his knees, as he pulled their arched necks back, as their eyes — the black lustrous full-stops of their souls — searched his being. 'Please, sir, please,' he murmured, and held his hand out.

This is what he saw.

He saw, as if in the strangely returned symmetry of a mirror, the long cupboard of his shop. He understood he was seeing his life then — not in a hallucination because this was so real — and he understood that this was a key moment in his life. Should he lie? Should he try to steal the jewel?

It was as if the young man's slightly effeminate hand, with the slim and dirty wrist, was holding in front of him temptation.

He could perhaps lose the shop, his business, his name. It was not good for a Jew to lose his name in a small town. It was dangerous. And dangerous for the other Jews.

This is what he understood the vision to mean: he must make some elemental decision here.

At the same time the brilliant jewel — it was a chandelier earring, of diamonds arranged around a central magnificent cabochon ruby — dangled there. What made it so peculiar was that it was all arranged in the form of an insect — a fly, no less! The body of the fly was made up of the single dazzling ruby.

It's costume jewellery, of course, he could have said. Or else he could have assumed a curious calmness, the stillness of a liar, and said to the young man, It's really quite interesting, that little bauble you have there. Perhaps you might like to leave it with me while I arrange with other jewellers to value it?

Of course, he might have continued, with a professional and faintly condescending smile, There is no way . . .

Where the conversation would go from here there was no telling. That it isn't actually terribly valuable, I'm sorry. The stones are cloudy, flawed, cracked, from a part of the world where they occur in too great abundance.

Linz understood the options immediately, and intensely. He understood, as the strange young man stood there so silently, holding the gem out so Linz seemed almost to hear the faint chime of some mystery just beyond his grasp — he understood that he must, on this occasion above all, declare himself.

Instead his body betrayed him. He would never afterwards forgive himself. He farted. It was a bodily expression of pure pleasure. The sound was unforgivable. The smell unfortunate, to say the least. The young man laughed. This was fortunate. It was as if they had turned some corner. He, Linz, laughed too, then said, 'Oh sir, how could I? How could I possibly?'

The young man, colouring, tossed the gem down, a little carelessly, onto the velvet.

Linz could not stop himself. He felt as if he were seeing a wounded bird treated clumsily. He stooped down to pick the earring up and cooed — yes, that was the only expression for it — he cooed to the jewel: 'Oh, do you mind, sir, if I hold it? If I inspect?'

And he reached for his jeweller's eyepiece, and attached it to his eye, and in vast size the wondrous beauty of the piece raced into his skull, occupied all the space that could possibly be there, arranged themselves in brilliant, shameless harlotry, took possession of him and announced that they would henceforth change his destiny.

'*Not invaluable?*' repeated the ravaged young man laying claim to the name of Samuel.

At last the Jew had unscrewed his false eye. A faint red rim was traced on his flesh, giving him a look of almost frozen surprise.

'I *know*, sir.' The young man said with disconcerting dryness. 'I know its exact value. I should do. It was purchased from Burlington Arcade, sir. In London.'

Linz recognised the authority in the accent of the young man.

'Oh, certainly, sir, I . . .' Linz now sprinted to catch up. He was aware he was sweating. 'I did not mean. Not for one moment. I would like to assure . . .'

He hesitated, then made a decision.

'Sir, I know this is entirely unusual in the circumstances. But could I offer . . . a small coffee, sir? My lady wife at this hour . . . always prepares . . . She would be . . . most honoured, I'm sure, if . . .'

The young man's face relaxed into indecision. Linz was aware of this. It was a crucial moment.

'Would you care, sir? It is not far to step. Through this curtain here. I think you can smell, sir, can you not? The scent of sweet Arabia, where the coffee beans come from.'

The stairwell was narrow, rising towards a window with coloured glass. The gem-like shade of ruby fell across Samuel's face as he rose, following behind Linz's suddenly athletic step. Linz was bounding up the stairs, two at a time, turning over his shoulder, looking down the steep descent towards Samuel — not speaking but smiling, pulling the calf onwards, lulling him and almost murmuring sweet nothings.

Samuel's hair, Linz saw from above, was thinning. He was losing his youth, this young man. His youth was bleeding away, had bled.

'Oh, Ada.' Linz pushed aside the door.

Samuel caught a glimpse of an over-decorated hall full of ferns on stands, pictures hanging out at slanting angles. Inside what appeared to be an upstairs back parlour he saw — or thought he saw, for one moment — a kind of religious image: Mary, with an infant Jesus, naked and plump on her knee.

The child was suckling greedily on the woman's breast and she was lost, lulled asleep in the connection. She looked downwards, and only a second later looked up — first into her husband's face, which returned to her a beam of pride, then, a little startled, to this awkward stranger.

Samuel felt staggered, breathless. The room, too small, was almost feverishly over-decorated, yet with a European *luxe* that instantly bade him welcome. Here was a language he understood, even if Linz and his wife were speaking, literally, a language he did not comprehend.

Mrs Linz rose, blushing, covering herself, pulling the child away with an audible soft plop.

The infant, finding himself thrust into a new world — deprived — turned his face, his brilliant unseeing eyes, towards the intrusion. Samuel. The child opened its mouth and began to bawl.

Linz, laughing, took the child, held it against his chest, was unmannish and soft with it, cooing and calling, and patting its back. Samuel thought for one awful moment that Linz might hand the bawling mass to him. Mrs Linz, who had buttoned up her dress, smiled at him with a becomingly pink face and returned his slight bow with a slighter, yet no less elegant curtsy. She left the room by a heavily curtained side door.

The child suddenly had fallen asleep.

Linz was standing by the door, behind which Samuel could hear Linz's wife preparing coffee. Linz was talking what Samuel identified as German.

Samuel took a seat on a rather over-exuberantly buttoned sofa. There was an oil painting on the wall opposite him. It was old, possibly from the fourteenth century. It was a strange scene — he could not quite stop looking at it. Behind a tormented-looking saint a ship was breaking up in a tempest. Strange stick-like figures hurtled out of the portals of the sinking ship. Changing as they did so into darkened, evil spirits. Smuts — they could have been smuts — but they were humans, transforming into angels. The waves rose up, wild and cavernous. One angel flew towards a break in the clouds, behind which could be seen a celestial calmness. But down below, in the storm, a ship was breaking apart, sinking.

An ugly painting, Samuel thought, shivering. He touched the jewel inside his pocket for luck.

'I am telling Ada of your marvellous gem,' Linz said, laying the child down inside a cushioned drawer.

'Our first,' he said to Samuel's unasked question. 'A boy. We call him Gershom — "stranger to this place" — since we are strangers here.'

Linz rubbed his hands.

His wife came in, carrying an elegant Limoges coffee set. The pot shook on a silver tray. There were tiny demitasses, and on a plate a fragrant orange and poppyseed cake. She set it all down, and, sitting like a hostess used to maintaining a salon, she began to pour.

There was a delicacy, an elegance in this over-stuffed upstairs parlour that discombobulated Samuel with all the force of memory. He found his hand shaking, unreasonably, as he took the cup — and for one moment the three humans sat there, gazing at the rinkling, tinkling sound of one human incapable of maintaining equilibrium.

Samuel found that tears had somehow attached themselves to his lashes — it was frightful.

'Ah, the wee babe,' he managed to say, and he felt his subterfuge work, for the fond parents softened, and smiled, and nodded.

Ada asked something, through her husband, in German.

'She is asking if you have long been here.'

Samuel shook his head, then nodded in confusion.

They all laughed.

What was 'long' here? An afternoon? Several hours? Years?

They understood. And fell, plummeting down the shaft that led them back to Europe.

Linz drained his cup in one. He had business. He felt sexually tense, ready almost to take his wife: his pretty pink and gilt wife with her frizzled hair, her slightly exhausted eyes — bulbous and watery amethyst — which were turned, in sympathy, upon their guest. Linz noticed that the young man was gazing speculatively at the piano.

He gestured lavishly. 'If you should wish . . . at any time . . .'

Strangely the young man stood up and went towards it, opened the lid and laid his hands upon the keys. He depressed a key slightly so that a single sound came out — low, pretty.

But then, seeing the sleeping babe, he sat down again, in almost a caricature of stillness. The parents relaxed.

'But truly — I mean this — if you would at any time like to play. My wife cannot . . . at the moment. But for both of us, music . . . music . . .'

Linz seemed to lose his poise. Now his lashes, too, wetted and he grew a little pensive, a little sad. Then shook himself.

'However,' he said, returning to the business at hand. He smiled a dashing cavalier smile at Samuel. He was almost bewitchingly handsome for a moment — no longer thirty-eight, no longer carrying memories, some of which were dark with pain, with loss.

'The lady . . .' he faltered for a moment. 'The lady who wore the gem?'

Samuel looked up slowly. His eyes went to the lacy curtain. He seemed to see something there so present that first Linz, then his wife followed his gaze. But there was nothing.

Only a fly caught against the glass, banging.

Linz, in one athletic jump, raised the window, let out the bluebottle. And into the room sprinkled all the alien sounds of the town, which had hitherto been cushioned: the hammering of nails, an iron hoop rolling through dust, a child crying.

The air that came in was sweeter too, fresher — there was the distant pound of waves.

'I do not wish, of course, to pry . . .' Linz said, turning around. Because he was standing he seemed too overpowering, so he made, with his hand, a gentle, deflecting gesture.

Samuel, he could see, was sweating.

'She was perhaps a person of some importance? You need not say her name. I understand completely — discretion. But sometimes a gem may gain added value when worn against the breast — the warm breast —' he added for Samuel's benefit, 'of someone well known.'

Mrs Linz sat there, uncomprehending, but smiling into the vague middle distance of one who does not understand a language; she even sympathetically nodded.

Samuel said nothing, but appeared deeply thoughtful. Or as if he could no longer quite understand Linz's implication.

'Even', and here Linz kissed the back of his own hand for some reason, with a delicate, yet lip-smacking relish — 'someone notorious.'

The word hung in the air.

Both men inspected it, from different angles.

Samuel shifted in his chair and sent the tiny demitasse skittering across the porcelain saucer. He caught it in mid-air.

Mrs Linz clapped her hands as if it were a trick. Samuel returned the precious cup to the silver tray.

Linz was thinking. He glimpsed the inside of a darkened bedroom. In a dagger of light, amid a cumulus of crumpled sheets, a fleshly woman was squatting over a basin, washing herself. Around her neck was a cascade of fabulous emeralds. She was Cora Pearl, whore to Napoleon III.

Linz had seen a pornographic engraving of the scene. This single earring, seemed to breathe the air of that profligate, immoral world. Linz returned across half the globe to that overheated room and glanced into the moistly sweating, closed face of the young man.

He too seemed to be on some private voyage.

'She was', he stuttered, as if each word were costing him, 'a woman . . . a woman who . . .'

Linz and his wife waited. But the young man's mouth refused to utter any sound, apart from a low baying of a moan, followed by painful clicks, as if his interior were a machine on the point of malfunctioning.

'Oh quite. Quite — no need to explain.' Linz hurried to relieve Samuel of the vulgarity of distress. 'We need say no more. The individual gems themselves are of huge value. I pledge to you —' Now he took the risk of reaching out and taking the young man's hand in his own. The flesh was disconcertingly cold, almost frozen, yet moist too, as if rivulets of panic were issuing unseen out of his flesh — tears? But, overlooking this unpleasant discovery, he clasped the young man's hand and turned, almost tearful with the genuineness of his emotions, to his young wife as witness.

'I pledge to you that I will obtain, for you, sir, and you alone, the very best price. If you trust, sir —'

Samuel in his chair made a small half bow. But he was held imprisoned by the older man's overheated grip. His crushing maw was powerful — impossible to withdraw.

'If you trust me, sir,' and at this Linz allowed himself to smile generously, as if the idea of *not* trusting him was so absurd he could allow a little humour here, 'I could take — with your permission, sir — the gem to Wellington, and perhaps from there — who knows? — to Melbourne, even San Francisco? The earring, sir, is too brilliant, too entirely *fabulous*, for this small town.'

Samuel's hand, of itself, jibbed. He had gone pale — paler than all the whitenesses he had gone before — inside that room.

'The other way of doing it is for me to pay to you . . .'

Samuel had taken his hand away.

'If you should prefer, I could pay you now, this moment, a deposit as a sign of goodwill, in sovereigns — fifty, say — and I will sell the gem on commission. Twelve and one half per cent. You say you know how much the jewellery cost, when it was bought?'

Samuel nodded.

'It was then worth?'

'Sixteen hundred guineas.'

Samuel's voice was low, almost ashamed for some reason.

Linz looked thoughtful.

'Of course,' he said, 'fashion has changed a little. Ladies, sir,' he said and kissed the end of his fingers and made a pantomime shrug of incomprehension. Mrs Linz did not seem to like the sight of this. She rose, took the tray in hand. Samuel rose also. Linz rose last. He looked inconvenienced, and Samuel thought he caught a reprimanding glance sent towards his wife. She flushed, cast her eyes down, then moved out of the room. Samuel listened to the rustle of her undergarments. She was wearing a simple white smock over what he could see was a pretty, slightly too elegant green gown — a gown such as you might have seen in Geneva, perhaps, in any middle-class suburb, several years earlier.

'You choose.'

Linz was standing there.

Samuel tried to think: of fifty sovereigns. What this might mean. Shifting out of the Haresnape hovel. Perhaps renting one of the new wooden houses high on the Hill. Once he had harvested the full amount of money from the jewel he could escape. To some more civilised city. Assume a new identity, but take up his old life. Return to his self, albeit in another, slightly altered form. He ached. He wanted.

'I . . .', he said.

Then Linz, seeming to scent his indecision, went to a small escritoire, placed atop the piano. It was boulle; Linz touched a small part and an unseen drawer slid out.

Linz scooped out sovereigns. He didn't bother to count them. Samuel thought: perhaps he knows how many are in there? He poured them into Samuel's hands: the gold glittered in his palms.

A heap, a heat of gold. On his flesh. Its lovely weight sent licks of warmth up his arms.

'Take. Take. I trust. You trust me. I trust you,' Linz said. 'And think about what you want. Leave the gem with me for safety — I have a safe. If this house burnt to the ground, the earring would survive.' He smiled at the ridiculousness of this, and fell delicately silent.

Samuel was aware of Mrs Linz standing behind the curtain in the next room.

She had no need of language, perhaps, to know what was happening.

Samuel could not let the lovely gold escape.

He could not stop himself.

He handed over the jewel.

'I will let you know . . . how I would like you to sell . . .' Samuel said.

He began to put the gold into his pockets when Linz, leaning forward and making small tsk! tsk! sounds, reached around behind him — to a small suede bag his wife was holding out, and he slid the gold into the bag, tightened its little neck, then handed the small fortune to his captive.

Delirium and a Hat

The door behind him clicked to, and Samuel was released. He was staggering almost. He felt drunk. He could escape. He was rich. Well, he was almost rich. Suddenly his surroundings which had, up until that moment, hardly ever ceased to chafe him changed. He could leave. As soon as the money was harvested. Perhaps it would be best to let the Jew go to San Francisco? He would leave behind his wife, the baby, the piano . . .

Samuel stepped out rashly into sunlight, humming. It was two o'clock. It was impossible that so much time had rushed by. Where had it gone? It was as if Samuel had lost count of his own memory, his grip on time. That weight that almost, otherwise, crushed him. He found himself turning instinctively into the private bar of the Masonic Hotel. At this time in the afternoon the bar was pleasantly sunlit, with a single man, who looked like a commercial traveller of some kind, sitting with his legs outstretched, half asleep over a jar of beer. The man, who had a long drooping moustache, nodded companionably to Samuel.

Samuel went to the bar and ordered a tot of brandy. While he waited, he saw through into the public bar where a group of men were bent over, playing billiards. The room was plunged into a sort of eternal darkness. There were lugubrious murmurs, the soft *pock!* of a billiard ball, a background rumble of unseen males.

In the distance there were double doors opened wide, through which Samuel could see a hitched horse, and then an empty section on which four men were sawing wood. They seemed to stand in a vista of mud, raising a beam to vertical. The staccato of hammering. Angry saw back and forth.

The barmaid, a snub-nosed, rather distant woman, who looked as if she dreamt her way through the mornings and only came awake later in the day, pushed the brandy towards him.

He started sipping. But too quickly his hunger for numbness outgrew his modesty. The glass, conspiratorially, sat there empty. It demanded to be filled again. He indicated to the wench. She, silently drifting like a ballerina through rehearsed steps, opened the bottle, filled the glass, replaced the cork, put the bottle back, slid across the glass.

He emptied that more slowly. The desired numbness was descending. He relaxed. He began to contemplate how he would fill his day.

Perhaps a wander up on the Hill? It helped him at times to contemplate the horizon. It acted on his soul like some purifying agent. That is, when it wasn't forming itself into a prison bar. A walk up on the Hill. Perhaps he could then inspect one of the new wooden cottages that were going up so quickly. He might hire one? Perhaps obtain a piano? Instantly he saw a snugly wallpapered room, a soirée of sorts — there was Mrs Linz . . . and Miss Perrett perhaps? Then his vision faded. I'd only hire the house. And then when the Jew comes back I can . . .

I can, I can, I can.

The loveliness of the chant deserved another glass, which was already sudsing down inside the glass. His insides were heated up, burning. It felt good. He felt alive. He wanted — he wanted to talk, that was it. He wanted someone to speak with.

'It's a beautiful winter's day,' he said to the young barmaid. She looked at him consciously before replying.

'Yes, thank goodness,' she said. She relaxed, polishing a glass. 'Me mum is doing me and the little ones' washing today, so I'm counting on it carrying on fine. What with all the rain we been having.'

This was not what he meant. He nodded, and, with his hand undisclosed, felt for his small suede bag. Only a fool would reveal so much money. He opened the bag discreetly and extracted a sovereign.

I'll buy a bonnet for Fanny.

He was in the Athenaeum Reading Room. He had been driven there by a desire to sit still. Collect himself. He didn't trust himself to go into another hotel. He didn't need another drink. He was drunk on possibility. On a whole cascading bolt of chance clanging against chance. He could get out of there now. Look at this room! A wooden shell, catching the boom of waves on shingle. The tick, the too loud tick of the clock on the wall. A public reading room for mechanics, with creaking bentwood chairs.

Not even a carpet on the floor.

Through a door Samuel could see the tiny darkened closet where the Philosophical Society was displaying its wares — greenstone mere, intricate carved paddles, two feather cloaks — arranged in heraldic form: elliptical, mysterious objects that refused, mutely, to disclose their story.

He could escape all this — that heavy bloated fly, which might have come straight from the butcher's shop, from alighting on a heavy coil of horseshit — he could escape the rapt bang of the fly against the windowpane.

To get out. Escape.

It was then he had his great revelation.

I'll buy a bonnet for Fanny!

It did not matter that Fanny might never get to wear it. It mattered nothing that she might never even place it upon her curls.

He had stood up so startlingly sudden, that he overturned the *Nineteenth Century* magazine he was leafing through. The other occupant, the Reverend William Tye, on duty in the reading room, turned to him, staring over his half-glasses. He paused, frowned, then licked the pad of his finger. He turned away, to crinkle over the page of what Samuel could see looked like a Royal Society journal.

There was a definite sense of reprimand.

'I beg your pardon, sir,' Samuel said to him.

The old gent, hairy and grim but with a sharp, intense look, nodded slightly, looked away.

Samuel felt he wanted to stamp. Or shout. He had about him the electricity of one who had won a lottery. He felt he wanted to acknowledge the blessing of the world.

'I didn't mean to disturb you, sir,' he said unnecessarily. 'I have been coming here all this while and never introduced myself.'

The old man frowned.

'There are some here who would be pleased not to shake my hand,' the old man said dryly. But held out his hand.

'Well, I am not one of them!' sang Samuel. He shook the old man's hand as if he might have just won a prize also. Or Samuel was congratulating him. He laughed.

His laugh had a lovely high quality: unexpected, musical.

'Oh, this is a grand reading room, this. I might, sir, be able even to provide a little financial assistance. In time, in time,' he said and almost touched the side of his nose. He was aware of the scrutiny of the old man, who, Samuel noted, did not deflatingly look at the state of Samuel's clothes. Sliding down to the full-stop of his wrecked shoes.

The old man simply and sagely nodded. Then he returned to his esoteric notes on nature and said, a little too dryly perhaps: 'The Athenaeum is only too pleased to accept donations from any source.'

Samuel was outside, in the brilliant daylight, before his mind caught up with the slight barb of what the silly old codger was saying. He'd heard something about him. Haresnape — Mrs Haresnape had said something about how she crossed the road rather than walk on the same path as him. He was a fallen vicar. He had lain with a Maori servant woman, who had had his child. Even while he was married and had his own family. The church had kicked him out.

Samuel for a moment contemplated the old man's predicament with real pity: he clearly could never go home. He was trapped here, in this — *place.*

Yet now Samuel was certainly leaving the place, he appreciated afresh the clement climate, the beauty of the Bay. He turned and glanced towards the waves. (He had walked out the side door of the Athenaeum, down two wooden steps and out onto the hot pebbles of the foreshore.)

A pure line of aquamarine heaped itself up, dazzling with light, then flung itself down on the pebbles. He staggered forward to look. The vast arc of Hawke's Bay — as big as a country — stretched out before him, in blinding phosphorescence.

Almost as if he were anticipating saying farewell he turned back in the other direction completely and looked inland — past the toy town, across a smudge of swamps, towards a rack of mountains, snow-tipped and the same pure white as the clouds.

He walked along the shore, immersing himself in the roar of waves onto shingle. Losing himself. Absolving himself. As if that were possible.

To Samuel's left was the hump of Scinde Island. The locals, laconic as to language, sparing with the price of a word, shortened Scinde Island to *the Hill*. It was as if everything here were so primal it had to be reduced to essentials: *sea, man, hill*. But in fact it was quite some 'hill'. More like a mount or an actual island — or a meteoric lump flung out as if by some angry god hurling it as far away as possible from the surrounding landscape. Which shrank away, leaving it alone, surrounding it with a desert of mosquito-plagued lagoons, sandbanks, braided, dangerous rivers.

Any other town was days away by boat. No fool would go inland because inland was a rack of mountains, cathedrals of stone and snow, narrow corridors of granite and icy water, all but impassable.

Isolated, alone — as much castle as keep — Scinde Island formed the nugget around which a town had accreted: twenty or so streets ran out in a desultory sort of way along what had once been a sandbar.

'*A more useless place for a town it is difficult to imagine,*' a scornful colonist had written.

Yet people had come. If there were mountains there were plains; if there were plains there was land. And if there was land, there was food for beasts of burden. Besides, that horizon was always beckoning with dreams, with possibility . . .

On the tip of the Hill was a military fort, to run to in times of danger. A port had been built on the further side of the Hill, and that was it: a few dozen streets, fifteen pubs, a lunatic asylum, a prison and a port.

It was an elemental landscape, but not without its majesty.

Loneliness was its curse, and its grandeur.

For a man running away it had undeniable attractions.

But at times its beauty could be a prison.

Not now, however; not today, when Samuel had a mission.

The waves sent a fume of air straight towards him. A faint, almost glamorous dust of light speckled out of the sea. Pale and silvery, vast and airy: it was almost as if distance were hammered into a gilt image.

Of freedom.

He took a deep breath. Oh, the sharp tang of freshness. It was unequalled.

He crushed his lids shut.

And remembered Fanny. On the day of his triumph. Of course. He was buying her a hat! What could be more idiotic — more sublime! He ran — he felt he almost ran — off the beach and back down Emerson Street, towards Towne & Neale.

*I*nside he fell down a tunnel of darkness. This is how it felt. He felt as if he had lost all sense of perspective and was within a cavern of objects so innumerable, so vast, that he had come awake in the middle of an Aladdin's cave.

Not that, he reflected ruefully to himself, he would ever — once! — have thought a drapery concern such as this, with its buckets, spades and dimity dresses, could be an emporium to excite him. He actually laughed to himself at this, pleasurably. Oh, the humour, the piquancy. If only he had someone — even that porcine dunce Will Alredy — beside him to share in the joke. How much easier it was when you moved with a group, a coterie of friends. They understood. They would have seen the joke.

But now a stiff young man, with a high quiff on top his head, slid towards him down the counter. Samuel recognised him as the young man choosing the engagement ring. The young man blushed becomingly. Samuel liked seeing young men blush. He felt a rush of pleasure.

'Good afternoon, sir,' the young man said, determined manfully to put aside his own personal discomfort. Samuel could not stop smiling at the young man's cat's-eye tie-pin. 'May I be of assistance?'

'Well, time will tell, time will tell!' Samuel said. He was suddenly all charm, all pleasantries. He smiled at the young man, trying to put him at his ease.

The young man waited.

'I am looking for a hat, sir.'

'Well, sir,' and he was off, the young shop assistant, sliding down towards where men's clothes — including coats, umbrellas, hats and shoes — were displayed. In all their dun and sparrow colourings.

Samuel raised a hand.

'A hat for a woman,' he said.

'Oh, sir. I understand. A young lady.'

Together, though separated by the long counter, the two young men walked along side by side.

'Well, sir, you are the luckiest of mortals, sir, if I may be so bold as to say. Towne & Neale,' he ran the words off his tongue with a certain grandeur that made Samuel smile to himself, 'have a new consignment. Of the very latest styles. Though I am afraid Miss Montgomery, who usually does for ladies' hats, is away. On a most unexpected inconvenience.'

Samuel felt that the young man was about to be indiscreet.

'Scarlet fever,' he murmured, obscured by a wall of fabric arranged as to tint and colour. 'Down by the port. They think it came in on the *Adelaide*.'

They were now in a forest of gowns, mannequins and hats. Samuel could not help jingling his coins in his pocket. The lovely sound rang out, muted.

'Sir, if you do not mind my being of assistance? If I can . . . ?' The young man glanced up the length of the shop, towards two male assistants who were turning plainly sarcastic faces towards him. Another older man — Towne himself? — was engaged in deep conversation with someone who looked like a tramp, but who was, quite possibly, a wealthy local farmer.

'I'm not sure if I — '

'You have a young fiancée, have you not?' Samuel was being practical. 'Let us throw all caution aside, young man, and let us just imagine what your fiancée — or mine! — might like.'

The young shop assistant flushed again, this time with pleasure, and nodded.

'Well, sir.' He reached across and took out of a box with an immense amount of tissue paper — a bonnet. 'This is the postillion style of hat, sir,' he said in a low voice. A hand bedecked with a rather suspect gem swept the fabric of the hat. 'Its name is *Fleurette*. It is a style favoured by, among others, the Empress Elizabeth of Austria, sir — one of the great beauties of Europe.'

He held the hat up. It was a deep emerald green, emphatically curled towards the front, with a froth of feathers riding up the side. In the somnolent air the feathers gently wavered.

'Sir, may I be so indiscreet as to ask about the young lady's colouring?'

'Oh —' Samuel seemed to have trouble taking his eyes off the hat. He had gone into some strange kind of trance. 'May I? Hold it. One needs,' he said, 'to get an idea of the thing close up.'

The assistant deferentially handed the hat over. Samuel held it away from him. He was looking towards the light, so the assistant had the odd sense of the purchaser's eyes moistening. He had the sensation that the pupils in the man's eyes had enlarged, grown brilliant. He seemed to be breathing in a rapid succession, almost in pants. The assistant began to feel uncomfortable; he glanced up towards the other men, who suddenly seemed a long way distant.

'You. Young man. You,' the stranger said to the assistant, appealing to him with what seemed, to the assistant, an appalling directness. 'What would you choose for yourself?'

'For my young lady, sir?'

'Yes. What speaks to your heart?'

'Speaks to my heart, sir?' The young assistant felt all at sea. He felt confused about who exactly the purchaser was speaking about. 'The *Fleurette* is a most stylish hat, in my own humble opinion,' he said. He flicked a glance up to the other men. He was speaking now with suppressed passion. 'But *La Condée* sir . . .' and here with almost a magician's flourish he buried his hands deep in a box of whispering tissue paper and brought up to the light an elaborate chapeau, shaped like a funnel, its rear end a firework of feather and sparkle. It was all in shades of a deeply drenched red. A single contrasting maroon feather rose higher than the rest, to the side.

'*La Condée, La Condée,*' the young assistant almost moaned. And held the hat out.

Samuel placed the hat on the pivot of his fingers and spun it around. It turned into a brilliant spinning wheel, revolving. As if staring into a gambling wheel, Samuel said, half thoughtfully, 'I do not know where Fanny will wear it.'

'Yes, sir. There is that. It may be a little . . . too *brilliant* for Napier.'

On the word 'brilliant' Samuel's eyes were irresistibly drawn to the shop assistant, who was pale now, and looking back at him directly. The shop assistant's eyes had taken on a strange glitter.

'You speak well of women's bonnets,' Samuel said to him, handing the hat back. He nodded. 'I will take *La Condée*. On your insistence, of course.'

The young shop assistant laughed, then seemed to choke back the wild free bird that was coming out of his mouth. Another assistant was drawing closer. Both he and Samuel could hear the heavy drum of the iron plates on the man's boots hitting the boards. He seemed to be bearing down on them.

'Toop,' the man said to the assistant, 'you're needed on pans and kerosene lanterns. When you've done.'

Samuel was aware of the newcomer looking between the two of them, of the young man blushing defensively.

'Here,' Samuel said, offering the young assistant three sovereigns towards the price of the hat.

'We are just concluding our business,' he said to the newcomer dismissively. He consciously used his London voice. The newcomer started, almost deferentially, but this was followed by an insulting, assessing glance at Samuel's clothes. The glance slid down, as always, to his shoes. It was at this point — Samuel would remember afterwards — his toothache began.

*I*t took control of his head, his bonce, his nonce, his skull. It jillyjagged away, dancing a dagger deep down inside his tooth, laminating the inside tray of his mouth with a dull, almost metallic taste; while the diamond point, of fever, of irreducible light, bore down through his jaw, rammed up to the side of his bite, then slid an iron mask of agony all over his skull.

Clamped on.

He managed, chattering with pain, to take his change. The young man, Toop, was looking at him from a vast distance. Samuel seemed to discern on his face a look of concern. He even spoke a few words — he seemed to want to join him as he ushered Samuel to the door — but with the hatbox in his hand, Samuel mouthed the words, 'Thank you. Thank you,' — heartfelt — and to the bully, 'He has given me excellent advice,' while he turned and, abject slave now, bore his toothache away.

Outside the light attacked him, leached into his pupils, rushed down the iris of his eye as if to say: See, you were fooled before, when you thought you could escape us — we hold you, inescapably, our prisoner. He staggered out, suddenly wondering why he had been so foolish as to weigh himself down with a cardboard box — wrapped up in brown paper, it is true, and tied tight with string — but why had he attached himself to a silly hat, made of nothing more than velvet, elastic hat-string, the feathers of an egret bird, plucked, dyed and arduously sewed in by some poor young woman in a darkened room, half a world away.

Why had he? Why was he holding himself hostage — to a hat?

He staggered along the wooden pavement, then bumped down into dust.

'Sir! Mr Barton, sir!'

Did Samuel only imagine a light sense of raillery attached to his name? Suggesting it was as unreal as himself?

It was Miss Perrett in her — he realised it now — eternal maroon-striped costume. She smiled at him a little uncertainly. She looked a little tired. Perhaps the force of his toothache was granting him a second sight. Even the slide of her gaze down to the hatbox, then up to his face, in ricochet, did not surprise him. Miss Perrett blushed. Suddenly she seemed to lose her power of speech.

Whatever she had been about to say had disappeared.

He half bowed to her.

She came awake, opened her reticule, dived in and fossicked around for a good while. She seemed to have lost her nerve, or self-composure. She kept glancing, as if he were holding a ticking bomb in his hand, not a hat. In the end he held it up, as if declaring it, and said, 'It is a hat. I have a friend — a distant friend, it's true.

But the idea — whimsy, really — came on me to treat her.'

'Whimsy?' Miss Perrett said hesitantly, as if it she were having trouble recognising such a distant, evanescent thing. She smiled a little bleakly, then handed over a handbill. As she did so, she shuddered at the vulgarity of her action.

Through the waterfall of his pain, from behind the slide and noisome splash and roar of it, he saw it was a Musical Evening. At the Oddfellows Hall. In Milton Road. Featuring, among others, Miss Perrett herself.

'To raise money for the church organ,' she said quickly. 'Otherwise of course I would not dream . . .'

Almost melodramatically, with great theatrical care, he folded the paper and placed it in his top pocket. To do this, he had to put the hatbox down. Miss Perrett darted forward, as if to place the box down in the dust would be to sully it.

'Oh, you couldn't, you mustn't . . .' she half articulated.

'I am afraid,' Samuel began — heroically, as he didn't want to speak.

'Oh, I quite understand!' Miss Perrett said, almost in fright, handing the hatbox back to him. 'So busy. It is difficult to fit things in. So much to —'

'No!' he said quite urgently, speaking too loudly because he could no longer trust — no, he could no longer trust anything. He felt an almost abject sense of fear.

He caught her mittened hands. She looked a little frightened, then moved closer to him, interested.

'I have the most terrible toothache.'

Instantly she understood. A kind of supreme intelligence slid over her features. She was nothing if not capable. She was nothing if not knowledgeable about how to make sense of this place — survive . . .

She pulled him along. He felt it forcibly, as if she had suddenly turned into a frigate with the wind behind her sails, and he a dinghy dipple-dappling in her wake. She was energised, almost made handsome by her quest.

She took him to the corner of Emerson Street.

'Sir, Mr Barton, can I recommend — and *reasonable* to boot —' and here she flung a mittened hand upwards to a window. On it was written, in somewhat showy gilt, DR. O.S. COGSWELL, and in a larger curving arch of letters, DENTIST.

At that moment clouds were sliding across a too blue sky, caught in the glass. It could have been a celestial painting.

'It is strictly cash,' she was whispering to him, looking at him a little scandalised at the fright of having to find the ready. 'But — oh!' she breathed, then seemed to wave something away. What was it? Pain? Or the unendurable difficulty of having to pay cash for something, on the spot?

She seemed to push him then, delicately, as one pushed a boat out across a still pond.

'You must not suffer — nobody must suffer!' she murmured to him. Then turned, sharply, abandoning him.

A Most
Unusual Visit

Samuel was seated in a high wooden chair. He was facing the window, a large double sash. Out it he could see the corner of the building next to the Masonic Hotel. A framework of sorts was etched into the sky, and a small manikin was banging a hammer, banging a hammer.

Or was that inside his head? His mouth? Was there a little devil inside his tooth, enjoying himself by pitching a fiery fork right into the pith of his being? Jabbing?

Samuel sat there, waiting, tense.

Behind him and slightly to the side, so he could no longer see him, was 'Doctor' Cogswell. He was the stranger Samuel had found bending over the footpath, looking for his eyeglass.

Now he came forward, alarmingly close to Samuel's face.

'Would you be so kind as to open wide.'

Cogswell came closer still. In the middle distance he appeared as a man in slightly too small a jacket, with a too insistent plaid, as if to make up for some hidden unquiet. Yet he also wore, unusually, a soft and floppy bow tie, of a strange deep blue, figured all over, it was apparent now that he was standing in such intimate proximity to Samuel, with little sprigs of forget-me-nots. These flowers seemed oddly joyful — as if to uplift the spirits of his patients.

Samuel's first impression of Cogswell, on negotiating the stairs — being told to wait; waiting in a long dream of pain — was of a loose-knit, rather casual, even gracefully moving man. There was something languorous, almost half asleep about him. This, in the circumstances, was soothing. He even seemed to speak slowly — his American accent having a comfortable upholstered quality so that certain words stretched out (wait, be so kind) and others were oddly hurried up, as if pain itself might be as quickly deleted.

A child and its mother had, in the end, been ushered out. The child was wan with pain. The mother was the more exhausted of the two, yet beaming.

'It is little less than a miracle! A miracle!' the mother was saying. And the doctor, if doctor he was, was standing there, holding a plucked goose in his hand. He was holding the plucked goose away from him, but a stooly pool of watery blood was speckling out from its beak. It formed a surreptitious ruby pool upon the floor.

Once their footsteps had died away, and the doctor too had disappeared through some private door, Samuel had a moment on his own.

Perhaps Cogswell was a quack?

Should he flee?

But as if by magic the 'doctor' had come back, was standing right beside him, apologising and recognising him as the man who had tried to find his eyeglass. (In the end, a workman had had to prise the board back.) By this time a young manservant — a youth, really — had come in, and was wiping away the blood. He did this without acknowledging either Cogswell's or Samuel's presence.

'Please,' Cogswell was saying to him. Bidding him step into his dental room. Seating him in the high-backed wooden chair, facing him towards the brilliant light coming through the window.

To Samuel's side stood a small, rickety, high-legged table, covered with a cloth, on which rested a metal spittoon.

It had just been cleansed, Samuel could see. Tiny beads of water prismed all over it, and in each of them, oddly distorted, he saw himself, a little pigmy crouched in terror, while the longer, larger Cogswell filled half the world. This strange sense of the occult was added to by a magnifying lens, and then, more disquieting, a series of metal forceps and other odd-seeming metallic instruments of torture. Some had ivory handles, some wooden. Some were all metal.

As Samuel sweated, his world went white with panic.

But Dr Cogswell gracefully swung his body into view. Once again, Samuel smelt something oddly metallic about him. (He had to assume the man was a doctor; he could only hope.) In fact, in his fright he realised that all he could do — the best he could do — was succumb. Like some animal placed in the infinite mercy of another stronger being, he could only, as it were, play dead.

Yet the American, almost irritatingly, would not let him. Oh, he was being charming, the American. Talking, almost ridiculously, about how he had come to New Zealand, on the mailboat that plied the route from San Francisco to Honolulu, and on to Auckland. He'd got off in Auckland, hearing of the gold rushes down at Thames. Though he had not struck gold. He'd kept on going.

'I'm like the piece of mail that's never been sent back! I just kept on travelling!'

He spoke in a leisurely, philosophical voice which, instead of calming Samuel, filled him with apprehension. He was sitting in the chair, extremely tense.

He hated Cogswell at that moment.

He hated the way he was standing there, looking down at something in the street he could see, but which Samuel could not.

He only wanted it to begin, and then to be over.

The doctor was saying, with a laugh, that his father was a Unitarian minister. In Boston.

'Not exactly a promising connection for a son on the lookout for gold!'

'I have a tooth that is causing me a certain degree of pain,' Samuel broke in, aware that his voice sounded, almost ludicrously, both prissy and angry. The doctor looked taken aback, then his instant fold of charm enveloped Samuel again, carried him away so that, in another moment, it seemed, the doctor had finished inspecting his tooth, making a small downward sigh as he explained that the tooth could be saved, though it might involve pain. But he could offer — yes, he went on smoothly — he could offer a quite particular pain relief that was the miracle — yes, the miracle of the modern age the mother had just been expounding upon.

Samuel was ripe for a miracle.

There were risks, Cogswell said, but minimal.

Samuel had taken too many risks to turn back now.

Now the doctor prepared, in a great arching dome of silence, a clean kerchief. Samuel watched him fold it once, twice, then again. The doctor had explained in his slow, deep voice that he would be placing the kerchief on Samuel's face. That Samuel must breathe in, slowly. He would fall asleep and then, the doctor said, the miracle would be performed. Cogswell said this in what Samuel could only conceive of as a deep brown, chestnut voice — a glossy chocolate voice of such compelling calm and good humour that Samuel felt his whole body sag, yes, fall down a precipice of relief. A relaxation so immense came over him that he let out a small sound, almost a whimper, which he prayed the doctor did not hear.

Cogswell turned his back briefly, and the smell Samuel had scented in the doctor's clothes made its reappearance. It was sharp, metallic. There was the sound of a glass stopper slithering out of a neck.

Instantly — almost as a magician might move, mid-trick — the doctor turned round and, without smiling but looking with what Samuel could only conceive as eerie calm, he placed the clean kerchief over Samuel's mouth and nose.

His eyes strained up, to take in what could as well be his murderer, but the handsome doctor simply arched an auburn eyebrow and his face relaxed into a smile as enigmatic as the moon when full.

There was light, then the door opened and Fanny bustled in, looking back over her shoulder.

She was carrying a collection of small boxes, wrapped, and her toy dog, Napoleon, was barking, barking with excitement that she was back. Fanny slithered off her wrap — it was the mauve silk edged with feathers — and began unbuttoning her glacé gloves. There was a faint smell of dog urine in the room.

It was late afternoon, winter.

'Lord,' she said, without looking at the man seated on the couch. 'I hope you took Nappy out for his doo-daas.'

The man said nothing. Fanny laughed a little, her vast silken skirts slithering over to the window. She pulled aside the lace a little and looked out for a moment. She sighed. There was the sound of horses' hooves hard on cobblestone — departing.

Fog pressed against the pane.

She let the curtain fall, went over to the fire. She disturbed the coals. Then she walked to the small walnut table, on which stood a gilt clock, a cupid raised on tiptoe, holding 'time' suspended in his pudgy hand.

Casually she threw a glove over the cupid's naked shoulder, covering his face. She took a Turkish cigarette out of a box, and turned round to face the man.

'I'm sorry, Freddie, if you've been waiting.'

The man still said nothing. She looked at him, inspecting his face for a moment. He was sitting on the sofa, his long legs thrust out in front of him. He

49

was sunk down in the sofa, very still. Fanny glanced, from beneath half-lowered lashes, at his legs. She had always liked Freddie's legs. The thighs were gratifyingly muscular.

She could tell he was in a snit.

Fanny went to the wall and rang the bell.

'Has the slut been looking after you?'

Freddie's pale grey eyes shifted from Fanny to the mirror, which was leaning outwards, returning a strange vertiginous view of the almost claustrophobically over-patterned, over-stuffed room. There was really only room for Fanny's immense dress, a side table, the two-seater sofa and a mediaeval-style side chair. The sofa and chair had been upholstered in shiny emerald green silk, which was echoed in the wallpaper. There was a chandelier overhead — a ridiculously artificial thing, a suspension of emerald glass and diamonds: it looked like the tiara for an impossible queen.

There was a muffled knock, a silence, then Fanny, looking directly at Freddie and half smiling, called, 'Come in! Come in!'

The maidservant was carrying a tray. On the tray were two crystal glasses and a bottle of Krug. The maidservant placed the tray down and took away the cake, which had had a single large slice taken out of it, then the slice laid down, a bite-mark visible in the wedge.

'He doesn't like our cake, Clara,' Fanny said. She laughed.

Clara's face showed no particular emotion.

'Tell Clara how you don't like our cake, Freddie.'

Freddie stirred.

Clara went on with her duties, sweeping the crumbs away with a small silver-backed crumb brush.

'Freddie. Are you sulking, Freddie?'

The man sighed.

'Tell Clara. Go on. She needs to know.'

The air in the room was a little tense. Clara did not look at the gentleman on the sofa, who, however, glanced at her, appealing to her as if to will the maidservant to speak up, to save his dignity. But Fanny now sailed straight towards Freddie, her skirts whispering and letting out an almost searing, slithering, slashing sound as she knelt down in front of him, on a little padded footstool. Her skirts settled all around her. She caught hold of Freddie's hand — his left hand, the one with the heavy, deeply engraved signet ring. She pulled the hand towards her and rained down on the back of it a storm of kisses. Freddie was aware she was kissing — no, she was licking his knuckles. It was more than embarrassing: it was physically painful, and exciting. He wanted to adjust the position of his . . . legs? — but she was holding him in a vice.

'Tell her, Freddie. Ask her pardon for not liking the cake.'

Fanny's voice was flat, hard. She bit into the skin of his hand.

He sat up.

'Look,' he said, colouring. 'Look, young Clara. It's nothing personal, it's just. . . well, I'm not a cake kind of man.'

Fanny laughed at this, and sat up. Her eyes, her blue eyes, were brilliant as she laughed. There was a trace of blood on her lower lip. Freddie was nursing his hand.

'Get out,' she said to the maidservant. Clara bobbed into a curtsy, and in silence carried the tray and the cake out. As she did so, she heard behind her what sounded like a woman in skirts being pushed backwards onto a carpeted floor, a footstool overturned. She heard a man let out a deep glottal groan, followed by a sharp slap, an intake of breath, then — as she held the door open just enough so she could continue listening — she heard Freddie saying proudly, yet as if he were whispering it right into the woman's face, 'Fanny, you bitch, you utter bitch, you cunning little whore.'

$\mathcal{D}$r Cogswell was standing in silhouette, with his back to Samuel, looking out the window, down at the street.

He appeared to be humming. His hands were crossed behind his back and his thumbs were playing some kind of ridiculous game, whirring in a wheel over each other. He was rocking back and forth on the heels of his boots, and humming.

Samuel tried to say something but his mouth would not work. He was still surfacing, still making his way up from that murky depth in which he had seemed to be trapped. This frightened him, this momentary stasis. He had seemed to be at the bottom of some brackish sea that barely moved. It was as if he were a dead fish, moving with the barely stirring currents. Then he had felt, at the end of the third finger on his left hand, a slight tingling in the blood. He was so pleased to feel something, he tried to touch this third finger with his thumb. But the thumb wouldn't work.

This is when he had surfaced.

This is when he had the confusion of who — where — he was.

The startling silhouette of a man against an oblong of light.

'Freddie?' he had murmured.

Then he sank again, but less deeply this time; he was already bobbing up to the surface, and this time he broke through.

He was, embarrassingly, sitting in the dental parlour of Dr Cogswell, who had turned, half smiling, and had now taken a few steps towards him, smiling as if Samuel were his own invention.

'Are you ready for me to work on the tooth, sir?' Cogswell said.

Samuel nodded.

'Yes.'

Cogswell laughed at this, then revealed the spittoon, which was bloody. The instruments were also in disarray.

'I have fixed your tooth, while you were under the ether,' Cogswell said. He was inviting Samuel to stand.

'It's all over, Mr . . . er . . . Barton.'

Samuel stood there, profoundly disoriented. His jaw felt sore, it was true, but of that terrible ache only the ghost of it, remained in his mind. It was as if he could hear its echo.

Cogswell was looking at him closely.

Samuel had an overpowering sense of the fine hairs of Cogswell's beard, which was quite closely cropped around his jaw. Samuel had the sense that hair did not grow easily on Dr Cogswell. The hair on his head, a pale sandy auburn, was brushed up into a showy crescent but had collapsed through lack of substance.

This perception — the intimacy of it — overwhelmed, destabilised Samuel.

He wanted to escape.

Instead: 'How can I thank you, Dr Cogswell?' Samuel had an odd feeling of nakedness. He was disturbed that he had been wrenched from such a complete hallucination to what was meant to be the real world — yet the real world had the disconcerting sense of being unreal, thin, glassy, even a trick.

'You have no need to thank me, Mr Barton. Or rather the price of my thanks is a simple one. Five shillings and sixpence.'

Samuel fumbled with his coins. He was glad to pay. He wanted to get out. He kept having the eerie feeling that Cogswell knew more about him than he knew about Cogswell. Cogswell, however, showed no sense of intimacy as he rattled open a small cashbox with a key, placed Samuel's coins within, counting them quickly as he did so, then handing back sixpence change.

The coin fell into Samuel's hand. He picked up his — as he saw it now — totally ridiculous hatbox. What would Fanny want with a hat bought in *Napier*, for heaven's sake?

'Ah, for Fanny?' Dr Cogswell said lightly, as Samuel turned to go.

Samuel felt a dead blush fall upon his face.

'You mentioned the lady, just once, when you were "trancing".'

Samuel's lips tried to say something but couldn't.

He began to walk quickly away, but Cogswell stopped him. He placed a light hand on the top of Samuel's shoulder. It was a delicate gesture, unthreatening.

'Please. I meant to say. I discovered a certain amount of decay in the tooth beside the one I tended. If you can find the time' — Samuel understood him to mean the money — 'I can see to that tooth. With', he added with his now well-established charm, half bowing, 'the same miraculous absence of pain. As you now know, Mr Barton.'

Old Tom

*I*t was night. It was beyond night; it was the dark hours of the morning. Only one person was awake — or at least walking the streets. His shadow slipped away from him, slithered back, joined to him. There were only three street lamps the length of Hastings Street — there were only three street lamps in all of Napier. This man, made small by all that was still around him, moved slowly, carefully. He looked at window fastenings, at locks on doors. Occasionally, when a room was lit, he would pause, grow still.

He believed, without expressing it to himself, that by stillness he could drain into himself all the sensations — the repercussions — of what might be happening in that lit cell.

He went towards a door, tried it, moved on.

It was a night of waxing moon. The vast scythe of sea was silver-licked, undulant, sending out its roar across the Bay, submerging the buildings in its rowdy music, pushing in against gaunt wood, closed glass. *The Hill, the Hill, the Hill.* It was almost the stilled heartbeat of that place — the Hill.

Where was it? It often seemed to change its shape. Was it St Michael's, in

Cornwall where he was born — a craggy, castle-topped piece of mystery? Or St Helena, the isle of exile where he had been sent as a young man, a soldier, to guard Napoleon? Or Scinde Island, Sinned Island, Sin Island in New Zealand, which he was sent to guard?

Old Tom, aged seventy-eight, night watchman.

For him the Hill was one thing only: the Old Men's Refuge in Tole Street, one thousand and four steps, up on the sunless side of the Hill. In one of the cleats, where the poor people lived. Those whose lives were spent in perennial shadow. Scarlet fever territory, home to tuberculosis, typhoid.

Old Tom liked counting things (three street lamps, one asylum, one hospital, one prison, one infants' home, one Oddfellows' Hall. Two jugs of ale, a pair of boots, a single pillow, one blanket (grey), a slightly greasy frock-coat (once owned by Colonel Whitmore, handed by his wife to a sergeant, on whose decease the sacred article was handed on, almost ceremoniously, to Old Tom). That it didn't quite fit, that it slid off his shoulders, was neither here nor there, against its inherited mana, its blessing. It was his dignity.

Old Tom with his lantern, which he never lit, except in exceptional circumstances. (Once a cat trapped inside a wall. Once a woman — no, a girl of twelve — giving birth under a house, a bloody mire. Once when he found himself tricked and all on his own: he thought he heard a Maori war cry echo across the swamp. Was it the cannibals about to attack and eat the eyeballs of every white man in Napier? Roast their gizzards over a flame? Would he have to sound the alarm — awake all the sleeping souls and get them to flee to the barracks up on Scinde Island's peak?)

This was the most testing time for Old Tom, night watchman, who had started his life as a young 'un, a corporal guarding 'the little corporal' who had humbled all of Europe. Old Tom who had been at Napoleon's funeral, firing a fusillade into the chill Atlantic. He now plodded the streets of Napier town, in the shade of Sin Island.

Old Tom was now on the corner of Tennyson Street, beneath the Golden Tooth of Dr Cogswell. There was a wind got up, a cool wind that made Old Tom's bones ache. He made a point of having no regular, clockwise movements about the town. He had a beat, it was true: up Tennyson, down Emerson, then back up Dickens — that was the commercial section — along Shakespeare, down the steps to Milton, a quieter walk along dim Carlyle: he might have been traversing the history of English literature, except he could not read.

He liked to creep along, as silent as the wind. He likened himself to a shadow falling out of a tree: you could not tell what was quivering leaf, what was the intense fibrillations of Old Tom's senses: he prided himself on his ears.

He listened to the metallic swing of the gilded tooth overhead.

Sometimes, even when the doctor's windows were not lit, he had heard upstairs what sounded like too wild merriment. Deranged footsteps, others running after, cascades of convulsive laughter, a decanter? dropped. Followed by suppressed laughter, then silence.

How many sighing ululations he had heard from behind half-opened windows. Some of them no more than the snuffle of an animal rooting, at other times a more peremptory sound. He did not envy any of them. He had left behind a 'wife' — and how many children? — in Nova Scotia. He listened to the sound of a child crying in the night. The wail of an abandoned babe, left alone in a piss-stinky mess, frightened of the dark.

The dark, the dark.

At times he conceived of a great overwhelming spirit, almost a sound, if he could only put a name to it. What this sound was, he could not precisely say. It arose out of the wind, or perhaps the wind's music as it passed over swamp. It was a crying, lost sound. At times he listened to it and other times it fell away to a murmur, on the very edge of sound.

This night it was absent. Curiously.

Old Tom continued his rounds.

And then, as night dawned into grey, he found himself, like clockwork, making his own one thousand, five hundred and ninety-four steps up towards the barracks, where he loitered, to salute the day.

The barracks were atop the highest point of the Hill: a stockade, a miniature castle.

Once the sun was risen and all was well, he then took five hundred and ninety steps down to Tole Street, finding himself in the Old Men's Refuge, where he joined all those other unwanted single men — old men who would never make it home. But this was his home, this cell, with a single cot, a grey blanket, a single pillow — and a lantern, laid down, seldom lit.

Old Tom, night watchman, had finished his rounds.

How the Mail Travels Overland from London to India

*S*aturday bloomed dark and wet. Samuel was captured in his room, fenced in. Listening to the sound of water puddling and piddling and pissing down the spouting, into the puddle, which became a pool, became a lake under the Haresnape shack. All around, outside, he saw mud, sheets of water.

The swamp to the back of the house sent off its nauseous gases: the distant reaches were used as a dumping ground for nightsoil, dead animals.

It would be a night of mosquitoes. Biting, buzzing, seeking any entry they could get to his skin, so they might set their septic needles in and draw out blood. He swirled away from the window. He had been standing there, his arm up against the damp wallpaper, looking out. Not seeing. Only feeling — captured.

Fanny. Why had she come back?

Haresnape was banging about the corridor, sweeping. She might have been trying to sweep him away. Except her hostility towards him had been allayed momentarily by the gold coins — four — he had slid into her palm. She was frankly surprised. Instantly swung around to an almost garrulous intimacy.

'Didja win?' she asked. Suspecting him of cards.

Had he won? He asked himself this as he inspected his own haughtiness. His inevitable response was to retreat to his room, murmuring idiotic prevarications: 'No. Indeed. Some money. Owed me.'

Closing the door on her inquiring face, eyes trying to rob him. He longed to say to her, I will be moving out, Mrs Haresnape. As soon as possible. But some survival instinct, wrought out of the months, the year of his flight, kept him mum. He would wait his moment.

So this time now was spent in pacing. He was wearing a dressing gown, a rather splendid soiled silken thing, tied around his waist. Below, trousers and shirt — smudged around the collar, smelling in a homely way of his own sweat. No tie. Slippers. He wished he had a scent — he wheeled around the room and found himself, accused, right by Fanny's face: Fanny on the wall.

'Why,' he asked her, 'are you chasing me? Can't I . . . *ever* . . . escape?'

Outside the door, in the hall, a sudden plunge to silence.

'Mr Barton, sir, is that you?'

She even tried the door handle.

'No!' he cried out in some pain. Then, sweating a little, turning into an actor (I will get a new room as soon as the rains stop): 'No, everything is in order, Mrs Haresnape. I was just . . . reminiscing. To myself. Out loud.'

He knew she wanted, almost demanded, that he open the door. But he would not. He would rather not announce his strangeness to her. She who by now was used to his moods — his sudden ebullience, his swishing cloak of manners and good humour, calling her 'Mistress Hatty Haresnake', to be followed, no less sequentially, by the slower, dandier dawdle down into a mute silence, almost an inability to run together words in speech. He might remain unshaved during these days. He would sleep in late. He would barely stir from behind his locked door. She suspected drink. At these times she had learnt to knock upon his door, lightly, leave behind a dinner plate, some cheese, a little bread. That was all. And then, in time (and usually following the mail from London, a monetary infusion) the toy that was his being would be animated again. Come awake.

Dispense its slightly suspect charm.

Oh, she knew everything about him, Hetty Haresnape thought: she saw him as if naked, as if she could stare into the insides of his being. Except . . .

'Sir, I would not disturb you normally . . .'

Her voice seemed inside the lock. Was she peering in?

He peeled the door back. Swung there, in the gale of her interest. Except that she was not looking at him, or behind him into his room. She was looking down.

At a damp missive. An envelope speckled all over, like a sparrow's wing, with darts and dashes of rain.

'A lassie dropped this in.'

She handed it over. And waited there. Now there was the tender negotiation — her ravenous interest in what was happening in his non-life. Her hunger for news. (She had already told him how Alf had gone off on a drunk down the port last night, with some of Samuel's gold. He was sleeping it off at that moment, in the darkened cesspit of the Haresnape bedroom.)

The children were rolling hoops in the kitchen, banging them against the wooden wall, yelling.

'You kids, pipe down. Or you'll feel more than the back of your dad's hand.'

A momentary silence.

Susie trailed in, sucking the edge of her sacking apron, wooden clogs clattering along the floor.

'Wipe your nose, young missus,' Hetty said and swooped down, roughly wiping the child's nose on a rag. As if she sought to wipe away the child's features. Susie's eyes moved from her mother to the letter in Samuel's hand.

'Not today, Susan, dear,' Samuel said.

Sometimes he took pity and allowed her into his room — on condition she touched nothing. He would teach her the ABCs. In his presence she changed into a silent wondering child: she was fascinated by the 'ladies' on the wall. Hetty Haresnape had gained most intelligence by interrogating her child when Samuel was absent.

'Who does he say they is?'

'Ladies.'

A threatening silence.

'I know they're *ladies*,' Hetty hissed. 'What else?'

But Susie kept to her alliance. She dandled her head down and played dumb.

'They are great . . . beauties,' she was quoting here, 'of the . . . *theatre*.'

She managed the word with difficulty. Yet she liked to run the embroidered richness of its sound through her teeth. It promised . . .

But today Mr Barton, sir, was closing the door. On her.

He turned around, went to the dim and dirty wash of light. He pulled the lace aside. The handwriting was unknown. But fanciful. *Mr S. Barton Esq.* A fluttering cloak of language laid across the puddle of his being. Yet the envelope was of an inferior quality — the sort any tradesman might buy, by the dozen. He slid his nail, his too long fingernail, under the pudgy weight of pulp paper. Slipped out a sheet, folded.

Rose Cottage
14 Carlyle Street,
Napier
September 5, 1872
Dear Mr Barton,
I am being so bold as to remind you of our little 'festivity' this evening. (Oddfellows' Hall, Milton Road, 8 p.m. sharp). I would not be so rash except the weather, having turned inclement, possibly means attendances will be smaller than we had hoped. And yet the purpose of the entertainment — to raise money for the church organ — is most worthy. I am sure you agree. In anticipation of your attendance, please accept my humble thanks, I remain etc, etc
Madeleine Perrett

Samuel stared down at the intimacy, the lovely floriferous nature of her Christian name. Its nakedness charmed him. To think that Miss Perrett was a Madeleine. He folded the paper up and abstractedly placed it on the corner of his writing table. To think she would imagine he cared whether Napier had an organ or not. It could go without music forever, so long as he was aboard a barque out of there.

At that moment a hoop hit his bedroom wall, hard. This was followed by a screel of kiddie laughter, wild and daring, followed by a walloping slap, a mother's harried voice: 'I told you kids to keep it down but what do you do but try me all the time . . .' accompanied by a screaming child — Samuel hung still, listened — it wasn't Susie. This was followed by jeering laughter, footsteps running up the passageway and *bang! bang! bang!* against his door, as if by accident each child kicked it as he — or she — went past. Hetty Haresnape's voice rose another octave. Mr Haresnape was roaring awake.

'You bloody brats! I'll wring your blasted necks, I'll . . .'

Samuel picked the letter up again, stared down at it. Could he wait until eight p.m.? Could he escape the house and, with dripping umbrella, go — where? The Athenaeum? The Masonic bar? The Linzes' even? Play their piano? He ached — he ached then to be up in that upstairs room. But he had dropped a card in to Mr Linz's shop to say he would call by on Sunday afternoon, at three p.m., if that was not an inconvenience.

Samuel needed to clarify how Linz might sell the earring.

He found himself turning to a book on top of his desk, opening the pages and breathing in the smell. (A painted woman leant down, out of her box, lighting a cigarette from a gas jet. Her jewels shimmered, her décolletage exposed. She breathed in the smoke then raised her face, bold, inscrutable, aware that a ring of men were gazing — not at the stage but at her. She smiled a little, then she sank back behind the brocade curtain of her box, into a suede darkness.)

Scent of powder, rouge, cigar smoke. Brandy. Dirt.

His shaking fingers felt within the leaves.

Thieved.

A single piece of rice-paper, folded in three, slipped out. Within it was another sheet, smaller, hidden.

He unfolded the first sheet. Shaking.

The handwriting, as against Miss Perrett's bold, almost masculine script, was over-elaborate, swift, a mincing gait of fineness.

Violet ink.

> *Darling, do come up tonight. Everybody is too drunk to mind.*
> *Stella is here and wants to see you. So come, love.*

The letter was unsigned. Except for an elegant semaphore of an initial — F? — ending on a few exaggerated stylish dots, like comets plunging off the page.

The second sheet was in different handwriting. More masculine.

It flowed across the page fast, urgent.

> *I love you darling. I am your slave. Do with me whatever*
> *you will. As I know you will. You fascinating being.*
> *P.S. Stella asks that you bring her umbrella. She left it*
> *behind. Her backhair, she says, comes uncurled in the rain.*

This letter was also unsigned.

Samuel glanced away in the darkness, as if seeing something. Then his eyes found the first note again, and for a moment a look of great sadness passed across his features.

The illuminated slides had just finished. Mr Liddle was packing them away, carefully. The kerosene lamps sent out their pungent odour and Miss Perrett curved over her shoulder to send an oblique apology to Samuel, who was sitting behind her, squeezed between Mr Mercer and Mrs Wren on a backless wooden pew. Mr Liddle was frowning, and Miss Perrett was wondering if he had diagnosed the final tepid applause as a reprimand for the fact that his illuminated lecture on The Route of the Overland Mail to India had, indeed, gone on far too long.

The earlier murmurs of astonishment at the palely coloured, pretty picturesqueness had faded into a mute silence that gradually, over forty-five minutes, turned into a rebellious withdrawal of any sound whatsoever, except the occasional sigh from Miss Perrett, to be followed by the rustling of her skirts, then, at one point — finally — the noisy collapse of her umbrella onto the floor, which seemed to awaken everyone.

But Mr Liddle, mid-stream in his oration, had just paused, then continued with his soliloquy about the marvels of the Indian subcontinent. Miss Perrett lectured herself silently: This is what you get when you have a Methodist — someone who preaches. She found herself rising to her feet.

Just at that point the rain and wind took up their furies and dashed themselves against the seaward side of the wooden building. The framework of the building shook, the flame within the kerosene lamps wobbled, shadows on the wall danced. Everyone in the darkened hall looked at the quickening fall of drips into the carefully placed bucket.

Miss Perrett saved the day by placing her finger on her lips conspiratorially, then walking down and saying, 'Please, I hate to interrupt, but I fear the bucket . . . ?'

And here she indicated the fact that the bucket was almost full. It would require replacing. Instantly the 'congregation' disassembled. Mr Mercer ran down the several steps to the room at the side. His wife wheezed in with another bucket.

'It's so wet today, ain't it?' she said asthmatically. Aware of minding her Ps and Qs with the dragon Perrett.

'Perhaps, given that time is marching on . . .' Madeleine Perrett melodramatically consulted the watch that hung off her breast, although actually she gave herself no time to look at the hands on the watch. 'Perhaps we all might like to show our appreciation . . . for Mr Liddle's really extremely . . . *educational* lantern show lecture?'

There was an appreciable moment of uncertainty before everyone — except Mr Liddle — realised he was being hustled off the stage. Then, believing they were about to be delivered, the audience broke out into a bright, fulsome falseness of applause. Mr Liddle, flushing, seemed to come awake, looked about the narrow hall at the eighteen people present, smiled a little uncertainly, then said in an excited tone of voice, 'If you would just let me . . . permit me . . .'

A huge vision of Lucknow flicked up upon the wall.

'Lucknow,' he began, in the low drone he took to be scientific, 'best known to Napierites as a terrace on Scinde Island, is in actual fact more famous for the frightful carnage of the Lucknow Siege, in which our brave army fought tooth and nail to free British women from the embattled embassy. The loss of life was dreadful and . . .'

$\mathcal{S}$amuel let out a low, punctured sigh. He was almost overcome with the smell of wet wool, warm flesh, sweating oilskin, kerosene. The slurpy drip of water in the bucket measured out his pain. The time in-between flowered into a plain — a vast windy steppe of unutterable boredom. *These people did not know how to entertain.* He longed to leap up, to jump onto the stage.

Instead he sat there, breathing out slowly, looking at the crêpe paper streamers dangling damply down and, to the side, an economical pile of wooden logs, the metal stove unlit.

A little further along, a photo-engravure of the Queen (God Bless Her) hung out, her pendulous German eyes glazed in disbelief.

Miss Perrett murmured to Samuel as she sat down, 'I tried, I tried, I tried!'

$\mathcal{E}$ventually, even the wonders of the Indian subcontinent and the marvels of the Royal Mail had their limits and Mr Liddle sat down, mystified at why the bright applause of half an hour ago had withered to a tepid pattering of hand on hand — barely polite, he said to himself, taking umbrage as he packed away his miracles.

Now a Mr Barnes was illustrating how a telephone worked. He had constructed wires between the hall in Milton Road and a cottage next door. He had in his hand a handpiece made of carved wood, with wires attached. First of all, with a daring glance at the audience, he spoke into the handpiece in a normal voice — or one raised just slightly, to be heard over rain pelting on tin. He had beside him an accomplice, Miss Tuxford, who, on the completion of his act, was to sing 'Oh for the Wings of a Dove'.

He held the handpiece out and Miss Tuxford, holding it to her ear uncertainly, listened in silence.

The small audience held still.

To receive sound over space. To puncture distance. Remove its sting. It would be a miracle.

But Miss Tuxford shook her curls. She was blushing with mortification. Mr Barnes snatched the handpiece, then listened. He presented his face, a complete simulacrum of honesty, towards the audience, furrowed his brow, as if he were taking part in a melodrama, shot his cuffs, listened again, rapturously. Then his expression dissolved and he looked, for a second, blank. He waited, but only the forlorn sound of rain on tin took up. Attacked their eardrums.

Wind, as if to intimate how humans are still held captive by the most ancient of forces, flung its fury against the small wooden building. It shook. Rain pounded down. Miss Perrett could hear the fuming roar of waves on shingle. Everyone held still, listened.

This was their miracle. A humble one. They were inside a hall. Dry for the moment, though soon enough they would have to set out.

Mr Barnes raised his voice over the roar and announced that, due to inclement conditions, which, he did not hesitate to say, if these conditions had been different, he could have delivered to them a living example of how a modern miracle, the telephone, worked . . .

Mr Liddle had the distinct irritation of hearing applause that was livelier than his second round, delivered to a miracle that hadn't even happened. He pursed his lips. Nursed his denigration.

He briefly hated Napier.

Miss Perrett rose, august, and made her way towards the piano. Two men, Mercer and Wren, raced forward, eager to be doing something, to justify their presence. They wheeled the piano carefully towards the front of the stage. Miss Perrett adjusted the stool, while Miss Tuxford arranged her curls, the folds of her dress, licked her lips, and made sure she stood near enough to the kerosene light so that she might be illuminated.

Miss Perrett pressed down the first note. She was thinking: A disappointing sum — only three pounds two shillings raised. They might as well have put the sum in themselves. But turning around to look out at the motley crew she accepted, blindly, the mute will of the people as to what could be done in a tiny place, almost without resources.

Perhaps this helped her overlook the trembling, banal little sound coming out of the virgin's mouth. The saccharine prettiness of the sound insulted Miss Perrett, who preferred something darker, stronger, richer. Music was her secret god — or rather she saw in music an expression of the force of life. And the little milkmaid, with her arched fingers and pretty pink cheeks, standing up on tippy-toe to make a point — her shallow renditions were but sketches of a blunt pencil on a blank canvas. Dutifully Miss Perrett played, careful not to overwhelm the slim sound. She held back. She concentrated. She made sure she did not outshine. And so the pretty maid sang on.

For her encore she did a crowd favourite (of course).

It was 'Home Sweet Home'.

And so the faces in the hall, all but one, softened, and lost their hardened looks, and the wax sank down, and each of them contemplated what they had lost, and what they had gained, and in what lay the difference, whether small or large;

and so in that little hall, amid the rain and storm, eighteen — or was it seventeen? — humans lost themselves and accepted, gratefully, the balm of art. Art as they did know it.

*S*amuel had lost himself. It was how he survived. He sank away from his chair, pulled himself away from contact with the human form on either side of him. He would have liked to laugh: outright, abrupt, furious, dismissive. He felt asleep, as if he were drowning under the weight of all the mediocrity — he wanted desperately to dash to the front of the hall. He longed to corral all of them and make them listen; instead he concentrated on withdrawing, on eliminating himself, on reducing his essence so that his body became his shell, and the shell was briefly empty.

He no longer saw the wooden tongue-in-groove walls with the cord from the Gothic windows blowing in the wind, the scuttle of the crêpe paper streamers eerily riding out, or the flames in the kerosene lamps swaying in the wind; he no longer saw the young maiden straining to reproduce a sound — or even the good woman Perrett as she laboured over the keys, her back braced as if to bear an insupportable pain. (Three pounds, two shillings!)

He saw that sinuous moment as the gas jet blew a beautiful yellow-green, the cigarette leant down. For one second the paper made contact with the flame and it scorched. All over the paper a blackened algebra of shape changed, turned rose, ruby, became inflamed. The beautiful painted woman — Fanny — raised the cigarette, to her lips. Her lips were scarlet — beyond scarlet. They were an emblem of desire, and they were curved into a strange smile. She placed the cigarette in her lips — her pale blue eyes glancing out from the box into the promenade of the Strand Theatre. In the heated bowl of her iris could be seen a clutch of men in evening dress, staring up at her. Hungrily.

Some were standing on chairs, hands balanced on the shoulders of those in front.

Others were crowded on the floor below, hindering people as they walked along, so they in turn gathered. Gazed upwards.

Behind these men, over their heads, limned with the lights coming off the stage, Fanny could sense, just sense, that the stage performance was still going on: it was the burlesque of the moment, *King Arthur*, or *The Days and Knights of the Round Table* (New Magnificent Scenery! Costumes! Machinery! Overture and Incidental Characters — Good, Bad and Indifferent!). The scene was set at 'Stonehenge at Sunrise' and Merlin was wandering around, with a bad head cold, attacked by a pesky dog. The audience was rippling and tittering with laughter. Yet the actor playing Merlin seemed to glance, once, out into the audience.

Any entertainer can sense an ebbing away of attention.

Fanny enjoyed this, rankly. She breathed in on her cigarette and glanced boldly across to the box opposite. The three plumes, arranged around a gilded crown, showed even in the dim light of the Strand Theatre. She thought she caught a glimpse of raddled blazing jewel. The Prince of Wales was sitting to the very back; he was bent over the — hand? — of a splendid creature whose back was turned to the stage. Her shoulder and back were beautifully naked, powdered, unutterably feminine. So Fanny enjoyed her moment of triumph, sensing that the Prince had dropped the hand, was looking directly over towards her. A gentleman wearing orders was leaning over the Prince of Wales' shoulder, whispering something. Both men now looked directly at her.

All about were looks, talk, suspended conversation — the limelight from the stage was burning her, was burning her up. She wished it had been her on the stage. She might have pushed her skirts behind her, opened her lovely throat and poured out 'My Pretty Jane', which was recognised as her song. She would have followed that with a lighter, comic turn.

She breathed out a beautiful fan of smoke and, genie-like, withdrew behind the veil of this smoke, into the shadows of Lord Frederick's box.

He was sitting there, watching her jealously. He wanted to get her home. But he also — and this was queer — enjoyed watching her power over other men. He enjoyed her performance.

She took up her fan and began to work it languidly.

'I think, dear Clinton, we might go for a little saunter?'

He nodded — blindly, dumbly. He was her creature: he knew that.

She came out of the box, graciously, fanning herself slowly as she moved through the crowd. Aware of the men turning to look at her, and of the women — the painted women, the whores — looking at her with a blaze of jealousy, of envy.

She was wearing the beautiful fly-shaped jewels that night, one in either ear. They glittered as she breathed. But as she walked along, or rather glided, bowing slightly to the left, to the right, she jerked to a halt. Someone had stood on the train of her dress. There was the sound — the terrible sound — of fabric tearing.

Lord Frederick had raised his monocle to his eye. His face showed no expression. Fanny wheeled round.

There was a youth standing there. Blushing, stammering.

'I am most . . . Oh. How can I apologise?'

Fanny looked at the young man. He had a fresh, unspent face. He was also blushing. His clothes were not those of a swell. A lawyer's clerk perhaps? Medical student? He looked terrified. Something in Fanny softened. The instant retort, the sharp reprimand, died on her lips. She who had flicked her fan shut, in distaste, now eased it open, began to ply it back and forth, back and forth, as if she were overheated.

'You may pay, young man. In some unaccountable way.' She smiled at him, raising her fan over her lips so that only her eyes gazed out at him. And her eyes were frank, ingenuous, full of ardour.

This was when Fanny first saw Samuel. When Samuel first saw Fanny. This was when he fell in love with her. Was conquered.

She was wounded. Would offer him everything.

'Young man,' she said. 'Follow me.'

And she tapped him on the shoulder lightly. He, Samuel, was aware that the gentleman with the beautiful creature was turning to him, looking at him intensely. He nodded to the gentleman, who looked away with infinite detachment.

Samuel separated himself from his law student friend, Cummings, who gave him a slight — congratulatory? — nudge forward. He had never been with such a supreme creature.

He prepared to walk behind her but she swivelled around, laughing a little to someone at the side, indicating with her gloved hand that she expected him to walk beside her. This he did. She slid her hand easily, quickly, into his crooked arm, and together now, almost as beau and belle, they sauntered along the promenade. Samuel, all the time deafened by his own excitement, changed in that instant into someone who had been accepted into a secret golden circle, where all would be laughter, and ease, and escape.

She took him to a small side room. There was a maidservant there, a rather bold moustached woman.

'Please pin me up, Maisie dear,' the beauty said. She seemed to know everybody there.

Looking out into the room, Fanny said, 'The usual crush.'

Samuel was so excited that he said, emphatically, 'Yes!' Then altered his tone, to catch some of her languor. 'Yes.'

She looked at him and laughed.

'You are — how old?'

He blushed. She looked at him more closely and laughed again, but this time a little tenderly. She leant forward to him — he thought she was going to kiss him for one terrible, shaming moment of desire . . . he had gone limp with wanting her . . .

Instead she pinched his arm lightly, through the material.

'Don't worry . . .' she seemed to be searching for a name.

'Samuel Barton,' he said, bowing. She held out her hand.

He kissed it lightly, feeling an instantaneous shock as his lips touched the heat of her gloved flesh. Expertly she removed her hand and looked at him quizzically. 'Don't worry, Samuel, we all have our little secrets.'

And she did not exactly laugh with him, but she leant her body into his for one second. Samuel could not quite explain it to himself, this is what he said later: he could explain nothing about the evening — including how he and his friend had gone to the Strand Theatre almost on a dare, each of them knowing that neither had the money for much more than an entrance ticket, knowing that it was a place where loose women were, but had almost instantly been caught up, swirled into depths he hardly knew existed. Yet, rapturously, he liked it all — he loved it. He was surprised he felt so at home.

She slithered past him, hesitating for a moment, saying, 'Join Lord Frederick and me in our box if you wish. But first of all, would you be so kind as to give Maisie a . . . coin?'

Maisie turned to him and waited expectantly.

He delved into his pockets, found his cab fare home — he had no smaller coin. He was not sure what she expected, so he handed over his crown and she, looking at him frankly in the face, took the coin, turned from him, then a second later, as if relenting, turned back and slid some coins into his hand. 'Here,' she said. 'I could not rob you blind, or pluck you out, though heaven knows, young man, you might as well hang a sign around your neck with the words painted on it.'

'Promise you will ask no questions?' she had said.

Samuel wanted, in one part of him, to go out and find Cummings. He wanted to say he would be late, or that Cummings could go. He wanted to say: *please, for God's sake, don't leave me here — alone with such a magnificent creature.* He didn't know what he wanted. He had lost himself; or rather, suddenly that old self had instantly dropped off him, like an insect skin that had blown away. He was living now in a delirious present. His skin, all his skin, was alive, was burning. The blaze of gas-light, the dazzle of the women's jewels, the curve of breast, the offering of desire — tasselled curtains, gilt on plaster, laughter, lazy conversation, something else insinuating, sexual, drizzling through from the supper room. Beautiful women everywhere, stopping, pausing on the turn, to glance meaningfully at him. Other men looking at him with a frank lust of jealousy. If only they. If only he.

Why him?

He had suddenly become handsome, desirable.

It was some mistake, surely?

He thought, for just a second, of Ursula back in Nottingham, to whom he was almost betrothed.

The beautiful creature was walking along now, quite quickly, looking neither left nor right. She had bent down and said to Lord Frederick, pressing her fan into the pit of his stomach, digging the end in, 'No, you wait here. I want a little adventure with this charming . . . boy.'

The way she said 'boy' made Samuel blush. With a rapt sexual excitement. Where were they going? Was it possible she had a room? Was she, indeed, so loose that she . . . ?

He followed closely behind her, talking — he did not know why, about his clerkship at the law firm in the city. She listened attentively — or was it not at all? He noticed Cummings had gone. Disappeared. No, there he was. Cummings was standing over there, all alone. He made some gesture to him, as if to indicate it was time to go. But Samuel no longer knew him. In his new life.

Besides, the violin strings in the orchestra were vibrating mightily, and on the stage the lights came up to reveal an enchanted forest. There were soft depths of scrim, and dazzling, glittering trees. Wafts of colours were coming and going like a perpetual rainbow. There was the sound of a harp: shimmering, glamorous as golden raindrops flecking through space.

She led him to a small side door and knocked upon it sharply.

'Oh, Fan.'

There was a broken-down-looking man in plaid pants. A soiled shirt. He was halfway through eating a chop. A plate sat on the top of a ladder.

'I want to show this darling boy behind the scenes . . .'

The broken-down man looked at him. Samuel afterwards tried to work out what exactly this glance had meant. (As time went on, he would come across this look again and again. It was not exactly insulting — rather it was like a swift swerve of a flame held against a silhouette, as if to diagnose something about him. Friend or foe?) But as easily the man relaxed and seemed to welcome Samuel as one of themselves. He closed the thin door on the noise outside.

A lamp lit up a dripping brick wall. It smelt dank and cold. Samuel shivered.

The dimmed light for one moment changed Fanny. She seemed — he could not quite put his finger on it. As if sensing his changed regard, she took a step further into the dark and then held out a hand to him.

'You must take my hand. There are steps. You mustn't tumble.'

*H*e followed behind her. He had no sense of perspective. Just her breath, which was even, deep. His own ragged. He wanted to. He had the mad desire to pull her to him, bury himself inside her. She would not?

'Fanny?' he asked, the first time he had used her name.

With an appreciable, almost impatient tug she pulled him into a room. It was a dressing room, and he was amazed to see the dancers he had seen earlier on the stage — the *Pas de Fascination* — lounging about on boxes, some smoking, others just sitting there, slumped and absent-looking. Up close, the faces of the women were almost grotesque with paint, their costumes coarse, smelling.

The room stank of stale sweat. An old hag was massaging the shoulders of the lead dancer, who had the top of her dress wound down, her head pulled forward so her hair cascaded over onto her lap. The old hag looked up at Fanny, the young man. She said something to the woman she was massaging. Cackled. Samuel had the sense it may not have been flattering, because the woman flicked her hair back, in one wild action of contempt, then looked at Fanny moving through the room.

'Oh, congratulations, dearie,' the woman said to Fanny.

Others, semi-dressed, murmured to her lazily, as if half dead with exhaustion — 'Oh, Fan. He's so pretty we could eat him.'

The women laughed. All about the room were plates with half-eaten chops on them, and bottles of cider and ale. A little alcoholic woman, like a depleted ballet dancer, was mumbling to herself, laughing hilariously.

The stage manager bustled in, all business.

'You're on next, dearie. Come on, wake up!'

Fanny led Samuel to the prompt side of the stage.

A man sat high on a stool, hunched over pages that had notes scribbled all over them. He glanced once at Fanny and her beau.

'You mustn't move an inch,' Fanny murmured.

Samuel was transfixed. From his viewpoint he was seeing everything in reverse. (He had never been backstage.) He saw the mechanics, faces lit from limelight, waiting to yank a thick-coiled rope attached to the next scene-drop. (A castle.)

The forest, too, which had appeared so entrancing from the pit, was revealed as coarse fabric, daubed all over in a mess of paint, with strips of metallic sheen sewn randomly on. The little gas flares of the footlights burnt his eyes.

The actors seemed strangely intense, yet somehow casual. A mechanic leant down and placed a sulphuric-smelling powder onto a burning piece of lime. A gorgeous green began to seep across the stage.

A slim woman in a trouser role, Vivien, stood gazing at a sleeping King Arthur. Vivien whispered in a loud stage voice to Merlin:

> *Look, perchance, he's in their power.*

Merlin: Not so; he's safe while sleep

> Shall from his eyes their soft enchantment keep.
>
> He knows no spell to shut folks up in trees
>
> — Or rocks as I do!

Vivien: *Do you? Teach me please!*

Merlin: Don't tease!

Vivien: *Do, please!*

Merlin: Let's prepare.

> This place is full of quagmires and pitfalls, you're aware
>
> Of magic mantraps and spring guns
>
> Of hidden mysteries and false suns.

Suddenly Merlin disappeared down a trapdoor. The audience roared and stamped. There was tumultuous applause, and Fanny, a beautiful fast creature if he had ever seen one, leant towards Samuel and said in the voice of a sister to a favourite brother: '*Welcome.*'

A Lone Soul

Solomon Linz had the eerie sense of being the only living human on the planet. But it was like this every Sunday morning, when he made his way back from the abattoir — if this was not too grand a word for the few pieces of corrugated iron slapped together on the compacted mud at the edge of the back lagoon.

He felt cleansed, as he always did, by his duties.

'*Blessed art Thou . . . who sanctified us with His commandments . . . concerning slaughtering.*'

The single slash of the blade through the jugular — between the windpipe, that fleshly, whitened tube, and the upper lobe of the lung — awarding a death as instant as possible. He who had grown used to lulling, to abstracting himself, to pretending not so much not to be a ritual slaughterer as someone whose job was an almost accidental outcome of an animal — a sheep, say — a knife and a religion. Yet he had to be expert: not to let the long knife slip, or the animal would become unfit. He who slaughtered for the four Jewish families in Napier, he who taught the children in his own sitting room, he who now walked home, the bled lamb warm in the crook of his arm, wrapped crudely in clean newspaper.

He was thinking of the earring.

He had dreamt of it the night before. A strange, chaotic, vivid dream. He was back in eastern Galicia. It was night. Winter. There was a fire lit. A torch. Slowly, and seemingly in a different time sequence, sound emerged. He had been asleep. He woke in a child's body. He was sitting upright. Through the room adults wreathed. His mother ran towards him, crying. Outside there was the sound of horses, breathing in the cold night air. Stamping. Soldiers had come into the room, they were pulling his father, yanking him out. His mother was trying to hold on to him. Wailing. Another soldier had come into the room, was smashing, piece by piece, everything he could find. The cabbala especially. Solomon climbed under the bed, then behind some barrels, under sacks. He hid. A sabre blade slid in around him. Thud. Hit the earth. Circled around him. Withdrew. He had shat himself. Now all he could hear was screaming. His mother's screaming.

Then it froze, and he realised he was looking through the other side of the jewel, and he was now an adult. And as he looked into the jewel, so all these events flowed backwards in time, then reversed themselves, so that he had simply come awake and his mother was preparing his older brother's food. It was not yet dawn and his brother was going on that long journey — the one on which he disappeared. His mother and brother were sitting at the table together, murmuring quietly as his mother passed over some coins, and Solomon smelt molasses, and corn and tar, and his mother reached her hand out across the table to his brother and they held hands, in silence, while his brother intoned a prayer. The soft murmuring sent him back to sleep again. The prayer.

*H*e passed the Anglican church in Shakespeare Road, a small wooden building like something cut out with shears by a child. Inside, a voice intoning.

'*O Lamb of God, that takest away the sins of the world, have mercy upon us.*'

He lingered for a moment, enjoying the sound of a plain man's voice, a maroon-coloured voice: ordinary, serviceable, yet at that moment raised to a kind of beauty by its use. Inside the wooden church he heard the mumbled voices in response. Voice upon voice upon voice.

The church was packed.

Not a soul alive on the streets.

Except a Jew, with a lamb in the crook of his arm.

A bled lamb.

The animal between his thighs. He could feel the panting bellows of its panic. The glassy eye looking backwards, upwards. Desperately. Yellow and black. The black of its pupil seeking. Wanting to know: *What is my future?* He used — this was his private knowledge — the tone he used with Ada when they lay together, the soft, seducing, calming sounds, a kind of pre-language: placating, calming. Inquiring. Answer me, these sounds said.

The sheep, head now turning, ears lifting, seeking to get a sense of what was happening. One hoof raised. Paused.

He had to slither down then and hold the animal around the neck, as if in an embrace. There was a stench of fear. He had to move beyond it. Fast. Often the animal voided. He always felt better if he slit its throat before this happened. He could not allow . . . Human feelings would be a luxury.

The blade was buried. A scarlet rope. The eyes lifted back, pupils wide and glassy, the accusation there for him to read. *You are taking my life? Why are you taking my life? Who are you to be taking my life?*

Is this all my life is?

Gradually the yellow and black globe of the eye clouded, set. Gelled. The whitened tube of the windpipe peeled back, the blood no longer coursing out, coursing out its accusation.

Is this all?

The slump. His own sense of release. Like orgasm, perhaps, except that he did not, a man, allow himself to think of that.

He could not think. He had to work seriously.

Examining the blade, running his fingernail along the edge. Keeping it sharp. The blade almost one foot in length.

He made a point, with each animal, of intoning the blessing: '*Blessed art Thou . . . sanctified us . . . commanded us . . .*'

This was all — nothing else, no sounds except those sounds: the slishing splash of blood coursing out, the stamp of hoof, sometimes agitated, the baying cry, the bleat, unending drip.

Even though he washed the pen down each time, the new animal sensed. All its senses working overtime. Ears back. And that question.

He passed the Presbyterian church, in Tennyson Street. From here he could see the Methodist, the Anglican churches and, further down, the squat hard assertion of the Congregational citadel. On his own holy day he could see, out his back window, the Congregational band preparing. A tuba, the drum and some tambourines. Marching back and forth. Forth and back. Bleating.

Is this all?

It was a beautiful morning, after the rain. Puddles on the road he avoided. The sky washed out, pure. The ground struggling awake. A dog, a mongrel, looking at him, deciding whether to bark. Scenting animal. Linz changed the lamb from one arm to the other. His mother would have to salt the meat, let it soak. It would be used for dinner later in the week. The Cohens and Abrahams would call to get their portions. He closed his shop on Saturdays, the only jeweller in Napier who did so. He lost business by it. He lost something more, too, in the small town — some almost undiagnosable difference was made obvious. He did not fit. This could be dangerous. Which was why he went out of his way to be courteous. Honest. Reliable. A good citizen.

He hurried up the back steps of his shop. As he did so he smelt — he smelt all the love and domesticity of his life. From the top of the stairs a sweet scent of honey and poppyseed and butter and lemon. His mother was showing his wife, the lovely Ada, how to bake his favourite cake. For the man Barton.

He came up the stairs at a run and, saying nothing, laid the lamb on the wooden bench in the kitchen. He heard his wife in the bedroom pouring water into the tin bath. He listened to the sound and thought: my life is good. He poked his head into the parlour and looked down at his son. His son was asleep, his finger in the corner of his mouth. A faint smell of faeces drifted off him. Solomon frowned.

Not all was perfect.

He went into the bedroom as his wife, as swiftly, moved through another door. They did not talk. Not yet.

He would bathe in peace. Cleanse himself.

*H*is body returned an image of himself, under water. Magnified slightly, his hairiness floating, anemone-like. He soaped himself carefully, scrubbed under his nails. He sank back under the water. The water slurped out onto the floor. He enjoyed himself. Ada, he could hear, was in the other room. She was humming to herself, and he could hear also the boy making sounds. She was changing him, perhaps. The cake began to smell baked. Her footsteps, capable, swift, moved across the wooden floor. Outside he could hear voices — the churches were out now.

The boom-poom of the Congregational band took up. It was marching down Tennyson Street, brazenly seeking to drown out other worshippers. The tambourine rattle, the enthusiastic, slightly-out-of tune wheeze of the tuba.

There was the sound of a cricket ball hitting wood. A window slid down.

A woman somewhere called to another, across a back section.

The wind changed its direction and the window shivered in its embrasure. He was getting cold.

He got out and reached for his towel. He wiped himself down, then dressed in the clean clothing laid out by Ada. He would sleep for a little. Then he would awaken and conclude his business with the strangeling Barton.

It wasn't that Barton was precisely dishonest, or shady. It wasn't that, Solomon argued with himself as he lay there, looking at the ceiling rose. It was just that there was something — unexpressed. Something to do with the jewel. This wasn't unusual. Anyone selling something had a story. More often than not, of pain, or want, or some small tragedy. But with Samuel Barton there was something else — or other.

There was something not quite right. He tried to think what it was, but as his body settled he thought about his reading of the Torah, and the word *Terefah* came to mind. His mind, now numb, now sinking into sleep, nibbled at the edge of the thought, inspecting the meaning. It was an unclean animal, a wounded animal. He thought of an animal once with diseased kidneys. He had had to kill it, then pass it on to the goyim. Charity. He saw his neighbours, to the right, the Millers thanking him. Suspecting him at the same time. Turning away and smelling it to see if it was off. His mind now took another detour. (He was used to this, this freefall, this limpid examination of his consciousness, allowing his mind to produce words and concepts for him to examine later.)

The word *Azazel* came up: scapegoat, the central part of the Day of Atonement, the animal selected to express all the sins of the world. The scapegoat placed in an isolated region, let go in the wilderness. Why did he see then that lagoon, glimpsed over the ragged cut of corrugated iron, with the distant vista of the hills, then behind them the mountains? Was *this* his wilderness? And what did it mean, this selection of a scapegoat, and the weight placed upon it, of having to bear the sins of everyone?

He slept.

And awoke to a loveliness of sound. He who loved music. Who relied on it to drown out those other sounds. The bleat, the bash of blood, the rough intake of breath. He could hear a woman singing. For a moment he lost where he was. The room was dark. He suffered a complete memory break. He was — who? And where was this darkened wooden ceiling, with boards running across it, a burnished gasolier in the ceiling rose? Outside he saw sky — brilliant acidic white and a gull cut into it, its mouth open, cawing. A black line, a series of wooden pilasters: elegant, a classical illusion.

The woman's voice was a deep and rich mezzo-soprano, clear in the upper register. She was singing something called 'Fading Away, Fading Away' while the piano played mellowly beneath it.

He was, of course — he realised this now — inside the body of a thirty-eight-year-old man. He was all his sins, weaknesses and failings. He was half erect, he was randy, and in the other room a woman, a strange woman was singing.

He got up, dashed some water on his face. In the mirror he caught a satyr, his hairy eyebrows drawn together in a concertina of lust. He disliked this grinning man. His moist lips parted. Teeth carnivorous. Hair coming out the bottom of his nostrils. He had suddenly got older. Face creased by sleep. He poured — poured water over his face, drenched away that look. He was a married man, respectable.

He straightened himself up, put on his waistcoat, tightened his tie at his throat. Put on his jacket. He searched in the mirror again for a moment. That other being — lecherous, eager, superably human, beseeching, a porcine animal — had evaporated. Now he was back being Solomon Linz, responsible Shokhet. Yet this other man winked back at him, only half believing.

The woman's voice sank back, to the close of the song. He heard his wife clapping, saying, in German, 'beautiful, lovely, gorgeous'.

He walked down the passageway and pushed back the door.

But there was only his wife there, an opened door, as if someone had just left, and their visitor, Samuel Barton.

*T*hey were walking down the stairs. Deliberately Solomon had not said a word about the jewel, the business in hand. It was better, more delicate, to leave it dammed up. Let Barton raise it with him. This was how men did business. Yet at times during the afternoon, as Ada leant forward with the coffee pot, or Barton suddenly looked up, a crumb on his fingers half raised to his mouth, Solomon felt the stranger's eyes fixed upon his own, not exactly imploringly but with a kind of blind, almost dumb attention. He had known this with certain animals, whose slaughter was made easier by their rapt succumbing. Yet he didn't like it — not in this man with whom he wanted to do business. He wanted — he wanted some sense of a game taken part in, and concluded. There were ways of conducting business. Bargaining for example. Solomon enjoyed this. He enjoyed all the subtle strategies, the hidden hands, the mock surprise, the intrepid tracking around until a point of pounce was reached.

But this person, this man, wanted none of this: he simply seemed to weigh Solomon down with trust. Attach all the baggage of his hope to him. This shackled

Solomon oddly, made him feel he could not walk, dart, stride — he could only hobble. Was this Barton's strategy? Solomon wondered, looking directly over at his guest, only to find, disconcertingly, that Samuel was looking back at him, and suddenly smiling rapturously, as if that moment they had silently, between themselves, come to some understanding.

Ada was looking between the two men.

'You like ... more coffee?' she asked Solomon quietly. His hand made a small dismissive gesture. Did she not understand that, without the words being exchanged, they had reached a point — of negotiation? Solomon's deep black eyes darted back to Samuel — who had, deflectingly, looked away, gazing back at the piano.

'Oh, please, by all means, do...' Solomon found himself saying, as to a pretty young lady. This annoyed him, as he felt he had no control over his responses. These — affectations — were being wired out of him by this unusual stranger. Barton stood up, put down his porcelain plate, wiped his pathetic whiskers and half bowed to Solomon's wife. She smiled. She was, Solomon saw with an abject sense of loss, happy. He had not understood how much she missed conversation, gallantry, the prettiness of all the rituals. He had thought — he had believed he was sufficient. He felt sore in some hidden part of his maleness to think that all of his being was insufficient for her — even when, naked together, he believed he fulfilled all that she might want, and perhaps more. He believed she should be modest in public, but she was perhaps too modest in the bed: too submissive, too silent. He could remember — but his thoughts, he was aware, were drifting dangerously, because he was a man given to treacly sinful thoughts of large breasts and broad swaying thighs — rumpled stale sheets, and rutting at dawn. All this was possible — possible — with Ada (he was schooling her, teaching her), but she also managed to elude him a little, as if this — animal — side of his being was his responsibility, and she would partake of it to a certain degree, but she was not pleased with what she saw. He had the disconcerting feeling that he was somehow naked, overbearing — and ugly.

Barton was playing the piano and turning over his shoulder, smiling. It was extraordinary the degree to which he came alive at the piano. The slack wax of his features suddenly took focus. His pale blue eyes sparked out meaning. Even if the only meaning was the nonsensical vapidities of the music hall.

Yet Samuel's eyes were almost flirtatiously engaging his own, and Solomon, oddly stirred, found himself rising to the occasion. In a way he instantly diagnosed. He reached for a napkin and carelessly — he thought — placed it over his thighs.

Ada, however, followed what he was doing, and seemed to look more intensely into his eyes. What was she saying? That she would be pleased? That it would be a relief? He felt a spurt of pure anger — an absolute loss of control — and looked back at her. She blushed, felt down randomly for the things on the table and rearranged them. She stood up a little too quickly and her dress caught a silver spoon, which clattered to the floor.

Samuel seemed unaware and went on playing. Now the child was crying. He had awoken. His cry was visceral, angry. Ada turned and left the room. Samuel, whose back was turned to Solomon, concluded with a grand clatter of sound, jumped up, heated, and turned.

Solomon felt distinctly uncomfortable. It was all too out of control. It was, he dimly perceived, or translated, some new way of doing business that he had never known before.

Samuel seemed taken aback by Ada's absence. Then he caught the bawl of the child.

Solomon said nothing but the sight of him picking up the silver, and packing up the cups, was a reprimand.

'Oh, I *am* sorry.'

The man called Barton leant across and touched Solomon on the back of his hand. Solomon looked down at the pale tapered fingers, with their too long nails, placed on his hand. For one second he hallucinated blood welling up between his knuckles, and he shook Samuel's hand off, too abruptly it seemed.

Samuel had, for one moment, caught a glimpse of the dark hairiness of Solomon's wrist, the way his strong arms disappeared into the blue cotton cuffs.

The two men stood there, looking at each other in surprise.

'We must talk,' Solomon said, surprising himself with the level, ordinary voice he used. In all his armoury of bargaining he had never used such a defenceless plan. Yet Samuel seemed to acknowledge this by shrugging, and murmuring, wiping some crumbs off his whiskers, 'Of course. Of course, Mr Linz. But first I must thank your lady wife.'

Samuel walked out of the room, abandoning Solomon, who once again returned to a perplexed state. He stood there, listening to Samuel murmuring, 'Je suis enchanté.' He then heard — he felt this somewhere down in his groin — the sound of the back of his wife's hand being kissed. He heard the low bubble of her laughter flecking the back of her throat. He felt an abject sense of jealousy, a sharp spear pressed right into his gut, slitting open and letting into his system some bile-like poison.

He would crush this man. If possible.

Samuel now came back into the room, smiling at him warmly, and reached out for his hand, shaking it and pulsing into his flesh a feeling of kindness, and thanks.

'I cannot . . . thank you enough. Enough . . .'

He seemed to be almost crying.

Solomon wanted his hand back. He disliked . . . Besides, he did not like being held. It was he who took. But Samuel was still working his hand.

'It is the *happiest* day . . . since I came to Napier.'

Solomon surprised himself — shocked himself — by saying, 'But you have not talked to me about the jewel. What you . . . want?'

He felt supplicant. Abject. A complete surrender.

Samuel himself seemed surprised. Slightly shocked. He let Solomon's hand drop. Was he offended? Was in fact the whole deal off? Samuel edged away from him, and his face, at the same time, leached by the light from the window, through which Solomon could almost abstractly hear the banal pomp of the city band, appeared furrowed.

'Oh, but I thought we had agreed!'

Solomon held still. This, he knew, just as he knew with an animal, was the crux. If he were slaughtering, this was the moment he would slash the razor through. Now, he thought to himself, he would see the ruby jewel pulse with blood, and slowly the animal would sag between his legs.

Instead he found himself saying, '*Agreed?*'

'Yes,' said Samuel, spinning away from him but half smiling — and it was this ellipsed smile that would stay with Solomon in the days ahead, it was this smile, taunting and implicit, that would haunt him. Samuel murmured quickly, 'You will take the jewel to wherever you need. To raise the highest price. Your percentage will be twelve and one half per cent.'

'Is that what you want?' Solomon found his voice was husky, complicit, almost drugged with something he could not quite understand.

Samuel had turned to him and was holding his hand again.

'Take the gem to wherever you need to go, Mr Linz. I trust you. You I trust.'

A Delicate Matter

Samuel found the gate, garlanded around with roving canes of blackberry. It was No 14 Carlyle Street. There was a small hand-painted sign: *Miss Perrett, Teacher of Pianoforte (Reasonable Rates)*.

Samuel wanted to apologise to Miss Perrett for his peremptory disappearance after the concert. He had stormed off into the night.

There was a shell path leading straight towards the open front door of a tiny wooden cottage. Once inside the blackberry hedge, Samuel felt he had entered another kingdom. There were ordered rows of vegetables (carrot, salsify, broad beans, cauliflower, asparagus) and then, towards the cottage, a fig, a peach tree, and on the walls of the cottage itself a grapevine, pruned and with the first pale leaflets of spring.

There was a figure to the left labouring over a hoe. He recognised Miss Perrett, wearing a large straw hat tied on by a scarf, and a brown wool outfit. Boots. She was working hard, in a rhythm, and did not see him.

He stood there.

'Miss Perrett?' he called. He had the hatbox in his hand. She stopped. He walked towards her, keeping to the path, which was bordered by geraniums, pinks amid sticks of rose cuttings.

'Oh, Mr Barton,' she said, and she raised a quick hand to her face. He saw she was sweating. She stopped hoeing and came towards him. She took out, from a sidepocket of an apron, a stained handkerchief, with which she mopped her face.

'I must apologise for calling without . . .'

'No, no, indeed,' she said, smiling at him almost radiantly. 'It is lovely to see you. Is everything all right, Samuel?'

It was the first time he could recall her using his Christian name. Her eyes went to the hatbox, then returned to his face, concerned.

At this moment, from out of the opened window, a voice called, 'Madeleine, dear, who is it?'

It was the voice of an elderly woman. Miss Perrett ignored the voice but there was the sound of someone making an arduous journey towards the door.

'Who it is, Madeleine? Who is it you are talking to?'

Madeleine turned away from Samuel but for a moment her eyes touched his. Her face had coloured.

'A gentleman, mother. Mr Barton.'

The sounds intensified of someone hurrying to the front door.

Madeleine, Miss Perrett, coloured deeply now: 'Let us go, perhaps, and sit in the shade of the tree?'

She pointed to a distant camphor tree. Samuel could see a rustic bench made out of manuka. But an elderly woman was now standing by the front door, holding on to the lintel, peering almost sightlessly out into the light. Samuel saw a beldame, a faded shawl over her shoulders and a widow's bonnet pulled down over her ears. Her face was like an older edition of Madeleine's but reduced: there was a gauntness to the older woman's face, an intimation of death. She peered in Samuel's direction, seeming almost to scent him.

'Good day, madam,' Samuel said, taking off his trusty straw hat.

'Good afternoon, Mr Barton,' the elderly woman said in the limpid voice of a gentlewoman. 'It is good to have a visitor.'

'Mother, you're getting cold,' Madeleine said to her mother, her voice fond but slightly irritated. She turned to Samuel, 'Can I — would you excuse me?'

Samuel watched her as she stripped her gardening gloves aside and, exasperated, yet with a real tenderness, guided her mother back indoors.

'No, no,' he overheard, 'don't be silly, Mother. I will bring you a tea. I know your headaches. Yes, it is better that . . .'

He idled away and went down the path, and sat under the camphor tree. From that vantage point, he grasped the industry involved in Miss Perrett's garden. In size it was possibly a full half-acre, yet the small cottage, of the sort a child might draw — two windows and a door, completely unornamented, a shingle roof, a chimney — occupied the only non-productive area. Every other part of the site was taken up with planting. The vegetable garden was enormous: nearing him a splendidly virile rhubarb patch; further out, a happy constellation of strawberries. Some of the paths showed cuttings — sticks stuck into a soil enriched with animal dung and straw. There was a buzz of bees. The sense of order, labour — yet also of decorum — softened something in Samuel. He let himself dream . . .

Then awoke to a clinking of china. Miss Perrett was walking towards him carrying a butler's tray. On it he saw a teapot, cups, cream and, as she lowered it onto a rustic table — a tree trunk sliced through evenly and smooth — he saw the gorgeous gem-like colour of several kinds of jam. And thin slices of freshly baked bread.

'Your own?' Samuel asked. He did not know why, since in England it was hardly a question you asked a gentlewoman.

Miss Perrett sank down with an appreciable sigh. She had washed her face, her hands. But she was clearly exhausted.

'Yes,' she said, and turned her eyes out onto the garden. For a moment she was silent. She turned the pot and said to him, 'It is my fifth year of making preserves.' There was a note of sturdy pride in her voice. 'My brother, George, has a sweet tooth.' She looked up at Samuel, a little surprised — 'But have you met?'

There was an edge of apprehension in her gaze.

'No.'

She relaxed and began to pour. 'He is most busy. Down at the port. He imports. . .' She stopped and passed a cup to Samuel. 'Business is not always as good as we might hope.'

'No,' Samuel conceded. He let his cup sit, but helped himself to bread and jam.

'I am planning my . . . escape,' he confessed. 'I don't know when, how soon, but. . .'

'Oh,' she said. She held her own cup and sighed. Her face seemed to darken.

'I could not go back, Samuel, to suffering the charity of others.'

She looked at him full in the face. Her eyes were passionate. 'I would rather be poor here, but independent — insofar as I can be — than a pauperish relation back at home.'

He bowed.

There was at this moment a suspension, a silence. Yet it was filled with the ample sequinning of bees, the spark and dash of sparrows.

'You know how the sparrow came to Napier, Samuel?'

He shook his head, bit into the sweet fresh bread and jam. He was hardly listening. The sweetness sang inside his mouth. But there was a cast of thoughtfulness on Madeleine's features. Her colouring had returned.

'It followed in the path of dung dropped by horses, oxen and other beasts of burden.' She looked at him. 'As the horses and carts made their way here, over the plains and mountains, so the sparrow followed. Dung by dung. Seeking out the seed. Of chaff.'

He took up his china cup, of pretty turquoise china, decorated with gold leaf.

'Are we not the chaff, Mr Barton?'

She looked out into her little kingdom.

He didn't know how to reply. He tried to think of something gentlemanly, yet not misleading. Witty yet not rude.

Miss Perrett seemed to awaken from her strange dream. She smiled at him.

'I have to confess,' she said, 'I run out on the road with my shovel when a horse passes!' She laughed. She suddenly seemed so much more free with him that he considered her afresh. She was — how old? Possibly in her early thirties. A handsome woman, in her own style. But trapped, perhaps, by the elderly mother and drunken brother.

'Mother would so much appreciate it if you looked in before you went, to speak to her. She hardly ever has the chance to enjoy conversation.'

'Of course.'

But now Madeleine's face changed. Became piquant with thought. He marvelled then at her features, the way they changed and moulded with an idea. An idea can give any face a startling mobility. So it was that in her little kingdom Miss Perrett appeared to Samuel as actually beautiful.

'I belong — oh, to many, many organisations,' she said, almost dismissively, 'but to one that is dear to my heart. An acclimatisation society. Next week Mr Mercer, our president, is obtaining — if the ship comes through — some two hundred birds, which we will be releasing. To remind us of home. And to try to control the pestilential insects. So it is both a practical exercise and a celebration. I wondered . . . if you might care? To be part of what promises to be . . . a happy event? Meaning much to our small town.'

Samuel had never heard of 'acclimatising', but suddenly the idea of a happy event fitted in with his plans for his future. He lifted his gaze and let his focus soften. This garden now, this swarming lively storm of green — could he not see in it a haze of summer England?

Was he not on the point of escape? Well, soon enough, after the matter of the gem was seen to. (He had no doubt about Solomon. He knew, at the very least, how to choose a man.) Why not, for once, relax and release the reins of pain whose spurs had been buried so deep that his flesh had almost grown around them? Why not, frankly, and in this pleasant company — *enjoy* himself? Suddenly the other face of colonial life swung into view, presented itself to him in all its startling candour.

'Oh, why not!' He breathed out. 'Why not, indeed! And could I? Could I be so bold as to ask . . .' He paused. He seemed to be having trouble speaking.

Madeleine smiled, a shadow of leaves moving over her face, dissolving and forming.

'I have some new acquaintances. Oh, charming people! So *sympathiques*,' he said, and kissed the end of his fingers. Madeleine's face for a moment quivered with the delicacy of a cat before something it instinctively disliked. Samuel seemed unaware.

'They would so much enjoy, I am sure, being out and about. In pleasant company.'

Madeleine said nothing for a moment.

'I am sure I can rely upon your testimony as to their being sympathetic,' she said smoothly, 'but may I be so rude as to ask their name?'

Samuel looked back at her.

'Napier is such a small tight ship in the end,' she said, brushing away imaginary crumbs, 'one feels one knows to *death* everyone aboard her.'

'Their name is Linz. He is the jeweller. In Tennyson Street.'

She understood what he was saying. She left a moment's pause. Then nodded. 'If you are sure . . .'

'Oh,' he said breezily, and she, in her turn, was frankly amazed at how youthful Samuel suddenly appeared. The years seemed to have rolled back, almost as clouds roll back across a sky to reveal the burning warmth of a summer sun. His very back had straightened. The frowns and furrows on his brow, around his mouth, smoothed out. He laughed.

She listened — loved — the musical freedom of his laughter. Inside the house, she seemed to hear her own mother relax. Then he said something strange: 'My life depends upon it.'

She said nothing. Then, 'I will send you a note. About a time. We shall hire a brougham probably. And all go out together.'

He laughed, as if this was the most delightful news.

'I have always loved — *loved* — a frolic. Of any kind,' he said.

She suspected him of a lack of seriousness.

He had stood. She unfolded, with difficulty, upwards. Held the brace of her lower back in her hand. Hoped he had not seen.

'I came to . . . apologise for running off into the night after the "entertainment",' he said, 'and to ask you something.'

He held up the hatbox.

Her silence was eloquent.

'It is whether you might like . . . this hat. I bought it on a whim and soon realised that the lady for whom it was bought . . . would perhaps not appreciate my attentions. A delicate matter.'

She let the silence sound.

'Well, of course . . . but is the lady . . . resident in Napier?'

They had reached the door.

Madeleine's mother called out from the dark interior. 'I am here. See? I am sitting up by the window!'

'No . . . I have no idea if she is still alive,' Samuel said quietly.

Madeleine turned to him in the doorway. It was as if she were considering all the proprieties of accepting a hat from an unmarried gentleman. Then her face softened.

'I would be pleased to accept.'

He handed the box over.

Miss Madeleine Perrett curtsied and Mr Samuel Barton bowed.

A Tongue
and a Cross

There was a cross on the door.

It had not been there, Solomon Linz was sure of it, when he went out. (But then when he closed the door he had not turned back. Perhaps he had not even noticed?)

Fasting made things seem sharper, more evident.

It was Yom Kippur, the tenth hour, and Solomon was on his way home from a walk up the Hill.

It was always a day for meditation, for thought, for atonement — curious word that, for asking for forgiveness for past sins. Solomon had gone for a walk to the highest point of the Hill. Looking out, he had meditated on how he would try to be a better husband to Ada, how he would try to quell that animal that seemed to always be alive within him, slurping and sucking on its fingers, gleaming and smiling sardonically at him, even now, when he tried to cleanse all his thoughts.

He had made a vow. He had felt uplifted.

And he had returned and found, chalked on the door, boldly, defiantly, in two strokes of yellow chalk, a rudimentary, even vehement cross.

Had a child done it? One of those surly little monsters who followed behind him, dancing in his steps, singing that stupid *Ikey Moses* taunt?

> Ikey Moses King of the Jews
>
> Sold his wife for a pair of shoes.

There was one boy above all who most seemed to enjoy calling out the taunts. Not that they exactly called it out. This was too obvious. Rather they let their chants and taunts drift into the outer perimeter of his consciousness, so that he was left to doubt what he was hearing.

> When the shoes began to wear,
>
> Ikey Moses began to swear.

They sang it while the girls twirled their skipping ropes, working up into a vehement rhythm.

> When the swearing began to stop,
>
> Ikey Moses bought a shop.
>
> When the shop began to sell,
>
> Ikey Moses went to H! E! L! L!

He raised his hand, spat on his fingers, tried to wipe the yellow off. (There was a dusting, like pollen, all against the green paint of the door). The door was obscured from view, down the side passage from the shop. Nobody would see. It was too high for a child. A child would not reach. But perhaps standing on the woodbox? Solomon could see it had been dragged towards the door — the scrawled semi-circle incised into the dust.

He felt better then.

It was better that it was a child. Less threatening in a way. But what did it mean, this infantile threat? He knew that in the plague days it had marked where a diseased body lay. Was that it? Whatever it was, it was sullying, a defamation.

On this holiest of days. When all he wanted was to go into a trance. To practise forgiveness.

Was this — he spat again, copiously, onto his handkerchief — a test of some sort? That he should forgive even this ignorance? This low-level hatred? He was aware all the time, in Napier, that he walked around as a marked man, nothing exactly said unless a man was drunk enough (and then what did it mean?). But he had spent his life ducking, as it were, the obvious, the unsaid — or what was said the moment he turned his back.

Forgive all this?

He seemed to be making a bigger mess by trying to wipe it off. The chalk was thicker than he realised. It was loosening into a yellow cloud, a liquid smudge. He would not like his wife to see.

'What is the mark on the door, Solly?'

His mother would be worse. More fearful. Instantly paranoid. She might go into her room and hide in the cupboard. It was the same with thunder. His mother changed back into the peasant who was never far below the surface. She went insane when it thundered. She sought, like an animal, any place inside the house to hide. It was mimicking another time when she sought to hide. That was what he hated about it. That, and the way he was ineffectual. He could do nothing to calm her. Until the thunder stopped. She would be inside the big wooden closet, a rag stuffed in her mouth, her eyes distended, bloodied from weeping, her hands clasped together, down on her knees. She was a wild animal, a cow that had become bogged down in a quicksand of mud, drowning. It was only when the thunder stopped, and the storm passed, that she bit by bit returned to being his mother.

Ada had not at first been able to understand. It frightened her. Then, when she understood, she pitied her mother-in-law. This had not helped. His mother did not want pity. She despised pity. Just as, in some way, Solly sensed that his mother despised his wife — her useless arts of gentility, her inability to labour as a beast of the field or go out into the world and negotiate.

'You have plucked a lily of the field,' his mother said to him in Yiddish when Ada was in labour. She often called her 'Lily' to him, as if this was some private code between them for the uselessness of his wife. The lily who had come from a superior family, an almost goyish family of superior Jewry. He had pursued her in Krakow and in the end she had, almost unbelievably, said that she loved him — loved him, he felt, as women in novels loved men. He was never sure if she knew what he meant. What his hardened penis meant. What his love meant.

But of course he loved everything about her: her fineness, her red hair, her violet eyes, seemingly lacking any knowledge of all the dirt and grease in his own life. He had never seen anything so fine. He liked, once he was married to her, to inspect her hands, to hold them and look down at them, palms up, so he could read their beautiful, almost waxen whiteness: the way the nails were unsplit, and even polished, delicately polished with — he saw her doing this (he loved to see her bent neck, its gentle incline) — a long pale white kid cushion, which she used to buff her nails to an ideal and beautiful pinkness. He had rained kisses on the insides of her palms; he had made love, let us be honest, to her hands, he had ravished her hands, he had taken, finally, her hands and placed them on that part of him he wished, above all, that she would understand.

Her eyes had widened a little and she had — this seemed indecorous for such a lady — laughed. It was a laugh of delight, as if she had discovered some new game. But it was ugly. It even looked ugly. He was aware of this, when he unbuttoned his trousers and revealed it to her. She had been unusual in this: she had wanted to see. He had thought that this was perhaps how gentlefolk carried on, as if all the usual struggling underneath clothes could be brought into the light and somehow changed. He was astonished, himself, at how ugly his penis was, in full distension. It was gorged with blood and wrapped around with one particular full, pulpy vein — which throbbed. He had lain her cool hand against it and she had, instinctively almost, wrapped her fingers around him. He had shuddered then; his legs had opened wide in a spasm and within a second — oh, the shame — she was looking down at the milky, sticky mess and asking him, with an actually concerned voice, 'Solomon, have I hurt you?'

He heard this in his dreams.

'Solomon, have I hurt you?'

No, he longed to say to her: you have made me the happiest man in the world.

It was not long before her words were put in his mouth.

'But Ada, Ada . . . have I hurt you?'

He had tried everything in his power to make it slow, gradual. Not to frighten her. But in the end there was no way around it, even though he had gone to extraordinary pains to warm her up (in the way a prostitute in Whitechapel had taught him — a prostitute he had patronised consecutively in some of the most miserable days of his life: when he realised he would have to become a butcher, not the scholar, the eternal student he longed to be — when he had, as he saw it, been forsaken by his God). But even with all these arts, which had changed her into a woman he did not quite recognise — panting and holding him against the back, moaning to him, saying '*Oh Solomon, Oh Solomon,*' — there was still that distance, when he sensed he was alone, alone with all the infuriating gods of concupiscence, when he changed into an animal rutting. In the end he had seen, as if from a vast distance, two large tears seep out of the corners of her eyes, her head turned away from him, as if she found him too gross to look at — as if he were a ghastly exhibition, an actual beast — and he had witnessed these two large tears — like liquid pearls, like pearls turned into liquid — slip out of the corners of her eyes and travel so slowly down her face. He was almost there, working away like an infernal machine, working away towards glimpsing his own God, and even though he had managed to swoon forward (still keeping up his machine attack), to lick the tears away, she had turned her head, quickly, as if she were avoiding him, except her eyes for one moment caught against his, and he saw what she was saying to him — she was looking right into his soul and he was naked before her as she silently said to him — So this is what you wanted me for? This is what you pursued me for, down all those streets? This is what I left my parents for, was thrown out of the house for? This moment now?

He found he was hard, even as he wiped the remains of the spit off the door. He went over to a bucket that had some rain in it. He threw it against the wood, and finally the last pollen of yellowness slid away. It would dry. It would be all right.

But he was sure, even as he slid the key into the lock and prepared to go upstairs — he was sure the cross was still there.

As he stepped inside he cursed himself for his randiness, saw himself as goat-like, cursed by being formed into something as abject as the animals he slaughtered.

*M*adeleine laboured over the vat, letting the heat permeate her skin. She felt her pores opening, the small of her back ache a little, as she lifted out and inspected the ox's tongue. She — Miss Perrett — was dressed as a working woman. That is, in clothes she had once worn down London streets when she had walked *fast, fast* towards Hanover Square Rooms to hear Clara Schumann play. The clothes — a green skirt, a once-violet plaid bodice — had got old. Worn.

There is always that point with any piece of clothing when it makes a transition from something you might wear in public to something you can wear only in private. But it is as if the scent of all the happiness, of all the secret pleasures experienced while wearing these clothes, still inhabits the fabric: is the invisible thread binding it together.

So, in wearing these old clothes, she still occupied the nimbus of past happiness.

Madeleine was skinning an ox tongue for her brother's supper.

She was enjoying herself, even as she laboured. She liked — no — she thrilled to the sense of purpose that passed through her now, sharp as an arrow. She, a spinster who was never likely to marry, felt she was filled with God's purpose. (She slid back the grey fur of the tongue, frowning. The tongue of a beast.) The fact was, she enjoyed work. She had discovered this most unlikely of attitudes — she thrilled to the fury of labour that overcame her as she, a woman brought up with servants, became a servant.

She welcomed the relief of exhaustion — though at times she could hardly walk, she ached so much. Of course it all depended on her mood, and there were times when she felt careworn, became overcome with headaches, felt wretched. Then she had to let her mother take over.

Occasionally she let her mind return to Harald Girten — the man she might have married in London. Their correspondence had grown hot, then, unaccountably, cold. He had written finally to reveal he was marrying, and that perhaps, in view of this, their correspondence should cease. After two years Girten wrote again. It seemed he needed some private ear. He never talked of his wife, yet her sheer absence from his thoughts, his words, seemed to express something. But he was not here.

Madeleine had been wearing this very dress, now stained with water, wrapped over with a rough apron fashioned from some flour sacks. She wiped the hair from her face with the back of her hand, and laughed. If he could see her now! She had aged, she was aware of that. Her skin, her once fine skin, had grown brown with the sun, even though she always wore a hat out of doors. But the wind had whipped into her. She had grown used to the leatherising of her skin. In time she felt it protected her. She came to inhabit the slight wrinkles of her flesh as her flesh grew older on her bones. But she was, when all is said and done, still only a woman of thirty-two — still marriageable in a colony too full of men.

There was a man who occasionally came to dinner with her brother. His name was Leyland. He was a Scot, a man of few words. She did not think much of him. Her brother was always, without asking, bringing men home for dinner. Their dinner table was part of his business.

She had heard that Samuel Barton possessed a beautiful voice. Would he perhaps sing in her choir? Become an ornament of the Lord? She had heard of his voice from Dr Cogswell, who had heard him singing one Sunday. He had gone into the Jew's shop on purpose, to inquire innocently after the source of so much magic.

Dr Cogswell had described the voice as one that lifted your cares away and made you drift into a trance, a dream. You no longer felt tired. You forgot where you were. Could there be any greater gift to a colonist?

She would ask Samuel Barton. She would be frank. She would even importune him. The Good Lord required beautiful voices.

Besides, there was that unpleasant young woman at church, Miss Violet Limbrick, who tried to make out that she knew true tone, while implying that she, Madeleine Perrett, teacher of pianoforte, did not.

Madeleine concentrated, wiping her hands quickly, quickly, on her flourbag apron. The skin was slipping off now.

She must act.

She must be quick.

The tongue was being revealed.

*S*olomon was used to the clarity hunger confirmed. He was studying the Talmud at the table in the parlour, and his mother was in the kitchen, sitting on a kitchen chair, not moving. This was her designated post: the kitchen. She chased Ada out when she tried to go in there. Ada was allowed to make Solomon his coffee. This decorative task, as befitted a lady, was the single thing Ada was allowed to do within the room of food. They ate as Jews, of course. This was portable, this was everlasting. Ada was not used to shtetl food, which to her refined city tastes was greasy, coarse. One day, on Solomon's mother's birthday, Ada had insisted on cooking a meal from her parents' house in Krakow. City food, *Austrian* food.

Ada had gone out with her mother-in-law as duenna and shopped, bought everything and spent hours locked in the kitchen. His mother had paced around the house, bad-tempered, scowling even at Gershom, who seemed to have picked up his *bobe*'s feeling and was restless, mewing. In the end, Ada had tremblingly served the elaborate four-course banquet, which his mother had eaten in complete silence, never taking a second helping of anything, and rewarding her daughter-in-law with a single 'Thank you, it was good.'

It had been difficult for months after this. Solly and his wife in bed. Solly seducing his wife away from tears. Solly seducing her into being his wife again. 'Forget about my mother,' he murmured to her. 'Forget about her.' 'How can I forget?' Ada had said out loud, in Yiddish, determined that his mother should hear. 'How can I forget her when she is just through there? Always?' He had not known what to say. What could he say? Her own mother was left behind in Krakow. Her own mother was effectively dead.

He turned the page.

Azazel.

Solomon, try as he might, could never quite work out which goat he would prefer to be. He could not help this putting himself in the position of the goats. Was it better to be the goat that was made into a sacrifice and killed, your consciousness terminated; or the goat — the scapegoat — that was loaded up with all the sins of the world, having to personify them, then led out into the wilderness and left there for all eternity?

When Solomon thought of this wilderness he could not help himself from seeing it as this place.

To be an animal, unknowing, incapable because of its very nature of grasping what its role was: to be dumb, not in the pejorative sense, but in the sense of simply being an animal without any higher consciousness; yet to be chosen to represent something as specific as all the sins, all the wicked acts, all the greed, all the deceit, all the adultery, the fucking — to dumbly represent it all, then be punished for what it could never understand?

To be flung into a wilderness, to be left there, to expire there; and never — this is what he always dwelt on — *never to know?*

Was this, in fact, for the best? Would it not be worse to actually realise that you were being banished, as it were, on behalf of everyone else? So they could go on merrily fucking, deceiving (painting crosses on your door for example), while you alone were chosen to live in a place where there were no other people (not even goats for company in your private hell)? Would you not feel a little, as it were, resentful? Would you not ask, *Why me?*

Or.

Is this all?

So perhaps it was better that a goat was chosen. A goat did not reason. A goat lived, bred and died. Perhaps this was part of God's infinite wisdom then — to choose a *goat*.

At this moment Ada walked through the room. She had Gershom over her shoulder and she was gently burping him.

Solomon's eyes went to his wife. He felt a brief sense of mortification. Of being over-blessed. He did not deserve . . . He had sinned too. (The sin of the flesh, of his too physical awareness. Of the way he could not stop thinking. Of the pleasure, the absolute and completely individual pleasure of. Sinking into his wife's flesh, burying himself in her. In all the pleasures that were abjectly human, not divine at all, in any way, unless you saw reproduction as in some ways divine, which perhaps it was — except any beast of the field could do it.)

Hunger was making his mind over-refined. Split into too many hairs of dispute. He was blessed, he knew that. He lived far away from violence, the pogroms. What was a mere cross daubed on his door? As nothing. He had his beautiful healthy son. His wife. His mother. And a business that was, if not doing tremendously well, at least ticking over. And now there was this . . . jewel.

He felt sure God had placed it in his way. It could change everything. He was blessed. He was sure of that.

Now his wife was walking back into the room. He smelt her milky flesh: clean, fresh. He smelt his son. She walked past slowly, treading over the boards so they creaked as she went. She paced along, as a ship in mid-ocean. Her eyes passed over his. Her pale lips shaped into an enigmatic smile.

Had she been reading his thoughts?

O God, you are the light by which we see the ones we love.

Did she also think they were — almost dangerously perhaps — blessed?

Was it good, then, that the goat knew nothing of why it was expelled?

He must tell his wife about Barton's invitation to the picnic. He knew his mother would produce a feast for him, his Ada. It might even coincide, more or less generally, with breaking the fast.

It was the first time they had been invited to a goyim event.

He returned to the page, placed his hands on either side of his face so he occluded the room, his wife, the window, Napier.

He went back to the vision of the goat.

'*I*'ve heard you have a lovely voice.'

Madeleine had asked Samuel to accompany her on a walk along the beach in the late afternoon. It had rained in the morning: wild, dark, heavy. Then the wind had turned sharp west and blown the storm away. The sky now was a brilliant but chill porcelain blue.

'. . . my voice?'

There was a long moment of consternation. Her dark eyes instantly read his face, the frozen moment of confusion.

'Oh, I did not mean to intrude.'

He said nothing, kept walking. There was a sense of all sorts of things not being said. Of something muffled, and painful.

'I did not mean — would never mean to intrude. But a beautiful voice for me,' she said, daring herself to go on, 'is an instrument,' her voice lowered here, '. . . an instrument of God.'

He said nothing, but laughed. There was something satiric, harsh in his laugh. She felt herself flushing. She was not sure she did not feel angry.

The wind was keening.

'What a small place this is, isn't it?'

He walked along, boots stabbing into the pebbles, sliding.

He accused her, she saw that. Of being a spy. Of being like everyone else — too interested in their non-lives, in all the things not happening to them. So certain something was happening to someone else. Wanting to make everyone fit within the smallness.

They walked in silence a moment, the only sound the angry shillyshalling slide of shingle on the beach. It seemed the very beauty of the sea mocked them. Her dress beat about her legs, whipping into her skin almost painfully.

'Can you not lend us your voice?' she asked in a lower tone, now, more vulnerable, naked.

He looked at her. 'I would. I would, indeed. But I swore — for private reasons — to keep to silence. A public silence,' he said. Then he said, 'I apologise, Madeleine. I do. But — you would not understand.'

She felt herself rebuffed, and seduced a little, by the mystery and sympathy of his using her Christian name. Its intimacy. She waited, but he said nothing, fell into a kind of muteness.

They walked the rest of the way in silence, then, having reached a point of mutual blankness, by common consent they turned back.

As they did so, an old Maori man on a skeletal horse, plodding along apathetically in the direction of town, looked at them intently, and for some unknown reason — hurtful to both of them — he laughed. He laughed scornfully, flagellated his old horse, then rode on.

*I*t was as they were parting that he said, as if incidentally, 'I don't want . . . to make myself too much at home here. I hope you don't misunderstand me. But I will be soon going and . . .'

She looked at him, felt betrayed. So you are going, she said to herself silently, while I will stay here, and grow older, and try to raise some elementary defences against the forces of anarchy and dissipation all around us.

She chose to say nothing.

He touched her then, on the arm, but lightly, lightly.

'If you would understand . . . how a voice may betray . . . may provide not only pleasure but also . . . in certain circumstances . . . reveal more than one might wish.'

She tried to read his face but he swivelled it aside. She saw that his cheeks were reddened, and his eyes seemed dry, haunted.

I would not cause you pain for anything in the world, she said then. But this voice was to herself, too naked to be spoken out loud.

Besides, he might not understand.

Instead she said, 'It was a simple — even idle — request. As you know, music for me is my dearest companion. So it would not occur . . .'

He nodded and their eyes grazed against each other for one moment. She knew, profoundly, that he was not of the marrying kind. She had received this information in silence — in certain moments of withdrawal, when a woman would have expected a man to come forward, even regretted that a man could be relied upon to come forward. Instead, with Samuel there was an avoidance, a silence, even a restful absence. But she longed, suddenly and acutely at that moment, to hear the beauty of his voice.

'You would not consider, perhaps, in privacy, accompanying me on the piano?' she felt her face grow hot.

He laughed then and said, 'I had no idea, Madeleine, my voice would be of such *compelling* interest.'

She said, more angrily then than she had intended, 'Music is the only thing in the world, Samuel, that means anything to me.'

But he said nothing, promised nothing.

The only sound — a small blessing — was a cessation of sound as their boots left the shingle and clambered over onto the muddy track. They passed as they went a small group of children — urchins really — playing with matches. Their heads were all turned intently inwards, to the miracle, and one — the smallest one — with a mean, arrow-shaped head, held in his grubby digits a flickering flame. He had just struck a match. But, as if sensing the adults' eyes upon him, the boy McSweeney flung the match at the girl nearest him. She shrieked as the match settled in, among her folds. There was a stench of something burning. The other children broke apart, screeching like gulls. The little girl screamed in pain.

Madeleine cut towards her, beat the flame out with her bare hands. She turned on the children but they had all run away shrieking, one of them — the boy who had flung the match — picking up a stone from the beach and sending it hurtling through the air so Samuel heard its zinging sound even as he ducked.

Soon it was all over; the crying girl had wrestled out of Madeleine's grip, then run off silently.

Together, shaken, Madeleine and Samuel turned back towards the town.

What is the nature of goodness, Madeleine raged to herself as she came in the door, when she is surrounded on every side by accomplices seemingly bent on making her be petty? It was no good. She had gone on to choir practice after her walk with Samuel and it had not gone well. Some sediment of her mood from the beach — fractured, dissonant — had clung to her.

Violet Limbrick was insistent that she knew the melodies better than

Madeleine. Violet with her slightly suspect prettiness, her moist mouth, her mauve glacé high-heeled boots which she brought in a muslin bag and changed into, *simply* for choir practice.

Madeleine threw her bonnet down. The wind had been almost maliciously beating into her face as she walked home. It could have been laughing at her. Tears had come, been whipped out of her eyes.

What is the nature of goodness? she had cried to herself. Is it being good to others, helping others, laying down your life for others? Did she not sit upon five committees in Napier? Play the organ for every service on Sunday? Train the choir? Serve luncheon every alternate Sunday at the Old Men's Refuge? Sing for them? Darn for them? Care for her mother, her brother?

Was this then to be her entire *use* in life?

She cried — with an inner rage she cried.

Then there were the tormenting questions. Why had her mother spent the small settlement of her late father coming to Napier? Here she, Madeleine, had had to get down on her haunches, like an animal, and scrub the mud off the wooden floor. She had, in the end, succumbed to the work, as if Godliness, or some sort of cleansing emotion, lay in making their tiny cottage homely. At times she had wept, wept hot coursing tears of disappointment, as she scrubbed the kauri plank floor.

Some days of peculiar angst, she took down and washed the curtains, beat the rugs, scrubbed the floors — then went on to the semi-salvation of baking a fruit cake and oat biscuits. She seemed impelled by some furious energy, as if to make something of her time here, to escape something.

George, her brother, would of course bring gentlemen home. It was nothing for him to bring two or three strangers home, coincident with his business. Madeleine would then share a bed with her mother. The strangers might sleep in the parlour, on the floor. They would eat whatever was to be eaten — eat them out of house and home, as Madeleine often said to herself silently — then they would stand around the piano, and some of the men would make eyes at her, or press their bodies, seemingly accidentally, against her flesh, as if by mute contact to make urgent their message that they needed — wanted — a decent woman.

She was not to be sold, bought or exchanged.

'*I will die an old maid & happy*' she had scrawled in furious lettering inside her diary. She had underlined it, as if to make it clearer to her subconscious she was happy with her lot. But she was only thirty-two. She wasn't an old maid so much as a maid growing older: oh, God — she wrenched her street clothes off with spurts of anger, stopping herself to undo the buttons of her old striped costume (it had to last, it had to last: she could not wreck what she could not replace) — oh, God, was there no delivery, no safety? Except in — and here she swung past the piano, looking at it accusingly, as if its very existence mocked her.

She must be calm! She must calm herself down. Mother would be wanting to know how her choir practice had been, and who was there, and what had they sung? And she, Madeleine, had to be careful not to flare up and fight, or find fault with what her mother said. It was nothing for Madeleine at times to have a terrible, crucifying headache — for her to hate everything and everyone who was here, in this horrid place.

Her mother trod carefully at times like this, insisting that Madeleine retire to lie on a bed in a darkened room, a cool compress on her face, which her mother might tiptoe into the room to replace. Could anything equal the sense of love, of complicity almost, when her mother lifted off the old moist cloth and replaced it with another, cooler one? At times like this, when the headache lessened its torment, when the opium drops began to seep into her being, Madeleine felt that she would be happy never to leave her darling mother, never to have her clean flour-smelling body far away from her. But at the same time she knew her mother would go, would leave her.

As George would.

'*M*adeleine, dear, is that you?'

As if it could be anyone else.

But Madeleine quelled that rebellious thought. And carefully laid aside the dress she was so sick of (and which she could only compare with Violet's pert, new blue dress, with its fresh tassels and bunched up back-skirt and crisp panniers — worn to a choir practice for heaven's sake!).

> We love the word of life,
> The word that tells of peace,
> Of comfort in the strife,
> And joys that never cease.

'Yes, Mother, I'm home.'

'Dear, I wonder if you could bear to help me. We have visitors coming around after George has finished business.'

> We love to sing below
> For mercies freely given;
> But Oh, we long to know
> The triumph-song of heaven.

'Of course, Mother.'

And later, when they were peeling the vegetables (Madeleine hacking at the coarse skin of a pumpkin with a tomahawk — she was enjoying herself with her own private massacre), 'And who, Mother, do we have the pleasure of eating with tonight?'

Mrs Perrett was silent a while and then spoke soothingly. 'Now I know, my dear, that you have no interest in him, but Mr Mercer from the school board . . .' and as an afterthought, 'Oh yes, that nice young Mr Leyland also. He's come into town to see about his sheep.'

To be busy is halfway to be being happy.

This motto might have been mockingly embroidered on a cushion. Madeleine did not care. She could not care less for either Leyland or Mercer. She walked out the back door, down the two simple wooden steps into her garden. She looked at it by the faltering light of the evening.

Amid the scurrying gloom of wind, the garden seemed to turn its face to her, to calm her with its familiarity, its productivity. *We, at least, you have created.* She scooped down and plucked some parsley. Its scent, brackish yet tart, refreshed her. She buried her face in the damp greenery.

Flowers, plants and music.

Were they the only things in the world that didn't disappoint?

Omnivorous Birds

The official part of the Acclimatisation Society proceedings was under way. Mr Mercer, before releasing the finches, rooks and larks into the air, was making a speech to the assembled crowd to the effect that 'between caterpillars, beetles, slugs and other destructive insects, half the crops grown in this province are, year after year, swept off the face of the earth. *The cure, and the only cure*, is a supply of omnivorous birds.'

At which point, a little flushed by his expenditure of so much energy on so many large words, and owing, too, to the gravity of the situation, Mr Mercer indicated with a prearranged signal that the birds in the first box should be released. But Mr O'Connell, his assistant, had been a little too nervous about this moment — had rehearsed it so often in his mind that when the signal came, he was daydreaming, gazing into the crowd, trying to find his Nelly, who at that very point was indicating to him that his tie was not straight — and so he bungled his part in the proceedings.

A ripple of amusement passed through the assembled crowd, about eighty in number. Some rude boys whistled towards the back, one yelling out, 'Wake up O'Connell!'

At which point, blushing a great deal, feeling that his collar was, indeed, too tight, he wrenched back the hatch, and the birds, a little stunned by the sudden change in their circumstances, did precisely — nothing.

The good-natured crowd laughed a little more. Mr Mercer, crucified by the loss of dignity, yet aware that a prospective mayor had to maintain the humour of the people, advanced on Mr O'Connell. He did not know whether he was going to kick him, in the behind, as befitted a piece of music hall tomfoolery, or whether he was actually in real anger, going to wrench the quails' box off him.

At which point the birds took fright. They fluttered out of the box, then stood there in the dirt, in seemingly stunned immobility. The crowd pulled back, widened away from them.

Four quails stood in total silence.

Was it at that moment that each person in the crowd sensed the importance of the occasion? But nobody could wait too long for there were, in all, fifteen boxes to be released. The plan, hatched at an interminable committee meeting, was that the wife of each official of the Hawke's Bay Acclimatisation Society was to be given a separate brand of bird to be released. Thus Mrs Mercer, the rooks. Mrs O'Connell, who normally provided tea and buns, the larks; down to Mrs Peabody, an inconsequential little thing, who could be trusted to liberate the thrushes. The birds were all, in their separate boxes, making anxious sounds — sounds as if they wished, above all, to be freed from their cramped conditions.

'Let the new chums come ashore . . .' a wag called out.

More vulgar laughter.

Mr Mercer understood what must happen. Ceremony must be curtailed, the birds' release expedited, even though the wives stood in an assembled group, slightly to the front of the crowd, each one carefully inspecting the costume of the other, then straightening a pleat, smoothing down a front-skirt, or modestly seeming to inspect a pearly button on the back of a glove. Mr Mercer must act — in this, he had to show the prospective electors that he was their man. He would take the situation in hand.

'O'Connell,' he said, 'hand me the next crate. And be smart about it.' (The latter sentence was hissed, his face obscured from the crowd. Mr O'Connell came awake, dreadfully. He walked, as an automaton, towards the crates, shaded under a willow tree. But the son of Mrs Peabody had got there first and was handing the box over to his mother. She was preparing to speak. This could be awkward. Mr Mercer raised a large hand, indicating solemnity — silence. (He wasn't a verger for nothing: in fact he was a verger to impress upon the congregation his own formidable form, his ability to be dignified in ceremony — to be, as it were, part of a larger pattern.)

'Please, ladies and gentlemen, good folk of Napier, I wonder in the circumstances whether the lady-wives who have helped the committee so much . . . ' He left a pause here, for the crowd perhaps to murmur appreciation, but unfortunately there was a yawning gap of silence, filled only with the cooing of a bird. This was followed by sniggers and larrikins at the back calling out, 'Let the poor blimming birds go!', at which point their voices were thankfully shushed — but Mr Mercer could sense that the ceremony was on the point of collapsing altogether.

'Whether the good lady-wives . . . '(he was wishing now he had not chosen his solemn black frock-coat, which bit under the armpits and smelt a little of rust — its heavy serge weighed him down so he felt betrayed by delicate little rolls of sweat feeling their way down his cheeks, fluttering like the hand of Joy down at the port — why was he thinking of her on this occasion? He had a vivid image of breasts swinging out as she squatted over an enamel bowl, washing herself. Could the assembled faces see what he was thinking of?)

He felt for his large folded handkerchief, ironed by Mrs Mercer just for this occasion — crisis? — '. . . might consider the propriety of, perhaps, Mr O'Connell freeing all the birds, one by one. Purely in the interests of expediting . . .'

No sooner had he spoken than the McSweeney brat raced towards the first box, his mother's wail failing to restrain him, and, in double-quick time (no doubt helped by having studied the catches on the boxes in private for quite some time) released the latches of over five crates.

The Napier Spit Brass Band quickly raised their instruments to mouth. Now the ceremony really was falling to pieces, Mr Mercer felt the stab wound of a headache behind his temples (at the same time he fixed on his face an austere look of majesty — or what he hoped was majesty, gained largely from studying photographs of Her Majesty herself). He signalled to the Band to start up.

The brass band began playing 'King of the Cannibal Isles', always a crowd favourite. This sound sent the birds hurtling from their crates, helped by another little larrikin standing behind them, his freckled face carved into a grin of mischief as he tapped the end of each crate.

A confusion of chaffinches, mynahs and thrushes speckled through the heavens.

*S*amuel, standing to the back of the crowd, alongside Mrs Linz, recognised the McSweeney brat as the one who had thrown the stone on the beach a few days before. Samuel was wary of street arabs: he knew both their price and their intense scrutiny. Usually they saw too much, and their knowledge, usually buyable for a few coins, could be very dangerous. Especially when you were coinless.

But that was then. This was now: him standing under the lovely shade of a ngaio tree, in his new tweed morning coat with matching waistcoat and plaid trousers. He had treated himself to a new bow tie in a deep red and he had even had his hair cut: his sandy hair was parted to the side and hung in a loose cloud towards the side of his head, romantically. He was smiling to himself: Mrs Linz had been laughing, frankly, a delicate little tinkle of absurdity.

The pomp of the band wore on. The birds in the sky had become little dots, then they had lost themselves in space. Had they disappeared? Only a single thrush had flown to the nearest branch of a ngaio tree and was sitting there, perhaps seasick, or overcome by the enormity of change in its circumstances.

Samuel felt he understood. But already brats — boys, and some girls too — were showing how adept they were at climbing trees. It appeared a competition. The bird gazed down upon them — why did Samuel, and Mrs Linz too, detect a trenchant sadness in the incline of the bird's head? It gazed down upon the children, one of whom, legs wrapped immodestly around the trunk of a branch was advancing towards it. Below, a mother called out, while tinier children stood in awe — gazing upwards in orotund silence. (Samuel recognised Susie, wearing a cleanly washed pinafore, bonnet and boots clearly two sizes too big — her elder sister's?)

The bird waited until the last moment. It seemed to be suffering a crisis of indecision. Would it leave its perch, which it had only just found? But the McSweeney lad was snaking along the bough, his mother below wailing while his father was saying, proudly, 'If he falls and breaks 'is bleeding neck, it's 'is own fault.'

The boy reached out. The thrush leant down its speckled neck, as if to inspect. Then, as the lad made a grab, in a flurry of wing-stretch the bird lifted into the air, suspended itself in motion for a seeming second. Then speed overtook it and in one whirring sound — Samuel below could hear the thrub of its wings — it flew over the crowd, an unfortunate splatter, one moment later, landing on the shoulder of Mr Mercer's frock-coat.

Mr O'Connell decided it would not be he who would inform Mr Mercer of the indignity. He buried himself in the crowd, an enigmatic smile lighting up his cadaverous features.

The Napier Spit Brass Band ended its rendition of 'God Save the Queen' on a triumphant note.

Mr Mercer called for three cheers for Her Majesty.

At the hip-hip-hooraying each person present felt the satisfying sense of occupying all sound, of sending a bold eminence from the inside of their chest, over space, over those leering silent hills in the distance, the shallow river speckling over stones, challenging the landscape itself to acknowledge the consequence of the occasion. Hats were thrown spinningly up into the air. Mock-birds, they plummeted into the crowd, leading to an undignified grabbing and lolly-scramble-like fracturing of the occasion. This marked the end of the formal part of proceedings.

Every little social group had fought for the best possie. There was the uneven earth under the shade of the largest and oldest ngaio — this was the Mercers. There was the smooth grassy area on which a striped tent had been erected — this was for the carriage folk. (The Monteiths had come out from their estate at Riverslea and were attended by servants. They were aware of being looked at but seemed not to see the crowd around them. They were entertaining the wife of the Governor and a countess visiting from England.)

There was a fringe of Maori watching from a distance, on the other side of the river.

Solomon Linz had taken it upon himself to find a particularly soft and grassy knoll — not too far from the river but not so isolated that they could not enjoy the spectacle of so many Napierites enjoying themselves in nature. Besides, after the picnic — each group having brought their own feast — there would be cricket, games and 'kiss-in-the-ring'. Later in the evening there would be a public ball, at the Oddfellows' Hall, starting at eight p.m. sharp. This could comfortably be expected to run until dawn. There was also rumour of a dinner put on by the Monteiths, but few people in the town could expect to be invited.

Solomon Linz was paying especial attention to Mrs Perrett, who had come to the picnic in a dogcart, accompanied by her daughter — and son. This was the first time Samuel had sighted the son. He was a brusque young man whose eyes always seemed to be straying away, looking into the distance. Every so often an intensely blue yet bloodshot gaze came back to focus, almost to finger nervously around Samuel's face. Several times Samuel caught Georgie Perrett gazing at him, but each time he caught him out Samuel sensed only a perplexed attempt to fit him in. Georgie soon enough managed to escape the confinement, as even Samuel could sense it, of his ancient mother and too attentive sister.

He strode off, going to, as he said, 'see a man about a dog'. Samuel glimpsed him later in the afternoon, flush-faced, clearly drinking beer with a rather suspect group of hearties, playing darts. He was dressed like a superior workman.

The moment Georgie had gone, Madeleine relaxed. The slightly creased, almost Chinese texture of her face smoothed out, grew blank. She was wearing a strange costume from which Samuel could discern eau de mothball. A faint red tinge on her cheekbones indicated that Madeleine herself was aware of this at times. (The costume was a poplin dress, in Havana brown stripes, multi-flounced, with an apron front, frillings of turquoise and dusky pink, brown fringings and epaulettes. Her boots, quite high in the heel, were of turquoise leather, well worn and polished to a sheen. She unfolded, delicately, a parasol which, Samuel felt, from the way she looked up at it appreciatively, might have been a treasure. It had a highly elaborate ivory handle in the shape of a twig, with Prussian blue fringes. Inside its construction, it was lined with the palest watermelon pink silk.)

'From China?' Samuel asked her. She smiled and said, 'Why, Samuel, how much you know about certain things . . .'

She left a tiny space here for a question mark, expecting him, perhaps, to say that his fiancée — for this is how Madeleine now conceptualised the previous owner of the hat — had a liking for parasols. She touched the hat, as if in gentle acknowledgement.

But Samuel just smiled vaguely, and smoothed out the check on his trousers.

They were all seated on a large blanket. Mrs Perrett was unpacking the picnic.

She had earlier said, significantly, to Samuel, 'How well Madeleine looks in her new hat.'

Samuel had looked at her and said nothing.

'We have you, I believe, to thank . . . ?'

Mrs Perrett believed she was speaking quietly but her deafness betrayed her. Solomon Linz looked directly at Samuel, who had blushed. As had Madeleine. In fact she had looked absolutely wretched.

'May I . . .' she had asked, as if to mask her pain. She was asking Mrs Linz if she might hold the baby. The baby was asleep, thankfully, cradled in Ada's arms.

Solomon had already explained that his wife did not understand much English, but this she understood well enough. Carefully she handed over the child to Madeleine, who held the child capably, and rocked him slightly, and made small peaceful sounds with her mouth. The baby seemed to sigh and fall into a deeper well of sleep. The two women smiled.

Now Madeleine, having handed the precious bundle back, was kneeling, helping unpack the feast. There was baked goose, rabbit pie, a leg of ham, currant bread, newly churned butter — her pride and the result of over two hours' hard work: that morning it refused to take (her shoulders still ached: she had been up at five o'clock in the morning, putting the finishing touches to the banquet). She uncovered small vials of jam (gooseberry, strawberry, blackcurrant) all her own and made from 'the acre', as she said to Mr Linz proudly.

There was an eel pie, a pork pie, a sweet lamb pie and, from a tin, a rich plum fruit cake, sequinned over its surface with almonds and glacé cherries.

As the riches were unpacked, there was a sense of wealth, of beneficence. It was as if each of the migrants saw, in physical form, the benefits of their migration. Solomon was boiling the billy, attending to the small fire which was to their side. He had asked Samuel to keep an eye on it, while he unpacked his wife's contribution. This Mrs Perrett was particularly interested to see. She hugged her old paisley shawl over her shoulders and a beady gleam glittered in her eye, behind her gold-rimmed spectacles, as she gazed down upon little treacly ears of pastry drenched, somewhat inadvisedly, in a glue of sticky honey; there were also some tartlets made with preserved fruits, plus what looked like a most unedifying dish: cold boiled carp in some kind of congealed jelly.

'And what is that?' Mrs Perrett inquired. Her voice emitted an almost scientific interest.

'That,' Mr Linz explained, 'is a sweet and sour boiled carp. Stuffed with almonds and raisins.'

'I see.'

There was a masked silence. Beside them the branches crackled. A pesky little Maori boy — naked except for a pair of clearly too large trousers, snot hanging out of his nose — had arrived and was standing nearby. But he stood just beyond the range of comment, in a neutral ground. He watched them all intently.

'A dear little piccaninny,' Mrs Perrett said, too loudly.

Madeleine busied herself pouring the boiling water from the billy into the teapot. She had brought, for the occasion, a large and serviceable enamel pot, slightly chipped. She had cut up the pies. Mr Linz carved the goose. (He did not touch the ham, she noticed.)

It was only when the plates were being handed around that Madeleine observed that neither Mr nor Mrs Linz had touched the rabbit or eel pie either. Mr Linz had also asked what was in the sweet lamb pie. Madeleine took a little umbrage at this, as if her cooking were being questioned. But then she understood something else, and it occurred to her how difficult these — mixed — situations were. Mrs Perrett threw a scrap out towards the little Maori boy who, like a gull, swooped on it and stuffed it in his mouth.

*I*t was towards the middle of their picnic that Madeleine was aware of some kind of commotion. Each of them had been apportioned part of the blanket as their own territory. Mrs Linz and her baby were protected, as it were, by Mr Linz stretched out and forming a bank between himself and Madeleine, who had her mother beside her, sitting upright, her back against the tree. Samuel lay at Mr Linz's feet, looking out into the assembled crowd.

It was some expression on Samuel's face, some stillness, that caught Solomon Linz's attention. He himself was balancing a cup of coffee — he had brought the coffee, which once again he and his wife chose to drink (ostentatiously, Madeleine thought as she supped her tea) — while he fed himself one of his wife's delicious tartlets. In the interests of international co-operation, Madeleine had enquired of Mr Linz how his wife had made them. He, in his turn, had been full of compliments for Miss Perrett's blackcurrant jam, and indeed, she had had the pleasure of seeing Mrs Linz (who appeared to have a cold) helping herself to three spoonfuls of the jam, which she ate, without bread and butter, as if it were a sweet in itself.

The drop on the end of Mrs Linz's slightly reddened nose had bobbed as she bowed in genuflection to Miss Perrett, who somewhat idiotically beamed back at her and said too loudly, in cut-crystal English, that she would share her recipe with Mrs Linz 'at the earliest convenience'.

But it was here, just at this opening hour of mellowness, when it was entirely possible that a promenade might be in order (during which a rather unsubtle checking of the delights of other people's picnics could occur) that Mr Linz turned over his shoulder, following the suddenly wary — captured — look on Samuel's face, to see a brilliantly shiny new buggy sparkle up.

The owner drove the buggy right into the centre of the paddock and, almost as if it were scheduled entertainment, handed the reins over to a youth, whom he appeared to tip carelessly if not lavishly (not even looking at the coin, Miss Perrett noted); yet it was the female companion in the buggy who was the cause of considerable sensation.

Nobody had ever seen her before. This would not have mattered if she had been drab, modest and homely. But she was not. She was — and there was no way around it — a startlingly bold beauty. She was a woman used to being looked at, moreover, and she knew how to wear the gaze of many men — and women too.

In short, she showed no awareness of anyone existing on the planet apart from herself. To start with, she opened wide her parasol. This was when Dr Cogswell — for it was he — handed her down. (He did this with an exaggerated courtliness, as if he were handing down not so much a dumpy Queen Victoria as an exquisite Empress Eugenie.)

She had unfolded — cascaded, poured — herself down from the buggy, laughing at the last moment in what Madeleine instantly diagnosed as a 'vulgar' manner: for the woman seemed almost to lose her step. All around her, men started up from whatever they were doing. Tea being poured from a billy briefly scalded a blanket as the pourer lost attention. But this was, it turned out, a little faux step — just a momentary lapse of the kind a really expert actress might attempt, to draw more attention to herself, to focus all eyes upon a person who might, at any moment, make a dreadful mistake: tumble, fall, rip apart the fabric of her dress.

It was then that the woman — as Madeleine saw her, instantly wrenching away any kinder term, such as 'lady' — had brazenly laughed.

It got worse. Dr Cogswell, with further ostentatious gallantry, crooked his arm for the creature. (It was really too much, Madeleine thought to herself. Since when did a *dentist* get himself up as a gentleman? This was precisely what was wrong with the colonies, she scalded herself with comment: everything was topsy-turvy. Besides, she decided, straightening her backbone, there was nothing *less* indicative of a person's background in a new place than *her clothes*. Anybody could obtain such vulgarly ostentatious plumage.)

Yet the fact was that every woman at the picnic was straining to obtain a better view of what the unknown woman was wearing. As if it were a fashion parade, rather than a picnic, Dr Cogswell and his guest were walking slowly along. It was as if Dr Cogswell were showing her off — the fact that her dress fitted her figure more tightly around the hips, had a low-cut bodice and less of a bustle than anyone had ever seen. It was also in a shade no one had seen before: neither precisely sage green nor eau de nil, but a seemingly shimmering layering of the two.

There was not a single woman present who had seen a dress like this before. In one blow — for it could be considered something almost physical, something akin to a shock — each woman understood that she was seeing a new fashion that rendered her entire wardrobe instantly out of date. They were all flung into the shade, a shade as bad and dark as a kind of early frost, and each woman had to further understand her inconsequence by grasping the fact that this woman was a new arrival, from somewhere metropolitan; almost as if she were a magic totem, she became the source of an excitement out of all proportion to mere cloth, mere draping, mere button and hook.

Mrs Linz, as if sensing an offensive, had turned to her baby, which itself had awoken and begun grizzling. The drop on the end of her nose fell down splat! upon the child's forehead — it was an unfortunate mistake — so the babe immediately began to bawl. She was trapped in her own maternity, Ada felt, flushing painfully, feeling humiliation as she bundled the baby into herself and felt down for milk.

Mrs Perrett decided — or rather did not decide but with the true instinct of a parent for humiliating its child announced — 'Who or what is that extraordinary creature? Is it perhaps the Countess?'

'Mother!' Madeleine said, 'Don't be so absolutely ridiculous — you can't see!'

'What is it, child?' the old lady asked innocently.

On the opposite side of the river, on a bank, the Maori were making a lot of noise. There was intemperate, extremely vulgar laughter and Samuel could see some — boy? — imitating the exaggerated femininity of the unknown woman's walk. It was a brazen exhibition. This was met, on the distant bank, with additional hilarity.

In contrast a profound silence seemed to have fallen on the side of the bank on which the Napierites picnicked. Dr Cogswell and his companion walked, arm in arm, slowly, seeming to have eyes only for each other, past the Monteiths, who in turn looked up at them with frankly amused, interested eyes. (The young Miss Monteith felt in particular a queer pain in her heart that she was instantly made into, as she said to herself, 'a frightful old frump'. Perhaps the unknown beauty might even come to the dinner that evening? It could get worse.)

Suddenly, and this is when Samuel began to feel both excited and rather full of dread, it became apparent that Dr Cogswell had seen him. He raised a yellow-gloved hand in eager recognition, and he almost pulled the unknown woman on a sharp semi-circle, beginning to advance on Samuel's little picnic party.

'*I* was looking for some friend I knew!' Dr Cogswell cried too heartily, from a distance. Samuel was standing on his knees. Then, aware of the indignity of his posture, he rose. Madeleine settled back. She was flushing, but not with anger. A sudden and dispossessing excitement had overcome her. Suddenly she no longer cared what anyone thought. It pleased her that Dr Cogswell and the strange woman had chosen their little party rather than, say, the Monteiths (whose daughter she taught piano). Now, indeed, the Monteiths were wanly looking over — the men, and perhaps some of the women, clearly longing to join their cosmopolitan little party.

There was the added excitement that this might actually happen.

Samuel had shaken Dr Cogswell's hand, and been introduced to the lady. He bent over and kissed her hand. The woman did not perhaps have, Madeleine thought, the best of manners. She had giggled, as if it were a novelty. Up close, Madeleine could see that the woman had a slightly heavy jaw. In fact everything about her was too large: brilliantly blue eyes under thick black lashes, cheeks of an unnatural redness, large lips that Madeleine told herself were 'meaty'; there was even the faint impression of black hairs on the woman's arms.

'Do join us,' Madeleine found her own mouth betraying her. She winced at the eagerness that poured out of her voice. She even scrabbled along, pushing herself into her aged mother. 'There is plenty of room, and as you see,' — she waved a hand over the partly despoiled feast — 'there is so much left here if you care to pick from our humble little picnic.'

The beautiful creature looked at Dr Cogswell and said she was feeling 'hungry as a horse'.

This unladylike statement was accepted at face value by Cogswell, who was swollen, Madeleine saw, as a cockscomb. He might as well have been blind.

He handed down the beautiful creature so that suddenly she was quite near — frighteningly near to Madeleine, right by Solomon Linz's feet.

Dr Cogswell made the introductions once he was seated. 'Miss Louise' was what he called her. She seemed to have no surname. She also clearly had no interest in any of them. That is, apart from a vividly presented slice of charm on saying hello. But this was soon cancelled. She was eating. She was sitting on her side, rather elegantly, Madeleine had to admit, but she was eating like a growing boy.

Dr Cogswell suddenly appeared to have absolved himself of all responsibility. He lay back down on the blanket and looked up at the sky.

Madeleine overheard him murmur to Samuel that he had 'gone at it too hard all night long'. She disliked — indeed feared — loose talk of all sorts. She had looked to Samuel to exchange a glance but she felt suddenly marooned. Lonely. Samuel was altering the way he lay on the blanket so all she had of him was his back and, occasionally when he turned, a side profile.

Dr Cogswell, Samuel and the soi-disant 'Miss Louise' chatted among themselves. Solomon Linz alone began to offer the visitor delicacies, including his wife's sticky pastries. Mrs Linz looked a little wan, Madeleine thought. Perhaps to settle her baby down she got to her feet, with difficulty, and walked a little distance away, holding the child to her, patting its back. The child was screaming. Madeleine longed to join her, yet felt trapped.

'. . . but *where* do you live exactly?'

This was her mother. She was using her deafness as an offensive weapon. Miss Louise, mid-gristle, scissored into the piece of fat with her strong milky white teeth, and a small globule of meat fell on her chin. Two men, Dr Cogswell and Solomon, instantly offered her a kerchief. She laughed, her mouth full.

'I've put down at the port for a while.'

Dr Cogswell said quickly, 'She has relatives there.'

'I did not catch their name . . . ' Mrs Perrett said.

There was a small pause.

'I feel like one of the tarts now,' their guest said, laughing at something Madeleine did not like to think on. She felt something old and dismal start up in her. She suddenly no longer liked the picnic and she felt a kind of anger at sitting beside this creature, whom she did not know at all — would never know. Madeleine was as invisible to her as were the Maori children who had waded across the river and were now collected around their blanket, all standing a respectful distance off but whispering in one another's ears, laughing, looking, all the time looking, as if the Linzes, Samuel, herself and this Miss Louise had each of them been changed into a chained-up zoo exhibit — *behind bars*, is how Madeleine conceived of it.

But the creature was looking directly at her.

'Where did you get your bonnet?' she asked.

In response she shamed herself completely — lost her own self-respect — by rearing up like a grateful animal, almost smiling dreadfully, saying to the creature, 'Oh. It was a gift. From a gentleman.' And she heard herself tittering, horribly, vulgarly, as if the style of the woman were somehow contagious.

Miss Louise said, 'It is a style I used to be partial to.' And then helped herself to another of Mrs Linz's sticky pastries. (She then licked the pad of every finger.) Madeleine, rightly, felt herself dismissed. Returned to some eternal shade. Often, in the future, lying in bed at four a.m., scalded by her own complicity, she would try to work out whether it had been an insult.

Solomon, meanwhile, was suffering a physical agony. His erection was so intense that he felt as if he were hallucinating. He felt as if his cock had changed into a form of growth with so much power he could do nothing but feel himself subservient to it. In a hallucination he sensed his cowed wife walking up and down, slipping into shade and light in a flicker of disapproval.

He thought to himself of the night before, when he had asked her to wear the jewel. He had asked her to be naked for him. She was standing by the side of the bed, about to pull the covers back. She was wearing that clean-smelling, ironed nightgown that he liked to lift. But this time she had pushed his hand away. She seemed tired, out of sorts. She had been like this for such a length of time. And though he told himself he loved her — and indeed, he did feel a powerful longing for love with her, the mother of his child — he had wanted something else that night. He wanted something more like lust with her; he wanted eclipse, celebration; he wanted to welcome in changed circumstance, good luck.

He had nuzzled himself into her, had pleaded with her. In the end she had given in, sighing like a martyr, which was not what he wanted. He had put the earring around her neck, on a golden thread. She had started at the coldness of the metal.

'Why? You funny boy. Why?' she had said in Yiddish. The rest had gone badly. It had gone like any rehearsed fantasy: better in the thought than the actuality. He was aware of her red nose, her slightly adenoidal breathing. The jewel had slid from around her neck, to the side, got lost under the pillow. What he wanted from her she had, in a prosaic, closed way, given; but he had not got what he longed for, and he felt a fool — a boy, or worse still, a craven old man — his shanks covered in long hairs, his reddened tool still arched up and pathetic so that he had had to go away into another room and finish himself off. All this he thought about as he looked at the young woman at his feet.

She had stretched herself out quite immodestly. She was leaning into Dr Cogswell as if he were her sweetheart. But her eyes, her mocking frank glance, were turned towards Solomon, as if she diagnosed and held in pleasurable anticipation all that he was feeling towards her: yet it meant nothing to her, also.

Solomon gazed down with a hypnotic intensity at her shoes. They were white kid high-heeled slippers, slightly bruised by juice from the grass. He could see their tiny little bronzed buttons in the shape of butterflies; he could feel, inside his thighs, the sharp angle of her anklebone, beautifully covered with the thinnest of silk stockings, then truncated by the tiny gathered pleats of her underskirt, each pleat shadowed by another follicle of lace (slightly dirty lace, he thought dry-throated). Her legs were shapely, one ankle resting on the bottom part of her leg, the draped stuff of her skirt puffing out. Each draping was lined with a shimmering fringe that shook slightly with each of her breaths; any movement was exaggerated, sent out a shimmy of contained excitement.

So much to undo. So long to unwrap. So many miles of string, bows, so many hundreds of miles of little expertly hidden slightly indecent indentations of stitches: his eye travelled further up this odalisque to the elaborate fringing and embroidery of her tightly laced bodice. This was a magnificent piece of architecture. Even as a male — that is, as someone supposedly rational and given to diagnosing methods of construction — he could appreciate this (as against the rank animal rutting against the coarse tweed of his trousers — his cock had somehow managed to elude his undergarments and in a further trial was now brazenly rubbing itself, oozing, he felt, against the coarse hairiness of tweed). He had to stop thinking of this — was his face a satyr's mask? Did he wear horns?

His wife, he was wanly aware, was looking over at him. No, it was worse. She had called him. He could not stand up and risk exposing the enormous need of his cock. He pretended not to hear.

Madeleine leant forward. She touched him, on the shoulder. He jumped — and spilt over the edge of Miss Louise's dress an unspent cup of tea. Horribly he watched the wetness spread through her garment. He groaned like someone in a kind of purgatory.

'I believe your wife is calling you,' Madeleine said. She might have been trying to be good, act well.

'Tell her,' he said abruptly — he had got his kerchief out, was about to mop the young woman's dress — 'I am busy just now.'

'What have you *done,* you naughty man?'

The circle of Maori children laughed hilariously, mockingly.

'Go away!' Solomon said to them.

'Go away!' they echoed, picking it up and making it into a chant. 'Go away, go away, go away!'

*S*amuel stood up, flushing, and separated himself from the debacle. He went and joined Mrs Linz, saying a few words to her that Madeleine, in some personal agony of embarrassment, could not hear. She felt rather than heard ripples of amusement, ribaldry, coming from the Monteith camp. She knew now she would never be invited to the celebratory dinner that night. All along she had been prepared for Miss Monteith to do more than recognise her — do more than acknowledge her as a needy 'good woman' of character. Briefly Miss Perrett hated the goodness of her name, her character. She wished only that she could escape. The hat was heavy on her head, causing a migraine. She began to load up the dirty dishes. All around her lay spoil.

Dr Cogswell said to her, 'Perhaps we might get rid of the little arabs if we gave them . . .'

He was about to offer them the remains of her plum cake! Which she had, in her own mind's eye, seen as possibly doing for another week in the lunches she got up and packed for Georgie each morning. She had long suspected he did not actually eat his prepared lunch, but it had been an article of her faith that food was an important balance against . . . other agents (alcohol).

But now, suddenly and personally devastated to a degree she could no longer accommodate, she said, 'Yes. Get rid of it by all means. Whatever is needed to grant us a little peace.'

Dr Cogswell got up and sauntered towards the children. They were soon enough joined by a tumult of shouting Pakeha children. He walked off, pied piper-like, cutting with his knife little chunks of the cake and feeding them out, to large whoops of excitement, accompanied by cries of abandonment and pain at being excluded.

Madeleine could not help but feel the exquisite strangeness of the atmosphere. Now there was only herself, noisily banging plates together, and the kneeling Linz, who was still attending to the young woman's dress. The two of them were speaking in low voices — apparently in banalities, but Madeleine felt herself and knew herself to be compromised. At one point she was surprised to turn and see her mother gazing with rapt attention at the man and woman. Madeleine glimpsed for one second something in her mother's face that was upsetting: an almost lewd appreciation of the very basic animal relationship occurring on the rug.

'Mother!' she said, a little too sharply. The old woman adjusted her gaze.

'What is it, child?'

'Can you not help me?'

The old woman said nothing, but, her face still showing the shadow of an ancient amusement, she began slowly, and with difficulty, passing the remains of the feast to her maiden daughter.

*I*t was towards the end of the picnic that the terrible event occurred. Nobody could say, afterwards, what had led up to it. It was, apparently, an event without explanation. It was when people were packing up — some, such as the Monteiths, had already left, hurrying off to prepare for their exclusive (excluding) dinner. Others were rounding up children, loading up carts, drays and buggies. Dr Cogswell and his brilliant companion had left: she with a stain on her frock, he in as high a good humour as when he came.

Samuel was exhausted. The day had been too long. Mrs Linz's baby had started screaming blue murder at least thirty minutes earlier and nothing would placate him. His face had become bright red, and Mrs Linz, through her husband, seemed to be under the impression the child had some sort of reaction to food he had mistakenly been fed. She must return, post haste, to town.

Solomon arranged for her to get on the cart of the O'Connell family. Samuel's last view of Mrs Linz was of her sitting on her own, round-shouldered, red-nosed, isolated. She did not turn to wave to her husband. Indeed, she seemed to have no words to speak to him at all.

Madeleine, her ancient mother and Samuel found themselves with the heavy boxes and wicker cases to carry. Solomon had disappeared in the crowds suddenly departing. There was something amiss — something not quite right here.

Samuel, manfully carrying the heavy wicker case, felt frankly bad-tempered. He had a sense that Dr Cogswell was arranging some kind of wild and risky entertainment for later that evening. It certainly involved Miss Louise, yet when Samuel had made the mistake of asking Dr Cogswell if there was anything happening later, Cogswell had peered as if into the far distance and said, 'Yes. Those snobs the Monteiths are having a dinner, but each of them would dance in hell before giving out an invitation.'

This was not what Samuel wanted to hear.

Madeleine had also succumbed to some strange silence. She had removed the hat from her head — 'it is giving me a headache,' she had said to nobody in particular. Mrs Perrett said to Samuel, in her overloud voice, 'Poor Madeleine does suffer the most frightful headaches. She is quite the martyr to them.'

At which point Madeleine had said, 'Mr Barton has no interest in our little pains and problems, Mama.'

It was then that it had happened.

They were midway towards the cart. Alongside them were the McSweeney family, squabbling about a lost china doll, a child bringing up the rear by banging, again and again, a wooden spoon on a cast-iron frying pan.

There was the loud sound of a shot. Followed by an agonising scream. Mr Mercer emerged from behind the bushes, hurriedly pulling up his trousers. (He had been answering the call of nature.) His mouth was panting open. He was yelling, but there was no sound. From the bushes a little further along came another figure.

It was a Maori, a seemingly fit and strong young man. He was holding in his hand a rifle. Half of his face had been blasted off. Flesh, including an eye, was hanging in one ripped hank. An artery had been sliced open, and an unending font of blood was pulsing out, pouring down his chest.

The man walked out in what looked like a bold semi-circle, staggering all the time as if he wanted to join the departing crowd. Which had fallen into silence. He walked as far as he could get, Mr Mercer walking backwards, stumbling to get out of his way, the crowd too rippling backwards as the man crumbled slowly and fell into a heap. Only at the last did he let his rifle fall, and it went off again, a bullet thwinging through the air, so that everybody with any presence of mind dropped to the ground.

A child was crying. A horse was straining against its leash, tied to a tree. A cloud passed over the sun, and some blowflies, alerted to a new scent, moved off from a crumb of rich plum cake and began to move towards a new source of attraction.

A View of
the Infinite

The view, for Madeleine, meant nothing. This was a betrayal, since she had always elevated the view from the top of Scinde Island into a symbol, almost, of all that was good about living where she did. But on this windy, buffeting day in late September she never once slid her glance aside to look at that vast blue-grey line that hinted at the infinite. She was huffing, as she walked along, almost grimacing, as if in some internal pain.

She stabbed at the ground with the end of her stout umbrella, carried as a walking stick. (It fended off mongrel dogs, gave her moral support.)

How had it happened? What did it mean? Who was the man?

It was all a mystery. The public ball had been cancelled. Some committee members of the Acclimatisation Society had voted for the ball to go ahead, but others were adamant that the festivities cease. So people retired to their separate homes, all of them conjuring up stories about what might have led to a young man — a Maori, it was true — taking his own life in such a reprehensibly public manner ('as to scar the little ones for life', as Mrs Mercer said, gathering her smallest children to her side, clutching at them. The children grew solemn at being at the centre of so much concern).

It had ruined everything, Madeleine decided. The afternoon, anyway, had gone to rot. She had felt tainted by proximity to that unsavoury, yet somehow delicious, woman from the port.

As she laboured up the steps from Shakespeare Road to Napier Terrace, she ordered herself to elevate her thoughts.

Nullify her feelings.

The sky was a vivid impasto of hurtling cloud. As far as the eye could see there was sea — a whole brilliant floor of molten silver. The sun had scorched out at that moment, burning a hole in the silver, turning it to white fire. And moving along slowly, closer to hand, was the schooner *Adamantine*, which was unable to dock, owing to an outbreak of measles among the immigrants aboard.

For one second she pitied the people aboard, sinking back in her own mind to her emotions just before landing: the terror of finally seeing at last all that had been promised — held out for.

Yet the restlessness too: the longing to begin a life held in stasis.

She stabbed at a dandelion flower, squashing its showy yellow heart.

Samuel had told her that Mr Linz was leaving on the *Adamantine*, on some important private business. She understood it was somehow connected to Samuel, but he did not elucidate, except to say that Mr Linz was going directly from Napier to Melbourne.

Madeleine understood that his return would be keenly awaited — not least by Mrs Linz, who appeared lost without her husband, her translator. Samuel and Mrs Linz were 'thick as thieves', as she reported to her mother.

Mrs Perrett had said nothing, but took up her embroidery and sighed.

'Women,' she said philosophically, and about what Madeleine was not sure, 'women in the colonies look worn so easily.'

'I expect it is the work,' Madeleine had not been able to resist saying tartly, gathering up her brother's washing and taking it outside, to the room in which she herself boiled all the family's thirty-seven pieces of clothing.

*S*he was on her way to give a piano lesson to Miss Ellie Monteith. It was the usual time, the accustomed day. Madeleine had, under her arm, her old valise, her fond old valise from dear old London, in which she kept her music.

She had now reached the brow of the hill. She was breathing hard, almost cursing, in a furious mood for some reason. A deep sense of dissatisfaction had overcome her. Usually such a walk, encountering, as she told herself, the infinite, would help her regain equilibrium. But somehow, on this suddenly cool day, the wind served only to razor into her complexion, to battle into her, seemingly to laugh at her.

The Monteiths' house was an early officers' mess, altered and to a degree gentrified by a long and deep veranda enclosing the building on three sides.

A carriage drive had been put in and two camellia bushes planted. Madeleine knew she was expected at the front door: indeed, it had been among her stipulations that as a lady, she expected to be treated as such. But this morning she swerved away from the door — closed on account of the wind — and went down the side veranda, towards the back, where she sensed Mrs Risington would be.

She pulled the tradesmen's bell, and somewhere within, a bell tongued out.

A shadow moved behind a curtain, there was the crisp sound of boots moving over wood, then the door was pulled back.

Mrs Risington had on her superior servant's costume — a severely plain brownstuff daydress, with no ornamentation whatsoever around the neck except for a single gold locket that was always there — attached to her throat as if a fleshly growth, Madeleine thought. She wore on her head a small and delicate lace cap, and she also wore a very fine linen apron: snowy white, quite small and decorative.

She had in her hand a silver-polishing cloth.

'Oh, Miss Perrett. You did give me a start. Such strange things are amiss at present that I don't know what else might happen.'

'Indeed, Mrs Risington,' Madeleine said, stepping inside while Mrs Risington held open the door for her. The wind sent the mat scudding along the waxed floor. Mrs Risington placed a highly polished black boot against it.

'A day for the Devil to be loose,' she said. And crossed herself.

Madeleine did not approve of heathenish superstitions, so said nothing.

She busied herself placing her umbrella in the rack, and handing over to Mrs Risington a small glass jar of 'my best blackberry jam', Madeleine said to her companion. 'For use in your own parlour,' she added.

Mrs Risington, turning somewhat regally, nodded and indicated that Madeleine should follow.

'Oh, they went ahead with the dinner all right,' Mrs Risington said, pouring. It was half an hour before the time of the piano lesson, and anyway Miss Ellie was habitually, rather prettily (in her own mind), unpunctual. Not that this meant that Miss Perrett could be late. She would have to sit on the hard wooden seat in the main hall, awaiting Miss Ellie's graceful appearance.

'You have been waiting? Not long, I hope, oh, I do hope!'

Madeleine had positioned her teacup on the starched white cloth and appeared to be considering its contents before she spoke.

'And a most jolly occasion it turned out to be,' Mrs Risington went on. 'No expense spared. There was the Bishop up from Wellington, and the Governor's lady, with a friend of hers from the Old Country. A countess, no less.'

'But when,' said Madeleine, considering, 'did the dreadful news come through?'

Mrs Risington was silent a moment. In the darkened back parlour Madeleine inspected the waxy jowls of her friend. There was the suspicion of a moustache above her dry, chapped lips. There was not, and had never been, any mention of a Mr Risington. But there was a child. Or rather now, a young man, in Auckland, who worked, said Mrs Risington somewhat proudly, in book-keeping. 'For a most important firm,' she added, the soul of discretion and slightly fudged appearances.

'The dreadful news?' Mrs Risington said, and began to blush. 'I did not look at the clock.'

'But who brought it?'

'One of the stable boys. He'd been sent down to the port to bring up some extra cases of champagne. And the surprise guest: a most glorious singer.'

'A singer?'

'A lady. Of sorts. But a real stunner.'

Madeleine knew instantly.

'She sang the most amusing airs.'

'They did not consider cancelling?' Madeleine said with a sharp tone of reprimand in her voice. Mrs Risington looked torn between defending her employer and a sense of personal scandal.

'Mrs Monteith said that, all things being equal, if people did not know about the death, they could not be expected to be — as she said — *morbid* about the matter. She would choose her moment when to tell, she said. "It is what one learns in life, my dear Martha," she said to me: "when to tell, and when it is best to say nothing."'

Madeleine barely nodded.

She had the feeling this house was no less indecent, perhaps, than that infamous house down at the port, which possibly even housed 'Miss Louise', the singer.

In one sense it was no business of hers. She checked her watch.

'But who was the wretched creature?' Mrs Risington asked raptly. It was her turn, now, to question.

'Who was he?' Madeleine answered slowly, and with difficulty. 'Some lost soul,' she said initially. But she could see this did not satisfy Martha Risington.

'From what I understand he was a young man who worked in the slaughterhouse. He seemed perfectly ordinary. Then some melancholy fit overtook him. There seems no logical explanation,' Madeleine said hopelessly.

She could not account for her own feelings of despair. At the waste of a life. And the view of a human, another human, staggering around in such extremis.

She herself had one view that stayed with her.

It was a blade of glass, sticky with blood. The red contrasted with the green so boldly she had not been aware what she was looking at. But then it had stained the side of her shoe. Its rust colour stayed there even now, as she sat, her boots hidden under the cloth. (She had polished them but the stain only sank in deeper.)

'There is talk he was a fighter in the saloons.'

Madeleine shrugged.

'I have heard he attended church, under the Reverend William Tye, and learned his scriptures perfectly.'

'Tye, did you say?' Mrs Risington drew herself up. 'A scandalous man if ever there was one. Chased out of the ministry, and good job about it. I would hate to think of all the Maoris he introduced to *religion*.'

Madeleine understood that Mrs Risington was referring to something else entirely. But what, she did not know.

Mrs Risington had left a disapproving silence.

'Well, let us not concern ourselves too much. It is not the greatest loss,' she said a little curtly.

Madeleine said nothing, but inwardly quailed. Her dark mood deepened and she looked at Mrs Risington as from a vast distance.

'Are we not all God's creatures?' she asked. She decided she would risk this.

'Not when they are heathen,' Mrs Risington said, plucking Madeleine's empty cup away from her and turning her back slightly. 'Or at the very least, only recently cannibals.'

The two women were silent.

'I think Miss Ellie may be awaiting you,' Mrs Risington said tonelessly.

To which Madeleine replied, as if her life depended upon it, ' . . . Yes, but *when* did they know? *When* were they told?'

Mrs Risington looked on her as if her old acquaintance had suddenly gone mad.

'Why, the following morning, of course. When it no longer mattered.'

A Fond Farewell

The rooks had come back, as had the chaffinches. One was seen on the roof of the Masonic Hotel, another on the roof of Linz, the jeweller's.

Of the partridges, most had been found dead.

'It is a worry,' intoned the *Daily Telegraph* two days later, 'that the great pains taken by settlers to introduce birds will come to naught when they are faced with their great enemy, the local hawk. The hawk is a most predatory bird. With regards to this, the Acclimatisation Society wishes to make it known that the reward for a hawk's head is now increased to one shilling: double the previous price.'

There was no report on the death at the picnic — just a note saying that no inquest would be held for 'the Maori who shot himself recently'.

The line below said: 'One Maori more or less is neither here nor there.'

These few curt words were all that were expended on the tragedy. It was as if, by diminishing it in print, so the ramifications of the messy incident might fade.

But it seemed to be tattooed inside Samuel's and Solomon's skulls as they took the cab over to the port.

Solomon was finally off to Melbourne.

Mrs Linz was sitting beside him, holding the baby. There was a kind of bruised silence between the pair. Samuel did not care to intervene.

'You must promise me, on your word of honour,' Solomon had said to Samuel, taking his hand between his own two hands — Samuel had the sense of dry warmth, of a caressively sandpapered texture that was entirely masculine — 'You must promise, while I'm away, to look after my little Ada.'

Ada was looking out the side window, enjoying the excursion.

The interior of the cab was relatively luxurious: it even boasted some out-of-date London magazines held in place by plaited maroon braid and a little silver-plate vase filled with freesias. Samuel's knees were bumping against Linz's.

'Of course, dear man. Of course.'

He slid his hands away and placed them on his thighs. He looked out the window.

Was the death bad luck? Did it presage an evil turn of events? It was difficult for the senseless act not to cast a shadow. No matter how you tried to shake it off. Samuel also had the feeling that Linz and his wife might have had an argument after the picnic. Ada's pale face seemed especially hurt, crumpled around the lips. Her lids were reddened and she was twisting, in her hand, a small, damp handkerchief.

Linz looked at Samuel urbanely, man to man, their knees knocking companionably, and raised his eyebrows. He seemed to be smiling enigmatically. He was feeling inside his jacket pocket, keeping his large brown eyes on Samuel's face. He pulled out his wallet, then slipped it back inside. Now even Ada was looking at him. He unfolded a square of newspaper.

'I did not show you this the other day. I did not want you to become over-excited.'

He handed over the paper and tapped the print in the middle of a column.

Samuel glanced at the paper's origin: it was not from Napier. In fact it was the *Melbourne Age*. It was a small gossip item that read:

REMARKABLE JEWEL.

There is talk afoot among the city's jewellers (who are a brethren much given to shared confidences) that any day soon a most remarkable jewel will be revealed in a certain Melbourne jewellery emporium not two hundred yards distant from these offices. It is said that the jewel may have graced the neck of more than one or two belles of great renown. Indeed, the jewel is said to be the price of virtue, bestowed on a *friend* of a French Emperor. Or should we say, an ex-emperor. Now the gentleman is living a little more quietly, in retreat, not two hundred miles from Chislehurst.

Samuel found himself blushing. It was pleasure, partly, but also shame. He handed the paper back. Ada followed it with her eyes. Just as he was putting it inside his jacket Solomon appeared to think better of it, and handed it to his wife.

'She can *read* English,' he said. Ada scanned the page, looked up quizzically. Samuel leant forward and tapped the page where the item was. He said, 'Your clever clever husband.'

Ada handed the paper back, after an appreciable moment.

'My . . . clever . . . husband,' she repeated a little slowly, looking from one man to the other. Samuel nodded; Linz laughed. He leant over, picked up his wife's hands and kissed them — each knuckle. 'My clever, lovely Ada,' he said. His wife smiled, quite beautifully, but it was at Samuel.

'My *clever-clever* husband,' she repeated.

$\mathcal{D}$own at the port, the three-hundred-and-four-ton schooner, the *Adamantine*, stood out in the midstream. All along the siding, however, a chaotic scene was occurring. This had been caused by several things. The migrants who had been kept aboard the *Adamantine* in quarantine, to guard against bringing in a measles epidemic, had finally — and then only on the insistence of the captain (against the advice of the ship's doctor) — been allowed to land. They were standing in confused bunches, trying to locate their luggage.

A flock of merino sheep had been loosed among them, and was pouring hither and thither, like rice scooting across a polished floor. A dog was harassing the sheep, barking madly. A man on a horse had been trying to direct a dray full of boxes away from the wharf but the top-heavy load had toppled over. Some of the boxes had broken apart and there was a muddle of things — tins of paint, iron bedsteads, bottles of figs, tins of sardines, buckets — all in disarray on the siding. Children, like flies, had suddenly appeared and the driver of the cart was trying both to pick up the boxes and keep the children at bay. His horse was agitated by the barking dog.

A stray pig wandered in, intent on its own business, snuffling up rubbish in a contented, self-absorbed way.

Linz was talking to a customs official, a rather grave man who appeared sublimely unaware of the bedlam about him. He held in his hand some documents clipped to a wooden board, on which were listed a series of carefully hand-written details. These were the number of consignments to be landed, and the number of consignments to be loaded in their place. As if he held all that was coherent, he looked through the noise, the mess, the chaos and appeared impervious to everything.

Linz returned, looking a little upset.

'He said there is a further delay.'

Mrs Linz looked at his face, reading his expression.

'How long?' asked Samuel. He had hoped to make the departure scene as swift as possible.

Linz shrugged. He turned and looked out at the boat. 'He said the crew broke into the alcohol on the boat last night and consumed everything they could lay their hands on. They need time to sleep it off.'

The *Adamantine* seemed especially enigmatic. There was no movement discernible upon it.

'What is it, Solomon?' Ada asked in German.

'A small problem. Nothing of importance.'

To Samuel he said, 'He recommends we wait in the coffee house over there. The boat will not be boarding for several hours at least.'

Samuel immediately felt very tired. He had not budgeted, emotionally, on small-talk dripped out over several hours. He was still recovering from the picnic and its horrors.

He felt strangely uneasy.

He acknowledged wearily that he would now need to find a sediment of energy inside himself and carry on. He nodded and, guiding Mrs Linz by holding the corner of her elbow, engineered their way around a dray loaded with greasy bales of tallow and wool, past a bullock team standing in contentment, pure and still, and then through the sheep, packed in tightly together now, raising their pupils in mute incomprehension, bleating as if they recognised, and saluted, the shokhet moving through their midst.

The coffee house was a rather poor establishment, much used in the port. It had only the basic facilities, which meant a rather dowdy set of tables, wooden benches and, to the side, under the bleary window, a built-in table and benches. This is what they took. An extremely fat woman behind the counter eyed them. Clearly she did not expect to move.

Samuel asked the others: 'Would you care for some refreshment?'

They needed, anyway, to purchase their right to sit there.

Mrs Linz had a lemonade. Linz, in a moment of inspiration, ordered a brandy.

'We might as well enjoy our time in the desert.'

It could have been his motto for life in the colonies. Samuel went to order the beverages. He felt he needed to leave the Linzes alone, for the sake of privacy, almost decency: in these last moments the couple might like to share some intimacies.

He stood with his back to the couple, while the woman laboured over the simple act of uncorking a bottle of lemonade, opening it, finding three glasses and the brandy. (None of the glasses, Samuel noted, was particularly clean.) The woman seemed to have a grudge against them — perhaps because they did not come from the port? Or because their middle-class mien and dress implied a rebuke to the frowsy surroundings?

When he turned around the Linzes were sitting marooned in silence, either baleful or companionable, depending on how you looked at it. They seemed no longer to need to speak — or was it that they no longer had anything to say to each other? Samuel felt that he was invading the intimate space simply by being there. But Linz seemed to come alive on Samuel's approach and kick-started the engine of his charm.

'My dear wife has just asked me if this is where the charming Miss Louise lives.' He laughed. Mrs Linz looked, with lively intelligence, up from the baby, to her husband and then Samuel.

Samuel understood that she was asking something more. As did perhaps Linz, who was being too urbane, too smooth. Was he, after all, Samuel wondered for the first time, completely reliable? If he lied to his wife, wouldn't he more easily lie to him? But Samuel also understood how a man might need to keep certain things from his wife.

'Well, does she?' Ada said to Solomon in a peeved tone that even Samuel could interpret.

Solomon appeared briefly baffled. 'I wouldn't know,' he said, lifting his glass up and saluting Samuel with it.

A moment too late, Ada lifted her glass, heaving the child onto the other thigh.

'*Salut.*'

'Success.'

'Good health and happiness.'

'To my speedy return.'

'And to my escape,' said Samuel last of all. On Solomon translating for Ada, they all laughed, and then fell through a hole into deep silence.

The door opened at that moment, perhaps fortunately, and the distinctive figure of the Reverend William Tye walked in. He removed his hat, ran a gnarled hand through his thinning white hair and paused while he took his bearings. He saw the Linz party, and Samuel raised his hat to him. He nodded in reply and made straight towards them.

'I have been kept waiting,' he said a little irascibly. As if Samuel, or the Linzes, were the cause.

'So have we,' said Samuel.

'My crate is . . . *most* important,' he said. 'The Royal Society in London is awaiting my consignment of ferns.'

Linz looked at Tye with frank curiosity: a colonial who had been living in New Zealand, in Napier, longer than anyone he knew. Was this what lent the slightly crazed air to the old man? As if he could hear or see things other people couldn't, and this knowledge drove him insane?

'Please, sir, please sit,' said Linz with natural courtesy for the old. And indeed there was something prophet-like, positively Old Testament, in Tye's look. Linz made way for him.

'Oh, well, thank you, indeed.'

Tye instantly undid himself by appearing almost childishly grateful to be included. He sat down with unbecoming eagerness, turning a bright and very clear blue gaze down at the babe. Mrs Linz, pleased at the attention being given to her treasure, held the baby up.

The baby, on cue, opened its eyes and looked directly towards what could almost have been the opposite pole of his life — his destiny, if he lived that long. The old man chuckled and reached out a hand.

'And what is his name?'

'Gershom.'

Tye blinked just infinitesimally, which indicated that he understood the Linzes were Jewish. He looked at them with deepened interest then. But said nothing.

'We were talking about the unfortunate incident at the picnic yesterday,' Samuel said smoothly.

Tye surprised them all by sighing deeply and seeming to slump down into an abject mood. This lively emotional performance, in one so old, made him a subject of interest to the Linz party.

'Indeed, indeed,' Tye said, and his large, awkward hands seemed to sweep the table clean — as if he could see some pattern there that they could not. They all found themselves staring down at the table top, to diagnose the portent of the rings stained on the wood — a multiplicity of them, a clutter. 'The very saddest business,' Tye said slowly. 'An unutterable waste.'

The vehemence with which he spoke surprised Samuel. Solomon, who had not witnessed the death, looked interested.

'You knew the man?' he asked.

Tye was silent a moment, and without answering directly said, 'He said he kept hearing voices.'

'He was a lunatic,' Samuel translated. Tye looked at him and Samuel was confused, humiliated, and more than slightly irritated to see Tye smile at him dismissively, then shake his head.

'That is one interpretation,' he said.

'There are others?' Linz asked.

'There are always others,' Tye said. 'There is always more than one way to see things, surely you would agree?'

Linz was silent.

'Mr Linz is about to go to Melbourne.'

Samuel felt he was adept at providing conversational clues. He felt slightly at a loss before the gravitas of the old man. He also wanted to imbue a little lightness, even frivolity, into their discourse. And by this way point out the old man's lack of wordiness.

Tye said nothing, but looked at Linz in a long, intense stare.

'I am going there . . . on a business matter,' Linz said, looking uncomfortable. 'For no more than a fortnight, I expect.'

Perhaps he might have liked to argue philosophy with the old man. For the first time Samuel witnessed Solomon not being in control of a situation. Solomon in fact looked suddenly full of longing, as if he had only at that moment, on the point of departure, sighted what he might have welcomed, living there.

Instead Mr Tye, sensing an opening, had taken up his favourite topic: New Zealand flora and fauna. He asked Solomon if he might like to join the Athenaeum, or the Debating Society. They were always looking for men of intellect in Napier.

'The place is a desert,' Tye said emphatically. 'A desert.'

Solomon was silent a moment, thoughtful.

'How does a man live in a desert?'

'He hopes to find an oasis,' Tye said after a moment of thought.

'I will not be away long,' Linz said, as if this were an answer.

At this point a boy ran into the room, calling out, 'Leavis. Is there a Dr Leavis in the house?'

'Linz?' said Samuel.

'A mister and a missus and a little 'un. Foreigners.'

Solomon, and a second later his wife, stood up. Suddenly, now that he was about to go, there was a clutch of sentiment. She looked alarmed. Her eyes swung from her husband to Samuel.

'You will have to look after her. Until I get back.'

'It won't be long,' Samuel said as much to Ada as to Solomon, who was shaking his hand too forcefully so that Samuel longed to slide his grasp away. The Reverend Tye was contemplating the small family group, looking suddenly haunted. Solomon was leaning over his wife's upturned face. He kissed her on each cheek, then, belatedly and rather hurriedly, on the lips. She seemed to cling to him, to yield her body to him. Her face was still upturned, and now tear-streaked, while Solomon said goodbye to his son. This seemed an especially poignant moment.

Then he was away, carrying his carpetbag, striding off. He had told them not to wait for the boat to leave. There were always delays down at the port, what with the tides and the uncertainty of everything — the crew, it seemed, included. He was anxious that they get on with things.

The Reverend Tye had disappeared also. He had gone off to check with the customs official that his ferns were, indeed, loaded and placed on the special part of the deck that he had paid for.

Ada and her baby and Samuel stood alone, amid an eddying crowd. There was a sudden forlornness in the air. Samuel slid his arm through Ada's. She was straining her eyes, trying to see if she could spy any sign of Solomon.

It was at this point Samuel — and Samuel alone — saw Miss Louise, in what looked like a startlingly ordinary travelling costume, dun-coloured and anonymous. She was lightly veiled. She was carrying her own suitcase.

Soon she was lost in the mêlée.

'We'll be all right, Ada,' Samuel murmured, thinking he could use her Christian name since she hardly understood what he was saying.

She turned to him, eyes reddened by weeping, and tentatively uttered her mantra: 'My husband . . . very clever?'

*S*everal days later Samuel ran into Dr Cogswell in Hastings Street. He reminded Samuel that he still had a pending appointment, and Samuel, feeling a little at a loose end, and wanting — he wasn't sure why — to be submerged again in that etherised dreamworld, agreed to turn up at the dentist's rooms on the morrow.

Before he turned away, Dr Cogswell seemed to recall something he wanted to share with Samuel.

'That delightful creature you saw me with — at the picnic?'

Samuel noted, almost indecently, the freshness of Dr Cogswell's lips as he spoke. He saw the glint of his teeth, and inside his mouth he was further aware of the ambulant slither of his tongue.

Suddenly he had fallen into a rapt focus.

'She picked up all she wanted to in Napier, then took off back to Melbourne.'

There was a small pause, then Dr Cogswell leant forward, as if he were about to divulge something indecent, which in a way he was.

'She works the ports in these small towns and picks up a *fortune*, dear fellow, singing songs and turning tricks. She earns in a few sweet hours what we poor sods have to slave over a lifetime to earn.'

Turning away, and roaring with a strange laughter, Dr Cogswell walked out of sight.

Book Two

'He might go out to one of the Colonies . . .'
   'Yes; — be sent away that he might kill himself with drink
in the bush, and so be got rid of.'

The Way We Live Now, by Anthony Trollope

Modern Babylon

1870

There was the sound of a gunshot. Explosive. Frightening. But it was only a sign for the great gas balloon to be loosened from the ropes that held it down to the earth.

Immediately the balloon bounded, like a big ball, up into the air.

'Oh, Fred!'

'What is it, darling?'

'You're not frightened are you, Fan?'

'Oh, Fred.' Fan closed her eyes. 'What bliss. What utter heaven.'

Stella was holding tight to the wicker sides with one hand. Her face was flushed, eyes glistening. Her other hand held on to her hat.

'Don't be frightened, Fan!'

But Fan was laughing, laughing. She could not stop laughing. It was like a seizure at the wonderful aeration of everything around her. The release!

Down below, Kennington Park seemed to sink suddenly.

'It's like a trapdoor! We've fallen through the trapdoor!' Stella screamed. She had turned around, was now holding on to the wicker sides with both hands. Her dress rose, in a wild rosette. She pushed it down, laughing.

The people who had gathered to watch the balloon's ascent changed into dots, surmounted by flat, upturned faces. Hands fluttering farewell.

The ground sank and sank below them.

'Fred, you utter darling!'

Fan gripped Fred's arm tight. Her face was white.

'What is it, darling?'

Fred had slipped around behind her and was holding her, his arms laced around her waist.

They skimmed over the top of some trees.

'Oh, Fred,' she murmured, leaning into him, eyes shut. 'You're a devil,' she murmured. 'A complete devil.'

He leant forward and nibbled her ear, whispered something. She laughed. His hands slid up to the nape of her neck. She pushed him away but Fred only came closer. He grabbed her. Fan shrieked.

Stella tut-tutted and said, 'Have a mind, dear, please, for some decorum.'

She indicated the mechanic aboard the balloon — a working man whose face held no emotion, as if he were deaf: yet observant. He was tightening the straps, testing the ropes.

*H*e had seen them getting out of their barouche. A fancy man and his two women. The two women, one in pale green, the other in violet, were both veiled, gloved, holding cloaks and furs. The gent had handed them down and the cabbie had carried over a blanket, a wicker basket. They were having an afternoon of pleasure. Ted Billington knew what this meant. Pleasure was a code-word for all sorts of things. The gent had been up there before. With other women. He had pressed into Ted's hand a gold coin as he got in. Ted knew this meant: you're not to look. You go and look out the side of the balloon once we're up in the air.

Don't pay no notice. And when it's over you turn around.

Ted didn't mind. He was glad of the coin. He had looked at the women as they got on board. The one in violet was a looker. Even through the veil you could see her eyes, pale blue and motionful, flickering and ardent. Maybe they were all a little drunk? They had that rallying, bantering tone. The women, of course, weren't ladies. That's to say, they had no modesty. No real modesty. Each of the ladies had looked at Ted intently, right into his eyes. The smaller of the two, in pale green, was very much painted, had a large mouth and a curious chuckling laugh. As if she knew something funny that you didn't. She would be a goer, Ted could tell that. Not that it mattered. They all looked right through him, as if he wasn't there. They had acknowledged his existence and would now ignore him. He became invisible to them. Which was how he liked it.

*T*he balloon skimmed over the tops of some trees. Suddenly they had a panorama of London at their feet — enormous, intoxicating, vast. Yet what was equally intoxicating was the strange sensation that they were floating in air, without actually moving. It appeared as if the earth itself were airborne — floating, weightless, away from them. There it went, sliding, panorama-like, beneath their feet, revealing ever more endless landscapes of streets, parks and buildings.

Fan and Fred were leaning over the basketry side, gazing down at the toy-like buildings below.

The balloon was floating above fields, in a line with the Thames towards Richmond. Voices rose, faint as the buzzing of bees. Yet the curious feeling continued: they seemed stationary, so still, in some strange dream-like freeze.

Fan's veil suddenly whipped aside.

She grabbed out at it but it escaped. She watched it go, changing form — becoming a sylph, a unicorn, a dragon, and then a tiny drifting kerchief.

The odd thing was it was only from the swift descent of the veil — its separation in space — that Fanny grasped they were actually moving ever upwards. They were caught in a corkscrew of vapour, turning higher, ever higher, revolving.

'It is so still — so beautifully still!' she called.

Fanny felt overcome, drunk — yet curiously awake, as if only at this moment had she come into consciousness. The rest of the day — the waking, dressing, getting there, almost her whole life up until that point — was a blank. It was like that moment when she walked out of the wings onto the stage: this strange sense of nakedness, of being upheld in the air — of walking out into space.

There was danger, but there was also something else: it was to do with feeling intoxicatingly alive.

She slid her glove down by Fred's wrist, where the black hairs licked. She stroked them and looked into his eyes for a moment.

'Thank you, darling,' she murmured.

He placed his hand — warm, rough — on top of her gloves. He squeezed her hand hard. She leant back into him and they joined silence to silence.

*F*irst Ted Billington heard what sounded like a moan. This was the first sound, after a long and purposeful silence. This silence was intense, occupied, full. Ted's hearing grew sharper. He thought he could hear the slither of fabric. He thought he heard something like fabric being pulled aside. Buttons. He heard a stopped breath, almost a sob. A woman's sob.

'*Oh, Jesus. Jesus.*'

The sounds all stopped at this point, held still, then gradually sound returned. He heard a man's groan, a man's groan when he's in the middle of pleasure and he doesn't want it to ever stop, but he senses, knows, that inevitably it will. The groan was a cry of passion, of anger, of entreaty. *Let me stay here forever, floating through the heavens.* He heard the low gurgle of a woman's laugh — he couldn't work out which woman it was. He thought it might be the little tart in green.

Ted felt his own pego, as he called it, engorge. He kept getting pictures. In his head. It was even worse than looking. He wanted to turn round. To catch a glimpse. But he knew. Knew that if he turned around, that sauceboat in green would be looking at him straight in the eye. He tried to shift his pego so it wasn't so stiffly sticking through his pants; somehow it was caught in his trousers. It was sore, but pleasurably sore, as if he were being made aware of only one thing: one source of pleasure. He could hear now, distinctly, the woman moan (he felt a sheath — deliciously moist, warm and tight), heard her moan, 'Oh, Fred.' The woman's voice was low. The man was saying, panting '*Oh, Fan, Fan, tell me you love me! Tell me you do.*'

It was at this point Ted felt a light caress by his left buttock. At first he thought it might be the wind. But no, there it was again. It was definitely a stroke. He shut his eyes tight. This wasn't happening. But it was. A woman's hand was slithering around, accurately, as if she knew it was always there: his stiff little pego. She rifled his pants, expertly opening the fly and pulling him slightly to the side. She drew his yardstick out into the open air. He almost scissored in again, it was so cold. Icicles attached to his prick. But instantly his cock was covered in her mouth. She was sliding soft velvet, unfolding it all down the length of his prick — the lady was down on her knees, gamahuching him!

She was unbelievably expert — that's to say, enthusiastic, industrious, losing herself completely in the pleasuring of his stalk. He didn't want to look. It was all too good. His own Susie would never do it like that. She said it wasn't proper English. Filthy French. But this girl, this woman, this tart could gamahuche God out of the heavens. He felt himself go loose. She grabbed him hard around his bum, pulled him into her mouth. She was dragging a spend out of him whether he wanted to or not, and God, he wanted. Oh God! What was he doing?

His eyes fluttered open. He saw, as in one instant flash of an image — indelible — the two others, just at the periphery of his sight. What were they doing? The woman's skirts were pushed up, over her back, they were — ? Was it possible? What did it matter? What did he care? He was being pleasured beyond his experience.

At that moment it happened. He heard the other man cry out. It was a strange naked cry, almost desolate. Then he felt utter shame, because the cry had come from his own mouth, like an arrow shooting straight out of his soul and his soul was naked. It was so needy and craving and thankful and blessed. In the same instant — although the timing here was all peculiar (just as afterwards he was never sure if he had really seen something quite strange under the skirts of the woman in mauve: something darkened and red, almost purple) — he saw very clearly a single thick clot of sperm splattering out into space, to be followed by quite a jet of it flashing straight out into the air, over the side of the basket. Where it disappeared. Oh, God. The shame. The terrible shame of it. He could not look at the others. He clamped his eyes shut.

Then opened them. He would have to do up his own trousers. He did this, slowly. The others said nothing to him. They had began to take up their conversation, as if nothing much had been happening. A little light laughter. As if they had been at a pleasant little play, seen something on the stage they quite enjoyed but now it was over, and they were on to their next enjoyment.

None of them said a word to him.

It had never really happened.

*E*liza Clarke looked at the green satin dress in the light. She was very still as she considered it. She picked up the hem and gazed down at the dirt on it. Her hands — thin, worn, pleated and pulpy almost — felt down to the stitching, which she rubbed. The stitching stayed firm. But there was a tidemark, from something like rain. Quickly she reversed the garment. It smelt of powder, of grease, and of that indefinable smell of use: sweat, agitation, longueurs of boredom, of inattention, sudden flares into excitement. There was also the smell of stale perfume. She buried her nose in it, then pushed it away.

'Phhsaw!' She made an expression of contempt, then dragged the slightly gorgeous, broken-down creature of a gown over to a shard of mirror. Eliza was in her bedroom, at the very top of No 36 Southampton Street, The Strand. It was her afternoon off, and she was taking the dress down to Petticoat Lane to sell.

Miss Fanny had given it to her.

It was one of the perks of being a servant. Or at least a servant in the house where Miss Fanny Clinton, singer and actress, lived.

Miss Fanny was, when she was in a good mood, generous to a fault. Almost absent-minded in her generosity. As if she had got sick of something and only wanted to see it go. Its charm was lost. At other times she was so tightly bound within herself that she hardly noticed Eliza. Hid from her. Waited until she, Eliza, had walked down the stairs, then opened the door and peeped to see if she had gone.

Miss Fanny was a creature of mood, of habits, of strangenesses.

For this stiff, creaking gown Eliza would forgive a lot.

She stood with the gown before the sliver of glass. Held it up against herself.

Its garish sheen lit up her features. She was ordinary in the extreme, Eliza, with a small uncertain nose, nostrils too pugnacious, cheeks a little too emphatic, but kind brown eyes that noticed things, such as dropped coins, unmeant comments, clothes that she could sell.

She was good at selling, good at trading. It was just something she did, begun from her earliest days in the countryside fairs when she had helped her da with a stall, begun at dawn. She had come down to London looking for work when she was twelve. By which time her da was dead.

She was no stranger to hard work — and expected it to be her lot, always.

This brilliant jewel of a gown, slightly flawed by its dirt and overuse, was a gift.

It did not flatter her. Its riotous shades made her seem too wan. It demanded, it was true, paint: makeup, vivid lips, rouge, powder, darkened lashes. It did not go with daylight, the pure light of day: it asked for gas-light, for candlelight — illusion.

She let the dress drop, looked into the glass, smiled.

Eliza turned left out of Southampton Street, began walking down the Strand. Humbly hugging to the buildings. She didn't particularly look up, being careful not to meet men's eyes. But every so often Eliza raised up her face, looked intensely round. She was wearing a brown skirt, which she had bought herself down the Lane, a cap on her head that she had spent over two months embroidering with careful, even stitches in an ivy-leaf pattern. (She liked to be decent.) She had on a bodice that had belonged to Stella — or, as Stella preferred to be called, after her favourite role, *Mrs Graham*. Eliza always felt a little uncomfortable in it, as it was low-cut, and tight. But she wore around the neckline, for modesty's sake, a paisley shawl, her own purchase. Her single pair of good boots, with a low heel (the left boot slightly too tight), completed her outfit. She was carrying the gown in a bundle, wrapped in a clean white sheet.

She waited for the omnibus going east, to Whitechapel via Holborn. All around her was the clatter, the clamour of horses' hooves on cobbles, the rumble of carriage and cartwheels turning, the hum of a thousand, a hundred thousand conversations of passers-by.

It was a quarter to three on a Friday afternoon.

She had reached the corner of Burleigh Street, just by the Strand Theatre.

A cross-sweeper, a little lad in rags, all sooty and scarecrow, with an ancient face, was sweeping, sweeping in front of a lady as she crossed a side road.

He was sweeping away horseshit, a great big dollop of it, flicking it expertly with the hard end of his sweep, then applying, with showy industry, the other end to the road. The lady, wearing a promenade dress, all glints of black satin embossed discreetly with velvet then lightly tickled all over with trimmed ostrich feather, was walking forward — not deigning to see the lad exactly, but having to time her promenade to his industry.

Like a ship slow in its turning, cumbersome yet rhythmic, rocking and somnolent, she moved along, a barge of state.

The lady reached the footpath.

The cross-sweeper none too delicately obstructed her path — yet standing a little to the side, staring up at her. She had, mid-walk, felt into her reticule, fumbled around for the correct coin. She slipped it down into his palm, all the immense artifice of the structures in which she was held — bonnet, hair, bustle, corset, tightly buttoned dress — creaking sideways as she leant down. The slither of her leather-clad hand, withdrawing.

The woman let down the tiny string within her skirt, which held up the bottom of her skirt from the dust. Moved on.

There was so much effort, Eliza thought, in being a lady.

Whereas she — Eliza — preferred her freedom, to walk about the streets. To be plain and in her ordinary boots. No bustle for her.

𝒯he omnibus arrived.

Eliza got on, squirmed her way up the narrow stairs and squeezed into a seat upstairs. There was a gent sitting beside her. She carefully looked about the 'bus. Gave everyone nearby an eyeful. It paid to make it clear you weren't in a dreamworld. Thieves worked the 'buses, just as they worked nearly every place the quality happened to be, and every so often a lady out shopping jumped on the 'bus.

For a moment Eliza let herself go into a daze. She was tired, exhausted from the work of the week. It caught up with her: the front steps and hall washed every morning, the boots cleaned (Fanny had such large feet); keeping coffee and boiling water always at the ready; sweeping the stairs, kitchen, pantry, larder and scullery; laying up fires; getting breakfasts; making beds (interesting that the two beds in Lord Frederick's chambers were not always slept in).

She went down to Fanny and Lord Frederick's rooms — the best in the house, on the first floor — each morning, knocking on the door. Sometimes they were still asleep. The quality liked lying in. Liked defying Nature in all its forms. Going out at dusk, when other folks were settling in for the night; waking up late, often as late as two in the afternoon. Reversing everything: a breakfast coffee in the mid-afternoon, then slipping out with their latchkeys to go somewhere 'tasty' for a late luncheon. And only really coming awake, it seemed, by six in the evening, when Mr Louis called, the hairdresser from Bridge Street, just up the road in Covent Garden.

The doors would be open then. The servants liked it, for Miss Fanny was often at the piano singing, while a froth of laughter and chatter could be heard. Sometimes they started to drink even then.

It seemed every rule existed only to be broken. They were delightful, theatre folk: contrary, either too bright and lustrous, calling out to Eliza if she would like a ticket to their latest 'fright', or silent as death, not stirring, sometimes even sleeping through entire days, still as if a body might be in that room, a knife plunged through the heart, like a *Police News* headline waiting to happen.

The girls all knew to keep a distance from Lord Frederick Clinton. He was after anyone, anything that wasn't suffering rigor mortis, said Mrs Peck, down in the basement, ironing. They liked to talk about the quality: what they got up to, who they liked — and disliked.

They had all been aflutter when Lord Frederick had arrived. Or rather his grand piano arrived, was carried up into the first-floor rooms. This was before he had even arranged with Mrs Peck to take the rooms. It was such a grand piano, shouting out quality, that the servants had all gathered to watch. He dawdled in later, making it all seem as if it had been prearranged. (He knew another gentleman in the building, a Mr Able who sold pictures.)

But then he never paid his bills, treated them as if they were invisible, a trifling clutter; had borrowed, Eliza knew, ten whole quid from the Missus, who must have been witless and clueless to give it. He was so ingratiating when he wanted something, gathering together all his magnetic, slightly metallic charm. Somehow Eliza saw him as being as intricate as his beautiful little toilette box, all ultra-polished ebony and silver and some strange dark-streaked wood. Under the lid — he had lifted it for her, standing behind her, before she realised — was a magic plain of bottles: silver-topped, engraved with the family crest, dancing unicorns and angry swans. Then she felt his hand sliding up under her dress, goosing her behind.

She had kicked him hard on the shins, then said, 'Oh, I do beg your pardon, sir, I thought it was some wretch trying to be low with me,' all the time looking at him straight in the eye, before she dropped into a curtsy, to show she knew her place.

He had nursed his bruise, looked furious for a moment, then burst out into a wild shout of a laugh (this frightened her more than the goosing). 'I like a gel with spunk,' he said, turning away, flipping the little box lid down. 'Now get out.'

She was only too glad.

Whereas Miss Fanny, or Lady Clinton as she liked to be called, wasn't like that. She had thrust out her hand when bold Clara had asked, 'We servants want to know, Miss, has he made an honest woman of you?' Miss Fanny had looked amused, flung her hand out and said, 'Well, here's the evidence. You look upon' — and here she drew herself up, a haughty stage dame — 'Lady Frederick Clinton, if you please,' and then sank into the deepest curtsy, such as one might do before The Widow herself. But she made it comical because she was wearing only a nightshirt, and over it a man's long dressing gown — maybe Lord Clinton's own, for it was made of a beautiful Chinese brocade, as costly as it was dirty.

Dirty. Dirty. That went for all of them: Clinton, Fanny and her 'sister', *Mrs Graham*. There was no telling who or what they really were. They was all slightly suspect, slightly dirty and flirty, and funny and gummy and sad: and regal and frightening and grand and — well, theren't enough words in the English tongue to curl around them lot.

*T*hey had fallen into complete silence. A vast cloud — a cumulus of exquisite shading: blues and a spheric smear of white — floated by. Fan leant out, her violet glacé gloves with the garnet-coloured buttons trying to snatch it, grab it, but it slid away, mercurial, swift. A vapour.

She turned back and faced Fred.

Fred was holding a bottle of Krug. Untwisting the wire. There was a wicker hamper at his feet, spilled open. For once he let the cork fly off, into space. There was a spurt, a rude torrent of champagne, which Stella rushed to quell: she held out a champagne glass. Fred poured out the foam, which rushed up and over the lip, dampened her gloves. She sucked the leather, laughing, laughing. It was as if they were all drunk. Without having drunk anything.

Instead they raised their flutes, gazed at one another and felt that special moment of communion that comes when good friends gather together: a serene sense of fate converging, delivering serendipity.

They clinked glasses and Fan, glancing down below, cried out, with child's delight, 'Look! Look! It's a train!'

And it was true. A thin metal line dissected the green baize tabletop and there, halfway across, was the tiniest puff of steam, such as would come out of the spout of a kettle.

It was a train on the south-western railway, hurtling towards London.

They hung over the edge, sipping their wine, murmuring, pointing out sights — and then falling into a deeper fold of silence.

'I feel so utterly peaceful,' murmured Fan. 'I feel as if nothing . . . could ever . . . hurt us. *Ever.*'

*T*his is when the stunner in violet sang.

Ted Billington would remember it all his born days. She placed her glass down, took up her position against the very edge of the basket.

Ted's eye caught hers and she smiled at him — generously, as if to intimate that he existed: was part of their tiny fête: could relax. But he wouldn't. Not after what had happened. He longed to . . . he wanted to dip his pego in some carbolic. Cleanse himself. He was dirty, dirty. As were they. Under all their silks and fine clothes. But this is when the one in violet surprised him. Her face, he noted, was very much painted, but there was something innocent there, some little unfound or unexplained childlike quality. This thought deepened while she sang. In fact, Ted thought, the longer she sang, the more she seemed to become cleaner, more child-like.

She sang a sad and moving ditty, 'My Pretty Jane'.

> Rose of the garden, blushing and gay
> E'en as we pluck there, fading away!

She began by making the lines seem a little silly. She fol-de-roled it. Rolled her eyes.

> Beams of the morning, promise of day,
> While we are gazing, fading away!

Her voice was pure and fresh. A full-toned mezzo-soprano, true to note.

Unaccountably it plucked the strings of Ted's heart. He could not help it . . . He was moved, moved. As were they, the others — the tart in green. They stood so silent amid the vast cathedral of air through which they moved.

144

All that is earthly, fadeth away,

But there's a land —

where nought shall decay,

Where there's no sorrow, no fading away!

Hope's fairy promise, charms to betray,

All that is earthly,

fadeth away.

When she finished, nobody said anything.

And then the threesome turned their backs on him and leant over the edge of the basket, gazing down at the world at their feet.

*T*here were no ladies down Petticoat Lane, no bustles (or *arse-warmers*, as they were called down here).

The distinct colours of mint-new gowns had dropped behind, been lost — just as the streets had got narrower, darker, more crowded. Everything here was noisome, bustling, contradictory: it looked less like a street or a lane than a sort of fairground of clothes — a lost-and-found depot for every kind of clothing that had ever existed.

But Eliza knew where she was going. She was heading for the stall she always preferred, which did good business.

She gripped her bundle to herself protectively. But she also relaxed, in part, because she liked coming here. She liked its liveliness, felt at home in its strident noise: the kids running up to her, asking her if she wanted a lemonade or a salted herring. She knew she would halt, at some point, and rest her bunions, as she said, while she savoured a roasted apple, or maybe a roasted chestnut — even treated herself to a tot of hot elder wine. That was, if her sale went well.

'It's not some old slop thing,' she was rehearsing in her mind. 'It's been worn by the famous Miss Fanny of *A Morning Call* herself. Though she had to be careful not to push this too far. It mightn't work. She might just end up looking ridiculous. (*Just who's this Miss Fanny when she's at 'ome, I'd like to ask?*) And Eliza would be hard pushed to make Miss Fanny out. 'She's performed, like, at the 'Gyptian Hall down the West End,' she might say, laying down her trump card. Or, 'Aven't you 'eard of Miss Fanny Clinton? Don't you ever get out of this 'ere delightful premises? Don't you ever travel *up west?*' Or 'She is the wife — sort of, in a manner of speaking — of a son of a duke, a real one too — and she's a masher of sorts, a real looker and . . .'

No, she had to be careful not to oversell.

The dress was dirty but would clean up a treat. Eliza knew this. She could almost feel the fall of the coin into her palm. She itched for its hard, prosaic safety. She'd add it to her other coins, saved up so arduously. She was of the saving kind, Eliza: she had a small nest-egg that she kept quiet about. She had plans, did Miss Eliza Clarke.

But now she was walking down a vista of shoes — some tawny, some port-shaded, some dull green. No piece of clothing seemed to have kept its original shade, as if some dun dust had fallen, pollinated everything — or was it the immense weight of past lives residually clinging to everything?

If things went well, Eliza would pop down and see her friend, Maryanne. She might suggest they meet up, on their next afternoon off, and maybe go and see *The Morning Call*. Though Maryanne had a strange obstinacy when it came to Miss Fanny. She usually said, 'No, I'm not really interested in seeing things of *that* type.' 'What *type?*' Eliza had wanted to know. But Maryanne just turned deaf and said, 'I'm too busy, you know, what with my sister and her kiddies.' She had her sister, it was true, abandoned with three under six and another on the way. Maryanne was a saint who tried to help out as much as she could. But she had turned into a slavey for her sister, in Eliza's mind.

Eliza preferred a little freedom herself. She preferred to have a sweetheart, but not to get too serious, as yet. She had a horror of being weighed down with children.

No, while she could (and she was only two and twenty) she preferred her own company.

Smell. The stench of old clothes. Corridors of them, heaps of them — mountains of them. Old knives, lanterns, detritus of a city. Kids running by. Fires burning. Voices yelling, selling. *Fried fish! Old knives! Rags! Bones! Ha'penny biscuits! Three-a-penny biscuits!*

She made her way to her favourite stall.

'G'day, dearie,' said the gummy old moll next door — she was sharp as a tack when it came to coin. 'What 'ave you there?'

'Oh, nothing for you, Mistress Waller,' Eliza said. 'Not today.'

'Oh, one of these days, dear, you'll see the light . . .'

Mr Amos was busy stitching. She had never come upon him when he wasn't working. He was always selling or cleaning or mending. Sleeves rolled back to reveal the long black hairs on his powdery white arms, balding head bent over intently; yet as if he sensed a customer, he pricked awake, looked at her.

'Oh, Mistress Eliza,' he said. 'What 'ave you there, dear?'

He had already seen the bundle. But first of all he glanced sideways, quickly. He motioned with his head and Eliza walked past Mistress Gummy and down a few steps, into a little stone enclave. Here, neatly folded, was Mr Amos's back catalogue — fold upon fold of washed second-hand clothing.

She unwrapped the bundle: 'I know it's —'

But he had leant down, was taking out the soiled, creased beast and was shaking it.

Eliza smoothed the silk with her hand.

'It's good-quality material, nothing cheap or nasty here . . .'

'A little bit Monmouth Street, ain't it?'

Eliza shook her head and prepared to take the gown away.

He stopped her hand.

'It's not a piece of slop,' said she, taking umbrage.

'Now, hold your peace, hold your peace.'

She knew they were now nearing some compromise.

'As worn by Miss Fanny Clinton, the actress,' she said.

He looked at her closely. She had the feeling he was looking at her strangely. But his fingers had gripped the top of the dress. He was still looking at it thoughtfully and she could read, as if she could see inside his brain, that something else was going on.

She reached forward as if to take it. He pulled her hand away.

'A decent clean and it will come up a beauty.'

He shook his head slowly, but the air of subterranean excitement remained. She noted that his fingers had not left the dress. He was holding it almost proprietorially.

'So what'll you give me for it?'

He closed his eyes as if listening for a sound that was coming to him, coming to him more clearly now, and he opened his mouth . . . but it was as if whatever was coming out shocked him: no sound came.

'Eh?' said Eliza, who knew she had to be tough.

'Miss Fanny wore this herself?' he asked intensely.

'Yes,' Eliza said, 'In her immortal role as Julia in *The Hunchback* if I'm not mistaken. Maybe even in *Witness for the Defence.*'

At the word 'witness' Mr Amos almost jumped.

'Well, of course,' he said, seeming to have come out of his trance, returning to his habitual self, at the same time as his eyes nervously — once too often to get away with — looked to see whether Eliza had noticed his dream-moment.

'It's the kind of toggery some fine girl will go for.'

Mr Amos's hands appeared to be doing something indecent. But in fact Eliza knew that under the dirty apron was his coin-purse — attached to his person like some inner tube or womb.

He looked at her intensely as his hands ran through the tube. He looked as if he was chasing after a coin placed in a dark and inaccessible place, but his face also had that rapt look of a great philosopher on the brink of a good idea. All was immanence. Then he reached forward, his hand still closed (she knew all this, it was part of their ritual), he turned his fist around, relaxed his fingers.

Not for the first time Eliza noticed how long his fingers were — almost elegant, except they were darkened by the black he put on waistcoats, and toughened by the sharp hood of needles pressed into cloth. But the hands seemed to Eliza independently beautiful, like objects that might have belonged in another place or time.

But she had to be all business. She felt herself torn at moments: business or dream-reverie. Sometimes the latter was so necessary, just to survive.

He was offering her a sovereign — gold.

The specificity of the coin was part of his ploy. A coin is physically almost in your palm.

She shook her head on some instinct — almost as if whatever was working her head came from some other intimation within her body. (Perhaps some fiery oil licking up her spinal cord.)

She actually at that moment appeared quite beautiful: that is to say, the force of life was present, expressed itself through the glistening of her eyes, the sharp intelligence focused around the corners of her lips. Her fingers ached — for the coin, for certitude, completion.

He saw her head turning, slowly, like a tree in the first wind that intimates an entirely new season: a colder season.

She was looking down at the clothes while his hand went back into his person. She affected not to notice. She knew that his face, lined already, worn and almost sutured with concern, would be here presenting such a mask as Covent Garden might applaud: tragedy, harshness, pain.

She might have been taking something from him.

Which she was.

Golden coin: two of them. Dancing into her palm.

There was the slightest physical contact, as the coins passed over. There always was, but today the frisson, the charged electricity of this momentary contact, was different. Had been raised a level in its excitement.

He abruptly turned away from her. He was inspecting the dress minutely. She no longer existed.

He said, almost absently, 'Goodbye, my dear,' then, as if remembering her, 'and remember, my dear, if you have any others' — he shook the dress, so it appeared faintly living, almost like the scales of a stage dragon — 'you have to remember your good friend Amos. Especially anything belonging to' — and here he leant forward as if to whisper something confidential, possibly even faintly dangerous — 'your Miss Fanny.'

He winked, grew silent, even priest-like, then disappeared, down the steps into a dim interior.

*I*t was getting to dusk. There was something about the winnowing of light. Far down below the drifting balloon the gas-lights were flickering on all over the city, in street after street. The whole face of the earth appeared to be covered with little illuminated lamps, like lights upon a Christmas tree. The balloon drifted some more. Smoke was coming from a forest of chimneys and as far as the eye could see there was street, brick wall, ant-like people going about their tasks. The further they looked, the more the lights melded together, became a swarm of fireflies. The whole city seemed alight. And the light was reflected in the low-lying cloud, so the city and the cloud seemed to be ensnared in some celestial — or was it infernal? — mist.

It was impossible to tell where the monster city began or ended. Buildings stretched away on every side, far into the distance, without end, seeming to blend into the smudge of darkness that was the lowering sky. Here and there little patches of green indicated parks, but most of the city seemed to possess an almost reptilian skin of brick, stone, smoke, fire, gas.

A faint wind had leapt up.

'Oh, lawd,' said Stella suddenly. They had drunk three bottles of Krug and they were still hanging over the basket sides, gazing down. 'To think that's our world down there. It quite gets to you, don't it?'

'What do you mean, Stell?'

This was Fan.

'I don't know . . . sometimes it quite makes you . . . sad. Not bad-sad. But glad-sad. To think of . . .'

'To think of what?'

'I don't know.' Stell shivered. 'It don't matter a jot, do it? As long as we're happy. And ain't we happy, eh, Fan? Ain't we the happiest gels in the whole wide friggin' world?'

*E*liza was leaning against a wall, enjoying her treat: a juicy roasted apple. She let the sweetness dribble down her throat, gave herself over to the minutest savouring of flavour, of relaxation.

It was over. It had been successful.

She licked her fingers.

When she was spotted by Clara. Clara as once worked for Mrs Peck at Southampton Street, then left. She was a stuck-up, devious piece of work. Besides, she was a poor worker, always looking to cut corners, shirk. *Slutswool.* She was wearing a dull green cape over a purple silk dress that had almost certainly belonged to a lady. It didn't fit well, and there was something a little flashy about it. It made Clara look cheap.

Defensively Eliza raised herself up off the wall.

'A treat to see you enjoying yourself,' Clara said a little too acidly, through lips sewn into a smile.

Eliza nodded rather than spoke.

Clara looked all over Eliza's face for an instant: it was a vivid, even avaricious glance.

'You must be terribly excited,' said Clara. Smiling still. The smile seemed to have set like an ugly gel across her face.

'Why?' asked Eliza. She had finished her treat. Clara had almost ruined it for her. She had saved the last piece of caramelised sugar to enjoy but now, almost without thinking, it was inside her mouth. It was over.

'Well, working in the house of someone so —' Clara appeared to be grasping for an adjective, 'so *notable* as "Lady" Fanny Clinton,' she said and then laughed.

'What do you want, Clara?'

'Oh, nothing. Nothing at all really. But I don't envy you — I don't envy you one little bit.'

Clara was shaking her head and looking around, as if she wanted to make her escape.

'In work, are you, Clara? Found somewhere else? I expected to see you hanging around the servants' exchange.'

Clara's head jerked back. She opened her mouth to make a retort but instead she said, 'Well, good luck,' and disappeared.

This last — strange — comment cast a shadow over Eliza's day.

What did she mean — '*good luck*'?

*T*he strangest thing happened the closer the balloon came down towards gravity.

They seemed to move out of one dreamy sphere and into another forcefield entirely. The extraordinary tranquillity that had entered each of their souls — soothing them, calming them, making them feel they were at peace with the world (pleasurably drunk) — gave way under them at this precise moment.

A rough wind snatched at the balloon.

The trees down below in Kennington Park were pulsing wildly. Above their heads, like the sails of a windjammer, the balloon began to buckle and thwack. A rope zinged through the air, slicing and hissing as it went.

Fred grabbed Fan by the shoulders and pulled her down. The two women's skirts beat wildly upwards, the hem of Stella's dress whipping into her face. Her eyes began to stream. Dust rose, and bit into their eyes.

Everything was moving very fast.

Ted, the mechanic, sprang into action. He threw down a rope, which was grabbed and attached to a grapnel. This only made the oscillations of the balloon more violent. It became like a boat caught on a rock in a rushing torrent of water.

Fan grabbed hold of Fred and, crouching down on the floor of the balloon, they kissed. It was as if the excitement only made Fred randier. But it became an unexpectedly tender kiss, this one: a form of saying farewell to something deeply pleasurable, a form of union.

The balloon bumped along the ground, strained wildly, whirled around on its pivot, span, skidded. Stell screamed and screamed, but she was secretly enjoying herself.

Then it was secured.

The balloon became taut, almost stationary.

Ted stood aside, making sure his eyes never for one moment so much as glanced at the sauceboat in green (he felt sure she would wink at him). The gentleman passed him a discreet coin, and the three pleasure-seekers alighted and got into the brougham that had been waiting for them since they had ascended.

Without a word, they left.

*I*t was a darker area, yet, of London. If light could be said to express power and money — and distance between humans — then darkness in London could be said to express poverty, proximity and something worse — something cramped, hooked in the human spirit, even a little deformed. Here the streets were no more than crooked corridors. In doorways stood skeletal women who seemed never to have seen the light, men thin as grass that grows perennially in the shade. There were filthy children, reeking pipes, starved cats.

Eliza was progressing towards the very centre of the labyrinth.

She was heading down to a damp place near the Thames called Sparrow Corner to visit her friend Maryanne. Maryanne worked in the place where fabric was picked apart. This was the last stage of any cloth, its final destination — to be picked apart and made into oakum and thrown as manure on the ground.

If Eliza was not careful, if she was having a fit of the melancholies (which came upon her at any ordinary time), the place gave her the heebie-jeebies. At these times it was as if she had been granted second sight: she saw not only those who had once worn all the clothes, but the fate that had brought them to sell the very clothes they wore. She heard the melancholy whisperings coming out of the abandoned raiment, some so threadbare it was difficult to think what rags replaced them. It was like a museum of selves, all heaped here in mildewy piles, placed in some purgatory, awaiting the heat of another body to chafe them into some semblance of life.

She saw all this, just as she saw — this twenty-two-year-old woman — all the history of romance in a gentleman's dove-grey velvet frock-coat bedecked with gilt buttons, bought with high expectations, worn with transparent pride — then converted into something as unseeing as habit, until the coat itself ceased to be a point of pride, became a flag of despair, of nothing much ever changing.

She who was a poor person knew this.

(Yet she also knew the price it would fetch. This saved her, guided her, to some extent allowed her to feel she could escape. As she planned. To go to New Zealand. She had heard a servant's life was really quite spectacular there.)

She went down some stone steps, then down a smaller flight, and down some stairs so ancient they were worn like a bow in the middle. Inside a low-ceilinged room there was the smudge of guttering lanterns. A group of women sat clench-shouldered on stools, picking apart rags. This was so like picking oakum in the prisons that Eliza always found it, standing there, an uncomfortable double vision.

But what made this situation different was that the women were always talking — or at least those who liked the sound of their own voices: exchanging gossip and stories, spinning them out to web over their boredom.

But today the women were all silent. They seemed to have reached a momentary pause. Heads down, they worked away, picking, pecking, disassembling. In some ways their hands were not unlike that convulsive plucking that overtakes the dying when they seem to revert to some almost electrical impulse, as if seeking to touch, for the last time, the fleeting texture of things.

Eliza's sneeze announced her — a newcomer always got snuffed up, for the air was a moving blizzard of cloth particles.

Maryanne, seemingly deep in thought, was nudged by the old crone beside her.

On seeing Eliza she looked instantly — and this was strange — both excited and proud. Maryanne glanced round the room, and seemed to whisper to the little old crone beside her, who gawped. The other women — and this was strange too — fled looks about the room, exchanged them, as if they shared some strange, almost thievish currency.

Eliza began to feel quite odd.

Good luck.

She rubbed the brass coin around her neck and she tried to glance into Maryanne's eyes as Maryanne led her back up the steps. But as they did so, a door down into a deeper depth of room was pulled back. Out of this room, as dust coming from a tomb, a wheezy flocculent storm came whooshing out. Cloying and unhealthy, it rushed down your throat. You seemed to be breathing in mould.

This inner room was the ultimate end of all garments. It was as if she had come to the wheezy heart of London, where all appearances ended.

Eliza sneezed again, vehemently. Her eyes watered.

'Bless you, my dear.'

Maryanne had actually taken hold of one of Eliza's arms and was looking at her as if she were sick.

'Why aren't you at home, lovey?' she asked.

'But I don't feel at all queer.'

'You haven't *heard.*'

This was said with the presage of an indrawn breath.

'*Heard what?*'

Maryanne looked triumphant: it is a singular moment in anyone's life when they are chosen to be the bearer of bad news.

'Your Miss Fanny. And Miss Stella. Are about to come a right cropper.'

'*What?*'

'My Bill that's a flatfooter. Told me. In the most strictest of confidences. And I swore I would never pass it on but . . .'

She wanted to take her time.

'But as you are my nearest and dearest . . .'

'*What?*'

'Their collars is about to be fingered. That's what. And their hijinks and frolics is all going to come to a right nasty end.'

A Curious Transformation Scene

The brougham took the gentleman and two ladies to a dusty little side street not far from Euston Station. All the buildings in this vicinity had a determinedly blowsy, uncared-for look — as if time had forgotten this particular part of London. It was near a square, it was true, but the square was only a faint echo of the greater squares to the left, in Bloomsbury, let alone those spaces, sparkling and cream, further away in Belgravia.

Regent's Square was rather like an overlooked space, filled with forgotten-looking four-storey terrace houses from which could be heard, at this hour of evening, children playing in hallways, domestic arguments. There was a smell of mutton bones and cooked herrings, of grease and coal dust, as if the stone itself were porous on this warm summer evening.

It was a strange place for gentlefolk in a brougham to fetch up; nevertheless, they came to a halt outside No 13 Wakefield Street, a tiny little passage of a street, just off Regent's Square. It was a lodging house, no less.

The beautiful woman in mauve got out, slipped a key into the door, glanced seemingly absently along the street, noticed a man lounging against a doorway smoking a clay pipe, thought nothing of it, then turned and called to the other two occupants of the carriage to follow her.

Sergeant Bill Williams, in plainclothes, had been observing the residence of No 13 Wakefield Street for over a fortnight. It was his observation that the two women — clearly women of the night — did not actually live there. Only every so often did they return to the place. This was the source of the complaint that had been sent, anonymously, to Bow Street. (The complaint came from No 16 diametrically opposite: he could just see the light — and was that a shadow at the window, observing?)

He glanced down at his watch. It was 7.20 p.m., 19 April, 1870.

The door had closed behind the three creatures but the brougham had not driven off. The driver was slumped in his seat, enjoying what looked like a tipple. Perhaps the threesome had gone inside for some private 'amusement'?

But no, pretty quickly really, that is, at five minutes past eight, the door opened again. And this was the source of the complaint. The women had now got themselves up as men. Not men exactly. As unconvincing, womenly sort of gentlemen. There was no mistaking it. The pretty one was pretending to be a foppish young man-about-town. Five foot six inches tall at a guess, pale blond hair, possibly blue eyes, slim build. Wearing a swallow-cut coat of an exceedingly fashionable type, low cut as to the neck of the waistcoat, with a cloth bow tie Williams had begun to see worn by the swells about the West End (a 'sailor's tie'). The other woman, the plumper of the two, was dressed similarly, but carrying a flat straw hat. Both carried canes, but their walk was all wrong — they had no idea how a man walked. They were all swaying hip and rolling shoulder motion. It was right laughable the way these 'ladies' had it so wrong.

What was the taste, Sergeant Williams wondered to himself, puffing on his pipe, for a woman to get herself up as a gent? Were they in on some sort of blackmailing racket? To tempt a poor sod who had a taste for Margeries and poofs, then bring him back to Wakefield Street, whereupon they would reveal themselves as women? Extortion?

A native Londoner, Bill Williams knew enough not to be shocked by anything: the greatest city on earth, after all, catered for every taste — from girls aged nine to soft velvety boys, women with hunchbacks. Anything you wanted could be found if you knew where to look.

The gent, he noticed, was still wearing the same clothes. He seemed anxious to get on. He kept banging his top hat against his leg, chafing.

'Come on, Fan. Get a breeze in your bloody sails, will you, goddammit.' His voice was that of a real toff — that peculiar confident stride.

'We'll drop you off near Berkeley Square on the way, Stell,' he overheard the pretty one say. 'We're running late. Caldicott'll be fucking furious.'

It was hardly genteel language.

The brougham trotted off. As it passed Sergeant Williams he carefully turned his back, gobbing on the pavement for good measure. He heard laughter, and the plump one gurgled out a nonsense rhyme that Sergeant Williams knew was all the craze among men-about-town and London layabouts generally. Something about double Gloucester cheese.

*T*he inside of the Adelphi Theatre, out at Chelmsford, was freezing. A single door lay open to the street but the pale square of gas-light could do nothing to heat the almost solid block of icy chill within the interior.

Up on the stage could be seen a single — economical — gas flame. The rest of the twelve-hundred-seat theatre was thrown into oppressive darkness and stillness.

Fan (dressed as a man) and Fred exaggerated the sound of their leather-soled shoes to counteract this stillness as they stamped up the side aisle.

An old grey-haired man was hobbling in front of them. He walked with a gilded shepherdess's crook, but with surprising speed. His hair was elaborately dressed in the 'beau' style of the earlier part of the century, and his clothes, which were almost rags, were the vestments of a stage gentleman from around 1840. (A faded ducal coachman's greatcoat.)

'They're 'ere!' he called out in a surprisingly fruity baritone. 'Their excellencies 'as favoured us with their presences.'

Up on the stage, now that their eyes had grown accustomed to the gloom, could be seen a single, bony young woman in the middle of a rather vacant-eyed plié. Her tights were grubby and wrinkled. As they got closer, it was clear that she was tubercular-pale, and not particularly young. Her tresses had the suspicious halo of a dye.

'Oh, hello, darlings,' she said in a vague, almost distant voice, as if she had only then and purely accidentally seen them.

'He-*llo*,' Fan replied, with the exaggerated tones of melodrama — that is, isolating every aspect of a word and drawing the syllables apart for maximum dramatic effect. Fan imitated a sonorous buffo bass.

At this point, stage door left fell back and a cross-looking little man came out. He was carrying sheaths of papers, a whistle around his neck and for whatever reason he was dressed in a rural smock, as if he were impersonating a farmer. On the top of his head he wore a hand-knitted hat in a mouldy-looking brown. His eyes were dark, snapping with anger.

He clapped his hands as he walked across the stage and made a large gesture down into the pit.

Fan bowed to the child sitting at the piano. It was Timmy, the son of the ballerina. He filled in at the piano during rehearsals.

Almost experimentally, Timmy ran his fingers over the keys and a slightly melancholy yet somehow perkily gay echo of a tune bounced back from within the deep cavern of the theatre.

'Now really, Timmy,' the director said, pursing his lips and quietening him with a single gesture. The child's mother stopped her pliés and skulked sulkily down on the edge of the stage, her legs dangling into the pit.

The child threw her some of his tobacco and she set about building herself a pipe.

'Thank you, your lordship,' said Mr Caldicott, director, not a little satirically, to Frederick, 'for being so gracious as to offer — '

'Dammit, I tried, Caldicott! But you try and get in the way of Fan and pleasure.'

Lord Frederick Clinton went and slumped down in a theatre seat. He lifted his legs up onto the back of a seat and sank back, gazing genially between his boots at the director.

There was a slight sensation of annoyance in the air.

Fan — that is, Ernest, to use the male name Fan went under — jumped lightly up the steps to the side door, which led to the stage. She walked out onto the stage and went into a deep stage curtsy before Caldicott.

(Frederick admired the elegance of Ernest's male impersonation as Fan rose up — an elasticised bow.)

'So sorry, dearie,' Fan (Ernest) said, speaking in a normal voice 'Truly. I can't tell you where we've been today. And how we had to fight to even get here.'

Caldicott looked at Ernest as if calculating how much he might destroy by losing his temper. Instead he melodramatically withdrew a large and somewhat brassy watch from his person, gazed at it in seeming astonishment — shook it, as if it must have stopped — gazed at it again, then slipped it, with one final look of utter annoyance, into his pantaloons pocket. Down in the pit the child gurgled, but the sound was cut off by a dark look from the director.

'One would never guess it was the day — or should I say *night* — before opening night.'

'Where do you want me?'

Fan sauntered downstage.

The elderly gentleman in the slightly greasy costume hobbled across the stage. He was holding much scribbled-upon notes — the script. He proffered these to Fan, who shook her head and called out into the dark theatre: 'Freddie, love, we know our stuff, don't we dear?'

Freddie made a grumpy harumph to indicate that they did.

'Could I . . . ?' Caldicott's voice was still a little sharp. Then, as if hearing it himself, he altered the tone dramatically into one of a sugary compliance. 'If your lordship would favour us with his presence upon the stage?'

Sarcasm hung heavily in the air.

Freddie put his feet off the chair, stood up, stretched mightily, and as he walked none too graciously up the steps to the stage he called out to Pirouette, the dancer, 'You've no idea how that dollymop of a girl wears a man out. Fan can never get enough of me.'

Fan took on the form, centre stage, of a gesturing antique statue, both hands raised above her head, fingers elegantly pointing.

Caldicott said to her, 'And darling, don't scamper away at the end. You've both got your costume fittings — '

'Oh,' said Fan, coming alive, or rather reverting from statue to human. 'Super. Cossies are always my favouritest part.'

'We know that, darling,' Pirouette said somewhat dourly, breathing out smoke.

Eliza had returned to Southampton Street as fast as she could. She found, down in the kitchen, Mrs Peck and the boy. They were peeling potatoes and Eliza, realising the importance of keeping quiet about what she knew, said she wanted to have a cup of tea before setting off again. She was going up west to do a little window-shopping.

The kitchen was dark, low-ceilinged and smelt just peripherally of earth, of something dank and chill. A fire burnt low in the grate and Mrs Peck, awkward of limb ever since her gout, moved slowly around the room. Eliza waited an agonising amount of time, blowing on the surface of her teabowl before she could introduce her casual question: 'Where are Miss Fanny and His Lordship this evening?'

'They ain't been 'ome for so long I'd 'ardly know if I'd even recognise 'em,' said Mrs Peck. 'Ain't they up in Scarborough again, doing their pranks?'

The boy whistled and said, 'They didn't need no Scarborough for them to get up to no good.'

Mrs Peck said, 'It ain't good for a lad like you to be knowing beyond your years.'

He — small, wizened, with a face creased and hard as a walnut — just looked at her.

'You silly old bint,' he said in a low voice.

Mrs Peck was hard of hearing but it grew instantly acute on suspicion of any cheek. Seemingly in contrast to her usual somnolent state, a ham-like arm sped out and banged hard into the boy's skull. It was quite some blow.

'Damn'n'blast yer eyes,' the boy muttered. He looked as if he might cry, but instead he bit his emotions back.

'They're off doin' their prancin' round on some stage somewhere,' was Mrs Peck's final remark.

Eliza rinsed her bowl and wiped it clean, placing it back on the shelf set aside for the servants' utensils.

'Why?' said the boy. 'Does you want to go?'

'No-ah,' said Eliza,' It's just as I have nothing much to do, for my night off, so to speak.'

From the stalls Caldicott observed Fan and Frederick's rehearsal. The programme was a two-hander, a burlesque piece called *A Morning Call* by Charles Dance (of *A Wonderful Woman*, *Dustman's Belle* fame), preceded by Lord Frederick doing a comic dialogue as Serjeant Buzfuz in *Pickwick Papers*. The evening would be finished off by Fan, as an encore, singing her popular song, 'Fading Away'.

They could expect a sell-out crowd.

But at the moment, while they waited for the old gentleman to set the lights, Fan was fooling around. Another of her definitive roles was Julia in *The Hunchback*. Julia had to decide between a young man with a hunchback (but actually a lord) and a man with a lot of money who was a commoner. Fan was declaiming some of Julia's lines: hand clenched on heart, other hand trembling to the side, eyes cast upwards as if to scan the very heavens — the correct stance for angst in theatre for several hundred years.

> Then take me! Stop — hear me, and take me then!
>
> Let not thy passion be my counsellor!
>
> Deal with me, Clifford, as my brother.

Fan turned to Frederick and grabbed his hand. She stooped down and, one hand raised in elegant gesture, planted her lips on Frederick's hand.

Caldicott rested his behind on the curve of a chair. He was tired. It never ceased to amaze him, this change in Ernest Boulton: how he could transform himself — even now, without costume — into another character: that of a woman. He took small, skimming steps, and his body ceased to focus all its force on his legs and his shoulders but became supple, pliant, ready to waver, dip and bend. His arms became soft and pliable and his eyes became the core of his being. And his voice, of course, lighter, more charming — fluting and pleasant.

He seemed also to glide on the balls of his feet. And bend from the waist only.

'*Be the jealous guardian of my spotless name!*' Ernest (Julia) now turned her head and looked back shyly at Frederick who, in turn, seemed to grow more masculine as Ernest grew more feminine.

> Let thy scrutiny o'erlook no point of it, —
>
> Nor turn it over once, but many a time —
>
> That flaw, speck, yea — the shade of one — a soil
>
> So slight, not one out of a thousand eyes
>
> Could find it out — may not escape thee; then —

She paused, placed the back of her hand on her forehead and fell back.

> Then take me, Clifford!

She fell into Frederick's opened arms and for one moment, in the exaggerated kabuki language of melodrama, Caldicott seemed to see something — something he could not quite name. But which he wished to present on the stage. Was it some brush with realism? Truth? But at that point the circle of a limelight roared onto them and the two actors, both men, collapsed in pratfalls onto the stage, unwrapped themselves, laughing, and rose to their feet, dusting themselves down.

Caldicott felt a rinse of disappointment. He had been on the verge of seeing . . . something. Sensing something. But now it eluded him.

'All right,' he bawled. 'Back to number ones.'

As Eliza left the house she thought she saw a suspicious man standing opposite, his shoulders bowed with exhaustion. Ostentatiously she turned aside, looking in the other direction, waiting for a dray full of unsold cabbages to go by before she crossed the street. She did not turn back to look.

She turned the corner to the right, even though it was taking her in the opposite direction to where she wanted to go. But she could cut back up Maiden Lane and then down the steps and through a corridor. She knew her way through the labyrinth of Covent Garden, which was, after all, only a few hundred yards from Mrs Peck's house. ('*A short hop, step and pirouette,*' as she liked to advertise her theatrical lodgings.)

Eliza walked through the night sounds: two women laughing, high, skittish, in an empty room upstairs; the first sounds of a violin coming out of a third-floor window, curving through the dark, feline and luxurious.

Closer to hand, the clank of chains as an elephant moved along slowly, majestically through the night crowds — like some kind of slave escaped from a Roman triumph, except that it was off to the back stage doors of Drury Lane Theatre, where it would appear on the stage at a climactic moment in a pantomime.

Eliza turned down a dark passage, feeling her way. She came to a black door, treacly with paint. A low flame burnt in a dirty-paned lantern. She knocked timidly against the door. Nothing.

She waited. She let out a deep sigh, took another breath, then knocked boldy, as one who was used to entering such a place.

After a considerable time she heard the scuffle of footsteps down stairs. A little hatch slid back.

'We ain't open yet.'

'I'm looking, most urgent-like, for Miss Fanny Clinton. I'm her lady servant. I . . .'

There was an appreciable moment of silence.

'Never heard of her. Besides, she ain't here.'

This latter comment was more hopeful.

'Could I leave a message? Will she be in later?'

'This ain't no bleedin' post office.'

Nevertheless, and seemingly unwillingly, a large key was turned and the door fell back.

A wrestler gone to seed was standing there looking down at her. Behind him were the stairs. He indicated, with a dismissive motion of his head, that she could ascend. She thanked him, climbed the rickety stairs painted the same treacly black as the door, the tread worn through to a smudge of wood. She climbed up to the second floor.

The doors all along the way were padlocked. There was a smell of urine, mixed in with the sourer taint of vomit, veiled incompletely by carbolic.

On the second floor a door was partially ajar, letting out a dagger of light.

She pushed the door back.

The room was brilliantly bright — almost overpoweringly so. Twenty gas-lights burnt overhead, in a gasolier. She cringed back for a moment, afraid. Then she saw opposite her a timid, ugly little creature. For one second she wondered what such a drab was doing there. Then felt mortified to realise she was looking at herself, in a brilliantly sardonic mirror. The place was all mirrors, she realised then.

She had never been in such a place. (*Mrs Graham* had once asked her to deliver a plain brown package to the downstairs door. This is what had given her the idea.)

Eliza grabbed her paisley shawl and laced it tightly over her shoulders. She could feel her face grow hot, her pulse race.

There was a manservant laying out a table. It appeared a banquet of some sort was taking place later that evening. He held in his hands a butler's tray on which was placed a mountainous pink glazed ham. He turned, seeing her, and looked her up and down.

He was about to call out.

Eliza put out a mittened hand — 'Please, kind sir,' she said, and bobbed down into a curtsy.

The grandee, dressed in slightly greasy-looking tails and white tie, waited.

'I'm looking for Miss Fanny Clinton, if you please. I'm her … maid. Something's come up. Most pressing.'

The grandee assessed.

'She don't appear here well before three or four in the mornin' usually. George?'

The grandee, for such a large man, had an unusually high fluting voice.

A man backed out through a swing door, carrying a tray loaded with coloured glasses. It was then Eliza noticed that a little man wearing what appeared to be an improbably yellow wig, seated at a piano. He was running his fingers over the keys.

They were all looking at her. Eliza, by sheer dint of character, sought to impress her respectability upon them — and her withdrawal of any moral comment.

The man carrying the coloured glasses looked over his shoulder.

'What's the arse-warmer up to tonight? Performing anywhere?'

'Dunno. Some two-piece fleapit where she can find an audience,' the grandee replied.

The man at the piano beckoned with his head for Eliza to come closer. As she drew nearer she realised he was a lot older than she thought. His cheeks were rouged, and she suspected he might even be wearing lipstick. But his eyes, aureoled though they were with white, were kind.

'She'll be here much later, dear. She usually favours us with her voice.'

The man putting down the glasses croaked out a laugh of a not very pleasing sort.

'Hoh yairs,' he said. 'Her voice. Her throat is more the instrument she uses most nights round here.'

The man behind the piano played a sharp note, then stopped.

'Miss Fanny Clinton has the voice of an angel,' he said with emphasis. 'And the voice of a female angel at that.'

'I didn't think angels 'ad 'oles and cocks and cunts, like?'

'Well, some does,' said the man at the piano with great dignity. He had gone back to his mellifluous playing — it was the lilting 'Bridesmaid's Song' from *Der Freischütz*. An uneaten plate of food sat on top of the piano — a wedge of pork pie, a pewter tankard filled with ale. His supper.

'Begging your pardon, my dear. Some as have no manners.'

Eliza felt uncomfortable with such raw language used in her presence. But she knew that theatricals of all descriptions were famously loose in their language and morals. It was part of their attraction, after all.

'Can I . . . come back . . . if I don't find her? Later, like?'

Eliza's usually quite firm voice had developed an unusual wobble, a querying urgency.

The waiter laughed in her face.

'Don't worry, ducks, no man round here'll be chasing your skirt.'

Eliza bit back her own retort: *what makes you think I'd like a flea like you, insect-face.*

The waiter walked out, letting the door swing to, with an air of expressive dismissal.

The piano man went back to his keys, seemingly wishing to express no opinion.

The grandee, however, sighed deeply, and yelled out to the wrestler standing idly by the door, watching all this with the mask-like expression of a perennial voyeur, 'Let the little baggage in later. But only to the top of the stairs, mind. She can send a message in. If Madame Muck so much as favours us with her presence.'

*E*rnest Boulton, gentleman, stood impatiently on the stage, lit by the lantern. His foot was tapping.

In the stalls the greasy old gentleman was asleep, his snoring every so often rising to a peak, then dropping away. A thin stage cat wound its way under the chairs. It was a feral grey, with peculiarly intense green eyes. Its attentions were focused on a cold chop that Caldicott had gnawed right down to the bone, then absent-mindedly dropped.

Everyone else had gone.

Ernest was wearing only pantaloons, a vest, and from his waist a vast petticoat, lit from behind by the lantern.

At his feet was a slight woman with a haze of springy ginger hair. Her mouth was full of pins and she was trying to talk.

'You did like your last dress though, Mr Boulton.'

Mr Boulton left a polite pause, and then sighed.

'I think I have a perfect dress — at home, dear Amy.'

She glanced up at him — she was pinning up the hem.

'Put the lamp a bit closer, there's a dearie,' she said to Timmy, who was stretched out on his back, his lids shut, smoking a meditative pipe. Without opening his lids, the child pushed the lamp a little closer.

'At home, you say.'

'Yes.'

'But your character is a widowed lady, Ernest.'

Amy only ever used Ernest's Christian name when she was most uncertain. Most plangent. He looked down at Amy's worn face: it was the ruin of a face really, but a kindly ruin.

'Of a general, no less,' Ernest said, flinging his thin arms out and taking a balletic stance. Then: 'Do you think my arms are getting too muscular, Amy?'

She sighed a little, through her pins, glanced up.

'No, dearie. If you'd only keep still.'

'Of course my own dress is, as entirely natural, that befitting the wife of a peer.'

'A pear? Or an apple? Or an orange?' asked Timmy, not even moving. 'Ha!' He sucked on his pipe.

Silence while Amy crept around on her knees a little further.

'You will be careful, won't you, Ernest dearie?'

'Careful?' He had just seen a shadow move at the back of the theatre. A figure disclosed itself. It was Freddie: Freddie harassed by the evil gods of boredom — those gods that sank their fangs into his neck and drained all the blood of reasonableness from him.

Ernest knew what was coming next. He could hardly listen to what Amy was saying. Her voice was particularly quiet.

'Yes, dear. But I've heard that you've been going out and about. In character, as 'twere.'

Amy raised her worn visage up to Ernest. She had known Ernest ever since he had come into the theatre as a sylvan lad of twelve. A sapling. (Even playing maids' parts then.) But there was danger — there were dangers in mixing the fantasy of the theatre with ordinary life. She knew, she knew . . .

'Ernest bloody Boulton!'

It was Frederick's midships roar. At times it thrilled Ernest, the way it vibrated in the core of his backbone, a sonic nerve vibrating in a solid bass hum. But at other times . . .

'In God's name, how much damned and blasted buggery longer are you going to bloody well be?'

Amy pricked herself.

'Oh dear!' she murmured. 'We're not even halfway there.'

'The widow of a general. The wife of a peer. There's only a few ranks between them, surely?'

Ernest was trying to walk away but Amy held him back, by his skirt. Ernest stood there in his underwear, imprisoned in his petticoat.

'I can't leave just yet, lovey,' he called out.

Frederick stormed back out the doors and slammed them shut.

'Oh diddums,' said Timmy, changing his position on the floor. 'Diddums can't get what he wants. Poor Diddums.'

'Ernest,' took up Amy again, forcing Ernest to pay attention. 'You are listening to me, aren't you? I've heard tell that you are going all over town in your outfits. It's dangerous.'

There was a stiff pause. Ernest did not like to be told.

'*How?*'

'Well, Mr Caldicott for one. He doesn't like it.' Amy was shaking her head. 'He says it's not good for business. Not one bit. If you're out and abouting in petticoats, as you are, why should anyone pay decent coin to see you up on stage?'

'Oh, don't worry about that, dear.'

Ernest suddenly wanted to reach down and ruffle Amy's silvery-ginger faded hair. He wanted to caress her and tell her how she knew almost nothing of the modern world, and how intricate and different and exhilarating it could be.

'I don't think I'll be interfering with the cut old Caldicott screws out of us down here by running around town in a petticoat.' There was a steely tone in his voice. He had become a gentleman again. Amy, on her knees, at his feet, did not like this. She disliked the way he went from being a chum in the theatre to being someone else. They said nothing for a moment, a long moment, and then Ernest seemed to relent, for he said, 'You'll never guess where I've been today, Amy, dearie? I've been to the very gates of heaven itself.' And then he told her about being up in the balloon, gilding the experience so she could see it. But Amy kept her head down, said nothing. Just kept crawling on her knees around the edge of his petticoat. Pulling him there. Yanking at him here.

When she stood up, with difficulty she looked him full in the eye — his pale blue glance sliding away.

'It's *dangerous*, Master Ernest. That's what it is. Men don't like to be made fools of. Not when it's in so particular and personal a department, as you might say. They get angry-like. And when men get angry, they turn into animals. Strike out. They turn vicious.'

As she walked off the stage, like a dirge, she said sharply to him — he was stepping out of his petticoat, 'You mark my words, Little Miss.'

A Green Boy

They had arranged to meet in Waterloo Place, near St James's Park, at half past two. It was a sultry day and the trees, just coming into leaf, already had a heaviness to them, as if already weighted down by grit, grime and smoke. Yet this same air lent a kind of murky glamour to the distances: across the verdant fall of St James's Park Samuel Barton could see two tiny women and a soldier, picked out in pink dawdling along, the women's parasols nodding, dipping, twirling. Behind him, a constant omnibus roar.

Samuel Barton was waiting for a fast woman. He had an afternoon appointment.

The possibility of the afternoon spread ahead of him, treacly, intriguing: a sort of infinite mist of possibilities, of sequinned becoming — explosions, lulls, engulfings. Or simply pleasure? It might just be pleasant to spend a dawdling afternoon with an intriguing actress.

He felt at the epicentre of cosmopolitan glamour: his life, which had seemed to lack form, now felt taut. He was an arrow seeking the target: yet what was the bullseye? Was it as contrary as — fun? Excitement? Looseness? He had known such privation that he longed now for the cool, long distance; or if not that, for the excitements of the night, the glittering illusion. He had been articled as a law clerk now for over three years: there was little chance — but chance enough — he might get to be a solicitor. But he had his own family to think of, back in Nottingham: their noble, too scrupulous support.

He had scrimped, saved, gone without. He had suffered beerhalls and mutton without really being aware he suffered from them. But now, as if in an instant, on meeting Fanny, he had become awake to his situation, and he felt an immense greed overtake him: he longed to lose himself in a gluttony — momentarily — of everything he had never had. He had a sense it might be the one time he might be free; it was a whistling corridor he stood within, liberally sprinkled with exploding stars.

Yet he'd come awake that morning in his own narrow cot, in his tiny Islington lodgings, three floors above a butcher's shop ('Dealer in Pickled Tongues, Sweetbreads Etc'): his bed narrow, clammy, his feet banging against the iron bed ends. It was too short and he had to sleep on a slant, sometimes on hot nights going to sleep with his hands clasped around the coldness of iron. It was comforting, in his aloneness.

But this day was the beginning of his crude awakening. In the morning light he looked at his attic room again: the peeling paint, the grimy window so fugged over as to appear to be opaque. (King's Cross Station the only 'dreaming spires' in the distance.)

Already the walls of the building had begun to shake: to emit the vibration that, he noticed when he first came to London, seemed to underlie everything. As if there were some hollow core within the great city: a dark void of oscillating black, a kind of infernal machine that was continually turning — or being turned — by lost souls, those lost souls he saw everywhere on the streets, sitting on pavements, sleeping in doorways, clustered around warm vents. The vibration from this hollow rotating core infiltrated everything as a palsied kind of tremor, which moved everything infinitesimally so that little revolving worlds of black — grit — were floating in the atmosphere.

Even the rich were grubby in London: there was no possibility of complete cleanliness for the air itself was a tint, a taint, of grime.

He had awoken to a knock.

He knew it instantly. Yet it was different. Cummings' normal morning knock was a rude awakening, telling him it was time to jump out of bed. Begin the day. It was a male knock, lacking any sense of mystery, subtlety. But this morning the knock was tentative.

Samuel called out, 'Is that you, Cummings?'

'Yes,' came the unusual reply — unusual as it was delivered from behind the door.

'Well, come in, man. You've seen me in the altogether enough times now for it not to be a shock.'

Samuel leapt out of bed and Cummings came in, as he always did, taking a seat on the desk chair (a broken-down kitchen chair, with a hollowed-out pillow placed upon it). The chair was placed at a three-quarters angle to Samuel, who turned a little away from Cummings as he reached for his trousers. Yet Cummings, as always, had had a vivid imprint of Barton's lithe physique. Samuel had made a sport of axing wood at home (thus doing something useful for his mother's kitchen as well as exercising his body), his colouring was olive-brown and his body was burnished all over with a light dusting of glistening, almost animal-like featherings of black hair.

In the broken oval mirror nailed to the wall Cummings glimpsed Barton pincering forwards, a thigh raised as he slid a hairy leg into pantaloons, for one second Samuel's John Thomas, morning-swollen, pod full, jostle-happy, joggled, leapt out alarmingly as Samuel stood up, then slithered into linen that Cummings could see was none too clean.

While this little opera was happening Cummings kept up, as always, a kind of joshing banter. He had no idea why he enjoyed looking on Samuel's nakedness, except that it was a custom between them. And it was as invisible to Samuel, who enjoyed walking about his tiny attic naked, as it was — seemingly — to Cummings. Who was aching to find out where his sweetheart was going. Not that either man conceived of the other in this way: it was just that they were provincials alone together in London, and there is hardly any more needy, nor intrusively intimate relationship than that.

In fact it was the first time Samuel had had a social engagement that excluded Cummings. The needy can smell freedom in others: Cummings snuffled it out of every movement in Samuel's motion around his room: the careless plash of water from the jug into the basin, the feckless drenching of his face: the happy splash of drips into the water as Samuel shook his head, his shaggy black curls sending out little spits and darts of water, one of which dashed itself right into Cummings' pale, watery eyes.

'Damn you, Barton!' Cummings said with more than usual vigour.

Samuel stood there, the water glistening on his face.

'What is it, Cubs?'

He looked over at his friend, with his scurfy, freckled skin, his thinning hair and pale blue protuberant eyes.

'I wondered if you'd like to come out today. A picnic maybe? A ride down the Thames to Greenwich? Or Madame Tussaud's? I know how you always love the waxworks — I'll pay, I'll pay!'

Cummings had risen to his feet in his wretchedness. Samuel was looking at him, slightly ashamed, even alarmed. Yet he turned curtly enough and said, his back to him, 'Can't, old Cubby. Can't.'

And Cummings witnessed in the mirror the despoiling of Samuel's face as he wiped it with a towel, finishing on a splendid rendition of a roguish smile into the glass.

Cummings, achingly, tried to smile back. He — with his thin stooped shoulders and dirty-blond hair going thin, even though he was a scant twenty-five — blushed. But it was the flush of defeat, of incipient humiliation.

This was an awkward moment and Samuel, as if aware of his old friend's pain (yet eerily immune to it at the same time; he thought to himself: *unhappiness is no longer my friend*), walked over to Cummings, who seemed to flinch a little. So Samuel stopped.

'Look, I'm sorry,' he said and finding a lie ready in his mouth spoke it: 'I've got something I can't get out of . . . I'd like to. Next Saturday afternoon? Yes? Shall we? Do you promise me? You won't go ahead and make some rash promise and disappoint me?'

The flush deepened on Cummings' plain face: yet plain people can be wounded as deeply as the handsome — perhaps more deeply. He looked down and Samuel had the awful sensation of hurt, that he was hurting Cummings, so he reached forward and punched him lightly — oh, lightly as a fluttering caress — on his chest. Cummings showed the disquieting possibility of actually rolling with the punch, onto the floor. But he straightened himself up, adjusted his worn little tie (he was always first up, first dressed). Now the gulf of a London Saturday evening opened up before his horrified stare — he would be alone. He would not be able to escape his own tiresome company.

Samuel was as if blind to his friend's pain. Though Cummings was one of the props of his life, and one he would miss if it disappeared, he had never, as it were, inspected the prop: like many handsome people he had taken Cummings' admiration for granted. It was what life was like. But he was no brute; he wasn't even hard: he was an indecisive young man of twenty-one, on the point of changing his life.

$\mathcal{F}$rederick sat there, legs wide apart, slumped in the armchair. There was a length of Japanese silk thrown over the chair but the brocade had been sat in, scrunched up: it had lost its form. Frederick was in his trousers. His boots lay beside him, scattered on the floor. He was bare-chested. He had a tattoo, surprisingly, on his forearm: of a hangman's noose, decorated at its base by wind-swept waves.

Frederick had the body of a sailor: he had been in the services since he was fourteen. He had started as a midshipman, and if the body of the sailor had been overtaken by the slackness of a clubman, there was still a vestigial masculine shape: the sag at least hung from muscles. He was unshaven, hung over and not really fully awake.

He and Fan had retreated to their hidey-hole at Wakefield Street after another wild night on the town. They had not been home to Southampton Street for two full days. The room, a shabby dressing room, was full of a languorous silence.

Fan, her body aching yet alive, drumming yet thrumming also, was standing there naked.

'What shall I wear today?' she was saying.

Frederick knew better than to offer comment. Fan gazed along the row of gowns and sighed.

'I have nothing new,' she said, her hand rifling among the silks, the satins, peplums, fine woollens. 'But I want to look good for — '

'Your succulent young plum,' Frederick said. He had an erection again, or a half erection: like a memory from the night before, of orificial pleasures, a glut. He was also half awake with memory, as if the sex had blossomed and bloomed in memory and after thought.

In the morning light Fan looked her most prosaic. She had the languor, it was true, that comes after a night of strenuous sex, but she had never looked more like a stripped boy, more like a slight ephebe than when she stood there, a little wretched at having nothing to wear.

Frederick almost groaned. 'Darling, pick one at will,' he said.

She sighed petulantly. 'It's all right for you.' She had a hangover too.

She kicked out venomously at the dress she had clawed off late in the night. Frederick always wanted her to wear it: it was an indispensable part of the play. A condition, almost. So her dress, once pretty and prim, was now greasy and suspect: smelling of semen around the inside skirts; other smells too.

She gave it a good kick.

'Bugger all this,' she said.

'What is it, love?'

It was the caramel accent of Stella. Stella had come into the room, wearing only a woman's camisole. Her penis, which was reddened and looked almost raw, hung out. 'You feeling a little queer?'

Fan said nothing. Her face set into a grimace. She looked quite ugly — hair in disarray, lacking her false plaits and cheveux (these lay on the table beside her, scattered where they had been flung in the battle the night before). The room was like the dressing room of a theatre — full of dresses, wigs, underwear.

Stella came back in with a glass of water for Fan, who made a facial expression of annoyance yet reached out and took it. She drained the glass, and handed it back.

She began to dress. First of all the drawers, which were split open at the crotch, at a time when public toilets did not exist for women; pale gossamer silk stockings, held up with garters; a lacy camisole; a bodice. Frederick always enjoyed watching Fanny's cock disappear. It was a brute of a cock: thick and long. Frederick always enjoyed seeing this — implement — sink down in a rising tide of lace, foamy silk, linen, jewels and hair. Fan had a big sac of balls too, low-slung. Frederick, who'd been in the navy, knew a big cock when he saw one.

He arched his back, yawning, and felt the companionable nuzzle of his cock up against his belly. Maybe Fan would bring the youngster back?

Next, with Fan, came the corset, then the bustle, then the dress. She had to step into this, as if she were garbing herself in a tent. She twisted around to the back, and rearranged the bustle.

It was her violet dress, the newest one she possessed. He watched her stuff the breasts with paddings of horsehair.

'More,' he said to her. 'Make 'em big. Lads like big bosoms,' he said. 'Your bosom friend!' He laughed a little idiotically at his joke.

Stell and Fan exchanged a glance.

'Bugger off, Clinton. Don't you have any jobs to do?'

It was Clinton's job to gather up the dirty washing and take it to the servants downstairs. This was a requisite of Clinton staying with Fanny. He had to do as much of the menial housework as possible. The strange thing was, he liked it. It gave him something to do. In between — waiting.

Now Fanny rushed towards the mirror. She actually did this — she rushed towards it, as if, finally, it had become her friend. She had placed her plaits on her head, was securing them with pins. She had pins in her mouth. Stell was in the other room playing something on the piano.

172

'Oh, Stell, shut the fuck up, will you darling?' Fan murmured. 'Tell the bitch to be quiet,' she ordered Fred.

Fred just sat and gazed at her.

'So you're going all out?' he said when she stood back from the mirror and, searching around for her parasol and gloves, smoothed the apron front of her dress.

She said nothing. Except, 'How do I look?'

She twirled for him.

'Good enough to eat.'

The first thing Samuel saw, as she alighted from the hansom cab, was a black kid shoe, high-heeled, with a coquille of pink silk, a steel buckle peeping out from the bottom of her skirt.

She was over forty minutes late. But she emerged from the cab as if it were he who had kept her waiting and she expected him to be full of apologies.

As she emerged further into sight he saw a cascading bloom of violet. She was wearing a double skirt, with a high waist of violet Irish poplin, its underskirt trimmed with folds and slashes of violet velvet. Such a cascade of textures and colours: parrot-pink, skeins of amethyst, fringes quivering, shimmering as if she were enclosed in a living thing.

She gave no appearance of seeing anyone else; she was absorbed in the infinitely intricate business of making an entrance. She stepped down lightly almost at the last moment, from the bottom step of the cab onto the footpath.

Samuel understood, in some part of his gut, that she was tightly corseted. Yet as if to counter this, to express her complete freedom of action, she opened her parasol. She did this in a showy, continuously moving way, which seemed to involve a continual kind of becoming, as if she were a chrysalis that was, on coming closer to him, evolving into her final shape — who she actually was.

Only then did she seem to see him, but it was as if, precisely then, she had snipped the garlands that attached her to the eyes of every man, and many of the women, in the street. In fact a frowsy children's maid, out for a walk with a pinafored girl, had lurched to a stop and was examining Fan from head to toe and back again.

'Did you ever see the like?' the maid said, a little gimlet-lipped. The young girl was looking mystified. She could not match the disapproval hidden in the maid's voice with the fairy-doll prettiness of the lady — all speckled and sparkly, motionful, a butterfly on first opening its wings.

Fanny slid her arm through Samuel's. She pulled him to her, into her body, quite savagely, so he felt for a moment she might have strong emotions, needs. This knowledge broke over him as a huge ocean wave breaks over the bow of a hardy steamer. For one moment he was stilled in thought — in wonder — and then his face lit up: he knew himself to be the proudest young man in London.

'What shall we do, little pal?'

She turned and looked at him, her face devoid of expression.

He had so expected her to have a complete programme of entertainments lined up that he felt at a loss.

'Oh, don't worry, don't worry at all,' she murmured, half laughing — at him? He was not sure. She pulled him by his arm quite tightly. They exited from Orange Street and went a few steps up an alley. He had never been up this alley, though it occurred to him he had walked by it unseeingly a thousand times, on his way to the law courts.

As they walked further down the alley, so the noises from the street fell away: the massed silence from the buildings high on either side sent out their pervasive chill. He heard two women talking high up on a first floor as sheets were thrown out a window and shaken; he heard water being thrown onto the floor; down some steep steps came a rush of cold air.

They passed a bookshop selling etchings. Several gentlemen were standing there looking in, but on Fan and the boy walking past they turned and Samuel had the uncomfortable feeling of being scrutinised: his whole body, from top to tail, in penetrating detail. Fanny seemed quite unaware and turned her head away. She was humming as she walked.

There was only the sound of her high heels on the uneven cobbles.

She avoided a puddle of uncertain-looking liquid.

'What's that song you keep humming?' he said, more out of embarrassment than anything else.

They had halted outside The Regal Cigar Divan. Fan slid her arm out.

'Song?' she said, as if she were surprised to find herself with Samuel. He felt momentarily lost, placed in strange company.

He hummed it.

'Oh, my dear,' Fanny said and smiled at him. 'That is my song "Fading Away". I shall sing it for you — for you alone. One day. Just you wait!' She squeezed his arm and passed into the cigar shop.

''Allo Fan. You're up and about a little early, ain't you?'

A hirsute, swell mob-man was polishing an ale handle. His eyes glanced at Samuel, then back to Fan. She made the slightest motion of her head — as if to say it's all right, but so slight that Samuel, hungry for everything about her, only just noticed. She said to the man, 'I feel like a wee pick-me-up.'

'Out late, was you, dear?' A blowsy woman in a none-too-clean satin dress came out, polishing a glass. 'Have any luck?'

Fan ignored this completely, turning round instead to Samuel, and raised her glass. (She had ordered two double brandies and soda).

Her ferocious intimacy seemed to block out everything around them. He saw only her face, and he was aware of her powdered nose, her lips, bewitchingly painted, and her pressing, intimate, moist eyes blinding him.

He had never drunk spirits in daylight. This was such a renversement for him that he was conscious of the alcohol sliding down his throat. It burnt. His whole body began to catch fire. Then he burst into a coughing fit.

At first Fan kept sipping, then, a shade of annoyance slipping over her face, she laughed to cover this annoyance and banged him lightly on his back.

'No! Please! I'm sorry.'

'Another, please.'

This was Fan. She was ignoring him.

She raised her second glass in a toast.

'This will set us up for a nice spot of shopping.'

Samuel hurried to catch up. He marvelled that he could so easily accept another drink. His senses were blurred and for some unknown reason, at that precise moment, the face of Cummings appeared before him — Cummings in all his plainness — and Cummings looked worried.

They had emerged into daylight at full sail. The drinks, Samuel decided, had been a marvellous idea. He realised he was entering a Valhalla of marvellous ideas, an enfiladed arcade in which, at each shop, there must be marvels to pause over, miracles to peruse. Fanny had shaken her reticule: it sent out a reassuringly heavy, almost drunken sway — of gold. She told him she wanted to 'look at' shoes, dresses, hats, gloves — oh, and some hair.

This last was penetratingly fascinating to Samuel. He couldn't help himself turning and glancing up at Fanny's immense 'do'. She had a chignon made up of puffs, edged on each side with a loop made of three additional braids. This was mounted up higher and higher into a sort of volcano of braided hair (tightly woven: as tight — he sensed — as her corsets might be). On its very top, slightly to the front, as if perched on a cliff face, were two hummingbirds, apparently either kissing or finding — this was amusing — some insect.

The insect theme was picked up on either ear: Fan wore large bejewelled flies as earrings, picked out in red glass.

Yet if Fan seemed extraordinary it was simply in the taste of her attire: Regent Street at four in the afternoon was full of women similarly bedecked, though differently comparisoned. Samuel had to admit she had the imprimatur of taste: she was an exquisite.

So was her hair — unreal?

She drew him along with her, drew him — that is to say — as if she were threading a particularly lustrous piece of silk through a glittering, slit-eyed needle. They moved along through the crowds, aware that people were turning, were looking, perhaps admiring Fanny's handsomeness, the extreme correctness of her dress, its fulsome fashionableness; perhaps, too, trying to diagnose the exact relationship between the two: a brother perhaps, with a rather fast older sister? She seemed flecked with laughter, foaming with some subterranean excitement.

They had gone through gloves at Dickens & Jones, gazed on shoes. (Samuel had never seen so many tiny boots, glistening in seemingly malevolent silence, awaiting impossibly small feet. Fan did not try anything on. He had the feeling her feet may have been rather large. She made a point of not revealing her shoe size. Not even the perspicacious shop girl — elegant, too sharp in her way — had been able to wrest this detail out of Fan.)

But now they lingered before a frankly scientific window. It was a brightly lit space lined with sky-blue velvet. Various cordovan leather cases were open, lined with lustrous purple velvet. In each of the boxes nestled a knotted fall of hair.

These hairpieces — chignons — were as glossy and heavy-seeming as a new pile of horse dung: heaviness was all, as well as the elaborately interwoven way the great weights and falls of false hair were melded.

There were falls of blonde hair, brunette hair, auburn hair. The cunning obscenity of it was echoed by every tint of hair possible on a human head. And each was attached to a Spanish comb, as if to illustrate how it might fall.

As if feeling a ghostly amputation, Fan reached up and tentatively touched her hairdo. Yet what did she feel? Of the tottering mass, how much was her own, Samuel numbly wondered?

It felt barbaric, cannibalistic. Samuel shuddered to think of the heads the hair had been removed from: their poverty, perhaps; their shame.

He recognised something here.

'Oh, Lord,' Fan said with longing. She seemed to be in some sort of dream. 'Oh, Lord, Lord, Lord.'

'Shall we go in?'

Fan sped a glance all across Samuel's face. He supposed it was the alcohol but everything she did seemed to have an almost physical effect on him. Her glance felt as if it touched him — actually touched him on his cheeks, on his lips.

She rustled forward and through into the shop. Her lips were parted and her eyes glittering. She had finally come awake.

*I*t was soon after this that she said, suddenly, 'Let's have our photograph taken.'

He was carrying the small box in which lay the weight of hair. He had been gentlemanly, stood outside the shop while she perused. But she had sent the small girl out — a child, really — to ask him in.

'The lady says she needs your opinion.'

He had gone into the overheated interior and been taken through brocade curtains to a glittering confusion of mirrors. In the epicentre sat Fanny. Her previous hairdo had been disassembled, and instead, on her head sat a gloriously thick, slightly blonde hairdo. It was so startling he had not known what to say. Fanny had laughed at him in the mirror.

'You don't recognise me?'

'No, no . . .' he said, blushing. 'You just look . . . different.'

Fan went back to looking at herself in the glass. She seemed to require a length of time, almost a swoon of time. Samuel was aware of the shop assistants trying to judge their relationship. Was he her fancy man? There was not the right weighting. Her amusement? But they could see Samuel was fresh-faced, slightly too rough around the edges, smelling too much of the ink pot and the ledger. Yet the shopwomen could appreciate the youth's handsomeness: poor clothes or tailoring off the peg didn't detract from such physicality.

In the end she had bought, instead of the lustrous coil, something that would add to her current tresses. He was startled at how much it cost. ('But it is real hair, my dear,' Fan had said, gathering up his arm again, having handed him the box.)

'But where is it from?'

Fan thought for a while, then shrugged.

'From people who don't need it?' she suggested. Then caught his eye and laughed with surprising coarseness.

He felt at sea, morally. He knew his sisters back in Nottingham did not approve of the buying of poor people's hair. They used their own hair. They could not afford any other. They had to 'make do'.

Perhaps he was sick of this endless matching up of carefulness to almost nothing. Wasn't there pleasure in freefall? At least for an afternoon. He enjoyed his moral numbness: his escape from morality.

Fan seemed this marvellous hummingbird of freedom to him — straining forward on her high heels, her bustle whispering along behind her, the tottering cliff face of her hairpiece, the slim defence of her parasol, the point of which she actually relied upon to keep her balance.

But if all of life was a hall of mirrors, couldn't it also be a funfair?

'Yes,' he said. What a lark. 'Let's have our photograph taken.'

The room, upstairs, had a rather grimy carpet set upon a dirty floor. There was a variety of painted backdrops to choose from. Arcadian landscape, book-lined living room, an urn against the Swiss Alps. There was also a choice of chairs, for example, a low-slung velvet drawing room chair, that went with a podium and fall of matching curtain. (This was better for a single, the photographer's wife said on a downward breath. She was an anxious, somewhat flustered woman who wore a florid rather over-emphatic dress, which Fan suspected matched the draperies. She was care-worn. The husband had explained that women felt 'most at ease' with another woman 'arranging them'.)

He — big bellied, wearing a morning coat that was a little too glossy and had the appearance of having been hurriedly placed on at the sound of footsteps climbing the stairs — was a mass of officiousness and high ceremony, not unlike a ringmaster at the circus.

Like the shopgirls, he was all agog at the possible relationship of the showy young miss and her drab but pretty clerk companion.

'And if we place your . . . brother . . . so?' he said, placing his meaty hands on Samuel, rearranging him as if he were a doll. Samuel stiffened under the male touch. Disliked it. Flushed a murky red. Looked pained.

Fan seemed to be laughing at him from under lowered lashes.

'My . . . brother?' she said, arranging the folds of her dress over her pink and silver shoes. 'Oh, you mean Mr Barton here? Let's just call him my afternoon beau.'

The worn wife tittered and looked and looked and tittered. She was down on her haunches, helping to arrange — and in arranging touch — the beautiful stuff of the fast young miss's skirt.

She could not help but make small sounds with her tongue, almost as if she were stroking a beautiful befurred animal.

Fan looked regnant. Proud.

The first arrangement was conventional: Fanny sitting in the low-slung chair, her arm out holding her folded parasol. Samuel stood behind her, to the side, one hand placed awkwardly, as if made of plaster, on Fan's shoulder.

The photographer's assistant, a pasty, pimpled individual who Samuel sensed did all the magical work, came out and dithered around, wearing a black apron of all things, hair plastered flat on his skull, prematurely balding and giving off the smell of poverty — of gas fires in grates and too many children. He adjusted the lightshade so a watery fall of light cascaded down, embalming our couple.

There was a momentary stillness as they waded out into eternity. Neither smiling of course, but staring down into a lens. The assistant disappeared beneath his shroud of black. There was silence, stillness — a flash, as their features were remade on photographic glass. A powerful chemical smell filled the air.

That image taken, Fan was all for experiment. She stood up, and said, 'Could we do a sweetheart picture?' Her tone bore only the lightest note of entreaty.

She demanded.

She had already taken her pose. She grabbed Samuel and placed him, putty in her hands, beside her. He stood, noble, chest puffed out, while she semi-collapsed beside him, half imploring, half begging — seducing him by look. He had his face half turned away. It was awkward, and would require a lot of fabric rearrangement.

The ringmaster humphed and hawed and said it would cost extra.

But his assistant, like a gas flame, glowed. For once he was doing something different. The lure of art, so often fatal, enticed.

The drab wife had sunk onto a rickety kitchen chair, taken up some sewing. She bent her head, every so often looking up, a frail smile playing over her features: it was like watching children playing.

But Fan — Fan was serious, gripped by a fever of creation. This photograph, she sensed, might be all she would have. Appearances were slippery, likely to disappear. If she could just for one moment arrest it all with a photograph . . . a carte de visite with which she might, with confidence, call upon the future. This is my reality, she might have been saying. *This is who I really am.*

Samuel was merely an adjunct — useful in his maleness, his prosaic certainty. His specifics: the slightly worn cuffs, the shoes that had been a little too clumsily resoled, the too bold tie attempting to eclipse all else; but more than this: the ordinariness, the unsayableness of his maleness. His ease with sitting with his legs spread apart, the supple trajectory of his trunk upholding limber arms that did not always seek to form subtle angles.

His even blink, his open, amused stare was gold coin here.

She — she was all a fever, a whirl of violet, a crush of purple, all palpitation and half-opened lips: she was in the middle of creation. She could hardly sit still. But she was at her happiest posing.

Photography, the modern masterpiece, would give her what she — this most modern miss — demanded: illusion, caught and captured, capable of being reproduced almost as a form of evidence. Evidence or illusion? She almost shrugged: either would do.

There was a click and the moment was over. Fanny stood and assumed a third pose. She had already edited it in her brain. Poor Samuel, a creaking virgin at this game, had to stand up, had to hold her arm, had to pose as a bridegroom. When for a moment his arm of its own volition jibbed, she took him afresh, curving around to look at him, saying, laughing, calling, 'It is only a joke, my dear. It is but a lark, a folly.'

Was nothing serious?

He was half drunk, loosened out into the palace of illusion. What did it matter?

He allowed himself, then, to pose, holding her arm proudly, staring down the lens, while she glanced down, only at the last moment, with an insouciant expression of extreme naughtiness, gleaming into the camera. She would elide the stillness of the frame. She would capture spontaneity, even in an art form that expressly forbade it. She would give, *give* utterly at this moment, sensing its importance. If all else faded, this could remain.

They could not take the images with them. They must call back, later in the afternoon. But pay, of course, pay now.

Fan did this. This was another moment in which Samuel's position seemed to be spotlit. What kind of man did not even need to pretend to be paying? To be holding the gold? And what kind of creature was she who had the money, the will for all these fantasies? She was from the demi-monde, that much was absolutely certain: of the upper classes, perhaps, in her light dismissal of other people's reality. But there was also about her something so wilful and strange that it was difficult to place her exactly: except as someone rapidly, giddily — almost gladly — fallen. It was almost offensive, the overworked photographer's wife thought, to see someone so excepted from the usual tyranny of rules. Yet, taking up her stitching, feeling the familiar ache at the back of her neck almost like an old friend, she also felt assured that the tyranny would bite back.

Nobody lived outside the rules.

*T*hey had gone then — almost run, it felt like — to the Globe restaurant in Coventry Street where, Fan said, she would 'treat' Samuel. Oh, he had been a little darling — the most gorgeous of manikins — to her this afternoon. Oh, how she had loved, even adored having him with her. He was so restful and silent, so observing and observant (so young and unplucked, she did not add): such a gorgeously dull and unpolished contrast (she also did not say) to her own too high polish, her almost blinding sheen. They made up an untold story, one that begged solution. She, who carried the story along, forced the story to be told — it was she who held all the power, just as she insisted on paying.

The afternoon was closing its petals. The light was sinking, growing moist; the gas-lights in the streets were going on. That vast floodtide of humanity was swapping course: the workers were beginning to go home; those who were idle were retreating to their private spheres; the night people, those who were out early, had made their first, brightly avaricious appearance. Was it this — this sense of disappearing time — that made Fanny grab hold of Samuel's arm and pull him along with her, an almost haunted look suddenly on her face?

He glanced at her: she was looking faded. He wondered how old she was, and he had a sense of her being alone, of being clamped by a loneliness so profound she was lost. She needed him at that moment, and her need was intoxicating for him.

She took him into the supper room at the Globe, which was almost empty. She asked for a booth, and the waiter, who appeared to know her, asked her how her day had been. He was of the too handsome variety; slim-waisted, broad-shouldered and so devastatingly gorgeous it was hard to work out what kept him as a waiter. He was Italian.

She answered him in an intimate way, then introduced Samuel, to whom the waiter bowed, and then said something to Fan in a quick and liquid undertone. She laughed, and said to Samuel, 'He says at least you are easy on the eye.'

Samuel did not know whether he liked being considered in such a way. Yet a man would have to have been made of stone not to be flattered. He half bowed back, and the waiter placed on the marble tabletop the big, gilded, slightly grubby menu.

'Oh, I think champagne,' said Fan after looking at it for a half-dazed moment.

Samuel sat with his back to the room. He did not know quite why he had taken this chair — or was he engineered into it? But the vast bevelled mirrors into which he looked returned a vista of marble, gas-light, an enfilade of gorgeous falseness.

The waiter, elastic to whatever might be demanded of him, disappeared.

Fanny let out a sigh. She seemed, for once in her life, lost for words.

It was so unusual for Samuel to have to carry the moment that he hardly knew where to begin. He made some comment about the rooms. She shrugged. A look of boredom flittered over her features.

'Fanny, where were you born?' he asked.

This seemed to startle her a little. She looked at him and laughed.

'Where was I born? Well, it depends, I suppose. In some senses I was born right here in London — not too far, indeed, from where we sit.'

He felt confused. How could someone be born 'in a sense'?

'Why do you ask, Samuel?'

'I don't know. I don't feel as if I know anything about you.'

She reached forward and squeezed his fingers.

'There isn't much to know. Take what you see. That's best.'

This slightly strange sentence hung in the air.

The waiter was back. Unctuously and with time-honoured ceremony, he uncorked the bottle and let the little death hang in the air, almost sexually. He was paying more attention to Samuel than to Fan. She watched this, expressionless. At long last, the waiter withdrew. They clinked glasses. Fan seemed utterly exhausted.

'To us, my dear,' she said. 'To our lovely afternoon.'

He said, 'To you.'

She said nothing.

Then she asked him what he wanted to do with his life.

He said, aware suddenly of how futile and small it sounded, that he wanted to help his family. He might go to the colonies, where, he had heard, they needed lawyers.

At the word 'colonies' it was as if a light went out in her eyes. He had never seen anything be of less interest to someone.

'Oh yes, the colonies,' she murmured, then took another sip, then fell into silence. A violin was being tuned up and there was the sound of a party of people arriving, settling down, talking. Samuel saw in the mirror the glances each of the people made towards Fan and, by inference, himself. He saw people lean in together, whisper, turn and look.

'You are quite notable, aren't you, Fan?' he asked.

She seemed momentarily startled.

'A lady does not like to be notorious,' she answered.

'That isn't quite what I said.'

She was silent a moment, then laughed. 'You're coming on, my dear,' she drawled. 'Half an afternoon and you've quite got a tongue in your head.' She leant forward suddenly — and it seemed to him this was part of her magic: she was all whim, all for doing things on the moment.

'I want to tell you something. Something important,' she said.

It was at this point that Samuel became aware of a sound — it was of table legs being pushed across the tiled floor: the dissonance of violence. This was followed by voices — one male and angry, the other softer, trying to placate. Samuel could see nothing in the mirror, except the people at the other table were straining around to look. Clearly something was happening.

As his eyes travelled over to look at Fan, her face was changing. He saw, for one second, a look of abject fear. This so crushed everything about her that she looked momentarily ugly. He had never seen her like this — returned to abject child. But this look was so fleetingly there that it seemed to have been a mirage, because it had instantaneously been replaced by a mask. She had straightened her back, grown taller in her seat, yet simultaneously she appeared to have relaxed. She had a curious half smile on her face and began playing with the rim of her glass.

At this exact point a man in evening dress appeared in the mirror. Samuel strained to turn around but Fan leant forward and grabbed his hand. He felt her need. She whispered, '*Take no notice.*'

When he tried to take his hand away she forbade him, implored: '*Pretend nothing is happening. Please.*'

The man was shouting. He was saying Fan should be thrown out. He said worse things. He said things it was impossible to believe.

Samuel wanted to leap to his feet. To hit the man. But Fan was imploring him to be still, to be silent. Her eyes cautioned him, begged him, warned him.

They need only be silent, she seemed to say, and the man, like a mirage, would disappear.

The Italian waiter pulled on the man's sleeve. The manager appeared, red-faced, asking what the matter was.

Fan judged her moment perfectly. She rose to her feet. Her face was pale with hauteur.

'Samuel,' she drawled, 'I really don't like the muck this place has in it. I think we might move on.'

It was an order.

He rose to his feet. The angry man lost control. The waiter and the manager were having to restrain him. The people at the other table were gazing, listening intently.

Fan, throwing some money on the table, sailed away.

Samuel was left to follow.

She was waiting outside, trembling. Whatever she had used up in getting away had left her drained. She looked at him, pale and haunted.

'The bastard,' she said.

Then she smiled. This smile cost an extreme amount — it was not real and she appeared old, worn.

'What an unpleasant end,' she tried to make light of it, 'to an entirely pleasant afternoon.'

He said nothing.

She did not touch him. She did not move. He didn't move either. The waiter looked out at them through the plate-glass doors, though without any sign of recognition. Then he looked about carefully, as if judging his moment, and slipped out.

He was carrying the box of hair.

'You forgot this, madam,' he said quickly, handing it over and silvering back within. The door swung to.

They were standing alone in the dark.

People were walking to and fro.

Their frolic was at an end.

'I must go home now, Samuel,' Fanny said to him, through stiff lips. 'Frederick is waiting for me.'

'I'll find a cab for you.'

He hailed one quickly, though it felt to Fan, at those ebbing moments, as if each second were taking an unendurable length of time. She was finding it difficult to stand upright, not to collapse. She seemed to have lost all will, all presence — suddenly it was as if all that was left behind was a collection of flesh and feather, hair and horse hair. She appeared quite ugly to Samuel for the first time. He noticed that her chin was large and slightly awkward, her nose a little too broad, her eyes flat, empty.

'I wanted to give you something,' she said. She opened her reticule, then pressed an envelope into his hand. 'I do not like to be untrue.'

She got into the cab, looked out for a moment, and waved farewell.

*S*amuel walked along Tottenham Court Road in a daze. He had slid his thumbnail under the gummed-up envelope in Charing Cross Road. He had come to a halt by the brilliantly gas-lit plate-glass window. (He glanced in once. A clever window-dresser had created a kind of imitation jungle out of paper palms, tiny stuffed birds, in the background a tropical sunset made of coloured foil.)

The crowds around him moved by, nobody glancing at him, although every so often a face would turn to him — a lonely face, with searching eyes — then move on.

He stood with the envelope in his hand, the handbill hanging down.

The handbill read:

TO SEE IS TO BELIEVE!!

Mr Ernest Boulton will be favouring the public with one of his highly esteemed impersonations, which have been delighting audiences from Scarborough to the Egyptian Hall, London. As Lady Chillington in *The Morning Call*, Lady Jane Desmond in *Killing Time*, Julia in *The Hunchback*, Etc Etc. Now for the first time at the Adelphi Theatre, Chelmsford. Two nights only.

TO SEE IS TO BELIEVE!

Photographic portraits of Mr Boulton in character available exclusively from Theatre. Post Performance – One Shilling Only.

A hand — Fanny's? Boulton's? — had written along the top: 'I would prefer you understood me. Then there is no misunderstanding.'

That was all.

It was unsigned.

No misunderstanding?

He took his eyes away from these words and, blushing, face hot, stared unseeing at the huge tide of humanity swilling along the street to Euston Station. In between he saw — as if for the first time — the odd brightly dressed unattached woman moving in a contrary direction, heading towards the Haymarket.

Was she in fact a woman?

He passed a hand over his face, like someone waking up.

Had he been a fool? Made a fool of himself?

Cummings. Had he been laughing at him?

I do not like to be untrue.

He did not understand. It was impossible that so cunningly feminine a creature could be a man. Then he recalled those last moments, when she was most haunted: the drop of her jaw, the broadness of her nose. It was all a frolic, a lark, surely? But anything was possible with theatricals. It was part of their magic — the dew of their magic. To change. To alter, to expand time, to collapse it in a moment.

To slide, to alter . . .

To see is to believe?

Then he noticed something else inside the envelope.

It was a ticket. To a performance of *A Morning Call.*

A Fan Flung Aside

*F*anny opened her fan, looked at it in contemplation a moment. Then she flung it aside and snatched up the letter.

Dear Fanny . . . she read the lines aloud. *Please for heaven's sake be warned. There is a man about who is after you.*

She glanced down at her maroon glacé boots with the tiny gilt buttons and slid her toes further out from under the silk fringe of the bottom of her dress. She admired them for a moment. She stood up and paced about the drawing-room carpet, smoothing her pannier as she walked. There was a pleasant slithering sound, of silk rubbing against satin, as she moved. She went back to the letter.

He is a good-looking, good-for-nothing fellow, and that's the truth. I only wish he would make love to me, she read aloud. Fanny smiled to herself, crumpled up the letter and threw it into the fire. She gazed at it a moment as it burnt.

Frederick had come into the room, noiselessly. He looked over at her. She was wearing another of her mauve dresses, which toned with her pale colouring. Her breasts, he noted, were pushed high, and her hair — her massive hairdo — was piled up on her head, giving her an imperious yet somehow frolicsome look. He felt an almost painful degree of desire for her.

'You've brought the coal?' she said. Her voice was cold. She did not move towards him.

'Ma'am?'

'Coal,' she said, turning away from him.

'Coal?' he said, his voice hollowed out. So, it was to be like this.

She turned over her shoulder, throwing him a brilliant glance. Her eyes were hard, almost blind, he noticed. He wanted her then. He would have liked to take her on the floor.

'Oh, pardon me, I'm sure,' she said to him, a little smile playing on her painted lips. 'I took you for my servant.'

'Would that you would keep me as your servant.'

'What wages do you ask?'

'I'll serve you for love.'

'You'll never get paid.'

She walked away from him.

'Never mind, engage me,' he asked. His voice was deep, throaty. He could hardly talk. He ached.

'You've got great confidence in yourself, sir,' she said, arranging the frills upon her pannier. She noted suddenly that they had become twisted and she concentrated for a moment, a little frown playing on her brow as she straightened them. For a moment there was only the hiss of flame, slithering, silken. She enjoyed keeping him waiting.

'I've heard a bad character of you from your last place.'

'Indeed! From whom?'

'From your *mistress*,' she said, her lips suddenly ugly. She moved past him, tormenting him with her scent, her dress brushing against his legs, against his body.

'What mistress?'

'Have you so many?'

'None. But I seek one, and that one — '

'Has a remarkably troublesome servant.'

'Please,' he said to her. 'Listen to me, I am serious — '

'It is hard taking someone seriously,' she said, 'standing with a coal scuttle in his hand.'

He flung some coal on the fire.

'Don't smother the fire, sir!' she said. He turned around, looked at her.

'You and I have known each other a long time,' he said in a small, wounded voice. 'Why say "sir?" It sounds very formal.'

She looked at him in silence a moment. Laughed.

'Suppose this were a play, sir. What would you say to me then?'

There was a ripple of appreciation through the audience. Fanny could sense it. She held them in her grip. It was like liquid love, like alcohol. She felt triumphant — in her pausing, her pacing.

She moved downstage, over the worn and slightly dirty drawing carpet, a prop of the Chelmsford Theatre, towards the carelessly painted backdrop of the drawing-room wall.

'Perhaps, Lady Chillington, you'll be good enough to furnish the plot?'

'I fancy, Sir Edward Ardent, it would be more in my way to act it out.'

She smiled into the footlights; the little gas flares reflected in her pupils. She sensed, more than anything, that moist being known as audience; if she had had any space left in her mind she might have thought: this is when I am most alive, most myself, playing a character in front of an audience. Instead she said, dawdling her lines a little, enjoying herself in the limelight, 'I'll try my hand just the same. I must begin, I believe, with the stage directions.'

*S*tella, standing backstage, changed her weight from one foot to another. Fan was taking her time this evening. Already the performance was running five minutes behind, and it had started over twenty minutes late. It was stiflingly hot backstage, the gas chandelier sucking out all the air. The audience's bodies, garbed and over-dressed, pressed together, added to the stench.

Stella glanced at Max, the mechanic, his hands in heavy leather gloves adjusting the hand-held limelight torch. The light caught on Fan's dress as she turned away. Close up, Stella could see the dress was quite dirty around the hem where it dragged.

'Well,' Fanny said in a loud voice, guaranteed to reach the back seats in the twelve-hundred-seat theatre (it was packed tonight): 'The stage represents a drawing room in Lady Chillington's country house. She is unexpectedly paid a morning call by a gentleman — one Sir Edward Ardent.'

'What — on the stage?' Freddie asked.

Stella noticed that Freddie didn't always articulate his lines as well as Fanny. He didn't throw them. But then he was hardly a professional. She sensed a ripple of unease through the audience.

Fanny would have to work harder to win them back.

'No, no,' Fanny said, moving quickly downstage towards the lights. She spoke directly out into the audience, confidentially. This was her skill — drawing the audience in, speaking to them directly, person to person. 'That is only for your information, to help you to know what to say. Now don't interrupt me, and don't speak until I tell you.'

There was a ripple, a whip-curl of laughter running through the audience. They liked hearing a man being stripped naked by language. Especially in such deliciously perverse circumstances.

'Sir Edward Ardent by name thinks it proper to ride over to Lady Chillington's, under the pretence of a morning call, although it is very evident to her he has some other object lurking behind.'

'How does she know that?'

'I'm writing a play, and I'm not bound to tell more than I like,' Fanny snapped.

'But I want information, madam.'

'You shall soon have more than you want.'

*S*amuel, sitting in the front row of the stalls, gazed up at her. His angle up to the stage was extreme: the bottom quarter of Fan's dress, when she was downstage, was cut off. But this was made up for by the gas flames hidden behind a wooden pelmet, highlighting the moulding on her skirt, her heavily made-up face, so she seemed to be boldly sculptural. He could see her bust moving up and down as she breathed. The quiver of her nostrils. The dilation of her pupils.

And the beads of perspiration on her forehead coming through the thick stage makeup.

Yet Fanny, by sheer willpower, forced a reality on the scene. She dared the audience not to believe.

'Sir Edward,' Fanny's voice was hard as she gazed out into the theatre confidentially, 'like hundreds of other moderately good-looking men, has been humoured by sundry weak women until he fancies himself utterly irresistible.'

The audience burst out into a clatter of laughter.

Frederick, who had been gazing lovingly into a mirror hanging over the mantelpiece on the backdrop, looked over. He had on the false moustache, the dark clothing of a stage villain.

'He may yet prove,' he said, just a little late for his cue.

Fanny threw another glance out there.

Samuel felt his heart hammering. Could she see him? Sense him? At one moment he was sure her eyes had flickered in his direction, seeming to sequin into recognition.

'Don't interrupt! Come, sit beside me.'

Fan patted the seat of an elegant couch. Frederick bowed. Took his seat.

'I can give it in five words,' he said.

'Not fewer?'

'Yes, in three — *I love you.*'

'Stay a minute.' Fanny rose from the couch, wandered downstage. 'Let me clearly understand. Are you carrying on the little drama I began, or are you, Sir Edward Ardent, Bart., in your own proper person, addressing yourself to me, Fanny Chillington, a widow?'

'I hope you don't take me for an actor,' said Lord Frederick Clinton, third son of the Duke of Newcastle.

The audience shouted with laughter. And kept on laughing.

Fanny picked up her fan and looked directly into the audience — a little too archly, thought Stella, who was aware of Billie, a fireman, standing directly behind her. She could feel the heat from his body. She had turned to him once, and in the dark he had nodded to her, almost subliminally. He had placed his hand lightly on the small of her back. She leant back into him, now, relaxing her body. She had made a decision.

'Well, in love affairs,' Fanny continued, 'there is not much difference between a man on and a man off the stage — one is a professional actor, the other is an actor full of false professions.'

Stella felt a light brush of Billie's moustache, then his lips against the back of her neck. The fireman was spooning her. She glanced behind her quickly to see if any of the stagehands had noticed but they were obscured by a backdrop. She bunted into Billie, pushing him off. He pulled her back into him. He came a step closer, pushing into her skirt with his legs.

'You think, then, that truth has no part in love affairs?'

She felt him lifting the weight of her dress up, behind her; she felt the draught, even through the split in her drawers. He was putting his hand, his thumb, into . . .

'Oh yes, it has. I wish it hadn't.'

'Why so?'

Billie was leaning into her, and biting her lightly on the back of the nape of her neck. How did he know she liked this: the tightness of the nerves there, the concentration of explosive power? She lulled back into him. Then she was aware, from high up, of a stagehand, no more than a lad really, looking down at them. She looked up at him directly and he looked down at her. She would not stop it happening.

'Because truth always comes too late,' Fanny said on stage.

'Always?'

'I speak from my own experience.'

'You think all men alike then?'

'Yes, in their disposition to deceive women.'

Stella gave one last intense look at the lad up in the rafters, then, giving in to the pressure from behind her, she eased back into the shadows, away from the coruscating limelight. There would be an empty dressing room probably. Or if not that, then up against a brick wall, down some dusty, shadowy passage — she enjoyed that. She liked everything that was risky, daring, bad. Stella Graham enjoyed life in the theatre.

'*I* was wondering,' Fanny (or Lady Chillington) was saying, 'which I would prefer: a deaf husband or a dumb one.'

'If you allude to me — ?'

'I did not.'

'I could not bear to be deaf, not to hear the liquid music of your voice.'

The audience, obediently, laughed. Fanny wondered for a moment at how different audiences could be: some nights listening acutely, other nights seemingly distant, critical, missing jokes, preoccupied with other things. Fortunately tonight they were blowing hot.

'It's very kind of you to think me so charming. But if you were dumb, you could not tell me so.'

More laughter. Obedient.

'What does it matter?' Frederick came and stood close to Fanny. She looked at him from under her heavy stage makeup. She was sweating, he could see, and he could smell her sweat: rank, high, animal. He liked it. He felt a blaze of adoration for her, for her daring. She was smiling at him a little — or was it for the audience? Fanny was well known for her 'charm', but he could also see, under the paint, by her heavily defined left eyebrow, a small muscle tugging away, urging him not to forget that it was also a play, and an audience was watching.

It was dangerous. Pleasingly — arousingly — dangerous.

The hero of the Lucknow Siege could not forget this. His stage moustache felt a little stiff on his upper lip. He worried that it was coming adrift so he randomly, as it were, touched his mouth, in seeming indecision. He could feel, warm as fresh blood — like the blood he had been drenched in, in the back streets of Lucknow during the madness of the siege — he could feel the attention of the audience bathing him and Fanny.

It was a delicious trick they were playing. It was wonderful. It made him want her. He could hardly wait . . .

'I could lie at your feet . . . ' He said his favourite lines, looking out at her through the mask of his cork-blacked eyes. His lashes felt heavy, thick, as if he were peering through a fencing mask. Sweat was pouring down his face, onto his shirt.

Her eyes were glittering: blind again, he noticed.

'Like a pet dog, with happy eyes to see you, with greedy ears to hear you, and express, by mute devotion, that deep affection I feel for you.'

Fanny, turning her head towards the audience, murmured an aside: 'Hang the fellow — how pleasantly he talks!'

'She's touched!' Freddie threw out as his aside.

Someone up in the gods yelled out, fully participating in the drama, 'I'd say she's been more than touched!' This was followed by crude laughter, whistling and an epidemic of foot-stamping. A few voices — women — called out for silence. Fanny waited then . . .

'There is only one thing I fear, Sir Edward.' She spoke crisply. Asserting her authority. The playhouse sank back into a rapt silence. Only the hiss of gas jets. Slither of her silk. Her dirty stage dress.

'What is it?'

'If you were to become my pet dog . . . '

'Yes?'

The tiniest cliff edge of a pause.

'I'm afraid you would expect me to wash and comb you every day.'

The audience burst into an explosion of laughter. It was relief. There was a happy smattering of applause, and from the pits one or two catcalls and fluting whistles. The foot-stamping took up again.

Joyful anarchy was alight in the air.

Freddie relaxed into the storm. He half smiled to Fanny on the stage but she was blind to him; she almost rebuked him for pausing for a moment, for risking losing his timing. She might almost have said to him: *there is not a moment to lose.* They must, remorselessly, move on towards their climax or they would risk — what? An audience leaving the theatre slightly disappointed, unwilling to come back, telling their acquaintances it wasn't worth the effort. The mirage might crumble, and it was there that danger lay.

And there was danger.

If the illusion crumbled.

So Fanny pushed on, almost before the audience had settled. She was implacable, this evening, she was all brilliance.

'Love delights in tormenting; women are weak creatures; men are full of deceit.'

Backstage, Stella's consort was rising to a soundless climax. He was embedded in her clothes, the marvellous cloth texture splayed all around him while he drove into her, hard, remorseless. Stell pushed back into him, fighting him, rising to his percussion, willing him to accelerate. She curled her mouth around so that he, leaning into her panting mouth, kissed her rapturously as he grunted, shoving hard into her, rising into his orgasm.

'I am the most devoted of your slaves.'

'I'm sorry to hear it: the best slaves make the worst masters.'

'I'll promise anything.'

The lad up in the rafters was watching, dividing his attention between the drama happening on the stage and the divertissement off.

'*I* am your slave. I beg you — make trial of your power.'

Frederick gazed at Fan. She made a small deflective action.

'All right. Fetch my bonnet and shawl.'

Freddie moved downstage, to a chair.

'Now put them on,' Fanny commanded.

Fred looked out into the audience a moment.

The house had fallen silent. Completely.

He lifted up his own hat.

'No,' Fannie said. 'Not your hat. My bonnet.'

Freddie to the audience: '*Not your bonnet!*'

A man in the row behind Samuel burst out into hysterical laughter. Samuel felt prickles on his neck. Red-hot needles. He felt, at the same time, a slither of sweat down from his armpits. The sweat trickled, tickled down his body. He could not quite explain his loss of self — even, if he put it to himself rationally, his fascination. Why was he there? Why was he — joyfully — losing himself?

Just at the perimeter of his mind he heard the name *Ursula* echo, then disappear, burnt by the lights.

Freddie moved down the stage to the sofa, picked up some women's clothes — a shawl furred around the edges with fluttering feathers. Plus Fanny's bonnet, a particularly lavishly made miniature castle of trailing feather, swaying ribbon, shimmering veil.

'Now put them both on,' Fanny commanded.

This set off ripple after ripple of laughs, in mocking disbelief. The laughter rose, then deepened.

'Yes, and the shawl,' Fanny said in a hard voice.

Lord Frederick Clinton, an honoured veteran of the Indian wars, and until recently a Member of Parliament, put on the bonnet and awkwardly placed the pretty shawl over his morning suit.

The audience howled. And stamped.

There was a kind of hysteria in the air, a sexual tension.

'Good. Now give me your hat,' Fanny said, her hand held out.

'What next, I wonder?'

Fanny stood there, an improbable top hat placed at a rakish angle atop the mountain of her false curls.

'Now, sir,' she said, moving a little downstage and looking out into the audience — Samuel frankly adored her at this moment: her power, the strength of her command. 'According to your own modest account, ladies have been making love to you all your life. I am curious to see how a lady looks when she so demeans herself.'

Frederick stood there, wearing the ridiculously feminine clothes.

'Fancy me the fascinating man,' Fan said directly to the audience, cocking her top hat, 'that you evidently fancy yourself. Down on your knees and — I must leave the rest up to you.'

Lord Frederick, emasculated, made ludicrous, and playing the part with a bewildered charm, sank to his knees.

'If I must. There. Hear me from down here, you captivating tyrant.'

Fanny still spoke directly out to the audience — to Samuel himself, he felt: 'I have him down at last, and I'll keep him at my feet.'

She dug the pointed toe of a high-heeled boot into his chest.

'I entreat you,' Lord Frederick pleaded from beneath his bonnet, 'to relieve me from a position that is not only painful' — she dug her heel in — 'but extremely inconvenient.' A pause. 'Do you love me?'

Fanny made a face. She was riding the wave now; she was dazzling in her insouciance. She wrenched the hat off, sent it careering off on a wild arc, into the wings. She turned her back.

'You do not love me, then?' Lord Frederick said.

'No. I was shamming.'

Lord Frederick rose to his feet and threw the bonnet and shawl onto the dirty stage floor.

'Well so was I.'

As an aside he said, 'I'm afraid all this will make me look ridiculous.'

'No more than you usually do,' Fanny said, turning about, her voice cold. They both were bathed in sweat now, dripping.

'There is but one way to make it bearable!' Lord Frederick cried.

'And that is . . . ?'

Lord Frederick caught Fanny's hand and pulled her towards the front of the stage. The closer he got, the more he could see out there. Beyond the little flickering flare of gas he caught sight of an adoring face staring up at Fanny — surely it was that young lovesick puppy? His face was carved into glee, into the release of suspense, forgetfulness.

'Union is strength,' he enunciated clearly.

He picked up Fanny's hand — it was slippery, almost slithery under his grasp. He carried it to his lips. Somewhere out there a man groaned. Others keened with laughter.

'Let us be married.' Frederick always said this line with particular emphasis, almost nobility. He kissed Fan's hand again and, holding it, stared into her eyes. 'And share the ridicule between us.'

Fanny, the footlights making her face appear almost burnished, smiled up at him.

'A very handsome offer,' she said, curtsying low. Frederick watched nervously as the edge of her dress swayed towards the gas-lights, nestled near the flame. 'Let half your ridicule be my marriage settlement.'

He bowed as low.

The audience clapped, screamed, cheered. The very floor seemed to shake with foot-stamping. There was a storm of whistling.

Fanny once again waited for the audience to settle.

'It seems that, like schoolboys, we have played until we have become in earnest,' said Fanny, née Ernest Boulton. Then, turning to the audience with an almost sneering yet triumphant smile (yet wasn't there also something infinitely succumbing about it — something pleading, winsome, coy almost?), she said ,'Well so be it! And let us hope that our friends — though they may laugh at us — will enjoy, another evening, some pleasant memory of — *A Morning Call.*'

And as the curtain fell, and the audience rose into a tumult of applause, Ernest Boulton and Lord Frederick Clinton kissed.

*S*amuel walked to the station through the night. He felt as if he had drunk something so powerful he had lost all his senses. He had not gone backstage. Didn't know what to say. Couldn't trust himself. All his earlier — raw — sense of hurt, of being gulled (if what Fanny's note said was true), had been overturned by the sheer daunting power of her performance on the stage. He was in love with her. He was in love — with all the performance involved in being her.

He did not think — did not allow his mind to hover — on any sexual specifics. He felt sure Fanny was enough of a lady not to, well . . .

(The fact that he was a virgin himself did not help.)

He was bewitched.

But then the words that man had yelled in the supper club came back. Surely these were lies? A perhaps understandable confusion . . .

It did not make sense.

As he walked further and further into the night, Samuel, drunk and dazed, argued with himself, tried to make sense of the conundrum. All the time seeing on stage that brilliantly lime-lit creature, her shimmering essence seeming to block out every question, just as the footlights were prevented by a bar of wood from dazzling the eyes of the onlookers: the audience.

Is that what he was?

A member of the audience?

Her audience?

What was true, real, life?

To see is to believe.

He would like to meet — not Fanny, but Ernest. Perhaps this would persuade him. Or was Ernest a hermaphrodite? He had read about these in an encyclopaedia but he wasn't sure if they were fabulous creatures, like sirens and unicorns.

Or is that what Fanny actually was?

Something fabulous.

He felt too confused to answer this.

He kept on walking. He must walk his drunkenness off. He must walk off his daze.

'*I*t ain't no use, missy. We don't allow nobody backstage.'

Eliza was standing at the stage door. She had not gone to the performance.

Could not afford to. She had heard, however, the roar of laughter, the great halo of an audience's warm applause. Then they had poured out, glistening, golden, whispering, talking — crowding around to buy a carte-de-visite of what the barker rashly anointed 'one of the True Eight Wonders of the World!'.

She had waited.

Until she could wait no more.

'Sorry, Miss. Strict orders. But the lovely lady 'erself will probably be slipping out soon. The marvellous and miraculous Mister–Missus Boulton.'

Eliza glanced at the stagehand, then spontaneously she made a bolt past him, through the door. He caught her arm, laughing.

'Steady on.' He dragged her back. 'You're quite some fan.'

She stood on his foot, hard.

'I work for Miss Fanny, you fool.'

He cursed her, let her hand go. She slipped past him into the dark.

Miss Stella was coming down towards her, arranging her wrap around her shoulders. She seemed deeply thoughtful — or maybe it was just the way her head was inclined. The light was behind her. She seemed some strange phantasmagorical creature moving into light, forming, unforming.

Stella looked up, startled, when Eliza reached out a hand and touched her tentatively. She shrank back.

'Oh, Lord, Lizzie. I thought you were a ghost!'

Stella laughed a loud, masculine laugh. Her face was sweaty with makeup. Her eyes, sexual and frank, looked up at Eliza.

'What is it, pet? You look like someone's walked over your grave.'

'I want to speak to Miss Fanny.'

Stell waited for the servant girl to go on, to explain. Was annoyed when, instead, the little slattern closed her lips and looked over her shoulder.

'Her ladyship's in there.'

Stell indicated with her head the dim darkness of the corridor behind her. There was a light on further down the passageway.

'You can't miss her. She's the only girl around.'

*E*liza came upon Fanny without her wig. For a moment she didn't know quite what to call her. Fanny looked up brightly into the mirror and seemed taken aback. But pleased.

'Lizzie, my pearl, what are you doing *here*?'

Eliza glanced behind her.

'I thought it was important, mum.'

'What was?'

'That I come. I've got some private *intelligence*.'

The way Eliza said the word, her whole air of importance, tugged a smile onto Fanny's face. She was putting on a fresh face for the evening's entertainment. It was a costume ball at which she would meet up with many of her friends. Admirers. The room was packed with her bouquets. She looked for a moment at Eliza in the mirror as she applied her eyebrow.

'What intelligence, dearest?'

Eliza closed the door. She came to the side of the mirror so she looked down upon Miss Fanny's face, not at a reflection. But Fanny appeared to be entranced with her own doings in the glass. Only for one second did her eyes slide to Eliza's face. She registered the servant girl's seriousness.

'Well, you know how my friend Maryanne's young man is in the force?'

Fanny's hand paused.

'Not really, but yes . . .'

'He says you is being watched. He says . . .' and here Eliza paused. She felt herself breathless, as if dissolving through the floor. She needed a glass of water. She felt herself to be a fool.

'Watched?' Fanny laughed. 'In what way? I hope he is paying. Where does he sit? In the gallery? Does it give the best view? And what does he think of my performance?'

Fanny was at an important moment in engineering her eyebrow line. The arch. It was important, when off the stage, not to put eyebrows on too thickly. Ernest didn't want people to get the wrong impression. He was very much a lady, not some common drab.

'It is important,' Eliza breathed. 'It is . . .' She searched for the right word.

She wanted to say dangerous. She wanted to say — to this moth-like creature, with her late hours, and gauzy dreams, her beautiful singing voice, her artful movement all over the stage, her male essence — Eliza wanted to say: *beware, beware, beware.*

But Fanny was standing up, was dusting down her dress.

'Eliza, dear, tell me if my dress is done up the back, will you be a darling?'

Eliza knew she was being dismissed.

She obediently inspected the tiny little bone buttons up Fanny's back.

'Mr Ernest, sir. I would not come all this way . . . It is a message.'

Eliza stood there, impressive, immovable.

Fanny had cocked her head to the side. She was sliding in the jewelled earrings that Eliza found so fascinating — the bejewelled flies, the ones with the huge glinting pigeon-blood rubies.

Fanny consulted the mirror.

'Why would we be "being watched"? We have done nothing wrong. We are actors upon the stage. There is no rule — is there? — against actors playing a part?'

Eliza did not know what to say. She fumbled. She did not want Miss Fanny — Mr Boulton, he of the impressive voice and presence on the stage — to think she was overstepping the mark.

'I wouldn't know about that, mum,' was all she could say, subtly defeated. But then she caught hold of Fanny's — Ernest's — hand.

'Be careful, mum. Be careful,' she said earnestly.

Fanny looked at Eliza intently for a moment, then some kind of curtain, gauze, scrim seemed to interpose. She smiled — was it even a little sadly? — then she rustled around and pressed a coin in Eliza's hand.

'This is for you, my dear. Take a cab home. We can't have a young lady like you wandering the streets at all hours, can we?'

And she laughed a lovely silvery breeze of laughter as she departed.

*I*t was getting on for five in the morning. Stell and Fan and Fred were getting out of their cab in Southampton Street. London had reached that peculiar moment of almost magical stillness. Stell was smothering laughter as Fan tried to hush her, which sent Stell off into further repercussions of laughter. She had been telling them about Billie, backstage, and about how he had declared his love for her so fervently during the act. But the moment it was over he recalled himself to his dignity, to his little wife back at home in Wandsworth, and by the time his trousers were buttoned he hardly knew who Stella was any more. He left her on her own, to complete her own dressing. This had been a lonely moment for Stella: an almost contemplative, philosophical moment. So this is the end product of — that? His echoing footsteps were all she had left, as further out there, on the stage, there had been an outbreak of ridiculing laughter. It must be, she had thought at the time, the bonnet scene.

She had gone and found a bucket of cold water, sponged herself down. The dirty devil had stained her petticoat. She had scrubbed it a little, rinsed out the water. Was this the reality of her life? A small stain, a tiny continent of incontinence? Covered with a silk overdress?

But at that hour in the morning she had reversed the defeat, proclaimed her own victory through ridicule. She talked of the tenderness of his foreskin, his mumbling protestations of 'amour', of how he would like to set her up in a little cottage in the countryside, a bower of flowers, just the two of them. It all appeared — in Stell's retelling — hilarious, stupid, absurd, an adventure. Freddie had paid the cabman, who listened in silence to the end of Stell's soliloquy.

Freddie had got the latch-key out of Fan's purse.

Fan was sitting on the upstairs step, looking out at the night. She seemed lost in contemplation.

It was then that she said, as Freddie bent down to help her to her feet, 'We made lots of lovely loot tonight. Let's spend it, Freddie. Let's blow the lot. Let's all go — let's all go to Paris!'

Shrinkage

'We ain't got no tin. And we sure as hell ain't got no paper.'

Lord Frederick Clinton stood there, pulling out his pockets comically, looking back at Ernest, grinning.

They were back from Paris. Penniless.

Ernest made a small grimace, walked away from him to the window and looked out, down at the busy pavement of Southampton Street.

Lord Frederick's name was no longer much good for anything, not since his bankruptcy. The rooms at Southampton Street had been paid for, a month in advance, and there were also the rooms at Wakefield Street, which Fan's mother unknowingly paid for and had been doing so for several years.

They had been blown back to London on an overdraft of extravagance, in a seedy half-awake state of exhaustion, somnolence. Stell had declared she needed a month to sleep, to 'get over' Paris. She and Fan had had a little altercation at one point on the train back to London — each put it down to the tiredness they felt, the over-stimulation.

They had put up at a discreet little hotel in the centre of Paris and they had not stopped until they had drained the cup, as Freddie put it, to the final, bitter dregs.

It was here that Fred introduced his favourite saying: 'If you're born to hang, you'll never drown.'

Yet something else had happened in Paris. Some change had come over their relationships: that of Stella and Fanny, and Fanny and Lord Frederick. Some basic truth about themselves had been announced. Like a glass falling to its level, each one had glimpsed in the other some essential, irreducible being, some need that was animal, pure and impure. Perhaps this was honest? Yet honesty can be an exhausting state to live in, to live with.

They were driven back to London by the very exploration of their own appetites. Frederick Clinton had learnt about himself in Paris many years before: he knew names, places. He could take his two companions there. Paris was superior to London in the extremity of its vice — or was it pleasure? Besides, Fanny and Stella were unknown in the epicentre of fashion. They had much to lose, and nobody to witness their loss. They learnt how provincial they were, how contained: rapturously, yet a little painfully also, it must be admitted, they sold off parts of themselves, their past beings.

They came back to London significantly changed.

And penniless.

'Can't you ask your aunt?'

Ernest was referring to the Countess of ——, Frederick's favourite source of a 'loan'.

'She says she's skint also. Her old man keeps her on a pretty tight rein. Besides, she stood me for my last lot of paper.'

Freddie grinned a little ineffectually, as if it were all a kind of joke. A thirty-thousand-pound one: the amount of his bankruptcy.

Ernest looked back over at his lover. Sighed.

Frederick had a sleepwalker's face, extremely pale. The most significant aspect of it was the architecture of his nose. His eyes were a faded kind of blue-grey, almost colourless, except at certain moments of excitement or cruelty. He was always minimally well-dressed. Or had been. By now, a year after the public humiliation of his bankruptcy — 'my little bit of bother' as he liked to call it — his clothes had a slightly more suspect, lived-in look. There was a look of incipient dirt about his collars. But he was the son of a duke nonetheless, and he could — at least in the immediate past — walk into the drawing rooms of the very best people in London. He still could, with many of them. What was a bankruptcy to them? Blood was what was important to Freddie's relations, to the people he had hitherto moved among. He had almost completely black hair, thick and lustrous, like the fur of some nocturnal animal. He was a debauched young man, who looked to others to provide his momentum, and his money. But he wasn't unhappy. Happiness was not a notion he possessed. It was beside the point. The real point was his ability to continue his life of pleasure. And he knew himself to be fortunate to have met up with Fanny. Who was his real wife. Or, if the truth be told, he was actually less Fanny's husband than Fanny's wife. But this was so contrary to appearances that nobody guessed it.

'Didn't we have fun in Paris?' he asked now.

'I'm more concerned with our time in London.'

Ernest's voice had a dangerous tone in it. He looked over at the son of the Duke of Newcastle and felt a kind of hopelessness mixed with anger.

'Well, I guess that means I have to make a visit home to my mother.'

Ernest's tone was tart. Depressed.

'Come off it, Fan. You knew it was always going to be difficult when we got back.'

Ernest said nothing, but went out the door. He didn't so much slam it as let it fall to. Freddie followed after her, quickly.

'Fan — Ernest?'

Ernest's steps down the stairwell were his answer, followed by the definite slam of the street door.

*F*reddie waited a moment, then considered his options. He could no longer go to his club — he owed so much at cards now it was better to keep a low profile. He had always in the past been able to find a berth with his aunt, the Countess, but she herself had been told in no uncertain terms by her husband that it did not help the family when they were trying to 'unload' — her husband's words — two rather unpretty daughters who had been on the market through three entire seasons.

Lord Frederick did not like to skulk, or go in up back stairs. But when times were tough he knew what side his bread was buttered on, and he was now pretty much reliant on what Fanny could pull.

Of course the handle helped, particularly with unsuspecting customers. But even in a town as big as London a man's name could become a byword. For not exactly probity. For being — how shall we put it? — somewhat less than trustworthy. Perhaps that was how he had come to fall in with two such extraordinary creatures as Fanny and Stella. Freddie counted it as good luck. They were such sharp 'uns, such lookers, such mashers, such extraordinary good gels that he felt, to a certain extent, protected.

When he was with them, everything was back to being a lark, such fun, such a frolic. He always became a little sad, a little grey, when things slowed down into talk of pounds and pence. He always got a little grey around the gills, as if he was back in the back streets of Lucknow, fighting hand to hand. Some kind of insanity had been unloosed then. Some kind of feral understanding of life — of kill or be killed. Some deadening of a moral nerve had occurred in those bloody streets. He had fought in the Lucknow Siege, but only one or two people knew the exact fact of whether, at a certain point, he fought — or ran. Whether he advanced, was left abandoned — or fled. It was all chaos, it was all madness, almost literal madness. That he had survived was the maddest thing of all. And after that, in some senses, he no longer cared.

Except of course for pleasure, burying himself in it as deeply as was humanly possible. For not feeling anything. For getting drunk as often as possible, for as long as possible. For feeling nothing. For abandoning feeling.

And then, at some loathsome stockbrokers' dinner he'd come across the most marvellous discovery of all, which was an *actress*, and what was even more marvellous was that this actress — pretty, sexual, acute, alive — was not an actress at all but a man. Under the dress, a prick. And pretty impressive equipage too. It was all quite extraordinary, the ruse, the trick, the mirage of it. It tickled his fancy. It was something he'd never tried before. They had left together, but not quite together. Some of them, the rowdiest, had gone to another drinking place after the extra-ordinarily boring dinner. Then they had rushed off, some of them — the actress included — to one of the finishes. There he had found himself roaringly drunk making love to the pretty little thing. There he had found himself supplicant and begging her to take him. There he had found himself with someone who would take him. Take him. Take him for all he was worth, which he knew, privately, was nothing. So maybe it was the best joke of all, to have this little actress, who was actually someone with a prick, a very big prick, take him, the son of a duke, who was actually worth nothing at all.

There was always a feeling of oppression attached to approaching his mother's house in Paddington. Perhaps it was the fact Ernest only ever went there when he needed something. Was beaten back there.

Or was it, he asked himself, breathing shallowly in little gulps of air, the fact that the streets at the back of Paddington Station were so dreary? There was no style here, no imagination: nothing but a careful, watchful sense of pounds and pence.

He always seemed to shrink when he came back here. He felt he was returning to some other, previous life — an uncomfortable one.

He had set out from here as a clerk in a bank. This was who Ernest Boulton once was. Not that he ever felt he was, exactly, a clerk in the London and County Bank, in the city. He could hardly do his job properly anyway. Live up to it. He spent his days in a daze, a dream, one part of him seeming to shrivel and die, lacking oxygen.

He came closer to his parents' house: No 23 Shirland Road, Paddington.

It was no different from any of the other porticoed houses, except the curtains were a different colour. He went up to the front door (by now he had shrunk down into a manikin so small he could hardly climb the Portland cement steps); he reached up and slid his key into the lock.

But Agnes had pounced and pulled the door back. She was dusting the hall — her story.

Ernest rehearsed his air of sparkling charm, as if he were somehow visiting someone star-struck. He smiled at her, and asked her how she was keeping and whether her sister was keeping well in Scarborough. (The sister who had seen Ernest in *A Morning Call* and written a delirious letter about Master Ernest being 'almost completely unbelievable' as Miss Fanny.)

Agnes, who had known him since he was eight, was impervious to his charm, its perfume even seemed to stink a little. While her features smiled a little grimly, as if chipped into plaster, her soul stayed cool, untouched, watchful. Ernest got the dispiriting sense she did not like him — what he had become. She was the oldest servant in the house. The only servant in the house, if you did not count the boy below stairs and the slattern who did the cooking.

'She's waiting for you, Master Ernest. She's always waiting for you,' Agnes said as she climbed, arduously, the old, faintly dirty stairs up to the drawing-room floor.

Ernest had seen a nudge of curtain by the second window that indicated his mother — seated perennially by the window — had seen him.

This depressed him as nothing else.

He felt he was caught in a play, the script of which he had read many years ago. He knew every line, he no longer needed to act. He wished, in a way, only to pass to the final lines.

Mother: Here, dear boy (passing some coin). But, please, I beg of you ...

Son: I know, Mother dear. My brother must not know, and I must be careful that I spend it only on what we agreed.

Mother (turning her head away, looking a little sad, but defiantly gay):

Well, dear, and what other news do you bring me?

They were sitting down, not too far apart, and Agnes had placed the burningly hot teapot within his mother's reach.

'You look too thin, darling,' his mother was saying as she poured. Her hand seemed to be shaking a little.

He laughed — he did not know why. She looked at him more closely then, and put the teapot down carefully.

He was not looking well. He had woken late in the morning — very late in the morning, if the truth be told — after a seedy and riotous night that had delivered . . . nothing. There were nights like that. When you set out with the best intentions, hoping you'd be delivered into some nirvana, instead of which you ended up treading some circle of hell, from the Strand to Evans, from the Bal Masqué at Highbury Barn to the Globe restaurant in Coventry Street, on to the Coal Hole in Maiden Lane, and then . . . one of the little clubs around the Haymarket, and then . . .

The night had taken his and Freddie's last coin. They had had an argument, a raw and ugly argument, because both knew the rent was due at Wakefield Street. In fact, it had been overdue for the past month — but the landlady there had delivered them a deadline. 'Lord or no lord,' she had said, 'I want my rent.'

Ernest had tried all his Fanny charms — Fanny seemed to possess so many more charms than Ernest, it was true — but she had stayed as obdurately unimpressed as Agnes opening his parents' front door, knowing he graced their home for one reason only: money.

His mother, too, Ernest knew, knew that. She had that patient, subtly wounded look on her face.

'But tell me, dear, when are you performing *A Morning Call* again? There are other appointments on the horizon?'

Ernest carelessly lied.

He knew what his mother wanted, and he delivered it to her. She always liked to know who had sponsored Ernest and Frederick's performances. (She had a marker in *Debrett's* under the Newcastle, but it wounded her when her acquaintances made tart retorts about 'tarnished' nobility.)

Mrs Prowse, whose husband had been a plasterer in Bristol — she was sure of this — had had the nerve to inquire, seemingly innocently, 'And is Lord Frederick the son of Lady Mary Hamilton by any chance?'

Mrs Boulton had flinched, for she knew what was coming next.

'The lady who appeared,' and here the thrust would be delivered *sotto voce*, which ensured that everyone around them at the card table listened — 'the lady who appeared in the *divorce* court? An adulteress by law?'

Worse was to come. 'The same as the aunt, Lady Jane Seymour Douglas. Both fallen from the high state of womanly virtue. They seem a somewhat *dubious* family.'

Mrs Boulton had had to rally. Fanny was not her daughter for nothing, as it were.

'They live differently from you and me,' she had said boldly.

But Mrs Prowse had said, 'Pray tell me, though, do we not share the same God? Stand before the same altar on the Judgement Day?' Shaking her black fringes, fingering her gnarled ivory cross, replete with coral thorns. (She had worn the thorns smooth, worn them down to nubs, to worry-beads.)

Mrs Boulton found after that that it was better to keep Lord Frederick out of the conversation.

She pushed her perennial fruitcake towards her son.

Ernest forced himself, as if it was some kind of penance, to have a second — large — piece of the cake, even though it was more than seven years since he had, in fact, even liked it. It was the taste of a growing boy, not an epicene whose evenings were spent on alcohol, opiates and other unnamed substances.

He felt a wave of nausea overtake him. He was still hung over.

'Dear? Are you well?'

His mother's mittened hand, cloaked in black needlework and jet, pushed his cup towards him.

He looked down, with a sudden vertigo of nausea, at the milky tea swinging to and fro. He had lost the thread. How they were connected.

Yes, their forthcoming performances.

'Mr Caldicott has booked us into the Royal at Scarborough again. Before that, we do some return nights at Chelmsford.'

He tried not to yawn.

'I'm not sure — ' His mother looked self-consciously decisive for a moment. 'I am not sure, Ernest, that I exactly approve of you taking to the boards. In such a, well, *public* manner.'

She managed to make the word 'public' sound scandalous.

He looked at her evenly. Venomously.

At times she found it hard to see in him that adorable little boy who had run to her and bunted his curls into her thigh, gurgling with laughter and seeming to take it for granted that the rest of his life would be a heaven in which he was always adored. She had had misgivings then. Some. Her husband had more. 'He must harden up. Life is not a gift to be accepted glibly. He must learn to fight.' He had arranged boxing lessons but Ernest had refused to go.

Where had he gone, that cherub with the lovely gilded hair? Who loved playing maidens' parts?

'Mother,' this rather supercilious wasted-looking ephebe was saying to her — lecturing her, 'Mother,' he was saying in a bored-sounding voice, 'it is all too highly respectable for words. Do you think a man of Lord Frederick's standing would countenance anything low?'

This was by way of a challenge.

Mrs Boulton felt her throat grow inchoate, choked with self-doubt. Wasn't he actually a bankrupt? The nephew and son respectively of two adulteresses shamed by the law? Hadn't he contracted a scandalous marriage with a Scottish actress? And been dunned by everyone, from a jeweller to his very washerwoman, in the public courts? For a scandalously enormous sum?

She had the dreadful sensation, this oppressively still summer afternoon, of more foreboding than she had ever had before.

Ernest had stopped being a bank clerk over three years ago. How exactly he lived, she no longer quite knew. But every so often there were these emergency calls.

It was all so strange — this exchange of an indifferent, dull clerk for the magnificent creature on stage who was Fanny. (She herself had gone to look at a performance. He had never asked her. She had taken herself off, alone, one evening. She had sat in the stalls, but far enough back for him not to see her. She had felt almost sick with apprehension. Then, when the emotion of the packed crowd took over, she had felt an odd somersault of the emotions. She felt — hectically — proud. She had told the person beside her, *that is my son*. It was only as the word passed out of her mouth — *son* — that she sensed how odd it was. But everyone adored the stage, loved illusion, welcomed the trance that, for an hour or so, lifted them away from the anxieties of life. And what better than this principal boy — no, not that term — but what better than someone mimicking another sex altogether: what could be more amusing?)

She had counted the bouquets. Fifteen in all, flung on the stage, Fanny herself graciously sinking into the deepest curtsy, with all the arts of a Sarah Siddons or Fanny Kemble (was that, Mrs Boulton wondered, the source of her son's improbable name?) She herself had always adored the theatre, and like practically every family in the land they had played home charades. (*Lacy's Home Plays, An Inexhaustible Source of Harmless Amusement, Adapted to all Stations & Locations, to Any Age and Either Sex.*) From the beginning Ernest had specialised in playing maidens. (His brother had always played King Arthur or Sir Lancelot.) From this fantasy, this *trick*, her son was now making a living.

Or not making a living.

She knew what his visit portended. There was no pretence any more, at hectic news. His visits were eviscerated of all this fancy business. She had the sense of looking at a bare theatre, a stage struck back to the rudest essentials.

Her thoughts were drifting, as were her son's. She glanced at him, caught him looking down, baffled, exhausted: not even trying to act triumphant. She longed, in this moment, to reach across the crumbs of the tea table, the half-eaten slice of fruitcake, to touch him. To reach for his hand. To bring his body towards her, nurture him.

Instead the door opened and Agnes came in, a little like a stage maid except she was more dilatory, even predatory, as if Mrs Boulton and her son were the extras. Agnes's old brown eyes assessed the damage of the afternoon. Five pounds at the very least, she thought. Probably a tenner. Maybe even more, by the brackish silence of the drawing room. All she could hear was the tick of the clock, and the crack of a bone in Mrs Boulton's neck as she turned to look at her.

'Yes . . . ' she said, her throat dry. 'More hot water, Agnes.'

Mrs Boulton was desperate for the maid to disappear. She did not like Agnes gazing at this wreck of a son. But, as if coming alive before the merest whiff of an audience, Ernest straightened, tautened, let out a gulp of a laugh and asked whether Agnes would like tickets to the Adelphi next Sunday. He had a pair — or he could at least have a pair sent out. If she wanted.

It was the same old same old. Lure, deceit, in exchange for cash.

'We've been to Paris,' Ernest then said in a seemingly bored, distant voice. Offhand. His mother jumped. Spilt her tea.

'Paris!'

'There is no rule, Mother, that one can only go to Paris once in a lifetime.' Then, as if hearing his own haughty tone and the damage it could do, he smiled, and said, 'Well, I don't think there is.'

His mother smiled. Perhaps things were a little better than . . . ?

Ernest waited for the door to close.

'I wondered, Mother —'

She looked at him. Once, she would have reached out beside her to the coins hidden in a small bag on her chaise. She would have put it in his hands, closing the fingers around it, bidding him to keep silent. As if this exchange were something sacred between understanding mother and forgiven son. But now, when it had all worn dangerously thin, she had a hankering to hear what he might plead.

'I wondered Mother, if you could possibly lend me — '

'*Lend* you!'

This had come out wrong. Too acidic. She who longed, only, to give him everything. If only he . . .

He had taken fright. She saw that. The blood had drained from his face. He was back to being Ernest the bank clerk, frightened before the start of each working day. But something happened — and in this was the change from the old Ernest, perhaps. He came back at her. He looked at her steadily, even serenely.

'Yes, Mother, indeed. Lend me. A temporary inconvenience. I swear of course I will repay. But I would be most grateful . . . '

He actually leant across the afternoon tea table, over the dismembered cake, and — in what she instantly assessed as a stage gesture — took her hand and kissed the fingertips. This was foreign muck. This was some affectation picked up in Paris.

'But what exactly' — she pulled her hand back and as if in consolation of a threatened self, placed her other hand over the just-kissed one. She was shocked at how cold her own flesh was. How icy. Unkissed — 'But what exactly is the great attraction of Paris?'

He looked at her with pitying eyes.

'The French stage is ahead of our own in matters of illusion.'

She looked at him, torn between believing what he wished her to believe, and her own knowledge that it was persiflage. She blinked.

'Oh, Mother, *please.*'

This last was said so urgently, so openly — so rawly — that she knew she was hearing the truth. He desperately needed some cash.

At this point the door opened again, and Agnes advanced towards the waning light and placed the teapot down.

'Is that all, m'lady?'

She turned, glancing closely at the state of play. She diagnosed that it was the crucial moment. She would linger outside, beside a door only partially closed.

As if to outstep her, Ernest's mother speedily — it was extraordinary how fast this seemingly inert, tepid creature could move — leant forward over the tea table and placed by Ernest's thigh a small bag of coin. He leant his flesh into it, nudging it as if to test its weight. Mother and son kept looking at each other as if nothing had happened.

'It is all I can afford,' his mother said to him, in a low, hurried voice.

'Mother,' the son said in the same low tone, 'I am so deeply — deeply — grateful. It is only a — '

But she raised her hand.

'Please,' she said. Her tone was firmer. 'Please, Ernest. Don't.'

*H*e counted the coins on his way back to the station. Not a bad haul. At least it would cover the rent. Make do.

He could remember when the going was good, and Freddie had bought him the earrings.

This was at the beginning of their affair. When Frederick's title still had, as it were, some power over her, over Fanny. When she believed. Frederick had got up first, and he had asked her if she wanted — cared to come with him. A surprise. Oh, nothing much. A canter up the Arcade.

She had been wary. The Arcade was known — as a place. No really respectable woman spent much time there. But Freddie was at his most seductively elusive, most sweetly insistent, his marbled grey eyes glinting at her. He was kissing her knuckles, pushing himself into her as if he wanted, all over again, to begin again . . .

They were in love then, or what counts for being in love.

That is to say, they cast themselves as two lovers in love. And perhaps — who knows? — they were.

He took her to Burlington Arcade. He had asked her to choose something. Some little bauble. This was before the bankruptcy of course. (A fortnight before.)

'Choose what you want, Fanny dear.'

Fanny was aware of the jeweller looking at her, intensely, closely. He looked at her over his half-glasses, his naked eye passing over Fanny's face and then staring straight into her pupil.

She was not sure if he recognised her. There had been that upsetting incident . . . She and Stell had been hustled out of the Arcade — physically manhandled — by that absurd beadle, that old stinking drunk who seemed to think he was something escaped from a Dickens tale. With all his toggery and frogging. Huffing and puffing about how 'we don't want types like you round here'.

Stell said later you had to grease his palm.

'Law knows,' she said, 'every whore in London uses the upstairs rooms when she wants to do a little jiggery-pokery.'

Fanny, standing in the shop, lightly veiled, had a sense the jeweller did recognise her. Saw through her defences.

But Lord Frederick, son of the Duke of Newcastle, was paying.

The man had bowed before Frederick, been unctuously accommodating. She had flown, as it were, in an aerial balloon over all the sparkling gems in the display. (At one point the jeweller had leant forward, and pressing a button, had revolved an entire stand from the window into the hushed shop. Fan had caught a glimpse of Eileen, an old drab who used to tread the boards in Drury Lane. There she was, coughing into a stained kerchief. Fan quickly looked away.)

The shop was so pleasantly silent, immured in seemingly expensive tissues of soundlessness.

The jeweller had got up and closed the door.

'Um,' said Fan, quite dumb with pleasure.

She liked the Egyptian-style jewels. There was a bracelet, heavy with twenty-two carat gold, a cabochon — garnet? Or could it actually be a ruby? — mounted on the top, surrounded by niello-work. Fan pretended this was what she was interested in, all the while keeping an eye trained on what she actually wanted.

Fred stood at the window looking out, whistling under his breath.

The jeweller had become quite intense. Intimate. His face was very close to Fan's. She hoped her makeup . . . her voice . . .

'Madam, if you want to try on this bracelet? The garnet has a *millegrain* setting that sets off the stone, I feel, particularly well.'

Fan exposed her wrist, placed the bracelet on, looked at it. Asked Fred what he thought.

'Whatever you want, my dear.'

'What about . . . '

Seemingly at the last moment she had pointed to the earrings. Made in the shape of flies. Insects were the *dernier cri* of fashion at the moment. Everyone had gone mad for them. Egyptian jewellery was so passé. A woman was barely alive unless she had a butterfly, a bejewelled praying mantis. But a fly! What a delightful illusion, what an absurdly expensive trifle. Only the truly wealthy would be enticed by something so — ghastly. A household pest. Rendered rare by stone.

'How many carats?'

This was Freddie, who had drifted back from the window and was standing behind Fan, pressing his leg into the back of her dress so the bustle slid sideways.

He pressed in there obscenely, intent, as if reminding her . . .

The jeweller — his eyeglass in — said the ruby was from Burma, was unflawed and was of the very highest quality. It was more than two carats. Its colour was extraordinary. So clear and of such depth and colour. He would venture his lordship would not find a finer stone this side of India.

There was that pause, that pause that often occurs before sexual action. It is duplicated in shopping, for the obvious reason.

'Yes,' said Fan, staring into the little mirror with the silvered frame. She turned from left to right, admiring the bejewelled earrings as they swung in her lobes.

'This is what I want, Freddie.'

So he had bought them.

'*L*ook!'

Ernest was as bad-tempered as he always was when he came back from Paddington.

Frederick knew to be careful. But he couldn't help himself.

'I say, Fan darling. Look!'

He was standing by the window, rocking back and forth on the heels of his shoes, a cheroot in his mouth, his hands deep in his pockets. Face a mask of glee.

Ernest was sitting on the little low green-striped sofa, massaging his toes. He looked up. He had a headache.

'What.'

His voice hardly had a question in it.

'There's some cove out here, watching the place. I'm sure of it.'

Fred took a deep breath in on his cheroot, which he held clamped between his teeth. He didn't take it out even when he spoke. He breathed out a deep blue fan of smoke, and coughed.

'What a lark,' he said, and laughed.

Ernest stood up, came up behind Frederick.

'Don't be such a dolt.'

Fred glanced at Fan. His face became glacial.

He is like a child, thought Ernest.

Ernest was used to Freddie's mood swings. Had occasion to be frightened of them when they went on too swift a descent. It was nothing for Fred to lie in his bed for days at a time, not answering, not even, seemingly, seeing Fan. He only got up to use the pot, then he ghosted back and lay there, in some somnambulant state that resembled the life-support system of some mollusc or piece of mould. This was such a contrast to Lord Frederick's occasionally brilliant public persona that Ernest felt, at first anyway, privileged to witness such a deeply personal moment. Of loss, of abnegation. But there were complications.

Frederick was occasionally almost hysterically jealous. Once he had beaten up Ernest — or was it Fanny? — so badly that neither Ernest nor Fanny had been able to appear in public for nearly a week. Nothing was broken exactly. Nothing, that is, apart from some veil that Ernest felt he had pierced, some opacity almost, as if he and he alone (mistakenly, he realised now) had access to some truth about Frederick's desolation of character.

Frederick had wept his remorse, begged Fanny's forgiveness, crawled to him. Frederick seemed shocked himself by what he had done. Ernest had a sense of some long-lasting injury in Frederick, sourced either in the horrors of combat at Lucknow or inside his own aristocratic family. They had made love, and even though Ernest was still in a state of shock — nobody had ever pummelled him or kicked him or hit him hard in the face — he succumbed.

Curiously, this act of violence, prompted by an unreasonable jealousy, seemed to seal their relationship, deepen it, join them together in a way that almost nothing else could. Ernest felt he had glimpsed some private hell within Frederick and felt — poor fool — that he could perhaps help heal or soothe this private pain. Frederick only needed the love of a good woman.

This is where it became a little complicated. Ernest was not so sure who Frederick was privately engaged to. (Frederick had come in the following morning, when Ernest was still lying in bed, hardly able to move without crying out, come in and said he wanted to give Ernest a family ring. He felt connected now to Ernest. He felt — they were together. But in the end it was more complicated than that, because if it was Fanny Frederick was engaging himself to, that was all very well: for all intents and purposes they could be engaged. But Ernest knew that Ernest could not be engaged to Frederick. This was more than impossible. It was unknown in the world.)

He accepted the ambiguity because he had to.

This was over two years ago now.

'Where?'

Down two storeys, at an acute angle, Ernest could see the teeming footpath of Southampton Street, just before three o'clock.

'He's not moving. Outside number thirty-four.'

It was true: outside the tallow and candle shop opposite was a rather idle man. He was standing propped up against the window, seeming to be waiting for someone. Except, at that precise moment he took his watch out of his inside waistcoat pocket — a surprisingly bright red waistcoat — looked at it, then glanced, seemingly straight up at the window at which Fred and Ernest were standing.

They both ducked.

And looked at each other.

Fred's face expressed nothing more than delight. He held the cheroot between his lips at a rakishly upward angle.

'He's dunning me for me debts, old boy,' he said to Ernest, and burst out laughing. 'I'm pretty sure I recognise the chap. He's from the coachmaker's.'

'Or jeweller's. Or suitmaker's. Cigarmaker's. Liquor merchant. Or is it the washerwoman this time?'

'You don't need to put the boot in, Fan.'

On hands and knees now, Frederick and Ernest crawled away from the window.

They opened the door of their rooms on the first floor and they went down the staircase, laughing and chasing each other down a flight until they came across Eliza, who turned, looked at them and sighed.

She was exhausted, midway through her day. She had been up since six o'clock, having lit the fires and cleaned the grate, and got the kettles ready. She had been carrying water and coal up flight after flight of stairs, like some beast of burden. Not that she minded. It was her role in life, she realised. But occasionally, just occasionally, she had reason to question why it was that some people could run up and down stairs, laughing, while she plodded up again, the backs of her hamstrings taut, the muscles of the backs of her legs aching and a sort of dim cloud of a headache darkening her pupils. All for five shillings a week, found.

It hurt her, too, that Miss Fanny had not listened to her warning. Had pushed it aside, as if nothing could touch her, harm her: she would always be within that shining raiment on the stage.

'Come on, Fan! Come on, man!'

Lord Frederick was laughing, laughing. He never so much as glanced at Eliza. She did not exist for him.

'Let's creep out the back door, eh?'

Eliza left them to their game.

She had delivered her warning. And Miss Fanny had chosen not to listen.

The Transit
of Venus

She came as Venus that night. There was no other way to regard her. Fan was wearing a low-cut green gown, her shoulders powdered, her arms bare too, except for her shoulder-length gloves. Her silk dress was all glinting sea depths of green, while in her hair was a single diamond star. It was placed centrally on her Grecian-style hairdo. This was the master-touch, the suggestion as to her persona: she was a Greek goddess this evening.

She walked into the Strand Theatre on Frederick Clinton's arm, mid-conversation with *Mrs Graham*. (Stell was Fan's lady in waiting, dressed in red — an echo, an addition, but there was no doubt this evening who was the star.)

Whatever the two actresses were talking about was so utterly fascinating that neither could stop. Fanny had her head down as she wandered along, her lips smiling inscrutably, mysteriously. Stell was whispering all the time, keeping up the same brilliant smile as she glanced around, vividly. She didn't recognise anyone in particular. It was as if she were showing off the brilliance of her companion.

They were obviously discussing the juiciest, dirtiest piece of gossip and there was not a person in the room — not even the Prince of Wales — who did not wish, suddenly, and desperately, to know what it was.

As they walked along the promenade, people cleared away from them. People curved around to look as they walked along, to get a better view. All over the theatre people were ending sentences. As word spread, first one man, then another, got up and stood on his seat in the stalls, and looked back.

The burlesque that was on that night, *Romeo and Juliet: Or the Blonde who Dyed for Love* was in intermission: it was the time when many people arrived.

They walked towards their box (purchased with the money from Mrs Boulton), laughing as they went. At one point, Fan and Stell burst out laughing, uproariously, with Fan however trying to quieten Stell down, saying, 'Now. Now!'

They sat down and Fan glanced surreptitiously towards the box where the royal party were seated. The Prince of Wales was sitting down, legs flung out in front of him in a position of royal gluttony, his slightly bulbous eyes looking directly towards their party.

Fan made a gesture of a swoon into a sitting royal curtsy; he appeared to nod, to acknowledge this, though later people said he was only speaking to his companion, who at that second bent down, whispered in his ear, and presented him with a programme.

'Good evening,' Samuel said. He had come in quietly, was bending over Fan's glove. He kissed the nape of her glove. Similarly Stella, whose hand was slightly more limp — unengaged.

Fan looked at him intensely, said, 'We forgot to pick up our photographs.'

And smiled. It was a quick smile, of complicity.

Frederick ignored Samuel.

Samuel said to Fan, 'I saw you in your play.'

Her eyes widened, and she looked back, away from the crowd, which was thickening in front of their box. She turned her massive mask-like face towards him. It was magnificent, both in its obdurate refusal to accept ugliness and in its insistence on being transformed into beauty, on being a mask, in its own way, of female beauty. The star in her hair dazzled.

Out there an initial drum roll started. The curtain was going up. It was the balcony scene, but, in keeping with the mood of burlesque there was a dog persistently barking throughout the tender conversations between Romeo and Juliet, both of whom, in addition, had heavy colds.

'Wherefore ard thou, Robeo?'

A racking cough came from the stage. Juliet sneezed in her balcony. The dog yapped.

'So you understand now, do you?' Fan murmured to her young conquest.

'It is a joke, isn't it?'

Everyone around them was laughing.

She was silent and looked hard into his eyes, sighed a little to herself, seemed to settle and looked away.

When she looked back she said, in a flat voice: 'You think it is a joke?'

He wanted to say so much, but he couldn't find the words. All he could do was look back at her, lustrously. His gaze said: *I accept whatever and whoever you are. I like being around you.*

She looked back at him, seeming to judge, in an intuitive flash, what he was offering. She accepted it almost humbly, yet this acceptance was so momentary that it was overtaken by a slightly metallic sheen, a guard, through which she peered, as if to see how much this might be worth. Then she spoke, as if casually.

'Would you like to visit me?'

'Visit you?'

'Yes. Perhaps one afternoon.' She appeared to glance momentarily over at Frederick, who was braying with laughter, gazing at the stage. 'I could sing for you. Privately.'

Samuel savoured for a moment all the meanings of the word 'private'. He was torn between desire — for danger, for the unknown, for loss itself perhaps, the intoxication of change — and something more primal.

'That would be . . . charming,' he said, hesitating a moment, as if to select a word that he sensed might be used in Fan's world.

'I shall not sing "Fading Away", but a song which I sense might be of special meaning.'

They looked into each other's eyes. It was a moment of great nakedness.

'Special meaning?'

'It is called "My Pretty Jane",' Fan said, a small — was it mocking? — smile creasing up on the corner of her painted lips.

'How does it go?'

> My pretty Jane, my pretty Jane,
>
> Never, never look so shy
>
> But meet me, meet me in the evening
>
> While the bloom is on the rye

'But who plays Jane?'

'Who indeed?'

They gazed at each other intensely. Then Samuel became aware that Frederick was staring at them.

The fact was that Samuel was feeling increasingly uncomfortable — out of his depth. Strange-looking men, men — he was sure of this — with painted faces, men actually wearing rouge and paint, were looking up into the box and murmuring to Stell, who was laughing, laughing — that private, dirty laugh. Were they all actors?

If so, was he part of their play?

He stood up, his face suddenly burning.

As if catching him out, sensing his anxiety, Fan looked up at him and tweaked his trousers.

'Darling you're not neglecting your studies, are you? I don't want you to miss that boat to — where was it? The *colonies*.'

Her painted lips formed sardonically. 'They need sturdy lads — strong and true, like you — out there.'

'*Out there*' had the sense of passing into spheres so distant as to become immaterial — as if one could move off the edge of the world into nothingness.

All around them, everyone was applauding. Juliet's nurse had disappeared, screaming, down a trap.

The music changed key. The 'Pas de Fascination' edged onto the stage — a comely line of 'beauties' in tights, with fixed smiles. They waggled their plump legs in unison.

'I must go now,' Samuel said, a small death in his voice. Fan already seemed to have forgotten him. She was gazing out at the stage. He was no longer at the centre of her intoxicating universe.

Frederick was staring up at him.

The limelight was burnishing Fan's features.

'I promised Cummings I would be home by eleven.'

Samuel's heart sank at the thought of his room, the silence — the only sound Cummings turning a page of *Fearne on Remainders*.

'We must all keep our promises, young man,' Fan said, turning her head away.

She did not say goodbye.

*F*an and Stell were *en promenade*. They were arm in arm, on their way back to their box after three brandies apiece. Fred was trailing along beside them. People were turning, again, to look.

It was often like this, but tonight — Fan could not quite put her finger on it — it felt different. There was something in the air. Was it her costume? Was it particularly successful, her transformation into Venus? She prayed she would be lucky tonight. They needed it.

There were some nights when there was no doubt. Fun was coming her way. Distraction. She settled into herself. She felt a glaze, almost, overcome her, sealing her within her powder, paint, the light and adjustable iron bars of her bustle, her horsehair. She was melding together, to form a kind of precious metal, a form of gold, almost giving out lustrous sparks. Her mouth felt thick, warm, almost as if a drug had been placed in her system — as if she were languorous from too much sex. Drowsy, almost, she was so relaxed.

She turned around, radiant.

Stell was saying, 'Let's go, darling. I'm so wretchedly bored I could faint.'

But Fan felt drunk. On immanence.

It was about to happen.

She was sure of it.

There was even, from the orchestra pit, the beginning frill of twenty violins. A drum began.

The lights on the stage were changing. A powdering gold light spangled all through Venus's hair. Her nostrils flared, her pupils dilated, her lips slightly parted.

She looked around.

At the hunters and the hunted.

This is my world, she thought.

Then she noticed Fred was standing there, looking strange — a little sick. What was the message on his face?

Something untoward was happening.

The men with painted faces were speaking to each other, leaving hurriedly.

Stell was turning to her, gripping her arm too tightly.

An extraordinary man had approached her directly to stand beside Stell.

He had hold of her arm. He reached out and grabbed Fan's, too.

'Now,' he said, 'if you two just come with us quiet-like, there'll be no fuss.'

'*How dare you, sir, address a lady in that manner?*'

Fan looked down at the man in the shabby lounge suit, pushing her bustle behind her with an expressive thrust of contempt.

She had not been on the stage for nothing.

She stuck her nose in the air and prepared to move, splendidly, away.

But the 'gentleman' did not move.

'The pair of yous. You're nabbed. Now get moving.'

Fan glanced quickly at Stell. Stell was never at a loss to put someone in their place. She was short yet imperious. But Stell seemed wordless.

Fan had the sensation of being pulled along.

The whole weight of her silk dress, with the awkward structure of the bustle, was caught in the man's weft. She was being pulled along in his wake. And she was, by force of nature, pulling Stell too.

People were turning to look. She was finding it difficult to keep her feet — her glacé leather boots, trimmed with a ribbon to match her gown, kept slithering, sliding on the dirty carpeted floor.

That floor over which she had walked up and down, up and down, *en promenade* a thousand times before.

Her chignon was bouncing. Her whole sense of herself — the composition and heft of her breasts, the great false palace of her hairdo, the swinging ricochet of her earrings, even the little diamond star placed in her hair — was now threatening to come undone.

Another man, this one bigger than the other, yet similarly dressed in a dingy lounge suit, was walking alongside her, 'escorting' her out of the theatre.

Frederick too had been fingered. The large gent was pulling him along as well.

The stage was ignored. The actors in a comic wrestling scene — Mercutio was sitting astride Romeo, who was bucking upwards — went on unobserved.

Voices rose up, all round them. Fan had the sense of each face, turned to her, receding almost violently, like a country left behind.

She felt sick.

Stell had gone white. There was a light glistening of sweat around the edges of her painted face, as if she were wearing a mask, and the mask was on the point of sliding off.

Fan glanced, one final time, back towards their triumph, but the box in which the Prince of Wales and his party had been sitting was empty. Discreetly, it occurred to Fan — yet with all the intricacy of a play in which they had an unknown part — they had withdrawn.

This scandal would be their own.

They were outside now, under the porch.

Stella was leaning towards the man in the shabby suit, confidentially, making it appear that she and the 'gentleman' were in some private conversation.

But the 'gentleman' seemed insistent on placing a good yard between his highly polished boots and the soiled perimeter at the bottom of Stella's dress: the intricate lace that had turned subtly and indecipherably grey over the weeks, then a faintly lustrous black.

'It will do you no good at all, old fellow, to take us to the station.'

Stella's voice was frank. But there was something else. The emergency was such she was speaking in the voice of Arthur Park, gentleman. A male.

Oddly, and this made Fan queasy in the stomach, the man with the malevolent gleam on his black Balmoral boots appeared not to be listening. He was looking ahead, beyond the perimeter of the brilliantly yellow gas-lights. Fan glanced round, to see what he was looking at.

It was the black maria.

It was backed up to the edge of the pavement.

And the back door was open.

'Anything you like to mention, you can have.'

Stella was bargaining with the detective, her voice urgent. The crowd was growing bigger by the second. And they were vocal. Laughing. Enjoying the spectacle. Of Stell and her humiliation.

Fan felt a sudden loss of stage presence. It was all too real — unscripted.

'*Anything,*' Stell pleaded. '*Just let us go.*'

The man in black boots pushed her. Pushed Stell as if she were a common bawd.

At this point Frederick made his getaway. Sensing that the attention was on the others, he swung about and ran, at full tilt, off into the darkness.

He had not been in the back streets of Lucknow during a bloody siege without working out when it is expeditious to retreat.

And on occasions, not to retreat is fatal.

(He had an urge to live.)

Fan looked momentarily taken aback: it was a further rung in her humiliation. The policeman pushed Stell again.

Then Stella took command of the situation.

She pulled up the hem of her red dress. She stepped into the black maria as if she were entering something quite joyful, like a carriage on its way to a ball.

Fan felt isolated standing there. She said to the man with the polished shoes, the unmoving face, 'I am sure, sir, this is all some dreadful mistake.'

But he pushed her into the police van and the door was slammed shut and Ernest Boulton found himself in darkness.

*T*he interior stank of excrement — of bowels loosened by fright. Her dress was stuffed in all around her and a metal rib from her bustle was bent, almost like some swollen internal organ, pressing into her sides. It was like being locked in a cupboard. The van was divided into cells so small a human could barely fit.

'*We'll tell them who we are.*'

She was sweating, drenched. She couldn't breathe — or even tell where she was. She pushed her hands up against the wall. There was someone singing riotously, in a sort of alcoholic frenzy, next door.

She cried out — '*Stell! Stell!*'

Or was it '*Fred! Fred!*'

Someone kicked the wall, hard — or was it punched it? She tried to calm down. Tried not to be overcome by the claustrophobia that came at her, cramping her legs and making acid spurt, skidding down the overheated nubs of her spine.

Mouth dry. She felt she couldn't even call out. She was going to pass out.

But she didn't.

She was betrayed even in this.

The wheels rattled over cobbles.

She pushed her face up to the grating, stared out.

The gas-lights of The Strand receded. The last pair of children running alongside the van had dropped back. One hit the side of the van. Someone within the van was sobbing, a continuous low sob.

Was it Stell? Let it not be Stell.

Out there in the murk Fan could just make out that constant sea motion of people walking about in the dark. This was the eternal hubbub of the night-time city. It sounded in her ears, as she was driven away, as if it were speaking to her, murmuring to her, calling out to her — was it fare-thee-well? Or was the hubbub unaware of her, oblivious?

Awakening

*H*e was dreaming of a hot-house: a hot-house full of the most spectacular palms and orchids. He was coming into the hot-house, he was opening the door and the heat was rushing out to hit his face. It dewed his whiskers, his eyebrows, stung his pupils until, the shock of heat over, he came inside. His vision cleared. It was a tropical world he was within: the Andes? There was the sound of a river rustling nearby. The palm trees were so real. But when he looked again, he was amazed to see that they were the trees he had seen on the stage at the Strand Theatre. They were made from tinsel and scrim. At least the flowers right beside him — the yearning, open-mouthed orchids — were real. But as he stooped to look at them more closely he realised it was difficult to tell. Yet there was smell of moist earth. Real earth.

He was meeting someone there. That's right. It was Fanny. He had an appointment. Fanny was going to sing for him. Him alone. But who had made the appointment? And was he really in a hot-house, or on a stage? Might a curtain go up, revealing him to an audience? An audience laughing? Was he in fact naked?

Or was she — he — Fanny — *Ernest* — naked too? For a second Samuel had the truly awful apprehension that Ernest stood naked at the end of the hot-house, waiting for him — a male body with its droopings and brushings of hair. Worst of all, Samuel felt himself tumesce, grow hard, in expectation.

What if he — if she . . .

He heard her singing now.

> My pretty Jane, my pretty Jane,
> Never, never look so shy
> But meet me, meet me in the evening
> While the bloom is on the rye
>
> The spring is waning fast
> My love, the corn is in the ear,
> The summer nights are coming, love,
> The moon shines bright and clear!

It was a beautiful naked woman down there.

His heart was bashing so loudly he could hear the slurp-slap-slurp of his blood.

He opened his eyes. Sound of footsteps banging up wooden stairs. He was in his attic room, at his lodgings. Pulteney Terrace, Islington. Stink of kidneys and liver from the butcher's shop, three floors below.

His door was pushed open. Cummings — Cummings who always knocked now, standing decorously outside waiting for Samuel to open the door — Cummings burst into his room, looking both upset and somehow victorious.

Waving a newspaper.

'Sam! Sam! Thank God you're awake! That creature you met — that person calling herself Fanny? — has got herself arrested. The night before last. Has appeared at Bow Street. The whole town's gone mad with it.'

He handed the newspaper over.

*S*amuel, his head in his hands as if nursing a hangover, sat reading the newspaper. Cummings stood to his side, gazing over his shoulder. There was no sound except from the streets below. A door slammed. Somewhere in the far distance a bell sounded — though whether a clock or church it was impossible to tell.

APPREHENSION OF MEN IN FEMALE CLOTHING.
At Bow Street police-station yesterday. Mr Flowers, the presiding magistrate. heard an extraordinary charge against the two young men of having been found personating women.

Samuel read in complete silence, letting out groans. 'Oh, my God,' he kept saying. 'Oh, my God.'

> The greatest curiosity was manifested yesterday to see the prisoners as they were brought from Bow Street station to the police court on the opposite side. Immediately they walked out of the station they were greeted with shouts of laughter, intermingled with groans and hisses . . .

Cummings did not want to say, 'I told you so.' He kept to a curious, almost tender silence. Barton was suffering enough. He kept hitting his head, then falling down into a deeper depth of silence.

> The court was crammed to suffocation.
> When the prisoners were placed in the dock, great surprise was manifest at the admirable manner in which Boulton and Park had 'made up'. Both had an unexceptional feminine cast of features.
> While listening to the evidence, Boulton rested her head on her right hand, but did not pay very particular attention, except when the detective stated that he had seen them about for some time, and produced photographs . . .

Photographs.

Samuel groaned. In fact he became subliminally aware of a curious shift in his perceptions: it was similar to what happens when you concentrate on a spot close to your eyes and the rest of the world simultaneously seems to shift backwards, almost vertiginously: the world becomes rearranged. An additional shift occurs too, to do with the hitherto unrealised novelty of seeing a word shaped into the serifs of print.

Photographs.

What a curious word.

Samuel shifted his gaze and, with an almost contemplative air, as if he had never quite seen him before, turned his starling-black gaze to Cummings. His stooped shoulders and deferentially lowered eyes seemed somehow medicinal: as if he were visiting someone sick in a hospital. But it was more than this. Just as Samuel's perception seemed in rapid evolution — so rapid as to amount to a revolution in his own feelings — so Cummings seemed part of a flat picture, as if he were merely part of a single screen of detail, not differentiated from the scurfed floorboards of Samuel's attic room, or the clothes thrown upon the floor, where Samuel had dropped them, like an excess skin.

Why did he get the unsettling feeling that he was viewing his own life as if from the outside, and as if he had already left it: been expelled from it? But before he could express this new thought to himself he was impelled — as if his life depended on it — to read further. And as he did so, his gaze took on a powerful force so that his eyes, reading the words, seemed like a sharpened spade digging into the verbiage, as if a spade were actually required to unearth the 'real' (hitherto hidden) meaning of ordinary words such as 'women', 'men', 'she'.

> The complete ease with which they maintained their parts astonished everyone in the court. The magistrate and the most experienced detective officers had to admit that the 'get-up' was good enough to deceive even themselves.
> The first witness was the superintendent of E Division, Mr Thomas, who had had detectives on the watch for the past month . . .

Past month.

Samuel felt an additional sensation, this time internal. It was like a calibration, or vibration of anxiety inside his body. He felt his heartbeat increase, then run along at a hurried pace; he felt, physically felt, a weight of sweat breaking out on his forehead. Yet this sweat was cold. His eyes, again, almost with a sense of loss, strained towards Cummings whose own face was pincered with anxiety.

Cummings said, 'Have you finished reading?'

Samuel made a small sound — was surprised to hear the almost broken sound coming from his mouth. This was followed abruptly by something even more surprising, and somehow shocking. It was a guttural laugh, exploding up from his interior. Like a pocket of trapped air it released itself and both Cummings and he, as strangers, witnessed its arrogant air of anarchy. This laugh said, '*I do not care. I could not care less.*'

Cummings made a moue of dismay.

Almost like someone having a stroke — because he was simultaneously feeling despair and elation — Samuel became aware of a curious impersonality sliding over him, encasing him in a protective shell that murmured to him, even as he sweated, and his heart beat, and he still heard the echo of his wild laugh: *this is not your life. This is the life of somebody else. This is the life of someone caught up in a scandal.*

> William Chamberlain, detective officer, went to Wakefield Street without a warrant and searched the parlours occupied by Boulton and Park and some other gentlemen. He found a large quantity of photographs of Boulton and Park in both male and female attire as well as a large amount of female clothing, and chignons. Talking about the photographs he said they included 'the likenesses of many other men of apparently good birth, including the likeness of a young gentleman who went about with them sometimes'. The solicitor immediately said, 'Do not say that.' Chamberlain, however, reiterated 'I have seen him.'

'They have seen me,' Samuel whispered, looking directly at Cummings, who came forward, almost a second too soon, so responsive was he to his ill comrade (as he saw him). He leant over Samuel, craning to read the exact words (to see the exact damage). Samuel's finger tapped the line in the paragraph, and, as if to make it more real, he read it aloud, his eyes never leaving Cummings's watery, steady gaze.

'*I have seen him.*'

Cummings listened, said nothing — tactfully.

Then, 'It might not be you.'

Samuel was not listening. He was witnessing a swift cascade of images: his mother, his sisters sitting mending linen, as they were wont to do on an early winter evening. They were gathered around an economical fire, none of them speaking. There was a knock on the door. They all eagerly looked up. A young woman entered the room, not particularly tall, with cheeks reddened from the cold. She was wearing a green cloak which she slipped off, shaking off fresh flakes of snow, which fell, melting and turning into little crystals upon the rag rug. Her red hair was also speckled with snow.

'Oh, Ursula, how good it is to see you,' Samuel's mother said, rising.

Ursula came closer to the fire, saying, 'I've a letter from Samuel. I thought I might bring it round and read it to you.'

At this precise moment the image faded, as if a light had been turned out. The three faces of his mother and his sisters, Alice and Tess, were all looking up, animate with anticipation, the lovely licks of the fire lighting the lower parts of their faces so that Samuel saw, almost tasted, how fresh and untouched their complexions were, how honest and keen their perceptions.

And how much they expected of him.

How they had saved to send him to London. Gone without, for him. Expecting him to save them.

He felt shame, and he felt distraught.

Cummings's grip on his shoulder, placed there seemingly in perfect syncopation with this dimming vision, tightened. Or had Samuel actually groaned out loud again?

'What can I do?' he murmured.

> The solicitor for Boulton and Park, Mr Besley, said much of the evidence 'has taken me somewhat by surprise, but unless the two prisoners were engaged in some unlawful purpose, no offence against the statute of vagrancy has been committed'.
> The solicitor submitted that it was all 'an act of folly'.
> The magistrate answered sharply that the act of folly had been going on for a long time. 'Once is very different. There are two ways in which one may regard it – either as inciting people to commit an offence which, a short time before, was capital, or inveigling people into rooms to try to extort money. I know the system exists.'
> The solicitor broke in. 'There is no evidence.'

Samuel's eyes went on reading, trapped, as it were, by horror. By disbelief. By the pictures summoned up in his head.

> The magistrate replied by saying he would remand 'the two women, as I may call them'.
> Boulton and Park were described as being in a terrible state of anxiety on being placed inside the police van, which was followed, on entering the police cells, by depression.

'Poor Fanny,' he said to himself, almost subliminally.

Just as he had been presented involuntarily with an image of his mother, sisters and the woman to whom he was all but betrothed, Ursula, now he glimpsed a vivid image of Fanny turning to look over her shoulder at him. He was back with her at the Globe restaurant. That man had just made his accusation. She was turning to look. Her face was freezing.

> A large crowd was waiting outside the court to see them cross the road to the police station. The excitement was partly traceable to the morbid taste of the public, but partly traceable to the notoriety of the young men, who, it is said, for years past have visited public places of resort in female attire, without dreaming, apparently, of their liability to a criminal prosecution for the offence.'
>
> Their solicitor asked if Boulton and Park might be allowed to change out of their dresses before being removed in the police van. This was granted, but after several hours the male attire had still not arrived.
>
> The crowd in the street by this time had greatly increased so the superintendent thought it best to remove them as quickly as possibly.
>
> The filthy fellows were then and there removed by van to the House of Detention.

'*What shall I do?*'

Samuel's first instinct was flight. He tried to maintain his rationality. He was aware how important it was to maintain this capacity — to believe in only what he knew himself to be true. He reasoned then that the photographs of himself and Boulton — Fanny — were still at the photographer's. His first action should be to obtain them as quickly as possible.

Cummings was saying to him (seeming to speak from a vast distance, as if down a tube, or underwater): 'Are you sure, man, you're not in any danger? It might be best to take a week off. Go and visit your family.'

Samuel looked at him as if he was mad.

Go and visit his family?

That was the last thing he wanted to do. He wanted . . . to be alone. For Cummings to go. For Cummings to stop looking into his eyes, to the backs of his eyes, as if he — Cummings — could see there a small theatre, a stage on which he could see acted out all sorts of possibly indecent scenarios. Samuel's honesty and credibility were under scrutiny.

But Cummings surprised him by coming towards him, his pale blue eyes watering as if he had suddenly turned a corner and looked into a blasting wind. Did he have some grit caught in his lashes? But he was coming closer and opening his arms. God, he was about to embrace him. He was actually embracing Samuel, for one moment dissolving his flesh into Samuel's, then seeming to freeze as if an unfortunate thought had occurred to him — as if he feared the door might fall back and a photographer might appear.

Cummings brutally pounded him on the back in a way that was meant to be a sign of male affection but could just as easily have been someone shaking him awake, or warning him to stand back. So they stood apart. Cummings looked uncomfortable and said, 'I'll cover for you at Budge and Costley's today. If you need to . . . do anything. I know you'll have things you need to . . . catch up on.'

All these careful elisions.

Cummings had gathered up the newspaper. Samuel wanted to cry out: *but leave it! Leave it for me to read again! I want to make sure it is real.* Instead he watched Cummings crumple the paper up, as if in this one act, he was protecting him.

Samuel said, 'Thank you.'

He did not know quite what he was thanking Cummings for. Was it the forewarning? The chance he was giving Samuel, before he emerged into the street?

'Yes,' Samuel said in a curiously calm voice — a voice he himself heard as becalmed. 'I won't come in to work today. Say I have a cold. A fever. I'll be there tomorrow, though,' he said carefully. 'Make sure you tell Mr Budge that.'

Cummings nodded and, clutching his cargo, like a crumpled up map of the world that had been found inadequate, he left. Samuel stood in his attic, his world changed — forever? — listening to the diminuendo of Cummings's heavy footsteps down his stairwell, growing fainter until he heard him open the front door, to a sudden blooming of noise from the street. Then the door shut and the house fell silent.

'What do you mean someone has collected them?'

Samuel was at the photographer's. He was sweating. He had tried — tried so hard — to walk in a measured way to Beak Street, the little side alley off Regent Street. He had kept his promise to himself to stay calm, to walk slowly, to remember to breathe. Instead his footsteps of their own accord had hurried up. He had found his breath coming in sharp stabs. He kept hearing all around the newspaper boys ululating 'Read all about it! Read all about it! The men in petticoats! Revealed!' One of them even advanced towards him, as in some strange dream, waving the paper at Samuel threateningly, seeming to jeer into his face.

'You want to read about 'em dirty blighters?' the boy cried joyfully. 'The woman-mans?'

Samuel had found himself walking too quickly then, his heart pounding.

He had run up the stairs two, three at a time. Burst into the still lagoon of the studio. There was nobody there but the owner. He looked at Samuel, licked his lips, then asserted a flattened expression like a ship with its hatches bolted.

'Can I help, sir?'

Samuel, looking at the man more closely, thought: he has not shaved today — an irrelevant thought that seemed to portend something. Other business at hand? Something more urgent? Samuel could not believe the man did not recognise him.

'I've come to collect the likeness Miss . . . ' Here sound slowed and everything became tranquil and ominous. What term would Samuel use? If he did not use 'Miss Fanny' he would be showing his hand too clearly. But what other name could he use? It had suddenly become complex. Dangerous.

'The likeness of myself and one other.'

'. . . other?' said the man, and drifted away, turning his back on Samuel. He went towards a backdrop — the Swiss mountain, complete with tumbling brook. He seemed to see a speck of fly dirt there because he got the edge of his apron, spat on it well — even too expressively, making a small spurt of disgust — then he began to clean the mountainside.

'We came here a week or so ago. Myself and the other.'

The man turned around. He was smiling.

'You keep saying "the other" sir but I keep wondering to myself, the other *what?*'

At this there was the sound of woman's footsteps running up the staircase. The door fell back and a voice said, '*Alf? 'ave you seen? 'ave you seen?*'

It was the man's wife, bonnet strings undone. In her hand, wide open at the page, was a newspaper. When she saw Samuel she let out a small sound and her hands, of their own accord, closed the newspaper.

'I was explaining,' the plump man said urbanely, 'to our young *gentleman* 'ere' — there was an unpleasant emphasis on the word 'gentleman' — 'that the likeness 'e is after 'as been picked up. Already, like.'

His wife stood stock still, her eyes moving from her husband to Samuel, then swiftly back. She said nothing but went towards the backdrop, where there was an unfortunate smear.

'Oh, 'Enry, what in 'eaven's name 'ave you been doing, then?'

Samuel felt himself to be invisible. He was uncertain how to proceed.

'Who was this person who collected the photographs? Was it Miss — Fanny?'

He at last brought her name out.

The man airily turned away.

'I wouldn't know, sir. It was a gentleman — that's to say a man, certainly. So it couldn't have been, as you say, sir, *Miss* Fanny, now could it?'

Faithful Friends and True

Eliza had fought her way through the crowd. It began back in Long Acre and swelled towards Bow Street to the point where it was so dense you could not move.

People were standing on the tops of vans. Hanging out of windows. Eliza burrowed through. Used her elbows, squirming like a rabbit out of a burrow, murmuring the occasional "*Scuse me, pardon, surely.*' She forced her way past people who did not want to move, who had been — as they told her forcefully — waiting a good two hours themselves to see *the he–shes* emerge from the Bow Street cells and cross the road.

Eliza felt in her heart a kind of torpor. She had known crowds like this. Hanging crowds. It was only two years, after all, since the last public hanging outside Newgate Prison. Eliza, as befitted a good Londoner, had been there (it was that wretch the Fenian who had tried to blow up the House of Detention). There had been the same competition for a viewing position. The same sense of piety fuelled by the keener emotion of voyeurism: a blend of excitement and the vindictive.

The same raw sense of anticipation.

It was like the tumultuous moments before the curtain went up.

Eliza got to within fifty yards of the front doors of Bow Street and could get no further. The crowd was wedged tight. Then she glimpsed the little old man in the yellow wig — the piano player. He was perched on the very corner of a first-floor window ledge, being assaulted by two ruffians. They were standing on some boxes, pulling on his boots. He was smiting them ineffectually with a silver-topped cane.

Eliza pushed brutally towards the little bewigged man. Who, seeing her approach, welcomed her as his saviour. Because Eliza, using the toe-end of her boot right up into the soft fundaments of each lad (giving them a poke as hard she could, for good measure), had put the lads to flight.

'*Now clear off, you lot, and leave the gent alone.*'

The gent, Monsieur le Pin as he introduced himself, welcomed Eliza like an old friend. He seemed elated by the size of the crowd, yet sad.

'I am hoping our two friends are not in any too serious trouble. The law is not a kind beast to meddle with. Not at all, not at all . . .' He shook his head as if in melancholy remembrance.

Eliza wedged her backside up onto the window ledge. (They were against the window of a ballet supply shop — full of dusty old shoes and moth-like fairy wings, harlequin masks. On the walls were faded announcements of day-schools, penny theatres, advertisements for petition-writers.)

Eliza looked back down Bow Street and whistled. As far as she could see, there was a tow-haired monster made up of heads, all of them pushing in one direction. The police court.

And there, diametrically opposite the court, stood the elegant shape of the Royal Opera House, as if to affirm that theatre and justice were two sides of the same coin: one dealing in illusion, the other in cruel reality. At this moment they seemed to have come together, producing combustion.

Monsieur le Pin was leaning out, looking up and down the street. The noise was quite deafening. A veritable babble.

'They've certainly filled all the seats, gentle Eliza!' he cried gaily. 'Even the cheap seats such as what you and I have. I have a feeling Mesdemoiselles Graham and Clinton will be pleased. If you're going to appear in court, after all, it's best before a *full house!*'

They were not dressed for daylight. As Stell and Fan were thrust out through the lock-up door that first morning the light seemed hard, flat — glaring. Fan winced and instinctively lowered her face onto her chest. She had been worried that her beard might be coming through, but she also knew it usually took up to three days for the first fine hairs to betray her.

But if daylight was the first shock, the second was the crowd. As far as she could see, there were people — a crowd, an audience.

But this audience was molten, swaying, an energy particle unleashed and pushing — pouring towards her. Into the pupil of her eye, trying to gorge on the tiny black dot within. Stella was ruffling, rifling through her purse of self, rearranging herself so she was bold. She raised her head high and slid her arm — God, her flesh was icy! — through Fan's.

She held her there, locked.

They would do this together. They would go down together, if need be. They would fight together. Hadn't Stell told her tales of Marie Antoinette facing the mob? They would be like that.

A storm, a summer storm of hiss. A snake's breath hit against them, fractured all over by laughter: not only friendly laughter but a shouted-out bark of disbelief. Yet this laughter was all they had to hold on to.

Fan's instinctive knowledge of audience told her: *we can play this.*

You laugh with a crowd — even, if necessary, against yourself. A survival tactic, when walking through a mob.

*E*liza saw how daylight scorched all around them. It brilliantly lit their silks, green and scarlet, making them seem unreal, almost absurd. Drabs did not circulate in daylight. They hid, like people of the night, from the light. But here were Stella and Fanny being *thrust* — this is what it felt like — into the emetic solution of daytime. The light attacked them, almost calcified around the powder that was left on their faces. They looked haggard, worn — yet, upon their coming into contact with an audience, Eliza witnessed an almost primitive magical rite. They came alive. From the dead of their raiment, the corpse of their clothes, they emerged, living, sentient. Perhaps risk energised them. They were in danger, there was no doubt. The laughter all around was, initially anyway, hostile: it wanted to consume them like a fire, reduce them to ash.

Yet somehow, in that brief walk from lock-up to courtroom, something — something strange — happened.

They had managed to acknowledge the crowd; they had been gracious, almost. They had even half-laughed, as if joining in with the joke against themselves: as if they shared with the crowd what a jolly jape it all was, what a frolic.

Then it became a rush. A race. To see who could get into the courtroom. It became quite dangerous.

There was that silence of concentration. People kicked. If you went down, you would be crushed underfoot.

The single policeman on duty was swept aside.

Like an angry flood they poured into the building, filled up every space, then backed up and still kept pressing in.

It became packed so tight nobody could move.

Eliza was trapped in the doorway into the building. She and Monsieur le Pin had tried to stay together. She had even locked her arm around his skinny frame. But a sudden surge in the crowd had broken them apart. Monsieur le Pin was last seen, his wig awry, being successively moved backwards, backwards, away from Eliza who could only call out, '*Monsoor!*' knowing he could not hear, could not possibly hear.

She was wedged in the doorway. Stuck. She waited for possibly twenty minutes defending her position. Then she thought of something. She had run out of Southampton Street spontaneously, dropping everything. She had not asked. She risked dismissal. Nobody knew yet, back at Southampton Street. What if she lost her position?

She squirmed with her behind, pushing and shoving backwards. She explained as she went that she was but a servant and she was running late.

Finally she found herself as if extruded from the crowd. She had been prodded, poked, grabbed and fondled. But now she was in the open. She rearranged her shawl around her shoulders. And looked about.

The street looked as if riot had taken place.

Cabbages were trampled underfoot and there was a single shoe, a green satin high-heel, lying on its side, its heel snapped off.

It was not worth taking.

'*The* missus wants to see you, Lizzie.'

Eliza had just slipped in the back door, past the washing. She had opened the door as quietly as possible, only to find the boy looking at her. He looked pleased.

She had been caught out.

She clipped his ear hard.

'You know my proper name, slop-face.'

He turned to her, gritted his teeth.

'She ain't pleased,' he said, and whistled. 'She ain't pleased one little bit.'

Eliza took off her shawl. Tried to work out what she would say, how she would say it. It was important how it came out.

She took her time going up the stairs to the second-floor back parlour. Mrs Peck was sitting there, her spectacles on the end of her nose, looking at invoices. These were spread all over the table: a paper storm. She had beside her the large earthenware pot of tea, a glittering brown bowl and a large chipped teacup. Mrs Peck drank out of her late husband's teacup, a moustache cup, out of respect to Himself, Mrs Peck liked to say. To keep His memory alive.

There was a photograph of Himself on the wall: a heavily moustached Frenchman, a forty-niner, who had died of delirium tremens five years earlier.

Mrs Peck looked up, expelled a sound almost like a bleat of anger, then indicated with a weighty hand that Eliza could come in. Eliza had only ever been in Mrs Peck's back parlour once, on the day she had been hired.

She bobbed a curtsy to her employer.

'I can explain, Mum,' she said. She couldn't stop herself glancing at the teapot. She would kill, *kill*, for a cup of tea. And to sit down. To rest her tired plates of meat. But she was aware she was facing reprimand. So she thought it best to arrive at the point. Of what might save her.

'It's Mistress Fanny, Mum,' she said. She couldn't help the lilt of excitement, salted all over with distress. 'She's come a right cropper.'

Mrs Peck paused. She moved one invoice to her left, then her hand, of its own ghostly accord, lifted another invoice, which she made a play at looking at. She needed to take her time, perhaps.

There was an unsubtle air of danger in the room. The paper fell slowly from her grasp. It was no use. She could not stop herself.

Mrs Peck's mouth fell open. But no sound would come out. Instead, an old yellowy, befurred tongue slid out to saliva over her thin lips.

'. . . cropper, you say?'

'Yes, Mum. She and Miss Stella — as calls herself that — was picked up last night. At the Strand.'

'. . . picked up?'

'Nabbed, Mum. By the police.'

Mrs Peck's old wreck of a hand raised itself to her neck. She seemed to be fingering her own neck, as if it were in some danger. She stood up and went to the window: the dirty-paned back window, which looked out across the washing and single starved tree to the back of the other houses, which looked, in turn, into her house — it was an entirely unnatural landscape, enclosed and cluttered, drab and lifeless.

'. . . the police?' she breathed. 'Law's a mercy. What 'ave they been and done?'

Eliza felt her head sway in ghostly denial.

'I don't know, Mum. I went along, to find out like.'

There was a tintinnabulation of silence: a soundless cascade of so many questions that neither, for a moment, could speak. They had to inspect this soundlessness, these figurative suggestions, the shape of which neither liked to put into words — accusations. Mrs Peck was turning to her, opening her mouth, when down below, three flights down, there was a sharp rap on the front door.

Mrs Peck let out a small whimper, then clutched her throat.

'*The good Lord. Please be merciful.*'

The two women looked at each other, neither moving.

The knock sounded again.

Each knew the meaning of such a sound: abrupt, loud, demanding.

'Well, don't stand there like a waxwork, girl! Go and get the door!'

When Eliza turned to go, she was surprised to find Mrs Peck's hand on her sleeve. The fingers tightened. How such a slow mover as Mrs Peck had got close to her so quickly she could not work out, but then everything seemed to be out of joint, perspectives seemed on the point of going awry, and Mrs Peck whispered to her, in a gale of stale tea scent, 'And tell whoever's calling, I'm not in. I'm not in. Not in at all. I've gawn off down country. To see me sister.'

*C*ummings bustled into the chambers of Budge and Costley, barristers and solicitors of Bell Yard, near Lincoln's Inn. Bell Yard was a mere stroll from the soft green lawns of Lincoln's Inn Field, but it was as if a million miles distant. It was a mean little alley made up of soot-blackened brick. There were mirrors suspended by chains outside the first-floor windows, in a vain attempt to attract a ray of sunlight within. But the sun seldom if ever penetrated the obfuscating gloom of the various legal chambers in Bell Yard.

Cummings was always on time for work. He had never been late by so much as a half second. But today he hurried up the two flights of stairs to Mr Budge's chambers on a mission. He went straight into Mr Budge's room — a chaotic chamber lined to the ceiling with documents so yellow and dusty they seemed to have been there since time immemorial. (Mr Costley's chambers were a further flight up — larger and closer to the light. It was Cummings' dream in life to move upstairs, to the higher floor.)

Cummings had already told his first lie, to Mr Budge: 'Samuel is,' he said, 'unfortunately ill. Struck down with a sudden ague. Most unusual.'

'Really?' murmured kind Mr Budge. 'Should we think of sending him some victuals?' But then he got things muddled, as he always did. 'But where does the poor lad live? If only we knew . . .'

Smithson, the underclerk, had snuffled into his papers. He had waved the morning newspaper at Cummings when he first came in the door.

'Now here's a pretty pickle!' Smithson had cried joyously. He always turned, as a matter of course, to the accounts of trials and remands. 'Seeing as how it is our bread and butter,' Smithson said. He was cadaverously thin and always kept a cache of peanuts in his trouser pockets. He found consolation for his hunger pangs in using food metaphors.

Cummings had turned deaf. He never wasted a word on Smithson, who was his inferior. This morning in particular he sourly turned away, as if grave matters weighed upon his shoulders.

But even as he got down the *Impey's Practice* from the top shelf, Cummings found his mind drifting.

It went, as inevitably as the point of a compass, back to his friend. His sole friend in lonely London.

The fact was Cummings wanted to stand proud beside Samuel when he delivered him — untouched, he hoped — (or not too damaged) to the woman he would wed.

Cummings had met Ursula once, and conceived a great passion to see this marriage take place. He saw Ursula as everything he himself would like to wed. And he had taken it on as an almost religious mission when she had, without any serious thought, laid her hand on Cummings's arm and said to him, 'Look after my Samuel for me. He means well, poor boy, but he is unused to this worldly place.'

Cummings knew Samuel had come too close to the roaring engine of London pleasure: omnivorous, darkly attractive, wild, anarchic in its hunger, dazzling as a false jewel. Cummings had read the paleness of Samuel's late nights, the wanness of his mornings. He thought he knew what was happening.

He felt he was watching the betrayal of Samuel's innocence.

Yet.

He did not think.

It had ever. Got to *that*.

Whatever '*that*' might be.

He rattled a page over here and let out a dry cough. Smithson flicked a peanut up into the air and caught it with a wallop of sound, his mouth popping shut.

'They've been spotted at supper clubs all over town,' he called out. 'I'm sure I've seen those two queer birds down at Evans's.'

Cummings began to hatch a plan as he sat there. He would ask for time off to go to Chancery Lane, to look into a current case of great obfuscation. This was not unusual. Cummings was regarded as having a peculiarly terrier-like ability to ferret out a telling fact. But this time he would diverge. He would, instead, keep a watching brief on a possible case: The Queen v Boulton and Park. He would tell another lie, if need be. It would only be his second.

*E*liza had been sitting in the improbable grandeur of the downstairs front parlour of Southampton Street for a very long hour. She was waiting to be spoken to by Detective Chamberlain, who was upstairs, at that very moment, in the rooms occupied by Miss Fanny. Or Mr Boulton, as perhaps Eliza had to call him now. It was terrible.

The detective didn't even use the honorific 'Mr'. He called Fanny 'Boulton' as if he were a common criminal. It made Eliza scent danger. She grew — not stiff, because she knew stiffness would not save her. She knew she must remain supple, artful, careful. Every word she said, she knew, from now on, would have to be carefully thought out, apportioned out like a coin on a very long trip. She sensed that she had, already, without quite knowing it, departed.

Was it those first words with Maryanne down the lane? Or that witch Clara, with her horrible 'Good luck'? As good as a curse, really.

Upstairs she could hear furniture being moved around. She could hear footsteps: the tread of the heavy, beautifully shone shoes of the detective. She could hear — when she really concentrated — drawers being pulled out. Then there was a long, worrying, silence. As of someone going through things in great detail.

He had already asked, this man with the intense flat stare — a stare that gave nothing back but took in everything — he had already asked: and who else lives with Boulton?

She had felt her lips grow stiff. She had said, 'Well, sir, you had better ask that of Mrs Peck, as she is the owner of these here lodgings, sir. I am but a servant.'

He had left an appreciable pause.

Eliza heard some people walking by, out on the street, one of them murmuring in delighted tones: 'Really? That house? In there? Which floor?'

'Young lady,' said the detective. He sighed. 'There are two ways of doing this. One is to be called as a witness for the prosecution. The other is to be placed in the dock and to be quizzed by the prosecution. I don't need to remind a clever young lass like yourself,' he said, as if he had already made an assessment of her, 'which position it is better to be in. A position,' he went on, in the same even low voice, 'is something, I would believe, a clever young lass like yourself — a servant, as you say — is something you might value.'

There seemed to be a threat buried in this over-wrought sentence. The detective's eyes, which were a speckled brown to the point of being black, observed her response, as if every sentence he said was based on some scientific principle of response, reaction, observation, writing information down.

'You understand?' he said when she said nothing.

She nodded. It was better not to spend words.

'Good,' he said, as if they had agreed on something. 'Sit down. Wait here. I will be down pretty soon.'

She had already given him the keys. (Mrs Peck's last dictation to her had been: '*Hold nothing back, Eliza. The more we give 'em, the less we 'ave to be beholden to.*')

As he was going out of the room — she sitting there, imprisoned on a chair she never sat on (his chair: a leather throne with deeply incised mahogany scrollwork) — the detective asked, as if he had suddenly thought of it, 'And the other gent? How long has he been living in the same chambers?'

Eliza's mouth had come open. She knew he was referring to Lord Frederick. She found herself about to speak. She was aware, as if she could see them palpably in front of her own eyes, of a pair of scales rising up and down. She heard her breath. Felt the hairs on the back of her neck oscillate.

'Do you mean Mr Park, sir?'

The detective said nothing. Waited.

'I am not sure, sir,' she went on, as if he had answered. 'But,' she added quickly, not changing the expression on her face, 'those are things, sir, you rightfully have to ask my mistress. *Sir*,' she said, as a final rejoinder.

He said nothing and went upstairs.

As it Were

$\mathscr{C}$ummings had been waiting for the doors of Bow Street to open for over two hours. It had begun at five o'clock. He had arisen, washed his face in cold water, sluicing aside, as it were, the night. He had a mission. That he was accomplishing it for his friend Samuel ennobled it, if he thought like that. But Cummings never for one moment made the mistake of thinking anything was noble. A shrewd Mancunian, he had read, at a glance, Samuel Barton as a gullible provincial; but there was also some untouched, cold part of Cummings' heart that waited patiently to be touched and warmed by human feelings.

And as it was, Samuel Barton, a handsome enough lad, with his bright gaze and vivid colouring, his sculptured lips and olive skin — this freshling was everything Cummings was not. And so, in Cummings's uninspected heart, Samuel became an extension of himself: of what Cummings might do and see and feel if he were, as it were, draped in Samuel's comeliness.

He had no sexual feeling for Samuel: this would never have entered his mind. But there was something within himself that led him to make this exceptional trajectory: to tell his third lie at Budge and Costley, to go to the courtroom at

Bow Street for the second day's hearing, to test the waters 'as it were' (Cummings' favourite utterance, since it allowed circumlocution during which time he could more safely assess what he thought: he was the kind of law clerk who took pleasure from keeping people waiting, all the better that they could inspect their case and present it in a more organised fashion when he banged the little bell on his desk).

For Samuel's sake he would become, 'as it were', Samuel's eyes. He would not become Samuel's mind: Cummings' own mind, so superior in terms of rationality, cool reason and lack of gullibility, would replace Samuel's mind so that he, Cummings, could dictate a superior course of action for Samuel.

So he had waited. The queue outside Bow Street began even while the sky was still wrapped in gauze, through which the occasional star could be seen enjoying its final glitter. Then, as fires were lit in house after house and a grey pall of powdery light smeared over the heavens, all around in the streets leading to Covent Garden the traffic increased: carts and men and women carrying in barrow and box all the vegetables and flowers needed to feed and decorate London's stony heart.

*T*here was something almost cheerful in standing in the morning chill, warming his hands around a hot chestnut, letting his eyes run along the lines of the newspaper he had purchased, genially ignoring, on either side of him, the 'gentlemen' who were also waiting.

(One was a superior kind of servant who spent his time exchanging lugubrious comments with another servant behind Cummings. They had discussed their respective masters. They also talked, at length, about the theatre, about sighting *Miss Fanny* and *Mrs Graham* (as they called them almost reverentially) on the boards. As to the darker rumours — they did not believe them, 'not for one second'. 'Not for one second,' echoed the other servant, who nevertheless left a long and seemingly pregnant pause as if he wished his bookend servant to come back with something a little more tantalising.)

'And 'ave you 'eard,' murmured the stentorian gentleman to the lesser gentleman (who was in service, as he had extensively canvassed, with no lesser being than a baronet), 'about where the beak 'imself ought to send 'em?'

'Where's that then?'

'Why where else but — the *Middlesex* Sessions!'

The doors opened after that. Or rather, initially, there had been protracted sounds of bolts being pulled back, of ominous and important bangings and then a withering of human sound.

The queue, by this time snaking down Bow Street, became alert. People stopped leaning against walls. A pleasurable shade of anticipation animated chill faces (they were standing in the shade). Cummings then passed his only words of conversation to the elderly servant.

'About blasted time.'

But, as so often proves the case in the world of law and courts, it was a false dawn. The bolt was driven back and an elderly crone came out with a bucket of water smelling of carbolic. Telling those nearest to stand back, she set about washing the doorway and wiping down the doors, all the while murmuring to herself in a never-ending commentary that never once seemed to be in any known language. She knocked on the door, was admitted, the door slammed to, and those nearest were allowed to watch the steam slowly evaporate as the water cooled.

Everyone went back to their waiting position.

Then with almost brilliant militancy, all bolts were suddenly drawn back, the door was thrown open and the queue, taken unawares, recovered itself sufficiently to bundle in through the gap, then begin rushing to the miniaturised space of Courtroom Two.

Cummings, in this race, responded as a native Mancunian. He pushed with his elbows out, digging with them sharply so he took up the room of at least two people, meanwhile calling out comments like, 'Give us some room, won't you!' and ''Ere, stop shoving, why don't you!'

The two constables in the building clung to the walls as the human river swelled, rose and then engulfed the hallway of the miserable, antiquated building. An old lantern, just lit, sent out a Rembrandtesque light, murky and staining. The walls of the building, which dated back to the previous century, were filthy, the plaster smudged where bodies had successively banged against them, so that a tobacco-coloured fresco seemed to be artfully painted on every known surface, while frozen rivulets of tobacco-tinged murk marked the upper areas.

Everything in the courthouse was poor, broken down and overused. Courtroom Two had one window, a stall for the accused, a stall for the witness, and a single raised platform on which sat a table and chair for the magistrate. It was, after all, a court usually set aside for the drabs and dregs of London's nightlife. And yet it was as if the sheer weight of human misery of the vast city had so endlessly passed through such a small culvert that it had permanently stained the building: it was less a courtroom than a kind of human drain. It stank, was airless, and dark as a catacomb.

$\mathscr{C}$ummings felt himself entirely happy with his position. He had secured a seat on a bench in the third row. That is, he had secured a miserable space no more than eight inches wide, smaller than the human backside, into which he had wedged himself. He had opened wide his newspaper, the *Daily Telegraph*, 'With The Biggest Circulation in the World'. The pages almost flapped into the faces of the persons on either side of him. The younger of the two servants was on one side (his master was a mere 'honourable'). On the other side of Cummings sat a theatrical gentleman with a most unfortunate wig. This gentleman also had an annoying habit — of humming to himself continuously, like an untuned violin. (The elderly servant was having a highly vocal altercation with a lady's maid two rows back.)

Cummings, flicking his paper, was trying to decide whether it was worthwhile bringing this annoying humming to the creature's attention, but the fellow was engaged in gossip of a tedious theatrical character with the person behind him. Cummings had the feeling he was surrounded by people who all knew each other, and most of whom lived in the vicinity of Covent Garden or Drury Lane.

$\mathscr{O}$ver the next hour and a half, he had reason to look often and longingly through the doorway of the courtroom. Every so often a door banged open from behind the magistrate's bench. A robed solicitor entered with all the panache of a lead player in a drama, black robes flying, inscrutable pieces of paper bound with red tape clutched in his hands. He was followed, at varying intervals and through other doors, by other robed creatures. These appearances always seemed cunningly timed to fall in an especially long lacuna of boredom. But no sooner did they emerge than they departed. It was all a long tease.

Cummings returned again to the satisfactory sentiments of the paper's editorial.

THE SOCIAL MORALITY OF THE DAY.

The moral sense of the nation has of late received a severe shock. We have here a degradation of morals that recalls and reproduces the vices of the Roman Empire. A serious cause for disquietude is to be found in the growing disposition to trifle and coquette with forms of vice to which there is no excuse for men being even tempted . . .

While Cummings was again pondering these weighty prognostications, a lively smell began to emerge all around him. Someone was unwrapping, noisily, a newspaper that disgorged a corned-beef and pickled-onion sandwich. As if this were a signal, many other people began to unwrap or expose food that had hitherto been hidden on their person — inside shirts, under shawls, in large pockets. Cummings alone did not eat, and he felt a black sway of misery and anger descend on him.

There is something indescribably impudent about the manner in which these practices have been carried out within London itself.

> Here are two youths of respectable parentage and education
> not only playing female parts in theatrical representations
> throughout the country, but habitually walking the streets and
> frequenting places of public amusement in women's clothes,
> practising all the pretty arts of prostitutes, submitting to be
> entertained as such by gentlemen, and then suddenly resuming
> the privileges of their sex . . .

The eating frenzy had died down. Outside, in the filthy passage, where the stink of hundreds of unwashed bodies compounded and sought egress by floating into Courtroom Two, various policemen could be heard shouting at people to make way. This was answered by various levels of sauce: that people would give way if only they could move or had somewhere to give way to. Then, as if to intimate that the proper hour was at last drawing near, various gentlefolk began to appear. The servants on either side of Cummings had obediently stood up, bowed and handed over their warmed-up bench to their betters.

Cummings found himself sitting beside a highly perfumed lady, beautifully dressed in a pale, watery blue silk. She had smiled at him, but in such a vague way as to intimate that she could not be relied upon to ever recognise him again. Then she had spent a good ten minutes arranging herself for maximum display: turning over her shoulder, waving at newcomers, calling out little greetings ('So lovely to see you, darling. Isn't it frightfully early in the morning? I hardly feel human.') Cummings gathered she might be a great lady of the stage. Other people from the fashionable world — that is, the slightly slipshod world of late nights and intemperance, of men about town, swells and suchlike — came to take their seats, as for a performance.

It was as if a drinking den or low burlesque place had simply been transplanted to Bow Street.

Everyone expected to have a thoroughly good time.

To all of these people, drab little Cummings was completely invisible.

*S*uddenly the inert and smelly crowd that occupied the hallway, almost as if they were laying siege to the building, let out an exhalation that was like a shivering of leaves when a great wind is about to start up. This shivering, chattering vibration increased in velocity until everyone in Courtroom Two was also vibrating in tune with this gale of interest: all were looking in one direction.

'They're here, they've arrived!' could be heard, repeated on lip after lip. Heads out in the hallway could be seen turning in different directions. Various ragged children were hoisted onto shoulders. Everyone in Courtroom Two could hear a great deal of noise out in the street: cheering, whistling, clapping and something else, almost indecipherable as a human sound — hissing.

But at that precise moment, when everyone was straining to gaze out the door, a small door to the left of the central table fell back. A court official almost diffidently entered, as if aware he could in no way fulfil the expectations of such an audience, and, walking along in big awkward sideways steps, he led in, first, a rather plump and unexpectedly haggard young man, followed by a thin man seemingly blown in after him, as if by a contrary draught from that storm raging outside.

Oddly enough, everyone in the courtroom — apart from those men draped in black who had, as suddenly, poured in through another door — started to clap. Noisily.

This had an immediate effect on the two young men, whose faces lit up. The plumper of the two made a small bow and doffed his hat, while the thinner man — Cummings instantly surmised it must be Boulton — looked pleased, but a little embarrassed.

At this point another door opened, a large court official entered and, opening his mouth wide for a parade-ground roar, called for 'order and for the court to rise for his honour.'

At this point there was a sudden hollow 'whoosh' sound, as of fire leaping up a chimney.

Everyone stood.

And into the courtroom walked a small, insignificant man who only for one moment glanced out into the courtroom. He looked a little startled, but this impulse disappeared instantly and, taking his seat, he established his credentials as a man who had seen everything, understood a great deal of it, and was astonished by virtually nothing.

The Play's the Thing

From the start Cummings could not take his eyes off Boulton. He was trying to comprehend the source of Samuel's fascination. Yet for all the world, without the trappings of femininity, Boulton looked like the kind of clerk you might pass in the street, anywhere, without so much as a second look. He was undistinguished in every way, except that he was perhaps slighter than other men — certainly thinner. His hair was not very well dressed but he was wearing what Cummings diagnosed (without knowing anything about it in particular) as an exceedingly fashionable suit — tightly tailored at the waist, large lapels, bright buttons. He was also wearing a curious tie of a type Cummings, who was unerringly conformist in every way, would never wear: a sailor's tie.

Cummings dismissed this, almost angrily, as an effeminate affectation. The rational part of his brain could not understand why Boulton would wear something so potentially incriminating. He decided that Boulton was probably a person of rather low intelligence.

This made him feel better.

The initial address was from a sharp character by the name of Poland. He started off by apologising, saying that the matter had been placed in the hands of the solicitor to the Treasury only two days prior, 'because it became obvious to the police, after they had made inquiries, that the two prisoners had not assumed men's clothes for the purposes of a lark and certain inferences must be drawn'.

He began fidgeting with papers.

'The police,' he said, looking up and now speaking more dramatically, as if he had only just then found his lines, 'have been literally inundated with communications respecting the case from all over the country.' His eyes passing over Ernest and Arthur, he continued in a loud voice: 'It appears Park and Boulton have systematically been going around the countryside in women's clothes, frequenting places of public amusement and annoying persons who were there for the legitimate purpose of amusement. The inference of a very unfavourable nature may naturally be drawn from their conduct. Whether they did it to extort money, or whether they were doing it for something worse — a crime held in detestation in this country, an unspeakable crime, ladies and gentlemen, which until only comparatively recently was a capital offence — this inquiry will endeavour to show.'

At this point the courtroom grew particularly quiet. The magistrate gave the appearance of listening, but also being in some kind of abstract state. He nodded slightly.

Mr Poland sat down.

He was followed by the counsel for Boulton and Park, a Mr Besley.

Mr Besley was short, fussy and appeared short-sighted. But there was a look of crafty intelligence in his eyes.

He started off by turning to the bench and saying he felt the young 'gentlemen' were being ill-treated as they had not been charged with anything definite and the prosecution wanted to keep the case open, in the hope that something definite might one day turn up.

Mr Flowers, the magistrate, suddenly looked alert and said in a not unfriendly but firm voice that the hearing must go on without a definite charge being brought in, since new evidence was being found all the time.

'There are certain facts with regard to Boulton and Park,' he said, leaving a brief pause, 'that disturb me.'

Boulton and Park had assumed a diffident air and looked about the courtroom almost, Cummings thought reprovingly, as if they were there accidentally, through no fault of their own. At one point the creature known as Boulton even had the temerity to look directly and questioningly at Cummings himself, perhaps diagnosing someone of unusual interest in the room.

Cummings had looked away angrily. But when he looked back the creature's gaze had moved on and a settled miasma of distance seemed to have calcified all over his features, casting him into a statue. He did not seem to move at all after that.

*T*he first witness for the prosecution was a 'gent' in a loud checked suit, with a pronounced moustache and muscular upper body that seemed to strain against the armpits of his suit. From his waistcoat, differently checked, hung a cheap gold chain that could be heard to clatter every time he moved.

He gave his name, in a sonorous bass, as 'John Reeves, resident at 61 Frith Street, Soho'.

He was staff superintendent at the Alhambra Theatre, Leicester Square.

Boulton gazed languidly at him: why did Cummings get the sense that Boulton's gaze was the myopic one of a cat, squatting, purring and gazing into the middle distance? Park by contrast had sat up, was quite alert.

The superintendent said he had known Park by sight for three years, Boulton for two years. His attention had been first drawn to them 'when they were walking about as women. Their conduct was suspicious. I should think they were trying to entice gentlemen. I saw them moving their shoulders, looking over them, trying to attract the attention of men, I imagine.'

Mr Besley interposed: 'Pray do not imagine.'

The prosecuting counsel said: 'It is difficult to describe in language what would be obvious to persons seeing them.'

Boulton's solicitor then countered: 'We do not know what women "do". In courts of justice we must have evidence.'

After this sharp exchange the superintendent, pausing to see if it was all right for him to continue — the magistrate nodded sagely — said he had gone up to them in the lower promenade ('a great many women go there') and asked them to leave.

'A person who I had often seen in their company told me not to interfere; that it was a mistake. I said: "It is no mistake on my part. I think I have seen them before in men's clothes. I cannot tell what they are but I have my suspicions about them. They will have to leave." I called one of my assistants and we marched them out into the street.'

'Who is this gentleman you have often seen with them?'

Cummings felt his gaze concentrate.

'I know the gentleman by sight but I don't know his name.'

'Should you know his photograph?' asked Mr Poland quickly. As he moved, he looked directly and even victoriously at Boulton, who looked away. Park, however, met his gaze.

'I think so.'

There was a small murmur in the back row of the spectators.

Reeves went on to say that they had returned several times later. 'They were walking about looking at the people in a manner more like women than men. They were surrounded at times by twenty men dressed in a similar manner, wearing paint. People were complaining about them, saying they were women dressed in men's clothes. They wore flesh-coloured gloves. They made noises with their lips. They were giggling and chirping to one another, and chucking one another under the chin. When I said they must leave, they said "Let us have some brandy and soda." I said "No, you must leave." I told the box-keeper to return their guinea and on no account let them come in again.'

Cummings was aware of a particular stillness emanating from the magistrate. Only when Reeves finished speaking did he begin to — hurriedly, it appeared — write something down.

Flowers looked up.

'You said you have seen twenty persons with powdered faces and dressed in that manner talking to the accused?'

'Yes.'

'As friends of theirs?'

'Yes, as acquaintances. There are a number of them about.'

The magistrate, saying nothing, went back to making notes.

Boulton and Park exchanged a quick look. All around them, murmuring and chatter rose.

Reeves was allowed to stand down.

The next witness made an unexpectedly comic entrance. There was a long silence, then the door opened abruptly. It was as if the witness had been thrown bodily into the room by someone behind the door. He looked broken down, with vividly dyed ginger hair, a coarse skin, large lips and a pendulous, drinker's nose. He was also dressed formally in what was quite clearly second-hand and somewhat greasy finery — a magnificent but ill-fitting evening suit.

He began by making a deep bow to the bench.

(Boulton could be seen to lean towards Park, his hand placed over his mouth. As people throughout the courtroom broke out into ripples of barely suppressed laughter, a shy smile passed over Boulton's face. Park also seemed to chuckle.)

The magistrate touched his gavel on the tabletop, but relatively lightly. He looked over his glasses into the courtroom and nodded for the Crown solicitor to begin.

The witness described himself as George Smith, who lived at 14 Paradise Street, Marylebone. 'Former beadle of Burlington Arcade, your grace.'

A flitter of angst passed over the Crown's face. The body of Mr Besley suddenly seemed a bit more relaxed.

Smith took in a deep breath and began what was clearly a carefully prepared and rehearsed colloquy. Cummings had the distasteful impression he might even have prepared it staring into a mirror. The occasional slur on his words also gave the unfortunate impression that the man was at least partially drunk. As he talked he swayed slightly to and fro, liberally peppering his remarks with 'your graces' and small half bows.

He said he had seen Boulton about the arcade for about two years.

'I noticed Boulton's face, and observed it was thickly covered with rouge. Everybody turned to look at him. He spoke to me on one occasion when he was leaving. He said to me "Oh! you sweet little dear." I saw Boulton going up the Arcade several times after that, turning his head and smiling at gentlemen.'

'What do you mean — smiling at gentlemen?'

This was Mr Poland.

Smith then did a most unfortunate thing, and it was before Mr Poland could stop him. He engineered a pantomime dame's swaying walk, turning over his shoulder and casting languorous glances — at the magistrate.

The result was a storm of laughter.

The magistrate, unable to keep the shadow of a smile from passing over his lips for a moment, banged his gavel. The court official, a large gentleman who might in different circumstances be mistaken for a Cabinet minister, looked severely annoyed.

'Order,' he cried out. But even his voice was half-hearted. 'Order! Order!'

'I can't do it half as well as Boulton,' said Smith. This was followed by more laughter. Boulton himself smiled. The laughter mounted and grew tumultuous. There was even foot-stamping.

This time the magistrate looked annoyed. He banged his gavel again, and said, looking out into the courtroom as it settled down, 'It is a surprise to me that Englishmen would treat a serious matter of this type in such a frivolous way.'

The room felt rebuked.

Cummings himself felt sick. With rage. Everyone in that courtroom knew that

Burlington Arcade in the afternoon was the trolling ground of prostitutes. No even faintly respectable woman would be seen there between three and five. The rooms above the shops were quite openly used as places of assignation. He intuited that the prosecution was trying to establish a case whereby Boulton and Park were male prostitutes, masquerading as women; then, once they had obtained their victims, they would reveal themselves as men. This was a particularly cunning ploy for blackmail.

There was nothing so blackmailable as men who favoured Mollies.

Cummings felt righteously furious.

Samuel had obviously escaped by only a hair's breadth. (If he had escaped, which Cummings in his heart of hearts, was certain that he had. He could not have borne . . . not Samuel. His Samuel.)

'Boulton made a noise with his mouth,' Smith continued. 'I went up to him and said, "I have received several complaints about you. I have seen enough of your character to consider you an improper person, and you must leave at once." Directly they saw me they rushed into a hosier's shop in the arcade. I stood at the door till they came out. Boulton said to his companion, another young man dressed as a woman, painted and rouged, "Take no notice of that fellow." I said to Boulton, "I have cautioned you not to come in here." He said, "I shall go where I like." He tried to pass me but I ejected him as before. They went quietly away.'

When Smith had finished, Mr Besley, as if incidentally, asked him about whether he was still a beadle at the arcade.

'Oh no, your lordship, to my regret.'

At this point his tale unravelled. When Mr Besley questioned him sharply on whether he had taken money as a precondition to the prostitutes working the arcade, Smith's face turned a bright red. He began mopping his face with a rather suspect handkerchief and he turned to the magistrate, saying piteously, 'It is an open attack on my honour, my lord.'

'You need not call me, your "lord",' Mr Flowers said to him, not unkindly. 'And please answer the question, Mr Smith.'

The defrocked beadle winced slightly, pushed his handkerchief deep down inside his pocket and stood there, a picture of deflation.

'The less you say about honour the better,' Mr Besley said to him sharply. 'Were you not dismissed from the Arcade on account of your unreliability and acceptance of what amounted to bribes?'

'They was not bribes, sir,' Smith said in a querulous voice.

'And have you not partaken of liquor this morning, Mr Smith?'

'Only three half-pints, sir.'

'And are you currently in employment?'

'No sir, I am not.'

There was a significant pause.

'How do you live, Mr Smith?'

'I am living off the charity of my good and esteemed friends, sir, in Southend. I live the best way I can,' he added as a piteous afterthought. He looked wretched.

'And were you offered, sir, any inducement to come forward with your testimony this afternoon?'

He visibly brightened here.

Mr Poland's face showed no emotion.

'Oh yes sir,' he said, as if he had at last remembered something of use. 'Superintendent Thomas of the E Division, sir, said to me, "I will see you are paid for your trouble, Smith, if you know anything about the case." I was taken, sir, to the House of Detention, where I recognised the prisoners in the cell.'

'Thank you, sir,' the magistrate said courteously, as Smith, bowing again very low to the bench, was escorted from the room.

After this there was a break into a level of merriment, which pained Cummings exceedingly. He had once and once only been to the Strand Theatre and had been shocked at its indecency. It appeared to him the same level of ribald enjoyment was present in the courtroom. The sad fact was — it did not appear to be a real case at all. It had become a form of entertainment.

The hearing had now been in session for over four hours. Everyone was aware that it was long past the luncheon hour. Outside, in the direction of the Opera House, a woman's voice could be heard running up and down the scales endlessly.

In the hallway the crowd was growing more and more restless.

Cummings felt his stomach emit a loud and, as it were, protesting rumble. The lady beside him shifted her body fractionally away. Cummings had the decency to blush. He was about to murmur something to her when Mr Poland rose to his feet.

'Sir, we have reached the end of today's proceedings. I would like to make a plea. I ask that the prisoners be kept on remand — '

Mr Besley rose to his feet in alarm.

'Your honour, I must protest . . .'

Boulton and Park were paying attention suddenly. They realised this was a moment when they could be released.

Mr Poland went on. 'We have no doubt the money will be forthcoming for bail, but we know that the prisoners, once released, may not be so forthcoming for future hearings.'

Park and Boulton turned and looked at the magistrate, almost as if willing him to respond to an alternative argument.

But Mr Poland's words ground remorselessly on: 'Even on the existing evidence, sir, there seems to be a *prima facie* case of felony, and that of a very serious character.'

He looked, at that second, as if he were trying to assess how the magistrate would fall. But as if sensing he could not trust Mr Flowers' silence, he put his hand out in a dramatic gesture that would not have been out of place in Drury Lane.

Boulton and Park both looked at Poland, transfixed.

His clerk, an understudy of a bewigged and black-robed type, leant forward and placed in Mr Poland's hands a sheath of what looked like oversized cards.

'I hold in my hands, sir, some photographs.'

'Photographs?' said the magistrate, looking over his glasses.

'Over fifty-five, sir. Some taken from an album.'

'And all of them in feminine attire?'

'Yes, sir. Some appear to be maidenly photos, some are allegorical. Some feature gentlemen, as an accompaniment.'

Cummings felt himself retract. Felt something shrivel inside him.

'Do you know the identity of any of these gentlemen?'

'I imagine sir, that — '

'Pray do not imagine, sir,' broke in Mr Besley.

'One of the gentlemen is well known, sir. That is, he was constantly seen in the company of the two — of Boulton and Park, sir.'

There was a moment's silence — almost a deliquescence. The case was at a fork in the road. But the magistrate seemed blind to this. He simply shuffled some papers on his desk and said, dryly, 'Pray continue.'

The silence in the courtroom became cross-hatched with whispers.

'He was the gentleman with the two accused on the night of their apprehension.'

The magistrate nodded but took it no further. He seemed to write something down.

'At the moment, sir,' Mr Poland continued, 'there is nothing — as yet — to say that the men posing in these photographs are not completely innocent. But if they are not innocent, sir, the court can rest assured that no names — *not one name, sir* — will be kept from the court.'

Boulton looked down. Park looked into a neutral middle distance.

The courtroom had grown very silent.

Even out in the hallway a curious stillness fell.

Cummings felt his heart hammer.

Mr Besley turned to the magistrate, ignoring Mr Poland's latest evidence. He spoke in a deliberately conversational tone, as if by vocal range seeking to establish a different — less pejorative — context.

'We ask for bail, your honour, as nothing criminal has been established. Our clients are completely happy to have a most searching investigation and would of course turn up for the continued hearing, as they are most eager — indeed, quite insistent — your honour, on establishing their innocence.'

Mr Poland hardly waited for Mr Besley to finish. He jumped up.

'I ask you, sir,' he said tersely, 'in the interests of public justice, not to allow the prisoners to go out on bail. If you have further doubt, sir,' he said to Mr Flowers, whose face showed no emotion whatsoever, 'I will go on with the evidence. I have further evidence, sir.'

Mr Flowers altered the documents on his desk for a moment, as if putting them in order was what dominated his thoughts. Then he looked up.

'I cannot think,' he said carefully, 'excepting the photographs, which of themselves are not evidence of criminal intent, that there is enough evidence against the defendants to prevent my offering bail.'

There was an immediate outburst of voices, crying heartily, 'Hear hear!'

The ripple and the rumble of the magistrate's words spread from mouth to mouth out of doors, out into the street. But while a faint echo of cheering could be heard from the street, Mr Poland's clerk was already placing something further into Mr Poland's hands.

It looked like an envelope. With writing on it.

'Sir, I would request that you read this letter.'

The letter was handed up to the bench.

Again a curious silence fell.

'I shall retire to read the letter. The court will be adjourned for five minutes.'

He banged his gavel and left the court.

This interlude was peculiarly long, Cummings judged. The lady beside him, quite forgetting herself, turned to him and said breathlessly, 'What do you think it is? A programme from one of the plays, perhaps? Ernest is the very *genius* with his impersonations, don't you think?'

Other voices took up, and sentence after sentence sped about the dirty little room. Some people took the chance to cough. One or two persons stood up to get circulation back into their rear quarters. The counsel and the prosecution dropped their adversarial roles and exchanged information on where they would go for an extended luncheon. Park waved at various friends, making faces that seemed to intimate that he expected to be seeing them soon, outside. Boulton was inspecting a pattern on his trousers.

Cummings waited, in suspension.

The door opened and Mr Flowers walked in without looking out into the court. His demeanour had changed. He looked ominously serious.

He sat down.

He did not glance at Boulton or Park.

'Since reading the letter, my opinion of the case has entirely changed. It is my duty to remand the prisoners without bail.'

He banged his gavel down hard, stood up and removed himself from the court.

There was an immediate sensation in the courtroom. The court reporters began fighting their way out of the room. The scribe from the *Daily Telegraph*, a wiry little fellow, cut in front of and jostled the *Illustrated Police News* reporter, a portly gent who himself tried to outpace the *Times* crime reporter, a seasoned gentleman who knew well enough to obstruct the passage of the *Saturday Review* reporter.

Sound in the courtroom rose and rose, with the swiftness of a saucepan of milk boiling over.

As the *Daily Telegraph* reported the following morning: 'The prisoners assumed an air of indifference. They were then removed.'

The House
of Waiting

Ernest had been taken, on first arriving at the House of Detention, to a bath.

The guard had brought him into the room and said, 'Strip.'

> Is't a dream? Is't a phantasm? 'tis
>
> Too horrible for reality! for aught else
>
> Too palpable!

His life was now a matter of stripping, of undressing, perpetually taking off layer after layer. As if all they wanted was to reduce him to the one irreducible being. His maleness. His body. Fit him back within the rude parameters that had always restricted him, or never really been enough. Never been a precise enough description.

> Oh would it were a dream!
>
> How would I bless the sun that wak'd me from it!
>
> I perish!

So he had floated through, evading the name, inventing another. Become a whole other — possible, fantastical, being.

He had gone into some kind of numb freefall. He kept banging into things:

doorways, chair legs. It was as if he had lost control of his body. He was terrified that he was going to piss or shit, as if he had suddenly lost control of his physical container. As if, in revenge, it might betray him. Turn him into how he actually felt.

Besmirched. Dirty.

'Use the soap, why don't you!' the guard had barked, shifting his eyes for a moment, as if he — fully dressed in his blue serge uniform, with the buckles and belt, his shoes and moustache, the little arrows by his collar — disdained to let his eyes rest on such a poor creature, such a neither–nor, such a slackly feminine body on a man.

Ernest had clumsily soaped himself, all the time wondering about the number of bodies that had lain in that brine.

The bottom of the bath was a loathsome slime — a shifting squish of green. He got out as soon as he could.

'You're not clean yet,' the guard had said.

He would never be clean.

In the eyes of someone like that.

When he did get out, he rose up without any modesty and went over to the 'towel', a damp rag the size of a shaving towel.

He stood there naked, letting his own eyes — the eyes of Ernest Boulton, gentleman — look with deep anger back at the guard, who for one moment let his eyes drop, let his gaze falter. Then the guard no longer registered Remand Prisoner 5C, no longer made any attempt to select out his individuality. He let 5C wipe himself dry, dress in the male clothes that had been brought for him, let him pass on to the next stage of his humiliation.

*H*e was weighed, without his shoes. He was measured. His name, age, place and date of birth were taken. His current address was inquired about: trade or profession, married state, prison record, religion, ability to write and read.

In this way the fantastical being known as Fanny withered down into a nervous, depressed young man. Now almost totally monosyllabic, he was asked whether he had any friends who could supply him with changes of linen.

He was asked about his diseases.

> Like some desperate mariner
> Impatient of a strange, and hostile land,
> Who rashly hoists his sail, and puts to sea . . .

(He kept hearing in his head Julia's lines. They occurred to him in his hour of need as if they could protect him. Words alone. They mocked him, instead. Grinned at him. Spat at him.)

He was marched off down a long brick corridor, its floor gleaming with polished asphalt. He observed the malevolence of the extreme cleanliness, smelt the overpowering carbolic. The way there was nothing living here. Even mould was regarded as an enemy. A possible companion.

> . . . And being fast on reefs and quicksands borne,
>
> Essays in vain once more to make land,
>
> Whence wind and current drive him, — I'm wreck'd
>
> By my own act!

The guard stopped to unlock an iron door, which slid along with a final, echoing bang as it hit the wall. They entered the Cyclops's eye of the place. In each direction Ernest saw row upon row of iron balconies, with circular staircases curling up to each level, and door upon dismal door: all glinting metal, gloaming asphalt — all cold to the touch, impervious, washable. The same stink of carbolic.

To scrub away sin.

To cleanse.

Remand Prisoner 5C was handed on.

*U*p three flights of stairs, along a terrace past four doors, he arrived at an iron door with a grille in it.

The guard was an older man who had looked at Ernest's name and occupation but registered nothing — and for this lack of comment Ernest was suddenly and almost savagely grateful, as if at this moment he could sense how much better it might be to be forever Ernest, always male — so much easier. The guard selected a key from his belt and pushed back the iron door.

Cold. A wave of chill.

A cell, twelve feet by seven. The same diabolically polished asphalt, whitewashed walls without so much as a speck or scrawl. In the corner, and high up, three small shelves on which were placed a Bible, a hymnbook, a prayerbook, an enamelled plate, a tin mug, wooden spoon and salt box, a piece of soap. A squat three-legged stool sat on the floor. And a bundle for a bed, rolled up and tied by leather straps to the wall. A pot to piss and shit in. And a window: high up, but a window nevertheless. Not barred, but with opaque glass panes. Two panes within the window cantilevered back.

The guard indicated with his hand the regulations printed on the wall.

"'Ere's something for you to read. Pass the time like,' he said in a way that wasn't actually hostile. Ernest was pathetically grateful. The guard was late middle-aged, like a broken-down sergeant.

No prisoner shall receive or send any parcel.
All prisoners shall regularly attend Divine Service.
Every prisoner shall be furnished with the means of moral and
religious instruction, and with suitable books.

Then the door slammed to, the key turned and Ernest Boulton, gentleman, was alone.

What — no escape? No hope?

None!

He was dry, parched, insane. He was walking up and down his cell, all eight paces of it, turning, hearing the distant felted footsteps two levels down, the soft swish of the keys. He glared at the door, then hit his head. He was going insane, insane.

I will get out. This can't last. It is only a momentary inconvenience. You are a criminal now. This is not a play. You have no lines, you have no lines. This can't last. I can't get out.

He had to calm down. Think. If only he had a drink. Some laudanum. Stell had said it would all be all right. Not to panic. He would contact his father, the Master of the Common Pleas. He would contact his friends. They would get out. It was all a terrible mistake. God: could nobody spare him a drink? The terrible silence, the terribleness of the silence.

At least he was wearing his own clothes. They had finally brought them in but had taken — taken his golden cufflinks, his silver-backed hairbrush, his toothbrush, his silk handkerchief, his chased gold watch that his mother had given him on his eighteenth birthday (all of these written down, laboriously, by the clerk downstairs). He had had to sit a yard apart from Stella, not speaking. Not saying a word. Their eyes had met and Stell — Arthur — had tried to calm him down.

Stell had said to him (quickly quickly), '*Gold will buy anything once we're inside.*'

The guard had said, 'The rule here is silence. Do not speak unless you are spoken to.'

Stell managed to murmur as she arose, '*Don't panic. We'll get out.*'

At first he half believed it.

He was in shock. He did not believe it was happening. Or that it could continue.

Marks in his travesty. Stations in his cross. The first time the door of his cell was closed on him and he was left alone. *There is some mistake. I am not here.*

Getting his bed down and feeling the coarse blankets.

He had wept.

Waking in the cell he thought: *I am going mad. I am going insane.* Then there was the terror of what lay ahead. Going to court.

'*It will be all right. They've got nothing on us.*'

This was Stell again. They had these snatched conversations. Stell had become more and more Arthur. Using a gentleman's cadences, a male voice.

This isn't happening to us.

It was a shock to think they had been so closely observed for so long.

What might come out?

It was all a fucking nightmare. A terrible mistake.

*E*rnest was haunted by several things: by what lay ahead, certainly. For once in his life he did not want an audience. He felt like someone chilled, frozen, still in shock. Ernest Boulton was trapped in his cell, in his male clothes. As for Fanny, she was some faint shadow: elusive, allusive, disappearing.

If she knew what was good for her.

> On the brink
> Of what a precipice I'm standing! Back!
> Back! while the faculty remains to do't!
> A minute longer, not the whirlpool's self
> More sure to suck thee down!

*E*rnest realised that if he stood on his closet seat he could just see out the central cantilevered window to the looming dome of St Paul's. He watched the light blossom and fade.

The most poignant sound was the distant rattle of street traffic.

It was difficult not to succumb to moments of despair, hearing the sounds of people going about their daily lives.

He wondered then exactly what he had got himself involved in.

There was a lot of time for remorse.

At six o'clock in the morning, a time when he was usually sleeping off the night before, a large bell began to clang. A few moments later, his cell door was thrown open by the warder, who came into his cell, followed by the Deputy Governor and another warder who carried a book.

Ernest was handed two hard brushes with which to polish the floor of his cell.

His hammock was inspected. If it was not stowed correctly he had to take it down again and stow it away in regulation order.

All of this was deeply humiliating to Ernest Boulton, gent.

It was better that Fanny not know.

Each morning, on hands and knees, Ernest Boulton, gent, had to polish the floors of his cell. Scrub the table, stool, basin and water closet. This was how he was made to understand he had no ownership, even of the pathetic objects in the cell. It was also an act of remorse. He was to wipe away the dirt of crime and sin.

And the ritualistic way of having to repeat it day after day also implied the Sisyphean nature of the act: the purging would never end.

Breakfast was served through a small trap in the door: a pint of gruel and a piece of bread. This was always a difficult moment in Ernest's day. Ingesting the food. But eventually hunger got the better of him.

This was another cross in his station.

Chapel followed. For him who had not been to church for over three long years.

On stepping outside he found himself on the gallery. He was told to turn sharply around with his face to the cell door: just one of the million small humiliations by which a remand prisoner was reminded of his loss of freedom. The absurdity of the action also helped the prisoner realise that he could not question anything: he was a passive participant. The prisoner had to hold the Bible, prayer and hymnbook behind his back. And stand looking at the door for a long time.

Then, in line formation, spaced apart and in total silence, the chain of prisoners walked downstairs along a stone passage, past the doorway of a kitchen where they smelt the dinner they would later consume — as if to heighten the experience of what they did not have.

Taking a low winding stair into the chapel, the prisoners took their seats on backless forms. But even here they were made aware of the frightening nature of their imprisonment. Two cages, one thickly curtained for women, and another full of cropped and shaven male prisoners in rough grey prison clothing, pointed to an unenviable future: they were occupied by those who had been tried, found guilty and convicted.

They were about to be sent off to prisons.

This was an unsubtle reminder that there was a further depth beyond this current purgatory.

Once the Governor had taken his seat, and the door was locked, with a nod to the chaplain, the morning service could commence.

The sermon usually focused on the redemption of sin.

At the end of the service the prisoners filed back to their cells in silence, hands compulsorily placed behind them, in them the penitential weight of a Bible, prayer and hymnbook.

The door closed. The only interruption to the rest of the day was the exercise yard. This too was a perfect expression of containment, despair. Marched off into a stone-paved yard with high brick walls, the prisoners had to walk in an eternal circle, some three yards apart, watched over by two guards so no talk took place.

The walls were so high that you could only see the sky, and as it was early May, heating up into a promising summer, the exercise yard grew uncomfortably hot. At times it was like being placed in a roasting oven.

Exercise was followed by lunch. There was an hour in the afternoon for further exercise in the Dantesque circle of hell.

This was a remand prisoner's day, repeated day after day, like the toll of a funeral bell.

Frederick never came to visit Ernest in the House of Detention. Ernest longed to see him, longed to feel the touch of his hand, the comfort of his flesh, his body. But Ernest also knew it would be suicidal for Frederick, Lord Clinton, to show his face. All Ernest could hope was that Clinton's relations and friends had got him out of the country.

The Nature of Goodness

'Ah, it's you, true friend!'

Samuel was standing in the Brewster's Own Oyster-rooms, his face alert and pale. He quickly folded away the newspaper.

Cummings had come straight from Bow Street. It was the day of the third hearing: two weeks had passed and still no charges had been laid.

'What news?'

The oyster-rooms, in Star Yard, off Chancery Lane, were where he and Cummings had always eaten, before Samuel met Fanny. (Time was divided for

Cummings into *Before Fanny* and *After Fanny*.)

Cummings took his time replying. He wondered sometimes if he was not enjoying it too much: the decrepitude of Samuel's pleasure, the way it was being worm-eaten with anxiety. In fact he slowed his pace a little, to let Samuel wait a moment more, to enjoy his sickly angst.

Let him think, Cummings thought to himself, a little of how it might be for his Ursula: what sickness she would feel if she only knew. But his pity for Samuel only doubled when he saw his old friend look so wan. He also knew some kind of corruption in his pity: he felt an unpleasant spasm of joy in seeing his friend (who was so victorious in love, with life) so cast down — so dependent on him.

'How did it go today?'

Samuel's shoes sketched a pattern in the sawdust of the murky floor. The maid was bringing them, unasked, their usual lunchtime quaffing: two tankards of ale, an oyster pie apiece. Cummings almost ostentatiously left his drink untouched. (While Samuel, as if in a trance, reached out for his mug and began supping, slipping down the forgetfulness, the calm of oblivion.)

Cummings noted that melancholy became Samuel's looks: he just looked more Chatterton-like, his cheeks hollowed out, his lips — bitten — redder and fuller, more poisoned by worry.

'Tell me. Don't spare me.'

'Friend, your name was not spoken,' Cummings said. With gravity he raised his mug to his lips, and as if to emphasise how unsteady Samuel was, he merely let the ale brace and dance on his tongue. He would take his time — his killing.

'But tell me what Fanny — '

Cummings clanged his mug down. He felt an almost uncontrollable rinse of anger.

'Don't — *ever* — use that damnable name again,' he whispered, and glanced about the saloon. 'At least not in my ears. If your Ursula could but hear you!' He had tossed in his poisoned dart. Knowing it would flare and flush through Samuel's system.

And indeed Samuel's face looked briefly anguished.

'I must go and see Fanny.'

'*Her. She. Fanny.*' Cummings leant his face in closer to Samuel. He all but hissed. Then, at the last moment he recognised that his safety lay in assuming reasonableness. 'Barton, these are dangerous terms to use just now.'

Samuel's dark eyes flickered all over Cummings' face.

'Good friend,' Samuel said to him, lowering his head, so Cummings caught a glimpse of the nape of Samuel's neck — it looked so naked, so vulnerable. 'You are such a good friend to me, with your advice. But how did it go today? Tell me, Cubs. Quick.'

He appeared to brace himself.

Cummings was on the verge of saying what he himself thought: that the prosecution were building a case that was clearly predicated on the fact that Boulton and Park were male prostitutes: why else would men parade around as women? Except to ensnare, and once having ensnared, to live off the blackmail? The pretty play-acting was all just a ruse. And the prosecution was setting a trap for Boulton and Park to mince into: once having established their presence at places of gaiety, of acting and, simultaneously, prostitution, the trap would close.

They would be mincemeat.

But still no charges had been laid.

It was the longest hearing without charges being laid that he had ever attended but Cummings had sufficient legal knowledge to know that a charge of sodomy was peculiarly difficult to prove: it needed witnesses, and because of the taint involved in being associated in any way with such ungodly behaviour, people were unwilling to come forward. The taint was so terrible that even to be associated with the act, in whatever innocent capacity, meant ruin.

Cummings sensed that the prosecution were still gathering damning material. There was talk of a wider conspiracy, among the 'associates' of Boulton and Park, who met for costume balls and the like, to corrupt public morals. The newspapers were full of hints of it. There were reports of men hurriedly leaving London. The scandal was not diminishing: it grew, hearing by hearing.

'You still think it could go either way?'

Cummings read, at a glance, Samuel's state of mind.

He did not want bad news.

Cummings was expressively silent for a moment. He said nothing. Then, glancing into the despondent face of his friend, he said, 'Regardless of how the case is going, my friend, we both know they only need bail and then . . .' He made a flitting motion with his hand — and even went *Pffft!*'

Boulton and Park would slip across the Channel. Go into exile. Join their friends in dingy cafés in Dover, boarding houses in Boulogne. In time-honoured fashion.

'But there was,' Cummings found himself duty-bound to add, 'some damaging evidence brought in at the last. Further letters. Of an extremely personal nature.' A long pause. 'You never wrote to . . . the personage in question, did you?'

'No. I did not.'

Another pause.

'How did — Ernest look?'

The quick change, mid-sentence, did not escape Cummings, who winced but pretended it was the chill ale on a rotten tooth. He pushed the mug away.

'I have nothing to compare,' he said in a carefully flat voice. He enjoyed refusing. But Samuel had gathered his hand into his own, grasped his palm and quivered into Cummings' body wave after wave of emotion, anxiety, care. Or was it love?

'I'm going to the House of Detention. I've got to see Fan . . . Ernest.'

It was love, then. Misguided fool.

'There was mention again of photographs.'

Samuel went pale.

'I saw some on my way here. None of me, yet, thank heavens,' Samuel hurried to add. He put his hand up and ordered two — no, one — ale (Cummings shook his head, sober as a verger at a slightly too riotous wedding). 'But many of . . . you know who. With Clinton, mainly. And . . . others.'

'I suspect,' said Cummings, dryly, 'there may have been many . . . others.'

'Is it wrong to value friendship?'

This was abrupt. Samuel's face had drained of blood. He looked suspicious — drunk, certainly: Cummings had a suspicion Samuel might have been drinking while he waited. It was so unusual for Samuel to be drinking alone in the daytime that he looked at him afresh. Samuel loomed forward, aggressive, suddenly ugly. Then a light broke out in his eyes and his expression changed.

'Oh, dear friend Cubby,' he cried in an agonised voice. 'What am I doing, saying? To you who are my dearest friend of all.'

Samuel, ingenuously as far as Cummings was concerned, dragged him into a beery embrace and held his body captive, tight.

'I say, Barton,' Cummings said, after a moment.

Samuel's clasp lightened.

'Of course, Cummings, of course,' Samuel said, attending to the placement of the mugs on the scarred tabletop, as if his life depended on it. There was a glitter of moisture on his lashes.

Cummings felt a brief spasm of emotion — or was it mere pity? — for the object of his affection. At the same time he was framing a letter he would write that very evening.

Dear Ursula, it began. I think it is timely for you to pay a call to London. I have some unfortunate news that I feel, as a friend, I must divulge.

I must go, dear friend.

Samuel was standing a little unsteadily. He could have been off to Agincourt, thought Cummings a little grimly, smiling to himself as he watched Barton move towards the door.

Now that he was gone Cummings could, himself, get genially drunk. He might splash out tonight and find himself a whore. He had an urge. Well, he had an urge to . . . but perhaps there was no need to inspect where this urge may have led him: to what dark and small room, to what bed, or indeed to what room without so much as a bed. He was an economical lad and it was, after all, London.

*L*ord Frederick Clinton could hardly move, dress, shave. He was inert in his very essence. He occupied the shell of his being, as someone not at home. Without Fanny, Fred's life had no purpose. She was everything and nothing. He was unused to introspection, so this activity was peculiarly painful to him. He was like a man taking his first walk on stilts: he could only fall — and hope, in falling, that he rolled and did not break anything. An overpowering sense of bleakness had overcome him, an almost theatrical awareness of his life's futility.

Normally he would be happy to be drunk, to eat until he had gorged himself, to rut or be rutted into stupefaction. But now even these skills, such as they were, evaded his grasp. He could not get drunk enough: he was simply delivered into a morose state; worse, he got into fights. One night he woke to find himself saturated in spew, blood drying on his face. It was terrible, and in some cathartic part of himself he felt he deserved it. But it didn't bring him any closer to a sense of reality. He saw the world outside — people on the streets, inside carriages — as having a reality denied him.

He was sliding down.

*H*e was living in lodgings on the edge of a rookery in Seven Dials. He had had, in his grassier days, use for a room like this, which contained no more than a pallet on the floor, some stained wallpaper. He slept through whole days. He sent a boy out, when he came to consciousness, to get the newspapers. These newspapers lay now, spent, spread all over the boards of the room. He was waiting, waiting to see if his name was mentioned.

Time seemed to have slowed down and taken on an awful weight. Some horrible consciousness stayed, as if squatting in the corner of his room, watching him.

It was a strange beast, this watching, squatting figure: neither fully human, nor yet an animal. It was like some kind of hideous gargoyle that had slipped down off a mediaeval cathedral, then changed into toad-like flesh. It was all eye, all stale breath. Out of it came a pestilential stench that seemed part Thames, part other smell: decomposing bodies, faecal matter. He became obsessed that he smelt like that himself.

This had led him, finally, to get out of his bed and crawl on hands and knees to a ewer. Wherein he had washed himself.

He had sent a note to his aunt. He could use his childhood name: Dolly. Nobody would know it was from him.

He simply wrote: Can you help?

He had paid a child to take it to the esteemed address. He gave the child special instructions to pass the note only to the lady herself. No other. He had described her.

Once he had done this, he fell into a black and airless sleep.

The creature, he felt, as he slept, as he dreamed, had come closer to him, as a cat might come closer to someone ill, requiring warmth. The creature had crept onto his bed, snuggled in. Wrapped itself into the shape of his limbs. Made itself at home.

'*G*oodness!'

The single word had come almost involuntarily out of Ernest's mouth. It was as if he had diagnosed that quality in the pale young man who had arrived at his cell door.

Samuel was standing outside Ernest's cell at the House of Detention. It was early evening.

Fanny, or rather Ernest, had raised a hand, in an instinct of shame — to cover his face for one moment.

They had only the smallest window to talk through: it could just manage a face. There were perforations around the edges of steel that left a space smaller than a handkerchief. Yet this concentration on such a small space seemed to force the presence of another person into a hectic portrait: all emotions contained, expressed in the dilation of a quivering nostril, the glitter of a string of saliva caught inside the cave of a mouth poised to say something yet incapable of speaking.

'Goodness, Samuel!' Ernest said again, and he laughed. His slim hand with the Gothic-shaped nails crumpled down from his face. His faded blue eyes, slightly too close together, looked at Samuel intensely. (Why had Samuel never noticed how close together his eyes were? He had the sense of looking at someone monumentally naked, a face that was almost unformed, caught in a moment of irresolution. It was as if Ernest were saying: *I would rather you had never seen me so*, yet at the same time, and more poignantly, there was the rising emotion of: *thank God you have come to see me. Thank you.*)

'How are you?'

Even the most common phrase seemed stilted when surrounded by such sounds: the clack of boot heels on the metal floor. The guard walked up and down, up and down, during visiting hours, listening generously to all the whispered talk.

'I am well enough,' Ernest said, then that same pale hand rose and rifled through his hair, which looked, Samuel noted, like an ocean in disarray, wave rising against counter-wave.

'My friend Cummings attended the court today . . .'

Ernest said nothing. He seemed to be draining inwards every aspect of Samuel's visage: as if already he was faced with forgetting him. Ernest moved closer to the window. He seemed to shrug.

'My lawyer assures me we shall get bail at the next hearing.'

But Ernest's voice showed no conviction. Indeed Samuel had trouble — was having trouble — matching this reticent being and its lower, more hesitant voice with the magnificent Fanny. It was as if, being stripped of costume, paint and hair Ernest was like a leek, stripped layer by layer down to some pithy, almost pulpy essence: hardly even there.

His eyes seemed to want to look everywhere but at Samuel, yet at the same time — nervously, and again and again — his eyes were driven back to Samuel's.

'Can I bring you anything?' Samuel asked.

Ernest let out a little laugh and moved aside so Samuel could better see the inside of his cell. Samuel gained a vivid impression of spartan, even sadistic neatness and emptiness. It was all bareness, as if all the better for the incumbent to meditate upon his fallen state.

'Are you all right, Samuel? How are you faring?' Ernest's face came into focus. He seemed pale, nun-pale, hardly there. 'Perhaps it might be advisable to go away somewhere. Leave London.'

He seemed oppressed, heavy-laden.

'Why?'

Ernest seemed taken aback. He licked his lips but his tongue was dry. For a moment he seemed to struggle with something.

'I have a bad feeling,' he said finally. 'I keep thinking. All the words from one of the silly little plays I did come back.

> On the brink
>
> Of what a precipice I'm standing! Back!

Ernest ghosted out a laugh. 'I feel as if I'm staring into a whirlpool. And I don't know, at present, who will be sucked in. Destroyed.'

Samuel was about to answer manfully, but instead Fanny — no, Ernest — spoke again, almost as if Samuel barely existed. 'Even those standing on the outer are in danger.' He beckoned Samuel forward, whispered vehemently, 'Go away — escape. While you can.'

The guard had come to stand nearby.

'What's he saying . . . escape?'

Samuel turned and glanced at the guard.

'He is . . . romancing,' Samuel said, man to man. 'He is an actor. That is all.'

They listened to the guard's footsteps dying away. The diminuendo of his rattling keys.

There was a pearleen glisten in Ernest's pale blue eyes.

'I can't see why they see us as they do. It was all a frolic. It was only play-acting, after all. Where was the harm in it?'

They looked at each other in silence. Then Ernest spoke huskily, almost in memory of the lovely Fanny.

'Have you seen Freddie at all?'

'No.'

'I look for him every day on the way to court, but of course . . .'

Ernest let a fall of silence unfold. Shrugged.

'Once I thought I glimpsed him, as I was getting out of the police van. Of course there is such a crowd . . .'

More silence. Somewhere, down below a level, a woman was sobbing.

'Are *you* all right, dear boy?'

Samuel shrugged. 'I tried to buy our likeness, to keep it safe, but the man said someone else had purchased it.'

They gazed at each other, wondering what the implication was.

It was as if, all around them, unsaid, a thousand repercussions were at that very moment coming home. Transmuting. Whispered voices. Secrets shared and bought. Nobody knew where it would lead. Who would be captured in the thrall.

'If you see Freddie, tell him he must go abroad. Tell him, Samuel,' Ernest grew more Fanny-like in his emphasis. '*He must get away while he still can.*'

At this point there was a careful cough behind Samuel. He turned.

There was an old woman standing about two yards away. Deferentially looking down. She was dressed in servant's black, a vehemence of white. She had clasped in her gnarled hand, like the roots of a tree clamped around a rock that has become part and parcel of its being, a wicker basket. On the top was a clean chequered cloth.

Samuel thought he smelt cooked chicken — with sage stuffing.

The old woman looked frightened, yet intent upon doing what she regarded as her duty.

'I shall have to go now . . . Ernest.'

Samuel felt the strangeness of Fanny's male name in his mouth.

Some sense of decency, or possible indecency, kept the old woman standing where she was, a little distant. She prayed the young gentleman could not see her trembling. (She saw him as a mere slip of a boy, a callow youth who had hardly started off on life.)

For Agnes, to be standing in a House of Detention was one of the most terrible moments in her life. But to be visiting, as she saw it in her heart of hearts, her foster-child in prison, bringing him succour — this was the most terrible thing of all.

To think of her bright gilden star so fallen. So sullied.

She refused to read the newspapers. She refused to listen. To tittle-tattle. She held herself into herself, and trembled with the pity of it.

And she had prepared, lovingly, all the things she knew young Master Ernest had loved as a boy. She had made these with the tenderness of a young woman making delights for her lover. She had tried not to cry. But she was mystified by the intensity of her own unspoken grief.

She could not allow herself to grieve.

A servant, she could not afford this luxury.

'Thank you, Samuel dear boy, for coming,' she overheard the whisper of her master. 'And please, for your own sake, think on what I have told you. I beg you.'

The young man turned after a long suspended second. He bowed to her. He seemed, too, to be caught in some strange mood. They had exchanged in one glance, this old woman and stripling, something mute, something almost inexpressible.

Then she made her step forward.

She looked within.

She felt herself fall into a blank space of nothingness: her darling had grown so much older. His face was gaunt with pain, and tension lines gripped his mouth, his forehead, screwing up his eyes. His neck was thinner and he looked, suddenly, as if he had plunged into a premature old age.

Perhaps it was the light?

She repressed this thought and hoped her face showed nothing.

But it got worse.

She did not know what to do.

Instead, she pressed her old flesh against the chill metal and murmured through the steel enclosure, 'There now, don't cry, hush now, Master Ernest. I have brought you your favourite scrapings.'

Of Pinchbeck and Heartache

*E*liza Clarke woke up. Sound broke into her. Downstairs. It sounded like a tooth being wrenched. Inside her skull. Eliza froze in her bed, her narrow little berth up in the slope-roofed attic in Southampton Street. She could reach out with her hands and touch mouldering plaster. The tiny window, aperture to her soul, was open. There, in the far distance, like a ship blowing away, scudding over rooftops with ghostly billowing sails, the dome of St Paul's Cathedral.

She slipped out of her pallet, felt with her toes for her shoes. Ignored the acrid stench of piss in potty.

It was a moonlit summer's night.

The house had held still for a long moment. But there it was again, that sound. Like something being forced. Like when the tooth doctor had his wrench around your fang, was pulling it, first one way, then another, but the nerve ending — screaming, screeching — held on. Raw, pulpy.

She trembled down the first flight of stairs, really no more than a ladder, avoiding the sixth step down, which squealed.

Towards the door of No 7, on the third floor, the room of Mr and Miss

Able, impoverished brother and sister.

The sister, Miss Amelia, had approached Eliza that very afternoon.

'We as are respectable,' she had announced, spreading out her faded skirts and seeming to inspect them. 'We as have names to lose must take care of what we — stand on.'

She seemed to see something under her foot at that very moment and shifted her too high boots, made to elevate her into the sights of any oncoming gentlemen.

'Don't you agree, John?'

John had been inspecting his nails, then his reflection in the mirror. He was a pretty Englishman, all blue eyes and corn-coloured hair. Mr Able worked for a picture framer, in an art shop, down St Martins Lane: though Eliza suspected he was a work of art himself, put behind plate glass to attract the ladies.

Possibly even gentlemen? Who knew, in this strange roundabout world?

Mr Able had shook himself as if he had only just that moment come awake.

'We saw nothing untoward, though, did we, Amelia?'

She looked at him a little flummoxed. A flush spirited over her cheeks. Her curls shook.

'That is not the point. We as have reputations — whose name must remain unsullied . . .'

'Oh, quite, quite,' echoed her brother.

They were standing before the door of their room with its two single beds, a paltry screen placed in between. Eliza, as servant, had stared into their poverty, all the contrivances of their gentility: Miss Amelia who washed her own linen and hung it out to dry before the window; her curling papers restlessly tossing in the wind; she who had always loved to come downstairs and hear Miss Fanny sing. Who hung about the stairs, waiting for Miss Fanny, or especially Lord Frederick, to come in. And when the door opened she went back up a few steps, shook her curls, then appeared, innocently, to be dawdling downwards.

'Oh, good evening, Lord Frederick.'

It was as much as he could do to be civil to her. She was penniless and therefore useless.

'If the case takes a turn for the worse, we shall of course have to remove ourselves,' Miss Able had, that afternoon, a little too grandly, announced. When Mr John went and ruined it all.

'But ain't we paid up, Melia? Ain't we paid up for a month in advance?'

He seemed quite terrified.

She hissed to him as she pushed him in behind the door. 'They would have to give us our money back, you fool.'

Eliza, whose hearing was sharp — her means of obstructing attack — heard Mr John say in a voice of despair, 'But where would we go, Melia? Where?'

Everything had become fluid, unloosed.

All connections were coming unstuck.

Ever since Mrs Peck ran off to 'visit her sister'.

Leaving Eliza in charge.

It meant Eliza had to get up several hours earlier and not only do the fireplaces, the beds and tote up the shopping but also do the cooking. Her back ached, her eyes burnt. But what really kept her on edge was the perpetual sense of *vigilance*.

*S*he descended another step.

And saw that No 7's door was open a crack. There was Miss Amelia, paper curls in her head, muck all over her face, standing in a patched old nightgown: a regular Guy Fawkes, Eliza said to herself with savage satisfaction. At the same time Eliza raised a finger to her mouth. Miss Able nodded.

Eliza picked up the poker, which she had always told herself would come in useful one day.

She curled her fingers around it. She descended another crook in the stairs.

The angle was peculiar. She looked onto the head of the vagabond. Nobody she recognised. She took another step, soundlessly. Gripped the poker even harder.

The creature had jemmied open the padlock of No 2 — Fanny's room. Wrecking the architraves around Mrs Peck's door.

The door lay open.

The creature had turned, looked around, held still. The house itself seemed to be listening. The figure went in. Ghosted. She followed, quickly now, two steps at a time, around the banister, along the narrow stairwell to the door.

Fanny's room was dark. A cavern. Light came in through a street window and fell onto a scurfed rug, where there was a wooden box, its lid thrown open, gaping. The detective. Must have been through everything.

There were letters scattered all over the floor.

She held still — listened.

The figure — she could see him now. He was over there, before a mirror. It reflected the light from the window. The creature's silhouette was bent down, intent. Inspecting.

She crept closer.

She raised her weapon.

At that moment the creature seemed to sense something. Froze. Looked down into the mirror. Turned.

She was about to let out a primal yell.

But then the creature spoke.

'Eliza. For God's sake! What are you about?'

The face rose into moonlight, surfaced from the sea depths.

It was Lord Frederick himself. Wearing a strange old woman's mobcap. He had the grace to look embarrassed — at least partially so. He was grinning. He was laughing. At her.

'Collecting some of Fan's stuff,' he said to her, already backing out across the carpet. His voice — she hated its condescension.

He knew that as long as he kept walking and talking she would do nothing. Be frozen between two irreconcilable attitudes: you are lying; I must obey you, sir.

'She asked me to collect her earrings. She's particularly fond of them, poor gel.'

'The 'tective padlocked the door, sir. He didn't want no one —'

Frederick seemed to pause for a moment. He glanced down at the letters on the floor, then began pushing them around with his foot.

'Did he, now?' Frederick's elegant voice spoke. He kept searching with his foot.

'Did he ask for my name, girl?'

Eliza thought for a moment.

'No, sir. Not precisely.'

'Good lass. I always knew you were sterling.'

'Shall I light the room, sir?'

For the first time Eliza spoke in a normal voice.

He froze.

'Dammit girl, are you crackers?'

His voice jumped back into that of an ordinary man — afraid.

'I'm only taking what's mine.' He was down on his haunches, the jewel box under one arm, scooping up letters with his other hand, stuffing certain of them in his pockets.

She stood and watched. He ignored her. His actions were all wretched. Then Eliza thought she could hear footsteps on the stairs overhead. She went back and gently pulled the door to.

The door complained. Groaned.

He glanced up, insulted her by smiling, awarding her a partial grin — as if she cared, as if she cared for him one iota: he who was a nothing, an emptiness disguised with a title, a poor fool really, scrabbling around at her feet.

She wanted to say: How is Mr Boulton, sir?

She wanted to say: It is he I care for, sir. *It is he who I have seen, from my back seat high in the gods, gracing the stage, making me forget . . . forget almost everything.*

He made me feel free, is what she might have said, if she could have encapsulated it in words.

He makes me feel as if I levitate.

As if I'm up in one of them balloons that skim across the city.

Which one day might blow right away.

From this dirty hole.

Maybe all the way to New Zealand.

She looked at Lord Frederick Clinton down on his hands and knees. He was craven, frightened. She pitied him. In the midst of this emotion he glanced up at her, as if suddenly remembering she was there.

He smiled his lopsided, cynical grin.

'I say, Lizzie, you wouldn't be so kind as to nip downstairs and pour me some of your good lady's brandy? Make it a decent tot while you're at it. There's a good girl.'

*I*t was the nights that were the worst. When a black pall of despair settled down on Ernest, regardless of what he tried to do. Perhaps it was the sounds he could just make out: of London dampening down for supper, before it rose up again, bit by bit, gathering in intensity, deepening into the delirium of the night.

Inside, there was only restriction, avoidance, diminution.

The silence of his travail.

The Cyclops eye into the self.

Why did I? I didn't know . . . I didn't realise . . . Does it all really matter? Why does it matter so much to everyone? I am fundamentally innocent. But will I be found guilty?

Fred! he longed to cry out. Stell! But he only ever glimpsed Stell on the way to church service, or out in the yard. The guards seemed to find pleasure in keeping them apart. Except Guard C, who had a kinder face — or was he simply an idiot? — and who let them bump into each other. Soundlessly, wordlessly, each read the other's face, slumped into despair.

This is taking so much longer than we thought.

At six o'clock two warders tramped along the balcony, one turning on the top of the gas pipes — an awkward squeal: dry, unlubricated — the other letting down the trapdoor with a clatter (*you have no rights*), thrusting in a serge sleeve and a hand. Each time Ernest gazed at the hand almost hungrily, in order to work out which guard. This particular guard's hand was snub-fingered, with a giant welter of cauliflower warts on the end of his middle knuckle — his claw extended a small lantern in which burnt a flame.

Light.

Ernest lit his own lantern.

He could read.

Agnes had given him her own dog-eared copy of *Bleak House*. He read this numbly, yet as if his life depended upon it.

Outside, with military precision, the chief guard called out, 'Fall in!' and ''Tention!'

Ernest, in the periphery of his brain, listened to the numbers. Those who had arrived that day. Those who were on special watch. He always listened to make sure Stell, brave Stell, was not one of them. (She might have done something foolhardy.) Then Ernest heard, not listening now, trying to blot it out, the scuff of guards' boots, serried and in step, as they marched away.

This pseudo-army, in the house of waiting.

They got only as far as the outer door. Then keys — Ernest listened to all this his first night there, starved for sound, starved for anything living — the keys were handed in, their numbers yelled out.

An inner door slid along. Slid shut.

By seven o'clock, an unearthly silence had settled. There was only the tiniest sound, the faintest fleck of a stopped breath, a minute pant of despair — a flick of a page turning over, a sighing settling down on a stool.

This was their most luxurious, private hour.

At eight o'clock the double-locking of the cell doors began: a successive slamming of some hundred doors, followed by a double-locking. This final shock of sound heralded the greater gloom of night. A bell sounded, and a warder's footsteps were heard passing along the metal runway, as the night-light within each cell was individually but swiftly extinguished.

Darkness.

Dark.

The night. At a quarter past nine.

Soon it was as silent as a catacomb.

Only the faintest jangling of a warder's keys marked the movement of a guard.

All the rest was given over to silence and regret.

*H*e gave himself up to the sounds. The sounds that had only too quickly gathered a dreadful metronomic pace, as if he were the merest speck of dust caught within an infernal machine. The machine ground exceedingly slowly, as if at last that faint vibration within the London air had been traced back to its source, its dark heart: the House of Detention. A house of waiting, of pausing and thinking, of wondering and worrying, of time slowed down so that finally it came into equilibrium with that resonance that was always present to the most prescient ears in London: of voices whispering, of eyelashes falling as the eye moved away from the keyhole, the murmur of secrets being sold, the flutter of notes being paid, the clatter of coins falling into an upraised palm, the squeak of a nib as it moved across a page, the bang of a door as a policeman set out, the sigh of a detective as he stood watching, the rumble of steel wheels as a cart on its way to market passed the glossy carriage carrying the bejewelled woman who had left her lover, who now wearily climbed his way to bed, while the servant waiting to strip the linen carefully noted the stains . . . Each of these little transactions webbing strangers together, so that the violence of a nation that prided itself on not having had a revolution in an age of revolutions was expressed through another form of violence: psychological violence. The damage of a whisper, a murmur, a slipped coin, a sold secret . . .In this way there was a commerce in souls, a sale of souls no less dire than in any slave market, more cruel because it was more whispered, more to do with the glance, the sale of a hint, an insinuation . . . And so even in broad daylight there was in London, the unquiet roar of secrets being sold, all coming into focus at night . . . in that quietest of hours . . . in that house of waiting, the House of Detention, as if our friend Ernest Boulton had been brought to the source, so to speak — to pause, to wait, to scrutinise and — no longer — imagine.

It was the end of imagination.

Or its beginning.

*T*here was that first night in the Bow Street cells.

The door had opened.

Stell and he were separated.

They were still in drag.

Fanny was taken into a room. Brick walls, a gas-light on the wall. A young

policeman and standing over there an old man — a gent of sorts, Fan supposed.
He was the sort you might have recourse to on a slow evening. Fan knew his sort.
Pathetic. But this man. Was not this sort.

He was a doctor.

The policeman ordered Fan to undress.

She had demurred.

The policeman spoke to her roughly, as if she were a common bawd. She was
told she did not need airs and graces, not where she was going.

Fan was in the first stage of shock: banging into things, and finding that words
did not come. Her tongue was too heavy. She kept smelling her own sweat, its
peculiarly intense metallic flavour.

It was fear.

The doctor ordered her to undress.

'Kindly disrobe.'

He said this in a voice without emotion.

She hesitated a moment, and looked at him. He had old eyes that looked
as if they had seen everything. He let out a small explosion, almost as if from
indigestion, except it was impatience. He tapped the bench.

'Disrobe,' he said.

She was more used to being helped to undress — by Fred. But under that
glaring light, she felt compelled. She took off, first, the long white glove she was
wearing on her left hand. She unrolled it, then slid it off the end of her polished
fingernails. On her left hand, on the third finger, was an elegant signet ring.

She slid off the Egyptian bracelet.

The doctor gave the impression of having all the time in the world.

She bent down and unbuttoned her boots.

The moment she placed them down, still warm and reeking, the policeman
leant forward with his staring eyes, as if he couldn't help himself, sniffed them
deeply, then peered down into their interior.

'I have been asked to see whether you are women or men,' the old man said.

'We have said we are men. We have said we are sorry.'

Neither the doctor nor the policeman said anything. They appeared not to
hear.

They waited.

There was some almost pornographic eagerness in the way they waited: Fan
recognised it. Ernest was frightened of it.

She undid the buttons at the side of her bodice so it hung down. She undid the cords that held the bodice together. She took out — she took out the horsehair padding.

The doctor leant forward and took the padding in his hands. He squeezed it, pulped it, looked for one moment at Fan-turning-into-Ernest, and placed it down.

The policeman, with a pencil, laboriously wrote something.

She undid the tiny buttons at the side of her overskirt and reached down to the spring holding together her bustle. She undid her petticoats and let them fall to the floor. She stepped out of her overskirt. Took away the bustle. Removed her bodice.

As she took the lacy camisole over her head it dislodged a false plait, which was ripped from Fan's head.

For dignity's sake she unpinned the other plait and took away her false hair. But she could not refrain from bouffing up her hair underneath. Its silken wave.

The policeman looked disgusted, but fascinated. He could not look away.

The doctor, on the other hand, stood there like an old, tired husband who has seen his wife undress a thousand times. He was, after all, the police surgeon.

But this was something extraordinary, even for him.

A woman-turning-into-a-man.

Fan stood there in her stockings, pantaloons. She held her hand across her breast. Reached up with the other and unpinned the star from her hair.

She hesitated.

'Continue,' the doctor said in what sounded a dry voice. Lacking in saliva.

Fan took this moment as her own. She had known moments like this — parallel moments when she had worked her magic.

But the doctor had turned his back. He had gone to the gas-light. He had raised the flame.

Now the light was hard and flat.

The doctor came back. He stood very close.

Fan saw, by the doctor's nose, a deep pock that indicated he might have had smallpox as a child. She saw dust caught on the flecks of his tweed jacket. She seemed to smell some emetic, cleansing solution trapped in his clothes.

'Take your pantaloons down.'

Fan paused.

'You heard him,' the young policeman said, too quickly. Fan's gaze, or rather Ernest's, travelled to the doctor, who nodded.

'I . . . will not,' Fan said.

'You must,' the doctor said curtly.

Fan slowly undid the side pearl buttons. As she did this, she crushed her lids shut.

It had never been quite like this. She released the tiny mother-of-pearl button of the lacy garters that held up her stockings.

The pantaloons fell down.

'Over here,' the doctor said.

This was what Ernest had not been able, afterwards, to understand. Comprehend.

'Over there?' Fan had replied nonsensically, as if all her ability to comprehend language had deserted her. 'But why?'

'He said over there.'

The policeman spoke with a violence that hinted loss of control. A vein on the man's face reconfigured into a snake's tail flickering and flashing down his visage.

Fan could not look at him.

She went and stood by the doctor. Almost for protection. The doctor angled Fan so she looked into the light. The doctor squatted down on his haunches. For one second Fan glanced down. He was going bald. His cranium seemed oddly touching, defenceless. Like a baby's head. Or an eggshell.

But the doctor, almost an old man, was squatting down inspecting her — penis. He was looking at it with a distanced, scientific intensity she had never seen before. From various angles.

He had taken a clean piece of wood, a speculum, out of his top pocket. He — hesitatingly — touched her. Lifted its hood up.

As if it were some distant circumference of her being, Fan felt the nudge. She would turn into a statue. She would cease to be — herself. Or even human.

She concentrated on the gas flame.

She gazed into the iris.

She tried to remember. Anything really. But it was as if, at that moment, the memory of Fanny was ransacked. Found empty. She felt only panic. Who was she?

The doctor, again using the speculum, lifted up her balls.

She jumped.

The doctor looked for a long time, let out a sigh and stood up. Breathed out.

He was still holding the speculum.

He indicated a crude wooden chair. The back of the chair faced the gas-light.

The policeman and the doctor exchanged the slightest glance.

284

'Go to the chair.'

Ernest went to the chair.

'Lean on the back of the chair,' the doctor said.

Ernest did so.

'Pull your cheeks apart.'

Ernest, numb, in shock, did this. The doctor angled Ernest's buttocks quite abruptly so they faced into the light. Ernest felt the cold fingers of the doctor on his flesh. I am not here, he thought.

The doctor pushed the being known as Ernest roughly to a different angle. Ernest felt a peculiar oscillation of emotions. One was the human need for touch. He was frightened, terrified. He craved another human's touch. But the doctor's hands were so impartial, so withdrawn, they gave him nothing. They took. They stole.

'Pull your cheeks apart further.'

He did so. The doctor squatted down again.

'I said wider.'

He could feel his breath on his skin. It felt almost wet. A spray.

He waited. He fell within a world of blankness.

But from behind him there was nothing.

Except a long and scientific silence.

*T*hey were on their way back to court. Arthur Park engineered a moment alone with Ernest. (He had paid good coin for the opportunity: a crown. His family had more money than Ernest's.)

'*We'll get out at the next hearing — my father has assured me. We'll get bail. It will be expensive, but . . .*'

He tried to sound confident, and Stella had always been a confident little bagpipe. But he'd lost weight: his trouser belt had gone in four notches. His fashionable pants hung loose.

He tentatively went to touch Ernest's hand but a quick glance at the guard warned him to retreat.

They must needs keep acting as males.

'*They've got nothing on us. Nothing really.*'

He whispered this. His mantra.

Ernest just looked at him.

'*But I had no idea we were being watched.*'

The guard was ordering the other prisoners into the van in a military voice.

Arthur and Ernest were last in line.

They had hardly any time left.

Ernest came awake. He was troubled.

'A doctor inspected me.'

This came out almost involuntarily, as a thought that haunted.

Arthur broke into an abrupt laugh.

'Oh, God. You too?'

'Yes.'

Arthur laughed in an almost jolly, rubicund spurt. 'They'll hardly . . . '

They looked at each other.

'Come along, you two. No dawdling, now.'

It was the guard.

'Won't they?' said Fanny, as she entered the cart that took them back both to court.

The Hunter and the Hunted

The Countess had replied.

Handsomely.

She sent what she knew Frederick needed. Money. She also put in a note with a brief message: 'Come. Have courage.'

And it was through this thinnest of lifelines that he found himself now, in a state of complete unreality, ascending the red-carpeted stairs of the Royal Opera House with his aunt on his arm. He was impeccably dressed. To all outward appearances he was the Lord Frederick Clinton he had always been — perhaps a little more haunted around the eyes.

She had said to him, 'You must go out in public. You must.'

She had invited him then to go with her to *Der Freischütz*. She made a pretty attempt to make it seem as if he were helping her. She had no one to go with. Her husband abhorred opera. She needed an arm.

He rose another step. He knew himself to be surrounded on every side by his own sort. There were people who were distant relations. Men he had been to school with. Daughters he had danced with. He could not quite sense what knowledge lay in their pupils when they glanced at him. Nobody snubbed him but he had a sense, at certain moments, of a convergence of movement away from him: a kind of artful manoeuvre that meant backs were turned to him — beautiful powdered shoulders, glittering with precious gems. He also felt that he was being stared at, inscrutably. Yet no eye seemed to connect with his own.

He knew how to carry this off. His aunt and he talked to each other gaily as they climbed the stairs. Though by the time they reached the top, neither of them could recall what they had been saying.

It did not matter, really.

It was as if his aunt had arranged, with perfect decency, his farewell to society. Not that she saw it like this; she saw it only microscopically — that it was important he not act as a guilty man.

The Countess smiled. She entered her box, arranged her dress, and turned over her shoulder, using the manners of an old coquette, and said to him, 'See, Dolly dear, I told you it would be rather nice to step out, didn't I?'

Yet he was not looking. He was glancing over his shoulder.

He saw, in the edge of the box, that the watching gargoyle had already made itself at home. It nodded to him companionably. It settled in. It waited.

The opera began. Frederick prepared to slumber. Suddenly he was hit by a weight of utter exhaustion. He felt he could not maintain the stem of his neck. His lids were so heavy the one thing he wanted was to slip out of the little gilt chair and slither to the floor, and perhaps, hidden by his aunt's skirts, lie there, fetally crouched, asleep.

At the same time he realised that his burden was to remain conscious. He prised his heavy lids apart. He glanced down at his thigh. His aunt had just tapped him briskly on the trouser leg, with her fan. Had he said something out loud? Sighed? Groaned?

Her face seemed to hold some reprimand, then it turned like a sentinel into the limelight from the stage. She allowed the tight muscles of her face to relax, and the mask of a dissatisfied, intelligent, middle-aged woman — heavily made up, head weighed down under a diadem of diamonds and sapphires — presented itself like a sphinx.

Lord Frederick looked across the Opera House, past the boxes, to that of the reigning beauty of the hour. She was wearing a vast confection in the palest grey silk, with diamonds blazing from her naked shoulders. She was animate, with all eyes trained on her, but pretending she could see nothing.

He was struck by the unbelievable fantasy of it all. It hit him with all the force of a new idea but he had no way of articulating this to himself. He half turned to his aunt and nudged her arm. But she turned to him, sheathing her fan, a look of irritation calcified on her bones. He sensed, in his clairvoyant state, how bored she was: how utterly chillingly bored she was, beneath the slightly metallic flavour of her charm.

'What is it, Freddie?' she whispered, alarmed.

But he lacked the words.

Then the curtain went up and he looked into a forest — a deep, dark forest. The strings took up and he shivered. It was as if he had never heard music before — he who had slumbered through a thousand operas. He found himself fascinated. When the beautiful and mysterious *entr'acte* came to an end he was startled by gunshots.

Two of them.

He moved into a sharper state of consciousness.

This is my story, he said to himself. This is about me.

The characters on the stage seemed to be speaking to him. For him.

He hunched forward to the front of the box.

His listening became acute.

*W*hen the village people took up their rebarbative sound, suspended and reiterated, again and again (Heh!Heh!Heh!) ridiculing the young hunter whose marksmanship had gone awry, Frederick felt an almost hallucinatory clarity. He raised his eyes from the stage with a sense of physical difficulty, as if they were in fact mesmerised. He glanced around the theatre. His aunt's profile. Her lids seemed to be tremoring downwards. She was using the darkness as a cloak for a sleep. The other faces, lit from the stage, appeared dramatic — as dramatic in their own way as whatever was happening on the stage.

That ridiculing chorus echoed in Frederick's brain.

Heh!Heh!Heh!Heh!

He settled down to watch the desperate bargain by which the naïve young huntsman sold his soul to the Devil.

Woe is me! Luck abandons me!
If the powers of heaven so decree
Then bear the loss like a man!
May Fortune's wheel decide;

He who trusts in higher power

Defies vicissitude and loss!

Give up Agathe!

How could I bear that?

I could never bear the loss! Never!

But it was during the coven scene, when the naïve hunter made his pact with the Devil for the use of magic bullets, that Frederick felt himself begin to tremble. He was so intensely involved in the drama that he suddenly had a fear he might fall from the box and crash onto the stage.

He listened to the words of the Devil — their sonorous intensity.

You don't know who I am,

I'm the Huntsman inside your skin,

I'm after you.

You can't escape, don't even try to.

You're not even human —

But hunted game

That secretly calls out my name.

You seek to escape.

You cannot. You are mine.

Relax before my aim.

Freddie shuddered, even as he felt a sudden, wild exhilaration. *You are mine. Relax before my aim.* He began to feel his skin, his breathing gathered pace. He was sweating now. He was grinning. His life had found a purpose.

His aunt, touching the sapphires at her neck, happened to glance at him. She was arrested. Troubled. Was her nephew insane?

No, I can bear the torment no longer,

the fear that robs me of all hope!

What transgression am I paying for?

What brings ill fortune down upon me?

But I am ensnared by evil forces!

Gripped by despair, tortured by derision!

Oh, does no ray of light pierce this night?

Does blind fate rule? Is there then no God?

Gripped by despair, tortured by derision!

His aunt, half stifling a yawn, gathered up her fan. Frederick had not moved. His shoulders were stiff. He had become consumed by an idea, an image, a sound.

You are mine. Relax before my aim.

He felt at that moment, staring down at the stage, as if he had heard what he had come for. That strange sense almost of insanity had passed. He felt suddenly weak. He realised his linen was drenched. He felt like a dying man. And he felt he no longer had the energy to stand up, let alone to complete all the actions involved in the play-acting of leaving the theatre, among people of his own kind. (Or who had once been people of his own kind — he realised this now.)

He leant forward to his aunt, touched her hand. She jumped.

'I must go, Aunt. Thank you.'

He slipped away before he could scent her disappointment.

He did not care any more. He needed to go.

As he went outside he was struck, as if for the very first time, by the profound conjunction of the Opera House and the Bow Street police court. There it was, just across the road. As sharp as a hallucination.

But he must lose himself.

He must disappear.

As he walked along he had an overpowering longing to be with Fanny. It was crippling, this angst, this longing, for it was a particular moment above all he longed for: they were sitting in silence, in a room together. Neither was saying anything. There were sounds outside, down in the street. But Fanny — Ernest — had looked up and their eyes had met. That was all.

The Death Scene of Lady Fanny Clinton

By now Fanny and Stell had been in custody for over twenty days. Still no charges had been laid. And yet the crowds that thronged around Bow Street police court continued to be enormous. The *Morning Advertiser* estimated the crowd at about two thousand, with many standing on cabtops for a view. The courtroom was also uncomfortably crowded — 'a minimum of room with the maximum of discomfort', as one reporter acidly said. Looking 'a little careworn' and anxious, Park and Boulton took their places in the courtroom. The magistrate directed that they be given the courtesy of seats. It was noted that they 'showed considerable anxiety during the examination of several witnesses'. This anxiety began with the very first witness.

It was Clara Duffin, who had once worked at Southampton Street. She gave her address as Shoe Lane, Fleet Street.

The *Morning Advertiser* reported that, on entering the witness box, she looked at Boulton and Park 'sternly and with defiance'.

Ernest had looked at her, a little shocked.

What had she to say?

There seemed the shadow of a grim smile upon her face. This is my moment, she seemed to say: this is my payback for all the times you never so much as noticed me or gave me the time of day.

She was dressed in clothes she might have worn to church. A dark grey serge, blue cloth gloves and a hat the tinge of a blackbird's wing. But on her breast she wore a posy of cloth violets, as if she might have been going to some more celebratory event.

Her face, normally pasty and uneven, was tinged with a light pink on the cheeks. Her pale grey eyes glittered. She glanced out into the courtroom eagerly.

'When were you in the employ of Mrs Peck, 36 Southampton Street?'

Mr Poland's voice was pleasant, slow — his coaxing voice.

'Sir, I began there in July 1868,' she said, speaking in a low voice at first. 'I was a housemaid, and my job was to clean the stairs each morning, to bring in the coal, to sweep the chambers of the lodgers —'

'And can you clarify for us, Miss Duffin, who were the lodgers —'

'Well, sir,' she said, 'let me see. On the top floor of course there was us servants. On the next floor down there were a genteel enough pair, a brother and sister — do you want their names, sir?'

'No, Miss Duffin. Given the nature of the present case, it might be better not to implicate those who are, as it were, innocent bystanders.'

'And then there was the bedroom of herself, the landlady, Mrs Peck —'

'And?'

'Well, sir, the best rooms on the floor below was set aside for him as is sitting over there. The prisoner known as Ernest Boulton took the rooms, sir, along with Lord . . .'

Her voice unaccountably dimmed suddenly. She seemed to lack oxygen.

'Lord . . . ?'

The court had grown very still.

'Why, Lord Frederick Clinton, sir. They shared a bedroom and a sitting room.' She seemed breathless, as if she had just climbed the hump of a hill.

'So the prisoner Boulton and Lord Frederick Clinton . . .' Mr Poland articulated Frederick's name with the utmost clarity.

The pens of the newspaper writers flew across paper; they did not raise their heads.

Ernest looked haunted. He listened to a murmuring, a rustling tug of whispers all around the courtroom. Someone towards the back began pushing his way towards the exit. The other courtroom reporters briefly looked full of anguish: they had spotted a stringer for *Reynolds News*.

What was that sound in the air?

What was Ernest listening to?

Was it the sound of a thousand pens moving across paper, of newspaper presses beginning to revolve? Of newsprint being marshalled? Of crowds gathering in anticipation before a newsboy? It was like a calibration in the air, that faint oscillation of sound.

'Lord Frederick Clinton.' Once again Mr Poland spoke his name very clearly and slowly, so there could be no mistake. 'I take it you mean the son of the Duke of Newcastle, the same Lord Frederick Clinton who was until recently a member of Parliament? You are saying Lord Frederick Clinton and the prisoner Boulton shared the same bedroom?'

'Yes, sir.'

'Can you describe what was in the bedroom?'

'Why, sir, a set of drawers, a large dressing mirror . . . the usual "utilities", sir, if I may be so bold as to call them,' she hurried on, 'and of course a bed.'

'A bed, you say, Miss Duffin?'

'Yes, sir.'

'And who slept in this bed, Miss Duffin?'

'Have I also said there was a dressing room, sir?'

'No.'

Mr Poland's voice showed a certain coolness.

'There was a bed in there, sir, too. That is, a narrow couch.'

'So there were two beds?'

'Yes, sir. Mr Park, sir, as you see opposite, would sleep there when he occasionally came to spend the night.'

Mr Poland paused. He shuffled some papers on his desk.

Ernest felt he could not move. He felt, at that moment, that if he stayed still, if he did not blink, if he did not breathe . . .

'So Mr Boulton and Lord Frederick Clinton — ?'

'Mr Boulton, sir, slept in the same room as Lord Frederick Clinton.'

There was a moment of complete silence.

Even the newspaper presses seemed to have paused.

'The room with only one bed?'

'Yes, sir.'

'I see.'

The magistrate shook himself. It was as if everyone in the courtroom was subject to some kind of enchantment — some moral stillness.

'But it is not unusual for people to share a bed, Mr Poland, is it, without the dreadful imputation of something . . . unnatural?' said Mr Flowers.

The courtroom abruptly came awake.

Someone at the very back shouted, 'Hear! Hear!' as if it were a stage play.

There was a brisk ripple of applause. There was even a suspicion of foot stamping in the back row.

The beadle called out, 'Silence in the court!'

Ernest found he was breathing, almost despite himself. He could not risk a look at Arthur. This was too dangerous. But he sensed Arthur's complete stillness too.

'Pray tell us, Miss Duffin,' Mr Poland went on in a light voice, 'on what terms did Mr Boulton and Lord Frederick Clinton live?'

'Well, sir,' she said — there was a lilt of excitement in her voice — 'Lord Frederick used to speak to Boulton very familiar like — more as to a lady than a man. I have heard him often call Boulton "my dear" and "my darling". I once accused Boulton of being a man but he laughed and showed me his wedding ring. He told me he was Lord Frederick's wife.'

'Wife, you say? Was he dressed as a woman or a man when he said this?'

Clara thought for a moment.

'He was generally dressed as a lady, sir, though I have had occasion — once or twice — to see him dressed as a man.'

'Were there particular times when the prisoner dressed as a woman?'

'Oh, usually of a night, when he was going out with Lord Frederick.'

'Did Lord Frederick Clinton also dress as a lady?'

She giggled nervously.

'Oh no, sir. Not ever. Not once.' A pause. Then a calculating look settled on her features. 'At least that I saw.'

'Did you notice anything else unusual about their chambers?'

She thought for a moment.

'Well, sir, I could not help but notice, as I tidied up, that there was great numbers of letters about the place, most of them sent to Lord Frederick, and most of them, sir, signed, "*Your loving Fanny*".'

'And did you notice anything else about these letters?'

'Well, sir, most of the letters had the initial "C" engraved at the top, along with a coronet, and a sort of scroll that said "Fanny".'

'I see.'

'I also had occasion, sir, to pick up — from the floor where it had fallen, accidentally, like — a visiting card.'

'And what was on this visiting card?'

'The card was engraved, sir, with a crest and coronet entwined with an "F" and a "C" . . .'

'The name?'

'Lady Frederick Clinton.'

'Lady Frederick Clinton. I see. And who do you suppose that referred to?'

'Why, sir, the prisoner Boulton, of course, who went about as Lord Frederick's wife.'

There was an outburst of whispering, a susurration, an uneasy, bustling murmuring.

'Thank you, Miss Duffin. Just one question more. Why did you leave your employment at No 36 Southampton St?'

'I spoke to my mother, sir — I was not comfortable with all the goings on. My mother said to me I should think of my own good name. Consequently I left that place of employment, sir.'

Clara composed herself and fell into silence. She lowered her eyes as if she were going into a trance-like prayer.

'Thank you, Miss Duffin,' said Mr Flowers in a very gentle voice, as if not to awaken her from her trance, 'you may stand down.'

'Thank you, sir,' she murmured, throwing a glance around the courtroom, taking in the 'audience', the newspaper scribes, and finally her eyes passed, but in passing did not see, Ernest Boulton and Arthur Park. By this time they were non-people. They were vacant spaces. They were whatever anyone could say about them.

*T*he courtroom broke apart for lunch and, as it did so, throughout the room a single name could be heard: *Lord Frederick Clinton*, the name passing from tongue to tongue until it had been carried, like a body handed overhead — a dead body, a comatose reputation — out the door, through the packed corridor of the Bow Street court, out into the street outside. There the name fractured apart and fled in every which way so that only several hours later, as fathers on trains opened their newspapers, they already knew the name of the gentleman whose presence had been mentioned so many times during the hearings, but whose name, up to this point, had never been spoken out loud.

*C*ummings and Barton were in High Holborn, heading back towards Bell Yard. The footpaths were congested and everywhere Cummings looked he seemed to see newsagents, a proliferation of newsboards.

They reached the corner of Chancery Lane and paused.

Cummings had already heard the newspaper boy calling, 'Read all about it! Peer named in court! Lord's name revealed!'

Glancing into Samuel's face he could tell that he had heard nothing.

He was asleep, still, in his enchantment.

Right in the middle of the traffic a skeletal but tough-looking boy turned cartwheels, daring the horse's leg to stomp down on him, his hardened face fixed in a rictus — a desperate mask of glee. A woman — a lady — leant out of a carriage and dropped some coin. Immediately another fleeting of children, all as desperate, fled among the horses' hooves, past the flickering wheels. A fight began on the road, quite ugly.

A policeman waded out, began to clear the scrum. Meanwhile a clutter of carts, carriages, drays and 'buses crowded to a halt. There was much yelling.

Samuel turned around, through the force of what magnetism he did not know precisely, and saw a fellow sleepwalker. It was Frederick Clinton. It took a moment for Samuel's mouth to work. Lord Frederick looked different. More gaunt. He was standing there, glancing behind him at something that seemed to worry him.

Samuel leant back and touched him lightly on the sleeve.

At the touch, the flesh of Clinton jumped.

'It's Barton, sir. Samuel Barton.'

'Why so it, so it is,' Clinton said. Some final glint of charm kicked in. He smiled, or attempted to smile. Samuel noticed he had lost one of his side teeth.

They began walking in the same direction. (Though Samuel had the distinct impression Clinton wasn't going anywhere. He was drifting, almost being carried along the street by the crowds, willy-nilly, like flotsam.)

'This is my . . . friend. Cummings.'

Cummings executed a rather unfortunate, exceedingly low bow.

'Cummings at your service, milord.'

Frederick sketched a half bow.

They kept walking abreast. At a loss to know precisely where to take up. What to say.

Cummings was aware they were coming closer to another newspaper boy. He observed the number of people crowding around, waiting impatiently to buy a newspaper. Those who had a newspaper began reading it immediately, even as they walked, slowly, away.

'Are you on your way to court, sir?' Samuel asked.

Frederick started, then laughed.

It was a cool, dry laugh.

'Damn me if I won't!' he murmured.

'I saw . . . I saw Ernest — Mr Boulton — two nights ago.'

Frederick stopped still for a moment, and grabbed hold of Samuel's arm. His grip was terrifyingly tight.

'Damn me if you didn't,' he said, and looked down at Samuel. His eyes seemed to flare into Samuel's. He had gone pale.

'How is the poor lad?'

Samuel thought for a moment. He shrugged.

'He has trouble sleeping.'

Frederick laughed a strange, uproarious laugh. Cummings stared at him in disbelief. Clinton seemed a man deranged.

'Well, didn't he always, the lovely little scamp? That's how he got into trouble in the first place. Up till all hours.'

This seemed fundamentally silly to Samuel, who felt disappointed with Clinton.

'He would like to see you.'

There was an embarrassed silence. Samuel was not sure Frederick had heard.

'But he told me to tell you,' and Samuel leant in closer to speak. Immediately an almost imperceptible wince of agony flitted over Cummings' face. At being excluded. But as if to disguise this he began to whistle loudly to himself. Tunelessly.

'You must go abroad. Fanny said. As soon as possible.'

'Mind-reader! She must have read my mind. She always had the greatest sense. In fact, little Barton,' and Frederick slid a grimy envelope out of his top pocket, 'I have some trinkets of Fan's I'm just about to . . .' Frederick touched his nose, 'you know, cash in, so to speak. But here!'

Frederick stopped stock still in the street. Cummings stopped immediately also, and turned back.

'Damn, damn!' Frederick murmured, ripping open the packet, then extracting something — something which Cummings could see glittered. There was a brilliant blood-like flash for a moment.

'Damn me, if she don't deserve a wee surprise herself.'

He leant forward and closed Samuel's hand about whatever it was he had just placed there.

'Hand it over to her. When things quieten down. And tell her . . . tell her . . .'

Samuel passed the tiny object into the top pocket of his jacket without looking at it. He patted it nervously to ensure it had sunk in, down through the fabric.

'Tell her . . . you know the old motto, don't you — If you're born to hang, you'll never drown.'

Pleased with his witticism, Frederick let out another of his wild laughs, turned about in the opposite direction and disappeared up a grim side alley. It was as if he had never existed.

$\mathscr{C}$ummings said nothing. He did not like being excluded. He waited a long moment. He was aware that to Samuel he hardly even existed.

But he could not help himself.

'Have you heard, of late, from your acquaintance from up north?'

He spoke waspishly.

'Who do you mean? My sisters?' Samuel hit his forehead. 'I have not written to them of late! I have been selfish, Cummings. Too selfishly obsessed with my own . . . problems. Or the problems, rather, of one other.'

There was silence a moment.

They had come to one of those piles of dank dirt that indicated the irruptions of a changing London. The Holborn Viaduct had only just been completed and the earth all about was still heaped up, smelling sour and rank. There was the rumble, a vibration, of an underground train.

'No, my friend. I am thinking of your betrothed, Ursula.'

'She is not my betrothed!' Samuel spoke with considerable heat. He was blushing and he looked angry. Cummings had the terrible feeling he had misplayed his hand.

But Samuel laughed and said, 'Why Cubs, you are interested in the young lady yourself, I think!'

It was Cummings' turn to blush.

'You mistake me, friend,' he said vehemently, 'if you think I would be so dishonourable. I would not, for the world — '

'We are not betrothed,' Samuel said simply. 'I don't know what gave you that impression.'

She did, was what Cummings longed to say. But he knew better than to speak.

'She is a lovely girl.'

This was Samuel, speaking almost for Cummings. He spoke as if he were only just appreciating this fact but he also spoke as from a long distance, from the position of someone looking backwards. 'She is sweet, very sweet, Ursula,' Samuel said finally, but in a faintly dismissive voice.

He drifted away.

'What was it our noble English milord gave you?' Cummings called out, as if incidentally. His tone was sarcastic.

'Oh, some trifle. A little bauble. Worthless, probably.'

Silence a while between our two friends.

'More important as a memento.'

Cummings saw he would get nothing more. So they cut down Carey Street. But Cummings saw another newspaper stand ahead. The stand was aflutter with news headlines, a barrage of words. It was as if everyone in London lived within a cocoon of language and at this moment the words were spinning, sprouting.

Cummings could already hear the shrill, repetitive cry of the newspaper boy, without being able, precisely, to understand what he was saying. But he could tell from the tone of the boy's voice that he was excited. It was the sound of news, of scandal itself, the breathless pause, the desire to know.

A woman with a basket over her arm was running towards the newsboy. She had her arm outstretched as if she could not wait to exchange coin for newspaper.

From all different angles people were coming out of doors, flocking to the central point: the small disseminator of intelligence.

His face was joyous.

As Samuel and Cummings got closer they could hear what he was calling.

''orrible and revolting disclosures! The men in women's clothes! Truly 'orrible and reeeeeeeeevolting revelations! Read all about it!'

After luncheon, the beadle called for a Mr Richard Barwell, surgeon at Charing Cross Hospital.

There was a sense that the Crown, having waited through an interminable period of amusement and jollity, had this day decided to take their gloves off. They had marshalled their evidence and they would, in today's hearing, display it. They would present such evidence that a trial was unavoidable. And it would be on their terms: of the most serious of charges.

On Mr Barwell entering the dock, Park had looked quite ill. Yet so fascinated he could not look away.

'I recognise Park as an outpatient from three months ago,' Mr Barwell said in the measured tones of science. 'Even though the prisoner came to the hospital dressed in what could be described as 'common' clothes, under a pseudonym.'

'How did you recognise the prisoner then?'

'I was asked to go to the Bow Street police station for inspection purposes upon his arrest. I identified Park in a line-up that included, I have to say, the sweepings of the cells. Park was dressed for the identification in old, shabby clothes. But I still identified the prisoner — even though, I must say, I pay more attention to complaints than I do to countenances.'

This led to a most unfortunate ripple of tittering through the room.

Mr Poland cut in sharply.

'But why did the prisoner Park attend Charing Cross Hospital and, I suppose we could say, under a false identity?'

'I cannot comment as to his motives. Only his complaint. He complained about a sore at the back portion of his body.'

'Can you be more specific, please.'

'I found two sores on his anus.'

There was an appreciable pause as Mr Poland let the implications of this sink in.

'What kind of sores?'

'Of a syphilitic nature.'

Again a telling pause. Ernest could not help but admire the lawyer's sense of timing: he would do well on the stage.

'And how would these sores come to be found on Park's anus?'

'The sores would be created,' Mr Barwell said, again in the level, rather flat voice of science, 'by intercourse of . . . an unnatural kind.'

The courtroom was plunged into utter stillness.

Park gave the appearance of not moving at all. Boulton appeared to be willing himself into invisibility.

'Thank you, Mr Barwell.'

The lawyer for Park and Boulton, Mr Besley, had no questions.

It got worse.

'Please call Dr James Thomas Paul.'

The police doctor entered the room. He glanced about him cautiously, then assumed the mien of a man who was doing what he regarded as his public duty.

'My name is James Paul. I am a doctor and have been in practice for sixteen years. I spent seven years before that at the St Pancreas Dispensary. I am police surgeon for the E Division.'

Ernest tried not to move.

'On Friday 29 April,' he said, 'I was directed to examine Park and Boulton, by Superintendent Thomas. They had been arrested the night before. I was told to examine them to identify whether they were women or men. I examined them separately, Boulton first, at Bow Street police station. There was no conversation between me and the prisoner.'

'And what did you find?'

'I inspected the anus of the prisoner Boulton and found it was much dilated. The muscles readily opened.'

'Why would that be so?'

'Dilation is undoubtedly caused by the insertion of a foreign body.'

There was a nervous titter.

Dr Paul seemed not to hear it.

'Can you be more specific?'

'It is attributable to the prisoner Boulton having had frequent unnatural connections,' Dr Paul said simply.

Boulton, sitting in his chair, had gone very white.

'His penis and scrotum are also of inordinate size,' Paul continued in the same level, scientific voice. 'This is also often occasioned by unnatural connection, in my opinion and according to the reading that I have done. I examined the prisoner Park immediately afterwards. His anus showed signs of even more marked dilation.'

Stell and Fan did not dare exchange a glance. They had been stilled, turned into statues. In that courtroom. Only once had their eyes grazed past each other. As the doctor had been called Fanny had felt Ernest's body grow still. He was hardly capable of breathing. It was as if the engine of his body had stalled.

He had looked down with surprise to his wrist: he recognised, in some abstract state, the sandy hairs speckled there, amid the cleats and fainter imprint of the freckles. But he was a long way distant from that flesh, just as he suffered the extraordinarily volatile sense he was projecting out of his body — being flung, spiritually, out of that crowded, stinking courtroom, flying over the rooftops of Bow Street, being lifted over the whole streetscape of London. This lasted for one — beautiful — moment. (Like the balloon ride but sped up, hectic.)

He was seeking — who? Was it Frederick? Was that Frederick down below, sauntering along a street? He was lost. He had nothing to do. He had nowhere to go. Too many doors had closed against him. Frederick! He wanted to call to him.

But Frederick had seen someone. Who? Now Ernest was plummeting, vertiginously, being punched back inside his body — no wonder he lacked breath. He was being savagely thrust back into his male container: he looked down in surprise at his trousers, at the fly, the flat shoes of a male.

This is me? My container. Imprisonment. As much as the words of that man — that doctor, carefully not letting his eyes rest for one second upon his own — his own, the accused, Ernest Boulton, gentleman, 23 Shirland Road, Paddington.

He was being carried, brought arduously back into his container, being imprisoned within it.

That is your crime, Ernest, a little voice said within his ear.

That is your crime.

Not this . . . monstrous invasion, this deletion of your being, this wrenching apart for all the world to see, in glee, to laugh at.

To scorn, certainly; to point fingers at.

Park beside him (that disguise of a name: *Park*) let out an almost sublimated groan, a bleat of the soul as his body lodged sideways for a second. It was as if he were having a stroke — Fanny, no! Ernest saw that Arthur's eyelids were drooping, fluttering, then growing stiff. He was staring ahead, face bloodless. A mask.

The doctor was burying them in words.

Shameful, hideous words.

Everything they were, all their possibilities, were being limited to — *this*.

Dilation of an anus.

Ernest's solicitor was turning, in the terrible slow motion of a Greek mask, over his shoulder to glance right into Ernest's soul, right past all the fabulous camouflage, all the *possibilities* of Fanny — how she might be any number of characters on the stage, become Julia in *The Hunchback*, or Fanny Chillington in *A Morning Call.*

All of these, like the spokes of a fan closing one after the other, sinking back to reveal that one, abject orifice.

Is that all I am?

Not a human, nothing more than a — a shit hole.

$\mathscr{M}$r Besley was on his feet. He looked furious.

'On whose authority did this inspection take place?'

Dr Paul looked at him, left a pause then said in a surprised voice, 'Superintendent Thomas of the E Division. He asked me to inspect the prisoners.'

'On what basis?'

'To ascertain whether they were men or women.'

'And is it true that Messrs Boulton and Park were threatened with force if they did not comply?'

'I do not recall.'

'Did you ask the superintendent for written permission?'

'I have examined hundreds of cases as a divisional surgeon and have never had to ask permission of the prisoners before.'

'So you did not seek for permission from the magistrate?'

The doctor's eyebrows shot up. He said nothing for a moment, and looked slightly embarrassed.

Mr Flowers leant forward.

'It is correct, Dr Paul, that an order from the magistrate is required.'

'I did not see any reason, sir, to deviate from the ordinary course,' Paul said, addressing the magistrate directly. 'I undertook the examination on my own initiative. The only order I received was to examine them.'

'But what made you take the examination in the direction that you did?' asked Mr Besley incredulously.

'I had no idea of what the charge was. But there was something I had read once, in a medical book. I decided to take the examination a step further.'

Mr Besley now turned to the magistrate, and spoke with great indignation.

'Messrs Boulton and Park have been subjected to the grossest outrage. I wish to protest in the strongest possible terms.'

'I think,' said Mr Flowers, speaking slowly and looking over the top of his glasses down at Mr Besley, whose face had flushed a most unhealthy colour, 'I think Dr Paul has only been doing his duty. I myself actually thought they were women.'

Mr Poland spoke quickly. 'Sir, Dr Paul's evidence is the only evidence we have that they are not, in fact, women.'

'They have confessed quite freely that they are men!' cried Mr Besley.

'. . . and acted as women,' countered Mr Poland.

Mr Flowers left an expressive moment of silence. The courtroom, crowded and overheated, seemed to be rising too quickly in emotional register. He spent some time altering the papers on his desk, then smoothing them down,

'Even when they said they were men, I must admit that I myself was not quite convinced,' he said finally.

Ernest and Arthur kept their eyes down. Indeed, Ernest seemed to be far away.

He seemed to be listening to something.

For, at that second of almost ultimate diminution — of being placed in the psychological stocks, pelted with words, having to witness the horrible and revolting murder of Lady Fanny Clinton (this was her death scene) — just at that moment he heard from across the way, in the direction of the Opera House, a woman singing.

It was rehearsal time. He awoke. How many times in his early youth he had lingered. Oh, hungry, he had lingered under the windows. He now strained his ears. He grew alert, grew inside the dying body of Fanny Clinton: he fought his own death.

And he listened.

It was the lovely lilting song from *Der Freischütz*, when Agathe's maid teases her about her susceptibility to male beauty.

> A slender youth comes along,
>
> Blond his locks or brown,
>
> Bright of eye and red of cheek,
>
> Ah, he's good to look at!

Fan thought of Samuel. She saw him.

> She averts her gaze downwards
>
> In the manner of a bashful girl;
>
> But furtively raises it again
>
> When the lordling is not looking.
>
> And should their glances meet,
>
> Well, what's so wrong with that?
>
> What's so wrong with that?

The piano accompaniment broke off. There were voices, raised voices, then the song began again, in another key.

> You are not struck blind for that,
>
> You simply go a little red.
>
> A little glance here, another there,
>
> Until the lips find the courage to speak!

The courage to speak.

If only she had had the courage to speak.

> He sighs: Most beautiful one! She answers: Dearest!
>
> And soon they're suitor and bride.

It was one of the sopranos of the Opera House, practising for the evening's performance. Or was she sending Ernest a message?

He relaxed.

It was the beautiful delivery of art. It was something he understood. Not this. Not this courtroom with the reporters scribbling away, not the lines of faces peering intrusively into his soul, trying to hook out his being, exchange it for a gob of spit. Ernest became aware he was actually breathing. He could almost track, it felt, the air passing through his veins, palpitating his heart, forcing a pulse to hammer in his wrist.

All this will pass.

The death of Lady Fanny Clinton.

Even my grief will pass.

I shall survive.

Somehow I shall survive.

Even this.

If I can only hold on.

The *Daily Telegraph* that evening described Park and Boulton as looking 'thoughtful and subdued'.

The Nature
of Truth

'It just ain't true.'

Eliza had washed down the front steps and had come in from polishing up the front stoop. Her back ached — righteously: she was burning with anger. She had read Clara's evidence in the paper. One thing in particular stuck in her craw. Clara said she had left Southampton Street because she did not like, according to the *Police News*, 'the atmosphere'.

This implied that those who had remained behind had no morality. Whereas she, Eliza, knew for a fact that *Slutswool* herself was the very personification of unswept corners, of dirt pushed under beds, of poorly laundered sheets, of every ruse at getting out of labour.

She could stand it no longer.

I don't know nothing about doctors and inspections and the like. But I do know what I know. And what I know is, it just ain't true.

She rose up the stairs like a vengeful goddess, her dress hitched up over her skirts, her elbows bare and shiningly red from suds. Hair loose.

Mrs Peck jumped when she appeared in her back parlour still carrying her bucket and mop. Eliza let them drop, for musical emphasis.

'Oh, Eliza. You did give me a start.'

Mrs Peck was studying the news. She had newspapers laid out from end to end of her work table. Each one opened on 'The Horrible and Revolting Revelations'. (She had sent the boy out and he had staggered back in under the weight.) Mrs Peck was looking through her magnifying glass, half whimpering, half tutting. Her face flushed — angry at being interrupted. She let her pupils scald down Eliza's body to take in the bucket.

'Begging your pardon, Mum,' Eliza said, making the smallest of bobs. Defiant. Mrs Peck nodded. She had just got to a juicy part. With great regret — and irritation — she realised she would have to snip the bonds between eye and printed word.

'It ain't true, Mum,' Eliza said. She had a way of standing flat on her feet, her body perfectly at ease. There was something bordering on impertinence in it. If it weren't for the fact that she was such a good worker . . .

'What that Clara Duffin says, Mum. In there.'

Eliza indicated the papers with a jiggy finger. Mrs Peck got the idea that Eliza did not have proper respect for written language.

'You read what she says?'

A pause.

'Indeed.' Mrs Peck sank back into the slightly greasy seat of a balloon-back chair. She sat there pole-axed.

'I don't want to get involved,' she said in an unexpectedly timorous voice.

'You is involved, Mum, begging your pardon.' There was another pause. Mrs Peck with difficulty, but almost like a child to its parent, raised her eyes to take in her uppity maid of all work. 'The good name of this here establishment is being bruited round from one end of the land to the other.'

Eliza's head nodded to the paper expanse, which stretched from the *Times*, through the *Daily Telegraph* right down to the penny-dreadfuls, replete with fanciful steel engravings ('Caught!' with Fanny and Stella's hands in the air, standing in pantaloons).

'Have you paid close attention to what the lazy baggage alleges?'

Alleges.

Eliza gave this a special roll of the tongue. Mrs Peck shivered. She thought Eliza had quite the legal tone. There was something terrible within Eliza — something unrepentant. Whereas Mrs Peck carried in the back of her brain a tiny dot of terror which, if inspected, revealed her husband in trouble with the law after a certain set .

of silver candlesticks, replete with armorial engravings, was found on his person, late one night. There was humiliation aplenty after that. Mrs Peck never wanted to go near a court, because in her mind a court was only one step away from a prison. And she always averted her eyes when the 'bus took her anywhere near Newgate, or Clerkenwell, or Holloway, or Coldbath. Psychologically some part of her was always back in that tiny wretched cell, with its pisspot and rolled-up bed, bars on the window, her husband standing there helpless. '*So help me God, Elsie, I'll get out.*'

'Mum?'

Mrs Peck felt almost ashamed. As if Eliza had glimpsed in her face her darkest secret: not so much that her husband had been transported as the fact that she had had to abandon him: the hardest decision of her life and one she still grieved over.

'She says she chose to leave here because the atmosphere did not agree with her. The *moral* atmosphere.'

The terrifyingly unusual words that came out of Eliza's mouth. Allege. And atmosphere. Both of these implied a knowledge of the world of books. Come to think of it, she had noticed Eliza nodding off over some tomes. Mrs Peck stared at Eliza closely. She had the feeling she was only just getting to know her.

'But didn't you have to let her go because of the sloppy nature of her work?'

Mrs Peck nodded. 'Indeed.'

'Well, the no-good baggage is bruiting round high and low that none of us 'ere is good enough for her. She says she talked to her mum about the nasty goings-on with Mistress Fanny — *well, you-know-who* — and her mum advised her to leave toot sweet.'

'The no-good baggage.'

'Slutswool, as we called her.'

Eliza was enjoying herself, but came back to the business at hand. (She carried in her head a spheric picture of poor Mr Ernest, looking so still, so far away from everything that was happening to him. As if he might like to dream it all away. There was a shade of sadness there. She had slipped up to Bow Street. Called out, as he got in the black maria. But there was so much noise he did not look. He just hurried, head down, into the van. It was left to Stella to raise a hand and wave, like a music hall star, to the waiting crowd. They had not heard the doctor's news yet, so they cheered.)

'I want to testify, Mum. Begging your pardon. If you won't.'

'*Testify.*'

'I want at least to go down there and tell them that Clara Duffin left her employ at Southampton Street because she was no good at her work. I want to say that when we tried to send her things on, we was told that she had gone, with no forward address. That her references, Mum, turned out to be writ by someone else other than the lady at her last address. That she was a shocking worker, Mum, who skived out of everything. That, in short, she is unreliable in every which way you could possibly imagine. So her word, in short, is not worth the breath used to push it, all rubbishy and trumped up, out into the world. She is a no-good piece of work, Mum, who fully deserves her nickname: *Slutswool.*'

Eliza was almost out of breath.

'But Eliza, is it safe?'

'Safe, Mum?'

Mrs Peck wondered how to say this without it becoming self-incriminating. But that was the precise problem. The moment you became involved with anything like a court case, your words were twisted out of your mouth. If you so much as got a date wrong you were made to seem a liar. She shuddered. She saw her first husband disappearing down into the hulks, not even turning around to see if she was there, though she was — she couldn't help herself going down to see the dear boy away.

She wanted to wipe away a tear. But she was frightened, deeply frightened. Wasn't it better to let Ernest Boulton sink? What did it matter, after all?

'Miss Able,' she found herself saying instead, 'came to see me first thing this morning. Requesting an interview.' She twisted the edge of her apron. Twisted and twisted it. 'She said to me that in view of the damaged reputation of the house, and the fact that she and Master Able had paid in advance, she considered it only right that they should get back at least half of their lodgings paid. She said in view of all the unpleasantness, I could only understand that they both would begin to look about for more respectable-seeming premises.'

'She didn't!'

'But Eliza,' Mrs Peck could not keep her voice from wobbling, 'it is something awful to stand up in a court of law. You might as well be naked.'

Eliza thought about this. She had never seen it exactly this way. But she saw, now, what Mrs Peck was saying. She was saying that you had to expect to be attacked yourself. Discredited. But then, in the end, her own life had been so uneventful — so hardworking — that there was nothing she could exactly lay her hand on that would stain her own name. Except perhaps the time she had broken the Minton vase and hidden the piece on top of the pelmet where it stayed forever, peeping down at her, leering. But it was frightening, it was true — if you let yourself be frightened.

Naked.

'But Mum if I stick to what I know and seen, won't I be all right? I never saw anything nasty with Miss Fanny. Personally speaking. Lord Frederick was another kettle of fish but I ain't speaking for him. It's Mr . . . Ernest I'm thinking of, Mum. I keep hearing him singing. I keep hearing his voice. You know, Mum.'

And they both stopped for a moment, as if to recapture the sound of Fanny's voice, of an evening, a slow evening, when the day turned into night, and the day's work was by and large done, and then, throughout the rackety house, up and down the stairs, through a half-opened door, Miss Fanny's lovely cadences slipped over everyone. Mrs Peck halfway up to the attic, stopping to listen, no longer feeling her aches; Eliza down in the kitchen, going to the door to open it wider; someone out on the street. It was nothing for a small crowd to gather, to listen. It was for this that Eliza was willing to go, as it were, naked — a Daniel among the lions; it was for this that Eliza would speak.

*C*ummings got nearly every newspaper he could buy. He read them all, gorging himself on print. He felt as he read both more victorious and more — ? Some sediment was settling in the bottom of the glass of his being. Some dank sediment: darker, harsher.

Samuel had disappeared.

'I need to go for a walk. Clear my head,' was what Samuel had announced. Standing on the threshold of Cummings' room — not coming into the room. Samuel had spied the newspapers. His dark brown eyes, wounded, had shifted from the papers to Cummings' face: *et tu,* Cummings?

Cummings had risen: 'We need to know, Barton . . . we need to know the worst so we can be prepared . . .'

But before his sentence was out, Samuel had gone. He was down the stairs, silent as a wraith, disappearing into the hot London night.

Whenever in future summers there was a still, hot night, Cummings thought of this period in his life. There was an almost physical weight to the heat: as if all the pollution of the great city had accreted itself to particles of warmth — particles that had absorbed the coal, the stench of gas, the odour of millions upon millions of sweating people, labouring in their flannels, cottons, muslins and silks. The humidity was stagnant. It was hard to draw breath. London plane trees, in full leaf, stood still, like ghostly ships marooned.

So still, as if waiting . . .

Cummings wiped away a trickle of sweat running down his forehead.

And turned the page.

His world seemed to have broken apart into a mosaic of printed words, all streaming out now across his — and hundreds of thousands of other peoples' — consciousness. He had already seen, in a stationer's shop window, on his way home, an advertising poster:

THE LIFE AND EXAMINATION OF BOULTON AND PARK. THE MEN IN WOMEN'S CLOTHES.
Containing their Correct Portraits in Male & Female
Costumes, Together with Their Life & Full Report of the
Examination, Suppressed Letters & Details
Never Before Published

(Ask for the *Illustrated Police News* Editor,
G. Furkness, 286, The Strand.)
Notice to Newsagents 7/- per Gross.
Published Monday 23 May 1870, 1d, by post 2d.)

When he had gone in to browse, the newsagent had deftly placed beside it a singular document, printed on frail blue paper: 'Bigenie, The Hermaphrodite, or the Singular Adventure of the Man–Woman & Woman–Man. With a fine plate 1/6d.'

Cummings had glanced reprovingly at the man (who had a Londoner's placid profile, barnacled by moral neglect, as Cummings said to himself heatedly).

Do you think I am interested? he wanted to cry. He turned on his heel, walked out. On the door he spied another sign:

Notice: The Only Correct Portraits of the 'Gentlemen in
Ladies Dress' to be had of Frank Bridge,
27 Tichbourne Street, Piccadilly.
Single Cartes 13 Stamps, Groups 19 Stamps;
in either costume 15/6.

The *Pall Mall Gazette* that evening had noted:

Carte-de-visite photos are in the windows of most of the print
shops so that between newspapers and photographs we have, it
appears, an illustrated edition of these androgynous adventurers.
The public is in transports of indignation. Idleness, luxury and
effeminacy have destroyed nations in olden times and in all
probability, we fear, shall do so again. It is, in short, a message
about the disintegration of society, a society which seems happy
to have supported, indeed even celebrated a hermaphrodite
clique, who number among themselves a nobleman who is
the very epitome of a misspent life. Everybody has been
thinking about the trial. The sad fact is the public mind has
been penetrated with the idea of crimes it has hardly thought
about before.

All that night Cummings lay in bed, unable to sleep, too hot, and tortured by all sorts of images and thoughts, circuitous and never-ending. His mind, indeed, was penetrated by the idea of crimes it had hardly thought about before.

He listened for Samuel's footsteps on the stairs.

He did not hear them.

'You do understand, don't you?'

It was Albert, Ernest's brother, standing at Ernest's cell door. Ernest was in agony.

'You do understand quite what you've done?'

Albert would not take his eyes off him. He seemed intent on bearing down on Ernest, bringing on him all the weight of his barely suppressed anger.

Ernest let out a small moan. There was nothing he could say.

Outside a guard walked by, along the metal.

'Are you praying, Ernest?'

'We have prayers every morning,' Ernest said after a moment. 'We are awoken at six and go off to chapel.'

'Good,' said Albert. 'I hope you are praying for forgiveness.'

'How is Mother?'

There was a resentful silence.

'She is taken to her bed. She is ill.'

'Could you take a message to her?'

'It is better if she does not hear from you. Every time I mention your name she wails. It is not comfortable, Ernest. My wife is staying with our mother. But it is not easy. It is not easy.'

Ernest made another small penitential sound.

'We shall have to get the best counsel we can afford. We will have to fight this . . . infamous . . . implication.'

'Thank you, Albert,' the person called Ernest said.

'It will ruin us, *ruin* us,' Albert said in a low voice. 'We can mortgage the property and draw on our father's funds. We do not have the money of the Parks, nor the connections, alas. I have heard that the Parks have asked for some of the best legal advice in England, no less. We can try for someone less. It is important — very important for our case — that we have the best, the most learned of counsels. Which costs,' Albert said.

'I am sorry,' Ernest said. 'I am terribly terribly sorry.'

'Our mother has said she will shift into a lodging house if necessary. She has already sold her silver and jewellery. She says she needs only her mourning jewellery from now on.'

Ernest said nothing for a moment. He felt inadequately prepared, like an actor who has only a few pages from a script. He kept trying to guess what the intervening dialogue might be. He felt curiously numb, both extraordinarily tired and incapable of deep sleep. He was racked with remorse and an impending sense of doom, of helplessness. He felt penitentially thankful for his brother's assistance on another level. On this level, he was both hopeless and also, curiously, oblivious.

'Thank you, Albert,' he said a moment too late, as if he were late on stage with his pathetically small piece of dialogue. His brother had said to him: 'I will not ask you if it is true. I need not ask you.'

Arthur's face was pressed up against the grille; he was seemingly peering right into Ernest's soul. Ernest thought, in the hard part of him, the part that was iron: *this will one day be over. It will end.*

But that was a different person.

This person now, Ernest Boulton, could only say: 'Pray, do not ask me, Albert. Help me if you want to, but do not ask.'

There was a long moment of exasperated silence.

'We have obtained — or rather the Parks have obtained — at great cost,' — a meaningful pause — 'the services of an outstanding medical personage. Of much greater authority than that quack Paul. Ernest, listen to this: we have obtained the services of no less a person than Mr Le Gros Clarke, the most eminent medical specialist.'

Ernest said nothing. He was numb. He tried to work out the meaning of what Albert was saying.

'It does mean, however, Ernest, that you will have to undergo another . . .' — a moment's uncertainty, Albert's eyes slid away — 'another examination.'

'Examination?'

'Yes. In total privacy, of course. I have spoken to the prison authorities here. They understand the . . . delicacy.'

'Well, I don't see that *delicacy* is an issue after the whole blasted British Empire has been down on its hands and knees peering up my arsehole.'

Fanny's voice was tart.

There was an appalled silence. But Albert could not keep back a disbelieving laugh.

'Ernest, we must be serious. It is no joke. As no doubt you realise. All along you've been treating this as if it were one of your silly little capers on the boards. Well, it isn't. And you've had to learn the hard way.'

Ernest could not think of what to say. Fanny chose a spectral, heavily ironic silence.

'The examination will take probably half an hour at the most, and it is of the greatest importance, Ernest, in rebutting the infamous, vile evidence. I confess, I cannot get quite out of my mind the . . . .'

Ernest said nothing.

'You do agree? We . . . our family's good name . . . '

It was Ernest's turn to chuckle. Though his laugh was cynical. He could not help seeing the funny side.

'You may well laugh!'

Albert's face had flushed red with anger. Veins suddenly sprouted out all over his face. Ernest realised he had struck a sore — the sorest point.

'We are being ruined by this — financially, morally — utterly ruined.'

His voice had slipped down a notch: he was genuinely wretched, Ernest could see.

'I have not had connection with my wife ever since this happened. She cannot stand my touching her. Our mother is like someone facing death.'

Albert did not add: And it is left to me, and me alone, to carry on.

Somewhere in another cell someone dropped something metallic, and swore.

Ernest went back to his genuflections.

'I am sorry, Albert. I beg your pardon, surely. Whatever is needed . . . Whatever is necessary . . . I will undergo.'

*E*rnest tried to offer up all he could: the abjectness of his being.

Besides, he was waiting. He was hoping the sweet boy Samuel would come and see him again. It was curious what had happened in the time he had been in prison. He had never taken the boy seriously on meeting him. Yet there was some kind of unusual sweetness in being in the presence of such an . . . unplucked lad. Fanny had had her own ideas about what she might like to do with him. There might even have been a moment of reckless *joie de vivre*, an excess of spirits, a dulling of the senses with alcohol, a rhapsodic release: the boy might have been delivered to her gorgeously naked, either supplicant or demanding. Either would do. But as it was, nothing like this had precisely happened. Instead she had felt — Fanny had felt — a kind of wistful, almost maidenly adoration for the youth.

She did not exactly want fucking from him: rather she valued the aura, the nimbus of his ineffably male presence. Frederick was for all the delights and intensities of fucking. Samuel was for some indefinite yet definitely valuable suspension in space, of what might have been, could have been, if the world was entirely — or in just one or two particulars — different.

Fanny — as against Ernest — was such a strange mixture of street knowledge and something almost unformed, untouched, something virginal almost in its longing. On this altar was placed a young god: Samuel. That he was callow, slightly hopeless, probably undependable was another issue. It was more than likely he would fall in love, settle down with some pretty girl: prettiness meeting prettiness. Fanny could and would accept this when it happened. She might even contribute a jewel (might *have* — Ernest realised this now. The day of the surgeon's evidence had suddenly cast all of his life into a sequence: before and after. This was the shock he was living through.).

Was it that Samuel seemed some part of Fanny's own past, some lost aspect of Ernest that had never flowered, remained forever green?

But perhaps he might never come to see her again . . .

She didn't expect to see Frederick.

Frederick, she felt sure, was safe — sitting in some European café. Sent there by his relations. Got out of the way.

*I*n a seedy cigar place in a back street of Soho, seated on a divan, Fred was bent over, murmuring seductively to an acquaintance. Fred was living by cadging and pawning now: 'a thing that gets a chap down', as he'd just been explaining. He was enjoying rhapsodically, almost nostalgically, the Havana cigar his acquaintance had stood him for.

He sat there, wreathed in clouds of smoke, a faraway look on his face. He felt so utterly will-less. Whatever had occurred to him during that opera had propelled him along in his rudderless, aimless direction. He had never had much will — only a talent for pleasure, and now, God knows, for whatever reason the pleasures seemed few and far between. He had no wish to go back and see his aunt.

He sat very still.

'I say, old Fred, did you ever go to that little place of mine up in Shropshire?'

Fred thought for a moment. These days it took him a while to focus. He was always thinking of something else — and keeping a weather eye out for he knew not what.

He looked about himself now, suddenly suspicious. And here was this cove whom he'd only ever known on the other side of a card table banging on about his 'place' in the country. Fred almost winced. He could imagine how pretentious it would be. All deer antlers and tartan carpets.

The man opposite, who had a rather large canary diamond in his tie-pin, was looking at Fred closely.

'You might like to . . . rest up for a bit.'

Fred understood. Instantly. But he did not move. He knew that when an ambush was about to happen, you had to appear almost sensationally relaxed. He let himself nod slightly, however. God, he was enjoying the Havana.

'It's an out-of-the-way little place.'

Fred caught sight of his shoes. His own shoes. He felt shocked at how battered they'd become. Unpolished. Leather corrugated. The sole coming apart, on the inner left foot. He slid his foot out of view.

'Has some decent pheasants and whatnot. Might even get in some shooting, Fred.'

'Shootin', eh?' Fred's eyes narrowed and for a moment he looked contemplative.

He looked as if he was weighing things. Then a sublime smile passed over his features.

'I say, Doddy, this cigar is the nearest thing to heaven I've come across in quite some while. You *are* a chum.'

Fred finished the last of the cigar, almost regretfully, drawing into him the beautiful thick smoke, his face a rapt mask, eyelids looking downwards: he might have been imbibing opium. There was a small, sizzling silence as he laid the end of the cigar down on the ashtray.

Outside could be heard the voices of two men walking up the lane. They had evidently paused by the window, looking in at the range of 'French' engravings (Cora Pearl Enjoys An Early Morning Bathe).

'Heard this one?'

> There was an old Person of Sark
>
> Who buggered a pig in the dark;
>
> The swine in surprise
>
> Murmured: 'God blast your eyes,
>
> Do you take me for Boulton or Park?'

Fred laughed. He couldn't help himself. He jumped up.

A vast weight in that instant seemed to have fallen off his shoulders.

'Can I? Would you? Be such a chum? Can't thank you enough, Doddy. Won't be long, mind you. Just need to rest up and think out what's what.'

Doddy, who had won a small fortune off Clinton in cards over the years, shrugged, felt a moment's pleasurable sensation in helping a chum in a fix, gave him his card, then moved on.

He left behind on the table a gold coin. Fred scooped it up.

He headed off to a drinking den.

He needed to celebrate the change in his luck.

A Strange Vision

Quietly kneeling, I put my eye to the keyhole and found I had a famous view of all that was going on in the next room.

Lord Frederick and Fanny were standing before a large mirror. He had his hand around her waist, and every now and then drew Fanny's lips to his for a long, luscious kiss. His inamorata was not idle, for I could see her unbuttoning his trousers, and soon she let out a beautiful specimen of the abor vitae, *at least nine inches long and very thick. It was in glorious condition, with a great, glowing red head.*

Cummings had bought *The Sins of the Cities of the Plains: Confessions of a Mary-Anne* in order to, as he saw it, thrust it in Samuel's face. At long last, he thought to himself, heatedly, he must make Samuel understand. The evidence in the newspapers should have been enough to make the yokel comprehend the nature of the creature he had become enchanted by. But after Cummings' questioning, Samuel had said nothing. He had become, as it were, wordless, silent, unhearing. As if struck dumb.

In a state of apostasy Cummings had run back to a stationer's in St Martin's Lane, where he had seen a none-too-discreet advertisement for the volume he now held clasped in his right hand. (He was a south-paw.) He had wandered back to their lodgings in Islington, all the while aware, as if supernaturally, of a strange motion all around him: of photos of Boulton, now alongside Clinton, appearing in every photographer's window. There were huge newspaper billboards everywhere. 'Sensational and Revolting Revelations'. Word after word was being poured out in a torrent, all over London, all over England. And he held, in his hand, the key.

Give the volume to Samuel.

Say to him: Read this. This is the reality of the enchanting 'actress' you have known.

But first of all, to vet it so to speak (and to gain knowledge, himself, as a man of the world) he must continue to . . . turn the pages.

> *Fanny at once knelt down and kissed this jewel of love, and would have sucked him to a spend, but Lord Frederick was too impatient, as he raised his companion from her stooping posture and, passing his hands under Fanny's clothes, as she gave a very pretty scream and pretended to be shocked at this rudeness, he turned everything up and tossed her on the bed.*

Cummings feverishly turned the page.

> *As yet there was nothing to see but a beautiful pair of legs, lovely knicker-bocker drawers, prettily trimmed with the finest lace, also pink silk stockings and the most fascinating little shoes with silver buckles.*
>
> *His lordship quickly opened Fanny's thighs and, putting his hand into her drawers, soon brought to light as manly a weapon as any lady could desire to see, and very different from the crinkum-crankum one usually expects to find when one throws up a lady's petticoats. There seems such a peculiar fascination to gentlemen in the idea of having a beautiful lady to dance and flirt with, knowing all the while that his inamorata is a youth in disguise.*
>
> *'What's this beautiful plaything, Fanny darling? Are you an hermaphrodite, my love? Oh, I must kiss it; it's such a treasure! Will it spend like a man's love?'*

Cummings, once again, turned the page.

> *Lord Frederick fondled and caressed Boulton's prick, passing his hand up and down the ivory-white shaft and kissing the dark, ruby-coloured head every time it was uncovered.*
>
> *I could see that Fanny was greatly agitated. Her whole frame shook, whilst one of his lordship's hands seemed to be under Fanny's bottom, and no doubt*

was postillioning her bottomhole; and presently, seeing how agitated he had made her, he took that splendid prick fairly into his mouth and sucked away with all the ardour of a male gamahucher; his eyes almost emitted sparks as the crisis seemed to come, and he must have swallowed every drop of the creamy emission he had worked so hard to obtain.

His other hand frigged the shaft of Boulton's prick rapidly as he sucked its delicious head.

After a minute or two he wiped his mouth, and turned Fanny around so as to present her bottom over the edge of the bed. Then he threw up all the skirts over her back and, opening the drawers behind, he kissed each cheek of the lovely white bum and tickled the little hole with his tongue. But he was too impatient to waste much time in kissing, so at once presented his prick to Boulton's fundament, as he held the two cheeks of his pretty arse open with his hands.

Although such a fine cock . . .

Cummings flicked the page.

. . . it did not seem to have a difficult task to get in, and he was so excited that he appeared to come at once, but, keeping his place, he soon commenced a proper bottom fuck, which both of them gave signs of enjoying intensely, for I could fairly hear his belly slap against Boulton's buttocks at every home push, whilst each of them called the other by the most endearing terms, such as:

'Oh Fanny, Fanny, what a darling you are! Tell me, love, that you love me! Tell me it's a nice fuck!'

And the other would exclaim: 'Push; push; fuck me; ram your darling prick in as fast as it will go! oh! oh! oh! quicker, quicker; do come now, dearest Freddie; my love, my pet, oh! oh!! oh!!!

There was the slightest sound behind him.

'I am not interrupting, I hope?'

A woman's voice.

He turned, flushing painfully, dropping the book in what he hoped was a casual manner. He quickly turned it over, so the cover was placed downwards. He glanced towards his armchair and was relieved to see the headrest covered the lower part of his anatomy. He felt furious. Who was this woman who had walked into his room unannounced?

'I do beg your pardon, surely. Perhaps it is some mistake. But you are Mr Cummings, are you not, my Samuel's friend?'

Was it the light of that late afternoon of summer that irradiated the green of Ursula's cloak? She appeared, suddenly, the freshest, yet most nervous young woman he had ever seen. She had the palest of pale red hair. Her skin was moist, extremely white. She was thin, elegant — and awkward.

He stepped forward, his hand outstretched.

'Oh, Miss Wentworth. Of course. I do apologise.'

She placed down what she was carrying: it was a chequered cloth tied up around what looked like a bowl. It was touchingly home-made.

'Samuel's mother and sisters would not let me come to London without bringing some memories of fine old Derby cheese.'

She laughed. Her eyes, he noticed, were a pale grey-green, intense even while they flicked about his room, eagerly noting everything. They were long-lashed with lashes of a darker colour than her hair: the same as her very fine eyebrows. Her clothing was modest, yet carefully thought through as to colour: her gown, which rose high to her neck, was a fine sage green. In either ear was a single, swinging garnet. Her face radiated both a discreet intelligence and a resolve.

Oh, Cummings groaned to himself. *To think what Samuel has been missing* (*what is invisible to him*) . . .

Ursula smiled as if she had intuited his thought. Then her smile seemed to fade. She suddenly seemed tired, as if the effort in getting there had exhausted whatever slim resources she had.

'You wrote to me, sir. I am most decidedly in your debt. An uncle of mine was coming to London. I begged him . . .'

She seemed to have run out of breath.

'Sit. Please sit.'

Cummings cursed himself that he lived as such a sloven. He pulled aside the newspapers — quickly, quickly — then a slipper, then an old and suspicious-smelling towel. He had the grace to blush.

She, however, saw nothing.

'Is Samuel . . . around?'

'He went for a walk,' Cummings said, 'as far as I can tell. He is walking a lot just at the moment. Perhaps to clear his mind.'

'He is troubled . . . ?'

She looked up at him. And paused.

'I will not . . . presume,' Cummings said delicately, 'to tell you of his troubles. They may, indeed, not be grievous at all. But I felt it was a duty . . . of a friend . . . to tell someone who holds his interests most close to . . . remind him . . .'

'*Remind* him!' She looked alarmed.

'To remind him, dear lady, of who he is. He is under some . . . enchantment. Though it is possible he may be coming awake just at present. Which may be why he is finding it all so painful . . .'

As one ripped out from a dream, from the deepest sleep, he might have added. He could not help himself. He turned away. He himself had a double exposure on his brain and he could not help, on seeing the loveliness of Ursula, of thinking of what he had just been reading, and in reading, imagining . . .

'*But* I do not understand.'

Ursula was trying to walk alongside Samuel.

When Samuel had eventually returned, he had walked into Cummings' room, seemingly resolved on some direction. He looked the best he had looked for days.

Ursula had felt such a lurch — an almost savage lurch — of love, of want, on seeing him. He was not cleanly dressed, yet, such was his nature, this lent romance. He had looked up particularly quickly when Cummings, standing aside like a doorman, announced — 'And see who has come to see you!'

He had looked startled, then he had come towards her, in three enormous strides. He had pulled her up to himself, he had cried out, 'Oh, Ursula! My very own sweet Ursula!'

They had embraced. She had cried. Cummings had hummed and turned his back. Then she had realised she was still holding on, while he was extricating himself and standing slightly apart from her, yet to the side, so she could see him only in profile.

He asked her then, in the cautious voice of one visitor to another, 'And what brings you to London, Ursula?'

For one second her eye had flitted to Cummings, as if to summon his assistance. That one motion was enough for Samuel's personality to change its chemical composition. He seemed to curdle instantly. He lost his lively colouring, lost his rosiness, became grave, white around the nostrils.

He began to flick his fingernails against the wood of Cummings' desk.

'My . . . Uncle Servus was coming to London,' she said in a low voice, suddenly looking down. She was flushing painfully. A glitter of moisture in her lashes.

Cummings looked as if he wanted to be out of the room.

'Stay, Cummings,' Samuel said. 'You must entertain your guest.'

Then he had walked out of the room, as if he absolved himself of all responsibility.

They had both stood there, dumbstruck. Terrified.

'*P*lease — ' she called out now. 'Please. Will you not stop?'

She had followed him down the narrow stairs. She had lost all sense of personal propriety. She was terrified of this city, in which she knew precisely two people. The noise frightened her. She was dazed by the number of people pressing around her — the sheer force of faces, of so many consciousnesses jostling about her, she who was used to being on her own, or living in a small town where she knew everybody and everybody knew her.

Placed in the great city, it was as if her personality became detached from itself. She became as if made of tissue paper, with thousands upon thousands of eyes looking into her — men gazing at her, children, beggars brushing up against her.

They were walking down Caledonian Road into the tide of human traffic.

All she could do was keep Samuel's taut shoulders in her view. She tried to catch up, and then, once they were in Pentonville Road, he turned round once and saw her.

She was staggered by the force of dislike that was expressed in his face. She wanted to turn back, yet she was presented now with the fact that she could not turn back. She did not know where she was.

The street lamps were coming on. It was another claustral evening, hot and still; she felt herself to be sweating, and she felt the filth of the city infiltrating every pore in her skin. They were nearing King's Cross station. The crowds grew thicker. More impersonal.

He did not slow down. He did not turn back.

She could only keep walking.

Suddenly he disappeared down some steps.

She followed him. Into a gas-lit, reeking darkness.

It was a long, tiled tunnel, curved — stinking of coal dust and dirt. Faces loomed towards her. She felt an obscure yet real terror. What if she became lost? She had not thought to take money with her. She had simply followed her betrothed down the stairs. As if her life depended on it.

She passed a shoeless child, begging. He had fallen asleep, his hand still curved out in a plaintive cup. The child looked so fast asleep as to be dead. A painted woman — an echo of herself made bolder, harder, more desperate — passed in the opposite direction, rustling her soiled finery and seeming to sneer on catching Ursula's frightened glance.

She came to a crossroads in the tunnel. People around her were bustling along, tired and intense. It had the pulse of a great city: oblivious, like a living organism that must move at a certain pace, at a certain time, or it would die.

She suddenly saw him in the distance, down the end in the gloaming of a dark corridor.

She followed quickly.

*H*e was waiting at what looked like a train station platform. Underground. The air was sultry, dense, dead. She had never been underground in her life. It was like a world of trolls, yet inhabited by humans. There was a big sign that said 'Farringdon', then, in different lettering, 'The London Metropolitan Railway Co'.

Samuel was not moving, at least. He did not run away. He stood there.

Perhaps there was nowhere to run to?

She went and stood beside him. He was sweating and panting, like a cornered animal. He glanced at her for one moment. So unseeing.

Welcome to our modern world, he seemed to sneer at her. It has in it all sorts of marvels I am sure you have never heard of.

She tried very hard not to weep. She was a young woman of strong character: she did not weep. But she could not stop herself from trembling. At times these trembles ran up and down her form with such force it was like a sickness, an ague. But she did nothing.

She waited.

He never once looked at her, but he made no attempt to move away.

Gradually a stale, dead breath, like the exhalation of some monster, blew towards her. A paper on the platform began somersaulting along. Other people, on the platform, crowded forward.

With a roar, and a brilliant gas-light piercing the murk, the underground train arrived.

He got on. She followed, and she sat beside him. Other people took the seats facing them.

He said nothing. She said nothing. It was as if they lacked the words.

Yet to the people sitting opposite them, they were a completely transparent theorem: they were sweethearts and they were quarrelling. Provincials in London.

As to how it might end — sentimentally it would be nice if it ended happily. But realistically, the onlookers were too tired to care.

*E*rnest, alone in his cell, did not move. He could do nothing that evening. He did not read; his mind was blank. He just lay there and listened to all the sounds around him — not actually listening but seeming to seek to absolve himself of all the weight of his consciousness. Every so often, however, he could not stop a deep sigh coming out of his body. He did not know where this feeling came from, and it occurred to him that it was like something dying, giving its last gasp.

But he did not follow this thought.

He observed — yet it meant nothing to him — that the evening light had a peculiar fragile beauty.

He did not get up when the warder came to light his cell. He moved automatically, because there was less effort in it, when the warder came around later to quell the lights. He took his mattress down, prepared the coarse blanket.

He was aware, in some locked cell of his head, that it was summer outside.

But like so much else now, this appeared to belong to another world, a world he had left behind.

As he lay there, waiting for sleep to come — waiting for the wretched relief of unconsciousness — his mind, of its own accord, heard the singing at the Opera House. But even as it turned to that lovely aeration of sound, to which as a singer himself he felt deeply attuned, he also listened as if for the first time to the words of the hermit in *Der Freischütz*.

He had heard those words, too, that afternoon in Bow Street, but he had carefully not listened to them — so dreadful, harsh, almost biblical.

> He who is expelled from the world
>
> Must dwell forever in a no-man's-land,
>
> Neither fully human nor yet dead
>
> But rather living through his own death.

Was this what he had to learn to be — a hermit?

*S*amuel had got off when the train slowed down at Farringdon Station.

This is when he first spoke to her.

For she had not risen. She had stayed there, hunched, miserable.

'Coming?' he asked, his voice cold.

As if in a dream, as if she lacked any will, she followed after him. They climbed an endless darkness of stairs, alongside tired workers. Eventually, it took them up to the surface of the world again.

It was as if he were saying to her: This is my world now. This modern world of London.

They came out, bewilderingly, in a side street that was curiously quiet. She had no idea where they were but she knew enough of London to sense how far, and fast, they had travelled. That it was a form of miracle. But more of a miracle to her was the evening: there was a beautiful pale pink light falling, and in one of those freaks of London's nature, the great grim city suddenly appeared almost coquettish in its beauty: light in the soft tone of peach juice made all the old Portland stone buildings, usually as white as bleached bones and blacked with coal dust, gorgeous; the very air seemed pollinated with prettiness.

It was a beautiful summer's evening.

It was as if they had escaped into another consciousness.

But he seemed blind to it. He was walking along as if he were leading her somewhere. Eventually they turned a corner and she saw a grim stone building with barred gates. A lunatic asylum, perhaps. A prison.

He stood there intent, as if his eyes were searching for a particular window. She had the feeling he might have gone there every evening, stood there. Kept watch.

Who was within?

The building stood still, inviolate.

It was a very long moment, this, and she knew to say nothing.

To speak would be to risk losing everything.

And eventually he let out a low sigh. This sigh was so deep it seemed to have come from within the deepest recesses of his soul. He glanced at her, quickly.

She looked at him. He had softened a little. His eyes actually connected with hers.

He had been bewitched, she saw that now. He was like someone sick. She did not know the details. He needed to come home. But would he ever be the same? And would he come home? It was a calculated risk. But she was strong. Surprisingly strong. She had wanted him ever since she was a child. They had played together. In some senses, at least in her brain, they were joined together.

He was what she wanted. Even now, she wanted him. More perhaps than ever.

He looked at her again and for the first time there was a tentative warming of his corpse-visage. But he looked so ravaged, so eaten up inside. What was wrong with him? And could her love cure him?

She felt strong. She wanted him so much. Besides, there was something quite romantic in such a ravaged being. She would take him home. Look after him.

Mend him.

It might take time.

But all in all, it might work.

All he needed was a good woman.

'Do You Take Me for Boulton or Park?'

It started in that silent hour when the fashionables had left their balls and parties, the rakes had reached their homes and the houseless wanderers had found somewhere to lay their heads. It is the quietest hour in all of London. And at this time of silence, in the ghostly dawn, they could be seen arriving. Some on foot, some in carts, some pushing barrows, all drawn as if magnetically to the same point: Bow Street police court.

Barrowmen were already setting up stalls, fighting for the best positions. They called one to the other, saying, 'Oi, 'ave you 'eard. . . ' and then they chuckled and guffawed their way through a limerick that had been chalked up on the front doors of the court.

'*Do you take me for Boulton or Park?*' they chuckled to themselves as they lit their braziers, warmed their hands, toasted chestnuts, lined up bottles of ginger beer, iced lemonade, salted almonds, pies, dried figs, dates and puddings. It was going to be a big day, anybody could see that. It was the day the beak was going to make a call.

Commit the buggers to prison or set the blighters free.

'Eh, Dad, what's this they keep saying, "*Do you take me for Boulton or Park?*"'

'Well,' said the father and looked either way. He leant down and whispered into the child's ear. The child broke out into a screel of laughter, danced around and took up the chant, '*Oh, do you take me for Boulton or Park?*'

Heh!Heh!Heh!

Much later Cummings, who had joined the morning vigil, overheard the whole limerick, distasteful as it was.

'Do you take me for Boulton or Park?' The person next to him laughed.

Heh!Heh!Heh!

A wizened boy in rags appeared with a ladder, a pail of glue and some brushes. Another child, older than him, with a lolling tongue, was carrying rolls of paper. The boy set to work. On every wall he could find, every post, he lacquered a large paper announcement that said, in bold lettering, 'The One and True Account, with All the Details of the Examination of Boulton and Park'.

The simple child stood beside the boy pasting up the posters, chanting the limerick, over and over, ever louder.

Heh!Heh!Heh!

It was like something loosed, some spirit at large in the air: anarchic, wild. Nobody knew how it might end.

The street was getting noisier.

From out of the honeycomb of nearby streets they came: the wigmakers from Drury Lane, the corsetiers, the dressmakers, the costumiers, ballet girls, chorus singers, the men about town — those whose lives were spent mostly at night, the layabouts, the loungers, the card-sharps, the servants and the swells. It was as if Drury Lane and Covent Garden, The Strand and Soho had relocated for the day: converged on one spot and democratically declared it was a public holiday.

Heh!Heh!Heh!

The queue quickly grew into a small crowd, and the small crowd grew into a big crowd which, as dawn rose to day, suddenly revealed itself to be a mob — a generous, good-natured mob it was true — *Heh!Heh!Heh!Heh!* — but a mob just the same, besieging the courthouse.

The sun rose higher in the sky. It was another sultry day, still and hot, as summer seemed to have come early this year, and this affected the crowd's attitude. People became itchy, irritable, but it also added to the holiday atmosphere: part fairground, part hanging crowd.

Heh!Heh!Heh!Heh!

$\mathcal{C}$ummings tried to dust down his suit, as if to make it clear to those less savoury personages pressing in on all sides of him that he was a gentleman, almost. He pushed his arms out and glared about him.

On his way there he had already had 'an incident'. Passing a shop window he had seen a really rather lovely image (if you had no idea what it portended) of 'Lady Fanny Clinton' and Samuel Barton. They sat there staring out peacefully at all the passers-by, perfectly at ease with being stared at. (It was the 'sweetheart picture'.)

Cummings had felt only rage. The back of his collar started pressing into his windpipe. His cuffs were too tight around his wrists. All his clothes were heavy on his body, as if he had suddenly become a beast of burden given an impossible task.

Ursula, he thought.

He had gone in, laid a coin down on the counter — no, he had thrown it down, it was true. The woman, a little woman, had suddenly stood up from a box she was sitting on behind the counter. She had been darning something. She looked a little frightened.

'How much is the carte in the window?'

Heh!Heh!Heh!

Cummings tried to concentrate on bringing his voice down to a normal level. Instead it strained out, weird and almost tormented. He heard his own voice and wanted to laugh — laugh out loud, mockingly. *Heh!Heh!Heh!* But he could also see that he had to make sense, so he asked in a different voice, that almost of a breathless child, how much the photo was. The woman fetched a stack of cartes-de-visites out from the window. Cummings had gazed in bewilderment at image after image of Samuel alongside 'Fanny,' and realised how hopeless his self-appointed task was. Then he did something he normally never did (he who was so careful of his coin): he bought a silly little hand-embroidered piece of rubbish, as if that was what he had always intended to do.

Heh!Heh!Heh!

Even as he left, a hand, seemingly devoid of a body, was placing another image of Samuel and 'Fanny' alongside the shop's other two bestsellers: the lovely Eugenie, Empress of the French, and Charles Dickens, recently deceased.

$\mathcal{M}$r Caldicott had arrived early. He was accompanied by Miss Pirouette dressed in a harlequin costume, and Timmy dressed as a little black and white dog. They would busk to the crowds, providing a little entertainment. And when the doors opened they would abruptly become like everyone else. They would push. They would shove.

They would call out, '*Oi, stop that. There's room for everyone if everyone is fair,*' and keep pushing. Inside they would applaud when necessary, and send out disbelieving emanations when evidence was presented that was hostile to 'our lads'.

Timmy and Pirouette took up their positions to the left of the crowd, but far enough back for everyone to see. Timmy then climbed up on Pirouette's shoulders and they began to do acrobatics. Mr Caldicott, dressed up as Admiral Nelson — face covered in paint — acted as their barker, wielding an upturned admiral's hat (praying that nobody recognised him as Alistair Caldicott, theatrical director of distinction).

*T*he sun was high in the sky now. The crowd had been waiting, some of them for over four hours.

In the middle of the crowd stood a very still man. This was Ted, the balloon mechanic. He had been drawn to the spot by an irresistible force. He had come into the case late — too busy drifting across London, working the balloon to take much notice of what happened down on earth. But one of his mates, Elric (who filled the balloon with gas), had cracked back a *Police News*, and, patting the page almost as if it were an old friend, had presented the paper to Ted. *Heh!Heh!Heh!*

'Ain't they them rum customers we 'ad a while back?'

Ted had looked down at the steel engraving. There were severed heads. A nun was running along, hands outstretched. 'The Recent Greek Outrage', he read. He had no idea what Elric was going on about. Elric leant in and pressed — malevolently almost — a greasy black digit onto the page, but his finger was held suspended above the picture, as if he didn't want to soil it.

Ted looked down.

'The Capture of the Men in Petticoats,' he read. And there were two completely unrecognisable women, all aswish in evening gowns, being escorted into the black maria. A steel engraving.

'What was 'is nibs' name? 'is lordship?'

'What?'

'Who was up there with us a week or so back? With his fancy women?'

Ted thought back.

'Clinton, I think. Some name like that.'

Elric took the paper off him, as if he couldn't risk leaving something so valuable with him for a moment longer.

'Wasn't his lady friend called something like Fanny?' He made the word sound ugly. '*Lady Fanny Clinton.*'

Heh!Heh!Heh!

Ted went into a strange space. He could only associate it with certain moments up in the balloon. You were floating, but you had no idea what was actually moving. You appeared to be stationary, eerily still. While the world below, which actually had a curve on it — upwards rather than downwards, oddly enough — seemed to be moving away from you. As if you were losing contact with the earth. Gravity.

His stomach fell — he who prided himself on his familiarity with aerial flight.

It all came back to him then, as his eyes — his anxious, wounded eyes — passed over the words in the crime report. He felt the percussion of complete shock. It was as if someone had secretly let all the air out of the balloon. He was not so much plunging back to earth as waking to find he had never been up in the balloon at all.

It was this that drove him to stand in that crowd. He did not, particularly, know why he was there. Or even what he would do if he were given a chance to come close to the creature known as *Mrs Graham*. Perhaps he might strangle the creature with his bare hands and thus end all the memory of what had happened to him — how he had been delivered into such an exquisite ecstasy of pleasure. He did not know what he would do. But he felt he wanted to come along to see, to be a witness, to confront those creatures who had gulled him. It was terrible because as he stood there in the heat, dazed by the sun, he seemed to emit a chilliness, a coldness, as if from a grave. He waited — waited for the arrival of the prison van.

Then he would decide what he would do.

Albert Boulton began pushing his way into the concentrated mass. He started off by saying, ''Scuse me, 'scuse me do,' keeping up a momentum as if his very bearing indicated that he was someone important. He kept hearing the phrase '*Do you take me for?*' *Heh!Heh!Heh!* It had become one of those idiotic catchcries that take possession of a crowd. He had no idea what they were referring to, but as the crowd got denser, and each person more intent upon maintaining their position, the statement became increasingly aggressive. The stench of unwashed bodies also grew in intensity.

Albert felt tainted by being surrounded so closely by so much poverty: painted women, whores, theatricals, costers, ostlers, that peculiar little man in a yellow wig — where had he seen him?

This is all Ernest's fault.

He could not help but feel this — could not help but glance around him, to the left, to the right, as if he wanted to actually hit out at the people sandwiched in right by his face. It was a nightmare.

Heh!Heh!Heh!

He also didn't know whether to make it plain why it was important that he actually get to the front of the crowd.

Could he say, I am Ernest Boulton's brother?

Heh!Heh!Heh!

He could not. And this impossibility was clenched inside him, like a horrible fist that might come out at any moment. He felt aggressive and angry: confused, yet certain.

He had to get to the front.

'Ere, you interested in an intimate record, like, of the he–shes?'

He was wedged right up against a suspect-looking gentleman, with a long drooping moustache that looked as if it came from the Napoleonic wars. The creature smelt suspiciously of whisky. The creature dug down inside a large pocket in his greeny fur-collared jacket and came up with a pamphlet.

Bending his face closer into Albert's so the latter got an alarming view of the dirt-filled pores on his pendulous nose, the creature murmured, 'Go on. I bet a gent like you could get hours of enjoyment from something like this.'

Albert's almost frightened eyes glanced down at the pamphlet.

Bigenie, The Hermaphrodite, or the Singular Adventures and Excitements in the Private Life and Times of the Man–Woman & Woman–Man.
With a fine plate 1/6d.

Heh!Heh!Heh!

Now the creature was goosing him. Actually sliding his hand — or was it a pickpocket? — down his trousers. Albert went into almost a frenzy of feeling for his gold watch, his chain. Hands, little hands, seemed to feathering all over his lower body, but he was so trapped in the motionless crowd he could not get his own hands down there.

Heh!Heh!Heh!

'I do not want —' he hissed.

'Keep your wig on, guvnor,' the man said, and then, almost miraculously, in one of those surges that had begun to pass through the crowd — like tremors on the top of some glutinous mass — the man was swept away.

*T*immy, on the edge of the crowd, was extemporising on the theme of 'What do you take me for . . . ?' He acted out various roles that the crowd had to guess. Fagin stealing handkerchiefs. Mary Queen of Scots — both the axeman and the queen herself. Bill Sykes and Nancy. Ernest Boulton taking a curtain call. There was no end to his tricks.

Mr Caldicott, or rather Admiral Nelson, collected coin after coin. The crowd was quite good-natured at this time of the day. *Heh!Heh!Heh!Heh!* They craved entertainment to pass the time away. There was still one hour till the doors opened.

*E*rnest was sitting inside the prison van, one foot up against the wall, a knee braced against the other wall. He had worked out, over the past three weeks, how to wedge himself into the tiny space. He also twisted his body around so that, like an animal sensing the air, he stretched up and gazed out of the tiny window of the prison van — no bigger than a letter slot. He saw. He got glimpses.

At times he saw the bottoms of women's skirts swishing along the street. Going along Clerkenwell Road. They were working women's skirts, dun-coloured. He saw heavy boots, and baskets being carried along, big wads of washing. Once he saw for a moment a small black and white mongrel, sitting down on its legs, lost in a luxury of scratching, its mouth wide open, seemingly grinning, a big pink veld of a tongue rolled out, jiggling.

Ernest felt at this moment an almost sickening nostalgia for the ordinary. How was it that he had never noticed any of this? He had walked by, always thinking of something else. As if his own destination in life were so important that he never took time to linger. Notice.

The van began to rattle over cobbles. He thought he saw a poster. His name. His family name. Laminated all over a hoarding, repeated again and again, as nagging as a toothache.

Stell — no, he was Stell no more, he was Arthur Park, gent — had murmured to him while they waited to get into the van (Arthur had managed to slip a coin to the guard again — Arthur who had so much more coin than him) '*My father has got on the case. He is calling in all sorts of favours. It won't go ahead. Don't worry. It may cost a fortune — will cost a fortune — but we'll be all right. Have faith.*'

Ernest's pale blue eyes had grazed Arthur's eyes. Why did he get the eerie feeling that Arthur was speaking to himself? Repeating what he might say to himself when he was alone in his cell in the depth of the night? As if sensing this thought, this heresy, Arthur had leant down suddenly and squeezed Ernest's arm.

This was too much for Guard D, who was not bribed, and he ordered them to stand further apart.

'Regulations, sir. Two yards apart. Two yards apart. And keeping to the rule of silence. Sir.'

Arthur was dressed as a gent. Was it only Ernest who noticed how haggard Arthur had got? He was still plump, but whereas before his plumpness had been animate, now it seemed to drag him down: he had an old man's pot stomach, skinny haunches and the skin on his face looked yellowy and creased.

Ernest wondered where Frederick was. He often pictured him in his mind. He saw him, sometimes, sitting with his aunt, in what Ernest imagined as a very beautiful room, a kind of stage set. They might be having a glass of champagne, and Frederick would be beautifully attired in evening dress, toying with his signet ring. They were on the point of going out. They were in Monte Carlo perhaps. The Countess of —— would be wearing diamonds and what colour would be her gown?

But at this point the image always faltered, and was followed by a large almost flagrant image of Frederick's face on the stage towards the end of *The Morning Call*. Ernest was haunted by this moment: Frederick's face, bathed in sweat, turning to look into his face. What was the expression exactly? Why did he look so intense? Was it the black wig he wore, or the black eyebrows, corked on over his own fine lashes? Or the exhaustion, the exhilaration of performance?

If you're going to hang, you'll never drown.

Why did he think of that at this moment?

Ernest shuddered.

The van seemed to have hit some obstacle. It couldn't move. Ernest craned up and looked out of the slit. Faces. Face after face. Craning up. In the sunlight. They were all looking up at him apparently (though he realised they couldn't see where he was, even as they searched every aperture, every window). Their mouths were moving. Moving as if they were the orifices of one single beast, like an octopus slithering around the van, its tentacles wrapped around it, each one opening, shutting, flittering. They were all calling out something. *Heh!Heh!Heh!*

Now they were banging against the walls of the van.

What were they saying?

Heh!Heh!Heh!

Yelling? Laughing as they called it.

We cannot play this. We cannot play this.

Ernest's heart beat to this black tune.

What were they all saying?

'What do you take me for?'
If only he could hear it.
Make sense of it.

'I am Ernest Boulton's brother. I have to get through to the court.'
It had happened. Albert was not aware of when it had first come out, but it had appeared, finally, to be the only thing he could say. He said it now, over and over, as he pushed, slithered, slid. He was aware of his shoes being trampled on, ruined — he felt the side of his jacket parting from his body, had to get hold of it physically and yank it away, saw a child's hand, dirty, adept, slipping out of the inner pocket, saw his own notes — notes about the trial — disappearing.

'I am Ernest Boulton's brother!' he cried out, aware that there were tears in his eyes: tears of rage, of impotence. We have lost all the money that existed in my family, he wanted to yell at the people all around him: do you not understand what it means? There is nothing left now. I will have to work for the rest of my life to pay off the legal defence. I will never be able to stop. My children will not be able to go to the school I had in my heart of hearts wanted them to. My daughter will probably not be acceptable in marriage to the type of person she should rightfully be married to. My wife is sick. She lies on the bed, holding her stomach, groaning. She cannot stand me touching her. My mother is like someone facing a death. Everyone has collapsed and it is left to me — me alone — me who is fighting even to get into the courtroom.

Heh!Heh!Heh!

But he could say none of this — he could put none of this into words. He could only heave his way forward, feeling as he did so, all his gentlemen's credentials — the clothes he wore, his shoes, his gold chain, even the calmness and apparently unchallengeable quality that comes from birth and self-belief — he felt every aspect of this being stripped away from him, thieved, devalued, made worthless. He would end up as one of those men wearing the battered clothes of an ex-gentleman, sleeping in a doorway.

What do you take me for?

The back door of the police van was unlocked. First one warder, then another got out. Ernest was the first to emerge. He no longer looked around but scuttled head down into the court. There was a ragged cheer, which died out too quickly. A strange thing happened at this point. The crowd appeared to expand mutely. It was as if there had been some vibration from within. *Heh!Heh!Heh!* It pressed forward, desperately, so those in front found themselves propelled forward dangerously fast, flung against whatever was solid — a wall, the sides of the van, a lamppost.

Ted found himself in a whirlpool of people. He tried to push forward, and in one of those bewilderingly sudden eddies that occurs in large crowds, he was first pushed away from the building then suddenly sped back so he found himself pushed up hard against the side of the police van.

Mrs Graham had just got out. But it was all wrong. It wasn't *Mrs Graham* at all. It was a haggard young man who no longer fitted his clothes properly. He was unnaturally white, and though he was plump still, his fatness hung on him, as something he could not get rid of, escape. He looked terrified.

Heh!Heh!Heh!

At that precise moment someone yelled out, 'Dirty devil!' From out of the crowd flew a single rotten egg, which splattered on the black maria's side. A line of police now braced themselves, with interlocked arms, leaning back into the swelling tumult.

Arthur Park turned his face. His eyes caught sight of Ted, but there was no recognition. The sound around them swelled: became frightening, deafening.

Two policemen positioned themselves on either side of Stella, who seemed incapable of moving. He was frozen. They picked him up and briskly carried him into the building.

Testimony

Every so often the door into the court fell open and a wall of heat, the smell of human bodies, rushed in to hit her. Eliza felt an abject sense of fear. She could hear, through the wall, voices talking, talking endlessly, with only a change in tone indicating another speaker. One voice was slow, hesitant — the witness? The other voice sharper, more querying — Mr Poland? Every so often there was laughter — a strange sound in that cheerless place.

When would it be her turn?

She looked about her. The room was tiny, with dirty plaster walls. She would have taken a cleaning brush to them herself. The wooden floor needed a good sweep. And there were cobwebs all over the high barred window.

Was it deliberately like a cell? To remind witnesses of what might be ahead if they lied? She strained to listen but the foot-thick walls prevented this. She looked for a moment at the policeman sitting there looking at nothing and soundlessly whistling. He had asked her name, age, occupation and address. That was the end of it, apart from one human sentence: 'It'll be over soon enough.'

Unlike hell.

*A*t that moment the door to the courtroom opened and the policeman jumped up.

'Call the next witness!'

'Eliza Clarke, servant girl!'

'Servant girl, Elijah Smart!'

As Eliza stood up, it was as if the very act of moving had shaken some fundamental certainty out of her. She was like one of those fairground globes with coconut snow within. Inside was a blizzard: the stark outlines she was so sure of the moment before — all she recognised as real and true — became occluded. She panicked. Felt a trickle of sweat unfold down her backbone. Her hands turned to kapok.

She walked into the room.

And saw. Saw Mr Ernest turn his head slowly, his pale blue eyes finding her own, and then she saw. Saw the faintest shadow of a smile there. Recognition. This is what is true. He is true. Only him. Her. The slipperiness of it all, fell away. She heard, in that instant, Fanny's lovely mezzo-soprano voice. It was a particular point of evening. She was up in her room. It had stopped raining. The rain was caught in the light. The sky was yellow. Down by the Thames a network of sails formed a kind of cobweb, reaching up into the silvered disc of the sun. The raindrops were falling, flashing through a tawny sky, and each one turned purple, green, yellow. Fanny's voice rose higher and higher and for one moment Eliza came into some realisation about her life. *I am this person now: Eliza Clarke, a servant girl, and this moment shall pass, and I will go on to be another person.*

It was a strange thought, almost a spasm. And then it passed.

*T*he room was packed. To her right, in a high box, sat an elderly man with a not unkind face. He was looking at her over his small glasses, watching her intently, seemingly willing to suspend his judgement about her character until she spoke. He even nodded to her, lightly, as if to acknowledge she existed — might even find the situation frightening. Eliza almost bobbed a curtsy to him but was prevented. By some sense of survival.

The snowstorm had stopped. Still. As still as that moment up in her attic. The rain had paused.

There was this space in time now. This space in which she could form the words.

'Are you Eliza Clarke, servant girl at 36 Southampton Street, The Strand?'

'I am, sir. I am a maid of all work,' she said, clearing her throat. She was almost frightened of the sound of her own voice. As if she had never heard it before — the exact sound of her voice, its low register, its country origins. She shivered. And was aware that everyone was looking at her, waiting.

'Can you please describe your duties at Southampton Street?'

'Well, sir,' Eliza said, deciding to speak only to the kind-looking gentleman sitting up high on the bench. She trusted him. 'I would first like to clarify something.'

She felt a moment's misgiving at using such a word as 'clarify' — and it was true, her tongue almost stumbled, gave out, *traduced* her but she had seen these words ever since she had taken up reading, and she decided now was the time to *spend*. Spend everything really. But carefully.

'Clara Duffin was a scullery maid, sir, under me, but she was only a scullery maid at Southampton Street for less than two months. More like one month, really. And during that time Mr Boulton, sir, was mainly away, doing theatricals in Scarborough. I have double-checked this, sir, with Mrs Peck, my mistress. She looked into her books.'

'And can you *clarify* for us,' Mr Besley said, seeming to smile a little — was he making fun of her? — 'the nature of Mr Boulton's apartments.'

'Well, sir, I do not know how Clara Duffin said what she did.' Mr Besley seemed to frown. She decided to go back to the magistrate. 'Sir, both the beds in Mr Boulton's apartments was always occupied, quite separate, like.'

'Was Mr Boulton habitually dressed as a woman?'

'Only, sir, if I may say so, when he was being a theatrical.'

'A theatrical?'

'Only when he was getting into character, for one of his most popular performances.'

There was a titter somewhere at the back of the courtroom. A soft wave of assent seemed to flow down towards her. She did not dare look back there.

Where the quality were.

Was she *giving a performance?*

Mr Besley said to her, 'Thank you, Miss Clarke.'

A frightening-looking man, a smooth gentleman if ever she saw one, now turned to her.

'You say Miss Duffin was a servant for only one month, not the six months she said?'

'Yes, sir. She said she needed to leave because she was delicate and had consumption but she went to several places after ours, never stopping long at any of 'em.'

'Did she ever talk to you about the nature of the relationship between Lord Frederick Clinton and Boulton?'

'No, sir. Not that I recall.'

'Did you not say,' the man glanced down at a piece of paper, 'you thought the prisoners looked like "ladies dressed up in men's clothes"?'

Eliza thought for a moment.

'I may have, sir, when they first arrived, like. But once I got used to them, and how harmless they was, sir, I never once noticed after that.'

'How did Lord Frederick Clinton address the prisoner Boulton?'

Eliza thought carefully for a moment.

'I am not sure what you mean, sir.'

'Did he call the prisoner either Fanny or Lady Clinton?'

'Only when they was getting into character, sir, as I said, for their very popular entertainments.'

Again there was that warm breeze, followed by a titter. Some people applauded. Eliza felt emboldened.

'Sir, can I make it clear that Clara Duffin's work was belowstairs. She never went into the rooms, as far as I know. I mean, she had no right to go into their rooms at all. She certainly did not make their beds. She could not be trusted, sir. She was a most unreliable worker, sir, if I can make so bold.'

'Is that so, Miss Clarke? And on what basis do you find yourself here this afternoon?'

'I came of my own accord, sir. I didn't have to speak out.'

'Were you promised any money?'

'No, sir. I was not.'

'Did you ever notice a wedding ring on the prisoner's hand?'

'Not that I noticed, sir. To tell you the truth, I never particularly looked.'

'What about the hairdresser who called nightly to dress Boulton's hair?'

'He is a fellow from Brydges Street, opposite Drury Lane Theatre, sir. He is quite well known for the magnificent truth of his wigs, sir. He used to come once a week to curl Mr Boulton's hair. And then they would dress up in dresses such as you see on the stage, sir. On stage, sir, they is somethink quite brilliant. I have seen them with my own eyes and certainly, sir, I can tell you this, as they say in their public pronouncements, "to see is indeed to believe".'

This was followed by what the *Daily Telegraph* scribe called an 'indecent outburst of applause'.

'You are certainly a fan, Miss Clarke.'

She did not dignify this with a response. She was suddenly aware she may have overstated the case and perhaps called into question her own objectivity. She had been a fool, she now saw that. And was having trouble breathing. She had spent too much too quickly.

'And I take it Lord Frederick Clinton is still resident at that address?'

A pause. He was making a fool of her, she knew that. She frowned.

'No, sir. He is not.'

'I take it he will not be here then as a witness this afternoon,' the very superior gentleman asked directly across the floor, to Mr Besley.

Suddenly it was as if she did not exist. Was irrelevant.

This happened when you had spent all your coin too artlessly, ended up penniless.

Mr Besley stood up and addressed the bench. 'I'd have thought the Treasury would do one thing or another — put Lord Frederick either in the box as a witness or in the dock as a prisoner.'

'It is not always so easy to put people in the dock,' said Mr Poland.

'But it is very easy to avoid doing so.'

Eliza did not know what to do. Should she go? She was overpoweringly aware of everyone scrutinising her. Her eyes for one moment laid themselves against Mr Boulton's and he, for one second, let his own eyes connect. His face made a small and gentle motion downwards.

She would have liked to curtsy.

Except the magistrate was saying, looking at her not unkindly given the circumstances, 'You may stand down now, Miss Clarke.'

As she walked out of the court she overheard him say, 'My mind is made up.'

*H*e was coming through the wings; it was dark. There was a source of light out there and he knew, she knew almost by instinct how to get there. Not tripping over the ropes, nor banging into the sets, nor Williams the mechanic who moved aside, nodding slightly as she passed by. She was playing Fanny Chillington and as she walked through the wings she was . . . becoming Lady Fanny Chillington. It was happening. There was that heat out there: she could feel it against her cheeks. It was times like this when she loved the theatre. She felt a tingling down in her toes, and at the back of her throat was a dryness, an exhilarating oscillation. Through every pore in her suddenly beautiful body she was alive: monstrously, utterly, completely alive.

'*My* mind is made up.'

Mr Flowers had pulled his papers together, banged them on his desk to put them into alignment, then laid them down again. He had taken off his glasses, polished the lenses, then placed them on. He now looked down into the courtroom, at the lawyers from both sides.

Complete silence had fallen.

*O*ut on the stage she could see the circle of limelight. Burning. In it stood Frederick, looking out into the dark. That dark waterfall. The light bit around his costume, irradiating his silhouette. And his voice, projecting yet coming back in a two-second delay, made all his actions strange, hierarchic. She felt the hairs on her body lift up. She was getting near. She moved to the wing, stage left.

'*I* have had no doubt for some little time past,' Mr Flowers said, 'that it is my duty to commit Boulton and Park. I feel it is my duty to commit them on the most serious of charges: there is too great a conflict of evidence. I cannot discharge them.'

*S*he could see the seam in the back scene wall, the grubby handprints of the mechanics who were now standing about, poised, waiting for their cue. She smoothed down her skirt and let herself be lulled into that perfect state. You had to believe in this state, lie back into it. Relax or the words would not come.

She felt a trickle of sweat unfolding down her back. She felt the heaviness of makeup. The weight of her wig.

But she would soon find levitation. This would come.

She stood up on the balls of her feet. '*Take very tiny little skimming steps. Remember to keep the waist the centre of the circle when moving. Move from the knees rather than the hips.*'

She launched out from behind the flat, and walked out into the blinding flash of limelight.

'*I*t is my duty to commit you, Ernest Boulton, and you, Arthur Park, on the charge of conspiracy to commit buggery. I also commit you on the charge of conspiring with divers other persons to commit buggery, and conspiring to incite others to commit buggery. There is also the lesser charge, of a conspiracy against public decency and morality, so as to amount to an offence against common law.'

'Sir, can I ask that the prisoners be allowed bail? These are young men, sir, scarcely of age. They are just starting out in life.' Mr Besley was addressing the bench. In the name of common humanity, I ask this.'

Mr Flowers' face was grave. He appeared to have heard nothing of what Mr Besley said.

'The prisoners are committed to Newgate Prison, to await the next session at the Central Criminal Court. Bail is refused.'

Mr Flowers banged his gavel, stood up.

*T*he wall of heat from the audience smashed into her face. But there was also that lovelier sound, of applause drizzling, then breaking out, then beating fast hard all over her, so every atom in her body coruscated, flicked alive.

She moved further out there, onto the stage, to be closer to her audience.

She came and stood beside her lover, Frederick.

He turned to her: she felt a staggering blow. The experiment of being there with him. The risk.

'Union is strength,' he cried out into the darkness. 'Let us be married, and share the ridicule between us.'

She turned, strange, drenched, powerful. 'A very handsome offer; let half your ridicule be my marriage settlement.'

He held out his gloved hand.

She raised her hand to his.

He pulled her closer, closer to the burning lights.

There was now the smallest pause.

'Half of all I possess on earth,' he called out to the void, ' — nay, the whole: I gain the better half if I get you.'

He came closer to her, kissed her.

It was like this every night.

Someone out there. A face would isolate itself. Be kind. Be idolatrous. Be trusting. Be waiting. Be wanting.

She would give. She would give all she could.

This was the outpouring.

This was the loveliness of it. And amid all the falseness — the hair, the padding, the corsetry, the bobbing crinoline, the papered cracks in the back set, the chilliness coming off the brickwork backstage, the utter death of a place without light — all of it was worth it for these lovely moments now.

This was life.

'It seems,' she said, aware the curtain was about to descend, 'It seems that, like schoolboys, we have played till we have become in earnest.'

They turned, kissed and faded.

*A*s the court broke up, Arthur, rising and staggering slightly, advanced to the bench and cried out: 'I am entirely innocent of any thought of such a crime!'

Ernest rose too, a second too late, as if his mind were elsewhere.

He missed his cue.

'I say the same.'

Mr Flowers, about to leave, turned and said, 'You say you are entirely innocent of the charges?'

Arthur drew himself up. Or was it Stell? The very last emanation of the haughty bitch: 'Of any thought of committing such a gross crime.'

Having said this, as the *Daily Telegraph* scribe reported, 'Park appeared to faint. Both prisoners,' the scribe noted, 'appeared to be staggered by the decision of the magistrate. Park several times applied his kerchief to his eyes. Boulton, before being removed, spoke briefly to a male relative and a female witness, both of whom appeared to be offering him some comfort.

'The prisoners were then committed to Newgate Prison, to await their trial.

'An immense crowd watched them being driven away in the van. There were more cheers than boos. Park took off his hat and waved it, acknowledging the crowd. Portions of the crowd had been waiting all day.'

*T*he following day a warrant was issued for the arrest of Lord Frederick Clinton.

A Gentleman and His Suitcase

After two months and one week in prison on remand, Ernest Boulton and Arthur Park were released on bail, on 26 June 1870.

'A great number of persons had assembled for the purpose of seeing the prisoners,' reported the *Daily Telegraph*, 'and they were followed for some distance but no manifestations of feeling of any kind took place.'

Eliza left him alone. The house was empty anyway. The Ables had gone. Mrs Peck did not show herself. She said she had a terrible headache. Had to lie down. But then she lifted the damp handkerchief off her forehead and, her eyes suddenly acute, murmured to Eliza, 'Tell me what 'e's up to, like. Keep me informed. I feel I've been remiss in the past, not keeping up to date.'

Eliza went down the stairs and knocked lightly on the door.

He turned — slowly, very slowly. He was just standing in the middle of the room, as if lost in thought.

The way he turned. So slow.

He had changed, got thin, eaten into.

But he looked relieved. On seeing her. A gay smile played across his lips for a moment.

'Ah, Eliza, it's you,' he said. 'I'm trying to work out where to start.' He let out a laugh, a new laugh she had not heard before. It sounded bitter. 'Or whether it's worthwhile starting at all.'

'I came to see, sir, if you needed anything.'

His eyes grew moist. She thought: he is going to cry. She did not know quite what to do. To gather him into herself, to nurse him as a babe? He turned his back to her and went towards the window, which he opened wide.

'I suspect we shall not have too many visitors today.'

He stood there with his back to her.

She looked about the room. The sad evidence of all that had happened was everywhere. Drawers pulled out. Chairs askew.

As if abstracted, she picked up some cushions off the floor, dusted them down and placed them on the back of a chair.

'The afternoon mail has come?'

'Yes, sir,' she said. 'There was nothing for you.'

She knew he was waiting for some message from Lord Frederick. Who had not been heard of, since.

Most of Ernest's friends had fled abroad. And those others who called did so as if to a funeral: low voices, muffled glance. (Except Mr Caldicott, Timmy and Pirouette, who came the night Ernest had come home from Newgate. They had had a merry party up there, playing the piano, and much singing — not Mr Ernest though, Eliza noted.)

This was followed by a deeper furrow of silence. From this silence, nothing had grown, come, or begun.

'Thank you, Eliza,' he said. 'That is all.'

She curtsied and went downstairs.

Past all the closed doors.

At half past five that evening the doorbell rang. This was so unusual now, so startling, that everyone in the house became still. Mrs Peck in her room lay there, ghastly eyes staring up at the ceiling. The boy was downstairs lounging about, arms and face streaked with black since Eliza had got him to polish all the brass and copperware, keeping him busy during the quiet period, like. 'Otherwise she'll have to let you go, boy.'

During the trial there had been endless ringings of the bell. Urchins had taken it upon themselves to ring the bell as a lark. *Heh!heh!heh!* Eliza had had to go up and down the stairs constantly, answering the door. To find nothing — no one. Or, worse, a steaming pile of boy-turd. Once they even smeared it all over the lintel, inside the lock. *God blast your eyes.* Then, somehow, in between the commitment and the release from Newgate on bail, the bell-ringing had stopped.

This is when the glassy period of silence fell. It was no friendlier. It was a queer, unnatural silence, as in a sickroom.

Mr Ernest had been brought back by his brother, and installed.

'The family shall pay his rent for the next month. Then we will work out some new arrangement.'

Mr Albert made it sound as if he was capably measuring out a coffin size.

'You mean, sir, Mr Ernest will be looking for accommodation elsewhere?'

The brother, who was like an imprecise match, but somehow less than Mr Ernest — or perhaps more, because he was in every way ordinary — looked a little startled by the servant's presumption.

'I am deputising, sir,' she said with a faint curtsy, 'for Mrs Peck, who finds herself incommoded.'

'Yes, well,' said the brother, with the faint impression of a condescending smile, 'Ernest will be returning to his mother's lodgings. In Leamington Spa. To live in retirement, as it were. For a while.'

Terrible words.

In retirement.

This had been Mr Ernest's last visitor.

But now the bell rang again, pealing afresh.

As she opened the door she was surprised to see a lamination of sunlight on the top of the brickfront opposite. It was still summer. She had a sudden sense of other people's lives, of couples out walking on a summer's evening, children playing games.

She stood there with the door open, as if to let some of this promise leak into a house of mourning.

Standing there, on the lowest step, was a young gent. He was well formed, but he looked as if he might have been a clerk, certainly a provincial. Dressed in travelling clothes. Indeed, he was carrying a suitcase.

'Are you looking for lodgings, young man?' Eliza asked, on an upward inflection.

'Oh, no!' He laughed strangely. 'I am in fact leaving London.'

There was an awkward pause.

He glanced around him nervously.

'I wondered, in fact, if a . . . Mr Boulton' (whispered) 'still resides here?'

*S*he closed the door behind him and immediately Samuel had the sense of the great silence weighing down the house. There was not a sound apart from the tramp of their boots up the stairs. He also had the sense of other people listening — ravenously listening. He heard, up one flight of stairs, the sound of a door handle being turned swiftly.

Footsteps hurried to the stairwell.

'Ooooh! You!'

It was an expulsion of air, a kind of puncturing, somewhere between a sigh, a cry and a slight moan.

Ernest was standing there, backing away from him, then coming to a halt. Once again his hand, seemingly of its own volition, rose up to his face, making as if to cover it with a fan of flesh, then falling away.

Eliza said, with difficulty (as if to awaken him), 'It's a Mr Barton, sir.'

Not Lord Frederick, she could have been saying.

But her last unspoken thought was lost in the rustle of cloth as Samuel leapt upwards, two steps at a time, towards Ernest. There was a pause from Ernest's side — he seemed to draw back, as if frightened. (Did he see a *Police News* reporter standing unseen in an upper-level doorway? 'The prisoner then embraced the defendant in a most unmanly style.')

This disequilibrium somehow threw them slightly out of sync and they both laughed. This was a lovely, shy moment that broke the tension.

'Oh, come in, come in, young man,' said Ernest then, turning and walking into his rooms. He left the door open.

The prisoner left the door open, the servant girl said in court.

'Eliza, bring us some tea.'

Mr Barton raised his hand. He looked embarrassed.

'Ah, no. I will not be staying long. That is . . . ' He flushed. He indicated the suitcase he had dropped by the top of the stairs.

Ernest gazed at the young man's face. He seemed to be in the act of remembering the young man, as if he anticipated no longer seeing him. His glance was so intense it made Samuel blush. This only made Samuel more beautiful in Ernest's eyes.

'I have to meet . . . someone . . . I am leaving London. *Ernest?*' Samuel realised he was at a loss to know what to call 'Fanny'. 'I am going home for a while . . . I have been ill.' This last was a confession.

Ernest made a small gesture, not so much cutting something off as indicating that Samuel's comments did not signify in the larger scheme of things. It was as if he — Ernest — himself were immaterial. He kept walking further into his room. His deracinated, wrecked room. (Rooms have spirits of occupation and spirits of emptiness and abandonment. The room, though occupied by two people, felt empty.)

Samuel felt curiously clumsy in this new territory, with this — stranger.

'I am betrothed.'

It was best to be brutal. To end it.

'Ah,' Ernest said, as if needing a moment. He had begun to shiver, as if suddenly cold. 'And to think I have no champagne. And you will not even drink a cup of tea.'

'She is waiting.'

'Downstairs?'

Ernest went to the window, looked out. He stood with his back to the room, apparently searching the street downstairs.

'No, no,' Samuel said.

They were two men standing awkwardly in a room, one with his back to the other.

'Ursula is waiting at the station, with my good friend Cummings. He has promised to come up to Nottingham. To be my best man.'

'More congratulations,' Ernest said, in a light stinging tone that did not quite come off. *I do not like the role I am being asked to act*, he might have said. And Samuel might have answered, *Please don't play that role; I don't like the role I have any better.*

They stood apart, briefly silent.

'Please turn and look at me, Fanny.'

Ernest turned. His face looked very white. He felt an unendurable strain.

'*I cannot . . .*'

'*Nor can I . . .* ' Samuel's word came as quickly.

There was a longer pause here — of adjustments. Ernest gave a bleak yet defiant smile.

'Well, then,' he said, as if something had been settled. 'Congratulations.'

Samuel came awake. He felt inside his pocket.

'I have been given . . .' He took out a small suede bag. 'I bumped into

Frederick, Lord Frederick . . .'

'*You've seen him?*'

Ernest took a step forward. Staggered. Samuel had the hallucination that Ernest might almost have hit him. But it was rather as if some explosive force within Ernest had blown him forward. He held back, trembling.

'A while ago. I'm sorry. At least a month.'

'Oh.'

Ernest took the bag and almost absent-mindedly emptied out the contents onto his palm. Something showed like a spot of blood. It shimmered, then sank back into the suede. It was as if it burnt Ernest's skin.

'He said . . . '

Ernest looked at him. 'What did he say?'

Samuel felt foolish saying it.

'He said something strange. You might understand it. If you drown, at least you'll never hang. No, wait, I have it wrong . . .' Samuel struck his forehead, laughing, yet grimacing too. 'If you hang, at least you'll never drown.'

Ernest looked disbelieving, hurt — Samuel saw all these feelings quickly revolve over his friend's face. He had wanted to shield him, but instead he had wounded him.

Then Ernest laughed. He laughed loudly and fiercely — and bitterly too.

His laughter rang through the empty house, from room to room.

'He's got away. He's escaped!'

*A*fterwards Eliza, Mrs Peck and the boy asked how it had happened. There was not a breath of wind. Yet on this becalmed evening, of an almost supernatural stillness, a rogue wind had sprung up, and almost out of nowhere it had roared up the stairwell, snatched back the door of Mr Boulton's chamber, then sent it slamming shut with such violence it was the very echo of a gunshot.

'Oh, God! Oh, sweet Jesus in heaven,' Mr Ernest had cried. 'I am dead!'

But that was all.

No further wind took up.

A serene silence returned, submerging them in its glaze.

But Ernest was shaking.

'It was a door, a door. The door slammed shut, dear Fanny.' Samuel was holding him. 'That is all.'

Eliza had come up the stairs, thought of knocking, but there was something about the silence in that room. Its porous depth.

She retraced her path.

A long, long silence ensued.

It was a few minutes to seven.

Mrs Peck was lying there, half dazed with morphia. The boy was downstairs, kicking a brass scuttle resentfully, planning his next move: he would be out the door soon, looking for other employment. Eliza was in the kitchen polishing the silver serving spoons.

It was then that Ernest started singing.

He played the piano also. And all up and down the house his voice rang out: beautiful, pure and strong.

> Rose of the garden, blushing and gay
>
> E'en as we pluck there, fading away!

Mrs Peck rose from her bed, sat up, then, almost against her will, walked like a medium towards the door.

She had a sensation that if she did not open the door and stand there, something awful might happen.

She must hear.

> Beams of the morning, promise of day,
>
> While we are gazing, fading away!

The boy froze halfway out the door and tiptoed back.

Carefully he nudged down the door handle, then pushed the door open, praying it would not reveal him.

> All that is earthly, fadeth away,
>
> But there's a land
>
> Where nought shall decay,

Eliza stopped her polishing and stood up, blood rushing to her head. She too went to the door.

> Where there's no sorrow, no fading away!
>
> Hope's fairy promise, charms to betray,
>
> All that is earthly, fadeth away.

His beautiful voice filled every space in the house.

His voice shifted the position of their souls.

By the time the song ended, they were all remade.

'*And* that,' said Ernest, carefully placing down the lid of the piano, 'is the last performance of the wonderful and mysterious Miss Fanny Clinton.'

Samuel had his suitcase in his hand.

'You mean you will not take the piano? Where you're going?'

Ernest smiled but ventured no reply.

The two men said very little as they walked down the stairs together.

'It was the wind!' Eliza called out, almost cheerfully.

Mrs Peck called out drowsily, 'Eliza, how many times have I told you? Never leave the bottom door open! Heaven knows, some criminal could creep up the stairs and slit all our throats.'

The two men were not speaking.

Eliza cried out, 'Your beautiful song. It quite made me cry.'

Mr Samuel stood before the front door.

Mr Ernest was standing there, very still.

'Thank you,' Mr Samuel said. (Eliza was caught there on the landing: she could neither retreat nor disappear. She tried not to look.)

Mr Samuel stepped forward. He opened his arms wide. Mr Ernest did not move. Mr Samuel took another step forward. Mr Ernest did not move. Mr Samuel clasped Mr Ernest to his breast and there was a sound like a cry, a deep moan coming from Mr Ernest's breast.

Eliza thought he was crying. But she was wrong.

The sound had come from Mr Samuel, who, turning quickly on his heel, as if afraid of being unmanned, had snatched up his suitcase, flung the door wide open, and run out onto the street.

The door slammed shut and he was gone.

Albert, visiting his brother early in the morning, two days later, carefully placed a folded newspaper down on the piano keys.

They talked about the forthcoming case.

Or rather Albert did. (Ernest never answered, never murmured a word.)

'We've been advised it's best to let it all die down. It's got all out of proportion. The most absurd thing is accepted as fact. In six months — a year's time, nobody'll be able to remember it, quite. And that's the time to hold the case, you see?'

Ernest realised it was his cue. He nodded.

'This is Park's father's considered opinion. I've been to see him. A most saddened old man. But of sound opinion. Might even be of use to me in the future. Never know. But he says: hold off as long as possible. Park's father will see to it, I'm sure. We'll rebut that rogue doctor.'

All during this, Albert had the disconcerting sense that Ernest was not listening.

Or rather, with one part of his rational mind he was listening. But subconsciously he was waiting, and waiting for one thing only: a message from Frederick.

'I've got some good news, Ernie,' Albert said.

Ernest's pale blue eyes focused.

'We have managed to secure,' — Albert could not stop his voice being the slightest bit portentous — 'through the aegis of Arthur Park's father, the very best criminal lawyer in Britain. Digby Seymour, QC.'

Ernest showed no reaction.

'He has accepted the brief!' said Albert, as if he wanted to wake Ernest up.

'How much will it cost?' Ernest asked. In a low voice. A moment too late.

Albert had not replied for a moment. He had to let his anger subside. Besides, he also knew he must try, this morning of all mornings, to be tender.

'Let us just dwell for the moment on some good news, shall we?'

His gaze was pitying.

Then he had to go. He was already running late.

Ernest got the impression he was dying to get away.

He did not blame him.

Ernest was left alone.

He did not know, precisely, what to do. He went to the chimneypiece, and moved the vase of summer roses Eliza had placed there — two inches to the left. Then he pushed it back two inches. He thought of going out. Then he decided he would go after the afternoon post arrived.

He listened to the sounds of the house: he could just hear Eliza, in the room up above, humming to herself under her breath. She was preparing the room for future tenants.

Ernest sighed.

He found himself in front of the folded newspaper. Why had his brother brought it?

Some residual interest in the world meant that Ernest flicked open the paper. Immediately he saw it.

PEER IN FATAL SHOOTING ACCIDENT.

This was the single line that leapt out. Ernest sank down onto the piano stool.

He began to read what, over the next few hours, and days, and weeks, he would read again and again, as if seeking to fully comprehend the truth that lay behind it.

> It has been brought to our attention by our Northern reporter that an unfortunate accident took place at Craigiehead, the hunting lodge of Mr Augustus Abraham, the well-known textile

manufacturer, not twelve miles out of Shrewsbury yesterday.

Lord Frederick Clinton, third son of the Duke of Newcastle, was found shot dead.

Our reporter understands, from the housekeeper at Craigiehead, that Lord Frederick had gone out for the day in order to do some shooting. 'If anything,' Mrs Virtue said, 'he seemed in unusually high spirits.'

'He appeared to have been crossing a fence with his gun cocked and loaded,' said the local policeman, Constable Rankin. 'He must have tripped, crossing the stile.'

The bullet passed through the left side of Lord Clinton's jaw and the right side of his brain.

Death would have been instantaneous. The incident appeared to take place at 6.50 p.m. precisely as the deceased's watch had stopped at this time, apparently as an effect of the explosion.

Lord Clinton's family solicitor said there was no note. He said Lord Frederick Clinton emphatically denied the charges that had been levelled against him. He fully intended returning to London, at his earliest convenience, to answer the charges, when this most unexpected accident had taken place.

The police said there were no suspicious circumstances.

Book Three

The hours creep on a-pace,
My guilty heart is quak-ing!
Oh, that I might re-trace
The Step that I am ta-king.

HMS Pinafore, W.S.Gilbert

After the Storm

1880

Samuel cut up the scar in the side of Bluff Hill, his eyes streaming with tears. It was a keen sou'westerly, the prevalent wind of spring. He was walking into it, exhilarated.

As far as he could see was sea shimmering all over. The sky was molten with cloud, great aureoles streaked with darkness and light. The ocean seemed to slip off the horizon and evaporate into a tumbling sky.

Perhaps it was the effect of walking so quickly, his head looking downwards: when he looked up he felt as if he were tumbling himself. The earth — the Hill — slid sideways and the great ocean lifted and hit him in the face.

His heart beat wildly and he found his face fixed in a gulpy grin. Tears, warm and salty, trickled down onto his lips.

He was crying. And laughing. With joy.

He pushed his body along, forcing the muscles in the backs of his legs to keep up their punishing momentum. He had almost reached a pinnacle on the Hill, a track off Lighthouse Road where he could see down into the port. (Past the prison, the lunatic asylum.)

A dray came by and the carter touched his hat in acknowledgement.

Samuel almost felt like yelling.

He was so happy.

He was recognised, known, named.

Even with his false name, which was now appliquéd to himself so it was his actual identity.

He had left the identity of Ernest Boulton far behind him. It was like a dry leaf, pocked by an insect: if he let it loose (up on the Hill, in the midst of a dying sou'westerly) it would fly away, arching off into nothingness.

On his voyage out to New Zealand he had adopted his friend's identity. It was a whim: nothing more. It was a fantasy. A final farewell, the last clasp of a numbed fingertip. Ernest had taken Samuel's name in a moment of fright, of panic. He had selected the name — no, the name had come out of his mind, when challenged — and from there, he had had to assume it.

He often wondered what had happened to the authentic Samuel. Catching sight of a dawdling couple in the street with a child he speculated on whether his Samuel would be the same: not so much happy as complete. He held on to the name, in the end, as some sort of funereal ornament, and gradually — as two things part — so the reality of his friend and admirer, Samuel, parted from its original owner and was applied to his own new rendition.

When spoken to, mind elsewhere, ('Samuel!') he didn't recoil.

He had become Samuel.

He had reached the point on the road where he could look down to the port. But he did not see what he had hoped. The SS *Awatea* was stuck out in the slipstream: the sea was still running high. It had had to heave to.

After a three-day storm, which had buffeted the ship on its voyage down from Thames (normally a two-day voyage), it could still not put into port.

Great white scars of waves roared in and unfurled themselves upon the rocks. The ship was rising, falling like a brooch upon the breast of an excited woman.

Samuel — Ernest — imagined the feelings of the people aboard. The Royal English and Italian Opera Company were supposed to be performing in Napier that evening. They were bringing to Napier the very first performance of *HMS Pinafore*. The newspapers had been full of the Auckland triumph: 'On a Scale of Magnificence Never Attempted Before. Bringing to Napier all the Entrancing Effects and Splendid Scenery as used in the Opera Comique, London!'

And Samuel, leaving his job at Towne & Neale during his lunch-time, had sacrificed his usual apple and a sandwich for this pleasure: to walk up and joyously reconnect with a theatre troupe coming to Napier.

*H*e had to hurry now. By his watch he had at the most seven minutes to make it back behind the counter. Mr Toop, his supervisor, was punctilious — and as remorseless at keeping time as he was at counting up the small change. 'It is all in the halfpennies and farthings,' Mr Toop had informed Samuel when he had been taken on, most grudgingly, as a shop assistant. ('We like people to have some training, we do. This isn't some little entertainment anyone can turn to, on a whim.')

Mr Toop kept a sharp eye on waste, on time spent idly. But by dint of some special talent *Mr Barton*, as he became known, had ended up being in sole charge (ordering and serving) of the ladies' counter.

This was due, in part, to his almost seer-like knowledge of the whim and iron will of women's fashion. It was the talk of Napier's women, or rather *ladies*, how *Mr Barton* had an unerring ability to choose a ribbon which might lift an old ensemble to a bold freshness. He understood how a frilling might be all a person could afford. But it went beyond this: it moved into an intensity he awarded these contests, these almost jousting moments when a woman had to decide, with whatever amount of money she had (and when was it ever enough?), to splurge out, riotously if need be, on perhaps seventeen moiré-silk buttons of an almost feverishly purpled sheen or on a pair of gloves. The gloves could not be too tight as to be ridiculous or to make your hands look like salted pork soaking in brine, but with little crenellations of liquorice-black lines forming a subtle tracery they had the effect of slimming down mitts so they passed under the encomium 'lady-like'.

Barton had harnessed, it seemed, all the loose change hanging about in the back of drawers, placed into earthenware receptacles hidden high on smoke-reeking chimney breasts. Silently, astutely, but with a seemingly monomaniacal intensity of intention, he had accrued to the Ladies' Counter of Towne & Neale so much loose change that it swiftly became apparent he was some kind of lodestone, almost, for the ladies of Hawke's Bay: they could not stay away.

They could not stop walking, as if hypnotised, into the store and coming out with a new length of ribbon, an edging of lace, or some lovely yardage of shimmering material, which they would then have to spend many anxious hours at the sewing machine, or by hand, adjusting into a suitable costume of note. *Having to live up to Mr Barton* became almost an unspoken goal among the matrons of Napier, especially those who graced the hillside villas. Samuel had, quietly, unassumingly, come to be regarded as an essential component — at least to the ladies of the town.

And anyone who chose to think of him, his private life, his life outside the store, could only comment that he lived so quietly, and so privately, in that little worker's cottage (hardly more) off Carlyle Street, which was not a good street, being only two streets away from the pestilential swamp and hence subject to its odours. But those who cared to stare into his intensely private life could observe that Mrs Leyland, the previous Miss Madeleine Perrett, had favoured him with some of her discarded garden plants, and had even given him advice on planting: so his little worker's cottage was bedecked with vine (Chinese gooseberry and grape), its formal little front yard formed into a parterre of box and geranium and visceria so that it had an air of private, almost indolent splendour.

As for what happened behind those curtains, always drawn, nobody could comment. It helped, perhaps, that the cottage stood alone, sandwiched peculiarly between The Napier Gas Company and Mercer's Aerated Drink Factory — a sort of no-man's zone that was not subject to the gaze of a single neighbour.

*C*oming back down the zigzag of Shakespeare Road into town, Samuel passed the clutter of public houses that were first stop from the port: the Golden Fleece, the Clarendon. Servants in open doorways were sweeping out the water. The storm had been vicious. On the second day, waves had broken over the sea bank dividing the town from the shore and run their long tongues into the main streets of town. Properties facing the sea had been broken up. Trees had been blown down and roof metal, in exposed places, had peeled off and been sent flying. A horse had been killed in Byron Street.

'A good day to you, Samuel Barton.'

A dark-skinned man, bald head glinting, raised a hand. He was sweeping, sweeping. All around the streets there was still a detritus, a matting of leaf, branch and dirt. The sound of hammers driving nails into tin came from behind the man, high up on a roof.

'Good day to you, Mr Hunt. You survived the storm all right?'

'Takes more than that to kill a weed.'

Samuel turned right, past the new church of St John the Evangelist, and headed along Hastings Street towards the Emporium ('Everything of the Best Quality Delivered at the Most Reasonable Price Possible').

It was amazing how, in the eight years he had lived there, the town had grown and changed. The population had doubled and the townscape itself had softened:

hedges had grown, trees leapt up, little wooden villas and pretty cottages now speckled the cleats and brows of the massive hill — all peering out from their verandas, like so many eyelids, at the immense horizon.

And this day now had the cheerfulness of the human spirit having survived some endurance: coming to, after a storm.

*H*e was actually running late: he was sweating. The chill wind fell away as he entered Hastings Street. He was protected by the shoulder of the Hill. He heard the pounding of the waves onto the shingle. The waves were still dumpers, a pale disturbed aquamarine, tense with power. A drift of salt was latent in the air.

A line of cabs waited in front of the post office.

He passed by what had been Linz the Jeweller's window. He felt a stab of sadness. Solomon Linz had never come back. He had not, it appeared, even arrived in Melbourne. From the reports — and they were conflicting — Solomon Linz was last seen standing on the bow of the boat as it heaved and tossed, mid-Tasman. He was standing there alone. It was dawn. The boat would reach port the following day. Either a wave had curled over the deck, snatching him, or — and this was purely conjectural — something untoward had happened. His mood immediately beforehand, the porter said, was remarkable for being neither ebullient nor depressed. The night before he had been seen walking up and down the deck in the company of a conspicuously bold woman. They appeared deep in conversation. But beyond this there was nothing. No clues. He had disappeared.

The earring had disappeared with him.

It had been a shock, a horror — but, as with other shocks and horrors, Samuel had learnt over time how to absorb it.

He had even laughed. In disbelief. At how nothing can come from nothing. And had gone immediately to comfort his good friend, the widow Linz.

He was almost back at the Emporium. But ahead of Samuel stood a squadron of rooks. The bad weather had brought them down from the cliffs of the bluff — their normal habitat. Like a battalion they faced him. Wings folded. Bright eyes sequinned.

He moved towards them. Tentatively. They rippled to one side. Like seed settling, they followed him back, then, surrounding him on every side, held him prisoner.

He still wondered what had happened to Solomon. Was he living in Melbourne with Miss Louise, the jewel providing the wherewithal for a new start? But would he have abandoned Ada and his son so carelessly? Perhaps it was better to think of a freak wave wrapping him in its arms, clawing him down into the depths . . .

If anything, the loss of the jewel had freed Samuel.

He broke into a run and the birds rose in a cloud, cawing and flapping all around him; he burst through the front doors of Towne & Neale almost like some kind of mythological apparition: so Mr Samuel Barton, shop assistant, entered the silted-up silence of the store.

*M*rs Cogswell, lady wife of the Mayor, rose from the little bentwood that had been suffering under the imposition of her considerable weight.

She made a deflective gesture, as if it were all her fault, for arriving early.

Mr Toop anxiously hovered in the background, a visor shading the frown on his face.

He retreated as Samuel made his entrance, tying on his apron strings as he approached, half bowing and murmuring to Mrs Cogswell, who stood marooned in her largeness.

'I am most dreadfully sorry, Mrs Cogswell, my heart was all aflutter with this visiting troupe. I went up to see if they had got ashore . . .'

'. . . and?' she said, her hand raised to her throat in alarm. 'The poor things aren't locked in that dreadful wooden tub, are they? Being shaken to and fro like salt shakers?'

Samuel said nothing but took on the professional air of a doctor soothing a flighty patient. He made a strange heraldic movement with his hand, inviting the beldame into his lair. It could have been a leather couch but was, instead, a catacomb of hats, gloves, stockings, lace and gowns: a cave of colours, textures, shapes and, most blessed of all, flattering illusion.

I think the dark blue, don't you?'

'I . . . am not sure.'

Mrs Cogswell, née Mercer, made this dreadful admission.

'I do want to look . . .'

She waited for the words.

'Suitably attired,' Mr Barton said smoothly. He was unrolling some gorgeously dark cloth over the strident yellow she had instinctively chosen.

Mrs Cogswell, with a reddened face, moist from the heat, little pinpricks of dew on her faint moustache, nodded. She was grateful for Mr Barton's patient art of listening. If she looked into her heart, she might have realised she came there less for a swathe of cloth to add to her opera-going costume, and more for the relaxation of bathing in his confidential tones.

He calmed her curiously.

He made her feel as if this inherently trivial pursuit — the art of camouflage — was actually so important she must abandon everything: the nagging feeling that she had left behind a child with whooping cough in the care of a slipshod maid, the mutton cooking in the oven — was the heat too high, would it be stringy? And then there was that other, darker matter.

Mrs Cogswell, wife of the leading dentist in Napier, carried the knowledge that everyone was talking. But what they were talking about was a faint blur of noise, like a fly buzzing just on the edge of her consciousness. She was aware of people stopping talking when she walked unannounced into rooms. She felt the crease of awkwardness. She listened, herself, acutely at these moments. She felt every sense she possessed — battered by child-rearing, by incessant childish demands, by always another on the way, by her own hormones in perpetual disturbance — she felt her senses trying to grow acute: to listen.

But it was a dismal effort. It was as if her senses had grown frayed, then ceased to quite function, through lack of use. She could not hear. It was all a blur. (But the blur had a kind of sequence. She knew her husband's name was at the centre of the aureole. And she also knew something else — some other name, unpronounceable, a slur of consonants — existed somewhere out of doors, beyond the blue-tinted glass in the windows, beyond the lip of the burningly hot cup of tea.)

She did not know, precisely, what every man, woman and child in Napier did: that her husband had another wife, a Maori woman, and an entire other family of strapping half-caste sons at the end of the railway line in Waipukurau. She did not know this. She could not hear the gossip: which was its point: to capture and ensnare, as a spider does in its web.

She found herself mummified, delivered to this very spot, the fabric counter at Towne & Neale, seeking salvation from that 'nice and sympathetic' Mr Barton, a real gentleman, so silent and understanding in the way he slid, without a word, a grosgrain towards her; and only with a faintly pained look did he intimate that the bright yellow silk she favoured (as a way of trying to obtain a fevered glance from her husband) was not quite correct. Was a fright. Was a frightening mistake, which could bring the whole house of cards down upon her.

Why was it, she wondered as she stood there, as if naked before Mr Barton's careful glance, that she felt her house up on the Hill, in respectable Cameron Road — so solid, with its five bedrooms and capacious verandas looking out to the sea — was so feeble it might fall apart at any moment?

She felt both miserable and rich. She could not even enjoy this moment now, when the sibilant Mr Barton was bending over in a semi-bow, pushing towards her a truly regal lustre of deep navy-blue silk.

She touched the material and let out an almost embarrassing sigh. Then found herself saying — taking herself completely by surprise — 'Do you miss Mr Solomon Linz still? I find myself thinking of him. His watery death. Often.'

Her eyes welled up with tears.

She enjoyed, frankly, the embrace of sentimentality. It soothed her wounded heart.

Mr Barton looked taken by surprise.

'That was so long ago,' he said in a strangely muted whisper — there was something feverish about it — 'so long ago as to be another life. Another person,' he said, leaning forward and placing the cool silk as an ointment against her frictioned skin — 'entirely.'

'You're due at 'The Pah' at three-fifteen.'

This was Mr Toop again, reminding Samuel that his afternoon was one long chain of appointments. The arrival of the opera company had sent the town into a small frenzy of spending. Every woman, it seemed, had to have some new furbelow, at least, to celebrate her anointment back into civilisation. It was competitive, tribal almost. The joyful rattle of silver coins, of gold, had echoed musically, like an overture, throughout the Emporium.

Samuel was glancing into the tiny little piece of mirror allowed the staff at the back of the premises. He was smoothing down his tonsure — faded blond now, almost like a watercolour that has been placed carelessly in the line of brutal sun. His skin had the texture of paper that had been spotted with mould from the rampant humidity of the place. In the glass he saw a sport of himself, a distant relation to that other, earlier Ernest, who at least had been a gentleman. This one now was harried, hurried, running late.

He could just catch the three o'clock 'bus — a clattering public conveyance pulled by two lanky, almost ropey old nags who laboured up the labyrinthine roads that went up the Hill.

The 'bus would drop him off on Napier Terrace, a ribbon of dust laid along the back of Middle Hill. To the right could be found 'The Pah', the somewhat magnificent house of Mr Leyland, farmer: politician, occupant almost by right of a seat on the local council as well as Parliament: a magnate of sorts, a mean Scotsman who was probably almost a millionaire.

He did not know he was known as a thief by the local Maori tribe. To himself, and according to his own lights, he was a man of principle, of God, who gave generously and quite sincerely to needy charities. He simply believed that an aspect of godliness was thrift, industry and an incredibly sharp eye as to profit.

He had made himself a landed grandee and bought 'The Pah' when the Monteiths retreated to bankruptcy. He now owned more than fifty thousand acres.

*M*adeleine had been married to him for over seven years. The marriage had taken the maidens of Napier so by surprise (not least Madeleine herself) that there were whisperings that Miss Perrett had stolen him from under the nose of Miss Violet Limbrick. This was not so. Leyland had stalked Madeleine, as it were, in his search for a woman who would be a willing beast of burden: who would work hard, be conscious of his coin, scrimp, save and mend with the best of them. She was also to possess all the ineffable arts of being a lady — modesty, instinctive sincerity, musical gifts, the ability to set a dinner table for twenty at half an hour's notice, to manage servants, to wear jewels becomingly.

He had not counted on one aspect, though.

The lady had gone progressively deaf in the month following the disastrous Acclimatisation Society picnic. Deafness had entered her life like an incoming fog: first of all barely discernible, creeping over the ground, nullifying detail, blurring sharpness. She had fought it. Denied it. Trained herself to listen attentively. Shifted back her defences — as the fog advanced — to watching people's lips, studying their expressions.

This gave her the unjustified reputation of being eccentric: she often found herself guessing a reply and adding enthusiasm to it, as if to underscore her complete comprehension. What she did not realise was that she was making mistakes; she was offending people by being jolly when they required a tot of bracing melancholy. Or worse, she was mordant and slicked down with sorrow when they required hearty congratulation. Her deafness grew apace.

She often found herself playing her piano — the beautiful grand piano her husband had so grandiloquently purchased for her (from a mortgagee sale, it is true, when the Monteiths had gone under). She played the longer as if to soothe the savage nullity in her breast: but she could not hear. She could only remember.

And so remembrance came to have a special power for her.

She also had, as required, a series of children: five in seven years. Two of them

— twins Alice and Brownlee — were born partially deaf.

*N*aturally she did not hear the bell.

She was mending a shirt of her first son, making it suitable for her second. She was watching, and in watching being soothed by the sharp nip, dip and slide of her needle point through the calico: she was bathing herself in memory again.

She was remembering the walk she and Samuel had taken along the beach so many years before. Why had he refused to sing for her? She had pleaded with him. She had said he could sing, if necessary, just for her. But he hadn't. He had never sung. She had never heard his voice. His voice, this fabled rumour, had never been heard in Napier again. She strained, as if to listen.

When a blur to the side of her vision startled her. It was Mrs Risington, who had come to work for her after the failure of the Monteiths. (Swallowing her pride like a spoon of castor oil.)

'It is Barton, madam, from Towne & Neale.'

Mrs Risington always raised the volume of her voice, to the point she found it almost gave her a headache. She felt the veins on her forehead swell, her eyes almost seeming to pop out of her head.

But madam always turned her dreamy head to her as if she were made of vapour. Then pincered her forehead in concentration, trying to peer out of the whitened mist of sound that surrounded her on every side.

Madeleine had naturally become sharp-sighted. She saw sorrow, gratitude, indifference: now she saw something else — Mrs Risington was pointing to the hallway. Was making a sign that indicated a quarter past three. She stood to the side, like a stage dame awaiting the meeting of two more major characters.

*M*adeleine had been sitting in a pool of sunlight. The storm had been so violent as to be thrilling in her sturdy mansion atop the Hill — she had been driven to stand before the windows, watching the rain dash itself against the glass, driven by the wind so the long straws propelled towards her, then crashed and splattered and smeared to their deaths. She could not hear the mayhem of her children playing cricket down the main hall, nor Mrs Risington's wailing when the glass on a picture — of Queen Victoria being crowned Empress of India (a kind of mythological picture in which the great white queen was being lifted up to heaven by the sheer force of adoration of the coloured people of the globe) — was broken. Shattered.

But now the storm, like someone who had overstayed a visit, was bundling itself away with such speed that the sky was yawning open, in great swathes of the purest blue. A gorgeous gilt sun was shining everywhere. Almost tremblingly effulgent.

The sun had caught on the point of her needle, glittered.

She was in her private sitting room. The one with the daguerreotype of her dear Mama, now deceased by two years. Her few books.

Mrs Risington had clasped her hands under her bosom, as if nestling there, at home on the glistening slopes of black satin. Madeleine knew this was always a sign of impatience. She rose to her feet, put her mending down and followed behind the woman who was now her servant.

*H*e was sitting in the hall. On one of those uncomfortable shield chairs, the point of which was to make the sitter unwelcome.

He had beside him a wicker case of some considerable size.

It was Samuel.

She had made, she realised, a sound that was probably fog-horn loud, because he started. He turned to her a face that she had to overlay upon the face she had been remembering, only a few minutes before. She inspected the lines, the acuity of sight. If anything he had settled into himself more. But now he was rising to his feet and standing there, a little uncomfortable, it was true, in his modest position.

(Madeleine recalled, in a flash, her own sitting on such a seat, years before.)

Madeleine turned to Mrs Risington.

'I told you to take him immediately into the second sitting room.'

She spoke, she thought, with asperity.

But if Madeleine could not hear, so Mrs Risington could, annoyingly, play the same game. The lines on her ancient face did not move. She stood aside. She might have been deaf herself.

Madeleine read Samuel's expression. He had heard. He smiled at her, suddenly, engagingly. She took his arm as he came towards her.

'Mrs Risington. Bring us tea. And some of that simnel cake you baked. And bread and cape gooseberry jam. And also those shortbread biscuits.'

She would spend, spend wildly, in her husband's absence upcountry. The house always felt different when he had gone. Lighter, more like a holiday.

'And use my mother's silver.'

Samuel was standing right beside her. Holding his wicker case of samples.

'Dear friend,' she said to him and smiled. She touched him on the sleeve. 'Dear Samuel.'

*H*e had finished showing her the gloves. They lay all along the edge of the somewhat magnificent brocade sofa (from the fallen Monteiths): the gloves like so many ghosts of hands longing for flesh, animating nerve, fingertips. The colours were gem-like in their intensity: garnet red, sapphire blue, the tarnish of old gold. Then there was the most beautiful tissue of kid: a kind of powdered whiteness, perhaps a definition of whiteness itself.

Madeleine had felt, frankly, incompetent. She had got Mrs Risington (grud-gingly — she did not like to step outside her housekeeper's domain: she was not, after all, a lady's maid) to bring into the room the costumes she might wear.

Samuel had picked through them diplomatically. Laying the plaids and tartans and checks aside as 'more suitable for church'.

She had smiled. She could always understand Samuel.

'They are too sober?'

He could understand her blunt tones.

He made a gesture with his hand.

'Too . . . dun-coloured?'

'Opera is an occasion for flourish,' he said, raising his voice. She watched his lips, nodded sharply.

The tea table lay before them. It was a handsome room they were in. Bespeaking wealth, everything was over-scale. Vast folding doors had been drawn to, separating this, the smaller, more intimate sitting room from the formal drawing room with its semi-circle of long windows, facing out into the deepest depth of veranda, beyond which could be glimpsed the smartness of an Italianate garden — all cabbage palms, aloes and cannas.

This smaller room had French doors, one of them half open so the pale sun came in, tremblingly touching the end of Samuel's shoe.

Madeleine had found herself gazing at it. She was harpooned by memory. She could remember the extremity of fashion of the shoes he had worn when she first came upon him. A refugee in the town, almost, with his broken-backed gentlemen's clothes. His shoes had been exceptionally sharp: high in the heel, yet worn down at the edge, through to the wood. She had also seen the split in the side, which showed, in unseemly fashion, a stocking she suspected might even have been holed itself.

It was like a statement of his soul.

Now he wore boots that were almost those of a superior working man. She was fascinated by them. Her coachman wore similar boots: tough, made for longevity, and probably as ungiving as wood until broken in. But Samuel had clearly worn them in, anointed them greedily with polish, and they would last the distance.

Whatever that distance might be.

As if catching the line of her sight, Samuel — speaking to her, she gathered, at a great pace — withdrew his foot.

It might have been the antenna of a snail. On being touched.

He was still the same.

But now he had stopped speaking. He was waiting.

Experimentally she leant forward and took up the most expensive of the long kid gloves.

'These are "*as worn in Paris*",' he said, with the hint of an accomplice's smile. 'Well, let us say, a small town perhaps a hundred miles from Paris.'

This was too difficult for her — she looked at him mystified, her fingers feeling leather so soft as to be a membrane.

'How much do they cost?'

He drew a small lined pad, a blue-lead pencil, out of his top pocket, as if he had thought in advance of just this moment. She marvelled, in some private part of herself — that attached to the sacredness of memory — that he could ever be so organised.

He wrote the sum down.

She glanced down at it, was scorched by its terrible intensity.

'He would never . . .' she began, then was aware she was exposing her husband before an old friend.

This would not do.

There was the tremble of a knock, which Madeleine clearly did not hear, and two children sidled into the room, one nudging along the other, their eyes fixed on the target of the just-cut cake.

Samuel stood and semi-bowed to the two children, who gazed at him with the clear, untroubled fascination of children in a happy home. He might have been translucent. The little girl, Alice, then darted forward and took up, artfully, two biscuits, making it appear as if she had one.

'Alice!'

Her mother's sight was sharp.

The child unwillingly, yet with a show of great generosity, parted with one to her brother. But the boy had his eye on a piece of the cake. His mother, following his gaze, cut him a generous wedge. His face lit up.

Samuel, watching this small piece of family theatre, basked in it, was amused by it and saw a little of himself in both the girl and the boy. But he also was aware he must try and make a sale. Toop would not approve of his going personally to 'The Pah' again if he returned coinless. 'Leyland or no Leyland, their coin is only as good as the McSweeneys'.' (The McSweeneys were a notoriously profligate family, always in debt, always living on tick.)

Alice and Brownlee hung about their mother's skirts, nibbling with their palms curved under the treats, to catch the crumbs. Finally they wet their fingertips and picked off the crumbs one by one. Hungrily they eyed the remains of the cake. But the door opened noisily and a larger boy burst in. He was rolling a hoop, which appeared to belong to his sister. She was crying. He was laughing. The hoop rolled over the parquet, up across the Turkish carpet and banged into the table set for afternoon tea.

The cups rattled and all the children screamed.

Madeleine rose.

Samuel immediately felt he was supernumerary. She spoke to them, mainly by gesture but also by strange gulping sounds that were both imploring and ugly.

She pointed to the outside door.

'Don't want to,' the older boy said. He was standing right beside the cake. 'The others have all had some!' He looked directly at Samuel. 'Besides, if that cove from Towne & Neale can be fed like he's a regular visitor, I can't see why *I* . . .'

His mother, hissing like a goose, drove the children towards the open French doors.

'Go out and play. You have been cooped up inside for three days. Go out and play in the sunshine.'

'Why do I have to . . .' the boy said in a surly tone. But Madeleine had managed to cut them some cake, and bustle them out the doors. She turned around, harassed, fractured.

'Now, where were we? You were telling me about the time you visited Paris?'

*S*amuel took the 'bus back into town. He had managed to sell Madeleine the second most expensive pair of kid gloves. She had gone away for an embarrassing length of time before coming back with what was clearly her own personal money: it was all in small denominations. She had counted it up arduously. He seemed to glimpse something here, in this chatelaine of a mansion, counting out her sixpences. She had handed him, closing his hands around, the large amount of loose coin. She might have been a servant girl who had saved up for her first really grand hat.

'You are going to the theatre?' she had asked Samuel.

'Oh yes, indeed. I would not miss it for the world,' he said. 'I won't be going on the opening night, of course. But there is one night to which I would particularly like to go.'

She did not understand. She stood there looking at his lips. It was an awkward moment. He had stayed too long, but at least made a sale. His wicker basket was closed, the gloves all safely in their pockets. But there was, residually, some sense of things not connecting. Their positions had changed so radically: he was a shop assistant; she was the wife of a magnate, but she was also a mother with a family. He was an old friend — an important friend — and he sensed in her a desperate will to somehow maintain a line of contact, acknowledging that their shared past was important. But he could not help but register also, almost by her unconscious actions, the news that he must, necessarily, stand in a queue, and in front of him stood not only the five children, but that enigmatic man Mr Leyland himself: the gentleman who, if he happened to be in Napier at the time of the opera company, would prevent Madeleine from attending. This happened through no express commandment: Mr Leyland's power was such that he did not need to actually speak. It was understood.

If he was in residence at 'The Pah', he was the single most important attraction there could be in Napier, as far as Madeleine was concerned.

That was why he had purchased her.

Those were the terms on which she understood herself to be bought.

She had escaped the horribleness of her genteel poverty, but she was in some part still trapped, still unescaped, still caught. And in her deafness she felt a kind of perennial isolation, as if, in being separated from music — which was, above all, the phosphorescence of her life — some part of her had gone into eternal eclipse. Samuel's visiting was no more than the ineffectual act of a lightsman with a long taper, moving along a dimly lit street, lighting lamp after lamp. It did no real good. There was a gloaming darkness in her world, a lustrousness had escaped. She had stood there, on the point of parting from him, and had suddenly, impulsively, clasped his fingers, as if, like a small child, she did not want him to go.

'You will not forget?' she had barked to him.

(Mrs Risington discreetly standing on the return of the stairs, listening.)

He had not said, 'Forget what?'

He had instead sent surging through his fingers a pulse that answered her own, and it seemed that at that second she heard what she had never heard: the beauty of Samuel Barton's singing voice.

She turned from the door with the pale glimmering of its beauty still hanging on her features.

I shall go to the opera, she thought.

A Friendship
Posy

He extinguished the gas lamp and the entire plain of the Emporium sank back into a penumbral embrace — basins, chairs suspended from the ceiling, spades, parasols, umbrellas, hats, all washed away into a pitch of semi-darkness. Toop was standing in a block of icy-blue light by the door, anxious to be off. He was rattling a chain of keys against his trouser leg.

'You're not off to the opera tonight, are you, Barton?' he said semi-accusingly. As if it were a defect of Samuel's soul. 'Not much interested in music and higher things, are you?'

Samuel let the diaphanous strains of darkness wrap themselves around his smiling face.

It did not do, in Napier, to look sardonic. A simpler palette was required here. At least on the surface.

'No indeed, not tonight, sir.'

'My lady wife,' Toop announced with a self-conscious air, 'is gracing the back stalls. At a cost of seven shillings and sixpence.'

He seemed partially scandalised, as well as secretly thrilled, by the high price.

'Only for the opening night of such a masterpiece as *HMS Pinafore*, of course, Barton. Only for the best.'

'Goodnight, sir. I hope Mr Gilbert and Mr Sullivan live up to their high promise.'

Toop left a silence, as if Barton's last remarks were in bad taste. Strange cove, he thought as he walked away. Never knew what he was going to come out with next. But good at moving fabric. No doubt about it: the man had dancing fingers.

*S*amuel stood for a moment, getting his bearings. It was not yet dark, and after the oppression of the storm he had a sudden whim to wander. Living alone had its pleasures, some of them intense, but to be always ambushed by a series of empty rooms could sometimes feel claustrophobic. Besides, it was a beautiful evening. He was not due home, for his appointment, for another hour.

Samuel turned right and wandered along Hastings Street. Deep inside the Masonic he could hear singing. This was backed by a scurrying roar of voices — talking, yelling, exclaiming — as if illuminating, after so much isolation and loneliness, all the joys of company.

Word had spread that the *Awatea* had finally docked at 4.23 p.m. The operetta would go on this evening at the appointed time, come what may. Further word had followed that the theatricals were arriving, *en cavalcade*, down the main streets of Napier at six o'clock. They would be led into town by the Napier Spit Brass Band. The mechanics and stagehands were meanwhile feverishly unloading the three-hundred-odd trunks that held their costumes and stage sets outside the Theatre Royal in Milton Road.

If anything, this contest against time and circumstance added to the excitement.

There was a palpable hunger in the air — for drink, for food, for celebration. The streets echoed with the accents of the forestry workers from Dannevirke, from Waipukurau — the Danes, the Germans, the Scots, the English, the Maori, had all crowded into town.

Even now, as day darkened into night, there were carts wending their way along the streets, some of them so weighed down with people as to seem to be hardly moving. One creaked by now, a row of children's faces bright as starlings looking out at the 'city sights'.

Samuel smiled, sighed. He crossed the road. There was a cluster of people standing in front of the plate-glass window of what had been Solomon Linz's store. It had been taken over by the American Novelty Company — several years ago.

('The Little Store with Everything. World-Renowned Pearl Cement, Unrivalled for Mending any Broken Articles. Colonial Jewellery and Greenstone a Speciality'.)

Mr Leonard, the proprietor, had created a display of the jewellery owned by Mademoiselle Hortense, the prima donna of the Royal English and Italian Opera Company. This had been sent forward by the opera company, for publicity purposes.

The glow of gas-light burnished the faces of those looking in. A row of children had been passed to the front and various sticky fingers were placed on the plate glass, as if to probe the mystery within. Laid out on strident purple velvet were various glinting, glittering, refractive jewels.

Awarded as a Token of Esteem for the Artistry of Mademoiselle Hortense Oturra, Chief Artiste of the Royal English and Italian Opera Company BY MEMBERS OF THE PUBLIC!!! pronounced a card, the words written in elaborate curves.

'That's the one, there, second from the back,' announced a woman's voice.

'No, it's not, it's the amethyst necklace, just down from it, to the left.'

This voice was quite contesting.

'Mummy, why did the farmer come on board the boat at New Plymouth and ask for the necklace back? Hadn't he given it to Mademoiselle Hortense?'

A girl's dreamy voice murmured, 'He was in love with her, he was.'

Various rude boys hawked, giggled and elbowed.

A mother shushed.

'He didn't quite get what he wanted,' said a male voice, a little slurred and suggestive.

'Shame,' said a woman's voice, a pillar of the Temperance League. 'Have you no shame?'

'None,' replied the man, 'that's why I'm in Napier tonight.'

'Mum, it's Mr Samuel!'

It was the voice of Solomon's son, Gershom, as he ran up the stairs two at a time. He was an agile little stripling. He had his father's dark intense stare, a stillness in his being. Yet arranged around this stillness was a whirl of hyperactivity: he was all arms and thin legs, always fetching, carrying, helping. Already, aged nine, he was pleading with his mother to be allowed to leave the penny school.

He wanted to work for his mother, who ran a boarding house for the Danish forestry workers who came in to Napier for their periodic binges. She had come to hold such a position of regnant trust that they gave her their seasonal earnings and told her to inform them when they had gambled, drunk and otherwise frittered away the sum total.

Not that Mrs Linz's boarding house was anything other than respectable. Indeed, it was almost dainty. It was clean, good in its simple appointments: her secret lure was the food. Mrs Linz Senior, now a redoubtable eighty-six, ruled the kitchen like a tyrant — a benevolent tyrant, it was true — training up a slow-witted maid to cook all her favourite recipes: beef with sauerkraut, stewed lamb with paprika, veal goulash, baked lentils, grimslich, pear dumpling, food that brought comfort to these wanderers so far from home.

This evening the house was aroar. Every bedroom door was open, and inside, as he passed over the polished linoleum up the passage, Samuel glimpsed little set-pieces of men combing their hair, adjusting, painfully, ties around faces that had been shaved for the first time in months. A mélange of Mitteleuropa accents, and those of Scandinavia, filtered through the air.

(Samuel had already noticed the 'No Vacancy' sign up outside, on the narrow veranda.)

Mrs Linz raised her beautiful head. She was still a woman of culture, and even in her dull little sitting room with its faded wallpaper there was an air of cultivation. The same piano was there and, hung above it, the strange oil painting of a shipwreck Samuel had first seen so many years ago.

'Ah, Samu-elle.'

She smiled. Mrs Linz now spoke a form of English — heavily accented, unusual in its contortions of the vowels. All around her was a sea of paper fans. She had been making fans to sell at the evening performances. She knew how hot the tiny Theatre Royal could get when packed. Gershom, a superb little bargainer, was to be the salesman.

He was highly excited, taut as a bow.

'Have you finished them yet, Mum? You don't want to miss the dawdlers, do you? There's a crowd outside, watching the stuff being unpacked!'

All along the mantel, arranged in chipped enamel pots, were ladies' sprays: a gorgeous aroma of carnation, wallflower and the first roses of summer drenched the room. These were also to be sold.

'I am so very, very tired,' Mrs Linz murmured. She made an attempt to rise but Samuel quickly pressed her down, into her low chair. She made a gesture around the room.

'We shall sell well tonight? You think?'

He nodded.

'Mum, *of course* we will. So long as you let me stay out as late as I need to. We'll make a real killing.'

'You must be home by ten o'clock at the latest.'

'Oh, *Mum!*'

'The correct term is "Mother",' Samuel corrected the boy. Gershom (Jack was his Napier name) looked up at Samuel disbelievingly.

'But all my friends call their mothers "Mum",' he said, as if suspecting a trick. He had laced his fingers through Samuel's and was impatiently banging their joined hands against Samuel's thigh.

'Mr Samuel is good to us, Gershom. He knows what is best . . . is right.'

There was a ghost of a smile over Mrs Linz's exhausted features.

Nothing showed time more painfully, yet tenderly — how long ago the tragedy was — than Gershom. He went over to the chimneypiece and counted the cost of the posies out loud (each posy costing sixpence). Down the hall came the sound of a violin being tuned up, to a jig. Somewhere out on the street, a man walked by whistling — joyfully yet out of tune — 'We Sail the Ocean Blue' from *HMS Pinafore*. (The score sheets had arrived in Napier a long while before: another publicity gimmick for the forthcoming production.)

'You are going yourself tonight, Samuel?'

'No. I've chosen to go to a different opera.'

Ada Linz went on pleating more paper into fans as she sat there. Her hands seemed to have an almost neurotic force of their own. Of need, of a desire to accrue money — the protection of coin.

'Mum, the boat got in at 4.25; the men are already outside the theatre . . . Can't I go down and watch the band? I've *got* to sell some of those fans.'

The child chattered on.

'What is your opera?'

'*Der Freischütz.*'

'Mum — *can't* I?'

'Have you set the dining-room table? Have you emptied the kitchen scraps? Have you asked *bobe* what else she needs help with?'

'Of course.'

He spoke in tones of outraged adult dignity.

'Well, perhaps you may.'

The boy picked out ten fans, ran off.

'Make sure you count the change!'

They listened to the sound of the boy scampering down the stairs. He was whistling, perfectly in tune, 'We Sail the Ocean Blue'.

'*Der Freischütz*...' Mrs Linz said, her voice faint, distant. She seemed suddenly overcome with sadness.

'It is one that has memories for me,' Samuel said.

'Ah, memories,' Mrs Linz said, and she went on pleating the paper, not looking up. She glanced up when he said nothing.

'Would you care ... to accompany me? On the night?' Samuel suddenly said. He offered her one of her own posies. 'I have no one else I would rather ...'

She smiled.

'You do not want an old woman — a widow — by your side.'

'I could think of nothing better than to have you with me.'

There was a knock at the door behind Samuel. A brutally handsome Nordic male stood there helplessly, his huge red hands dangling by his side. He was wearing what were clearly new clothes, possibly even bought that very afternoon, at a lesser emporium than Towne & Neale. He was holding a limp bowtie made of spotted silk.

'I cannot ... I cannot ... Madame Linz?'

She made as if to get up.

'Here.'

Samuel placed himself at the man's disposal. They moved into an intimate space as Samuel's hands darted around the man's neck. He felt the breath of the man fanning over his face. For one second the man's almost impossibly blue gaze focused on Samuel's face but, as if seeing something there he could not quite understand — or, alternatively, that was so easy to read — he slid his gaze away and stood there, like a gorgeous statue offering up his beauty, but passively, and by his very passivity, awarding a prize.

'Thanking you, sir,' he said finally, walking away in his heavy boots, rolling from side to side slightly as he went. 'You are most agreeable gentleman.'

Mrs Linz had been watching this critically, yet with some amusement.

'Yes,' she said. 'I think you may need a lady as a companion ... on the night of Napier's grand fête.'

*I*t was still twenty minutes before his appointment.

The Visitor was always on time.

Outside, the sky had the lustre of the faintest blue porcelain, deepening down to a luminous radiant blue. The buildings all about seemed cut out of cardboard and then dressed in black. Single windows stood out as gleaming golden rectangles, the occasional silhouette passing to and fro — dressing.

From Samuel's left came a discordant sound. It had been sounding around the town all afternoon.

A slightly oppressed-looking man came up to Samuel, drowning his self-consciousness by constantly clanging a brass handbell. He was bedecked in a sandwich board that advertised the opera company's schedule:

Friday 8.30 p.m. *HMS Pinafore*, Saturday 8.00 p.m.
The Grand Duchess of Gerolstein, Monday 8.00 p.m.
Der Freischütz, Tuesday 7.30 p.m. *La Somnabula*.
EVERY OPERA IN ENGLISH.

Seeing Samuel, the man — it was a sweating, sozzled Mr Haresnape — stopped ringing the bell for one moment and chanted: '*The Grand, Topical, Comical, Historical, Mystical, Sophistical, Laughable, Chaffable, Too-Awfully-Jolly-by-Halfable . . . HMS Pinafore!*'

People were hurrying along the pavement. Talking, laughing.

'I shan't be going to that one, Mr Haresnape,' said Samuel. 'I'm afraid I can't.'

The man detached himself a little dolefully and went on.

*S*amuel could smell. He was on his way down Carlyle Street. He had almost no time left. But he was passing by a sailmaker's shop. And he could smell oil paint. It was so potent that he turned, as if automatically, into a darkened corridor. He felt his way along. Into Northey's, the sailmaker's, and there, at the far end, lit by three kerosene lanterns, was a man. He seemed about to plunge into a dungeon made of tree trunks. There was a brutally red sun in the background, an adumbration of rocks tumbling down into a chasm.

It was Mr Thomas Kemp, scene painter. He was scurrying a paintbrush all over the canvas. There were buckets placed by his feet. Paintbrushes obtruded, and by his side, on a kind of crude stand, were pots of various colour amid the clutter and impedimenta of a sailmaker.

Mr Kemp's rotund form was wrapped in a dirty, floor-length apron.

The room was still, apart from the whisper of paintbrush on canvas and the slight gasp of Mr Kemp as he lunged out to create his image.

For Samuel, standing there, the scene-making brought him to the brink.

He felt himself fall into a vertigo of memory. He felt all the instability of his present fissure and crack, become crazed. He felt his skin, his throat. He heard his own breathing.

This was going to be dangerous.

Mr Kemp at this point turned his head and, seeing someone standing there, called out, 'Come further into the light, whoever you are. Don't be shy. Shyness has no place in the theatre.'

He leant forward and placed a dob of brilliant white on the lip of a cloud. 'Boldness is what is at home in the theatre, newcomer. Come closer. Step forward into the light.'

Then he began to hum a tune from *HMS Pinafore* — 'Things are Seldom What They Seem'.

Things Are Seldom What They Seem

*I*s there anything that can equal the pleasure of seeing something first? Then describing it to someone who has not had the lucky pleasure?

Mr Toop had spoken to Samuel at length about the crescendo of pleasure he experienced on the curtain first going up, to reveal, of all things — and occupying the entire stage — the deck of a ship!

Toop showed a neophyte's abandon to delirium: he was truly stage-struck. But Samuel also had the distinctly uncomfortable sense that Toop got at least as much pleasure from the fact that he was describing what Samuel had been excluded from.

Samuel did not tell him that at ten o'clock in the evening he had arisen from his bed, exhausted but at peace. After the Visitor had left, Samuel had fallen into a pleasant swoon of sleep. On waking, he had washed himself, then gone back up Carlyle Street. At the bottom of Milton Road he came across a phenomenon. The Theatre Royal was completely silent, seemingly in a state of queer enchantment, until out through the windows (thrown wide open to alleviate the heat) came the curlicued tones of Mademoiselle Hortense, singing 'Song of the Buttercup'.

This had only just finished when the house erupted into a storm of applause. She had to do an encore. At its conclusion the applause was as thirsty, this time accompanied by foot-stamping of a distinctly boorish variety.

Samuel had come closer. The evening was not warm but it was unsurpassingly clear. After the storm there had come a curious peace. Up in the sky was a waxing moon: its brilliance changed the heavens into a star-splattered nimbus. He felt gloriously alive. His whole body thrummed and ached and yet felt softened, pummelled. The Visitor always returned Samuel to himself, placed him back, neatly, within his physical sac: as if all his wandering thoughts could be relocated, focused.

Samuel walked closer still. He could see urchins sitting astride the window ledges, peering in. High up in the ngaio tree, nearer the stage, he saw child after child, like so many Christmas tree decorations, staring with particular intensity down towards the stage.

(These were the McSweeney children: hungry, dirty but in a state of quiet ecstasy.)

Within, voices had renewed their chant, '*Buttercup! Buttercup! Buttercup!*'

They were insisting that Mademoiselle Hortense do a second encore. But Samuel heard what he interpreted as a musical tempo directed from front of stage. It was a holding beat. The roar of the crowd rose. They were lost in a delirium: stamping their feet, calling back the singer. But gradually silence — a tapering silence — fell.

'Ladies and Gentlemen, we appreciate most sincerely the warmth of your approbation, but we do ask, in the name of the drama itself, as well as your sincere intentions towards Mademoiselle Hortense, who is still valiantly battling her recent seasickness, that you do not interrupt the drama after each song, and thus allow the operetta to continue.'

Chastened, the audience fell quiet. The orchestra of ten (four violins, a double bass, flute, clarinet, cornet, drums and the conductor doubling on the piano) took up with special verve.

Samuel stood there, smiling to himself. He let himself drift a little. He listened to the music, the pert accents of musical operetta. His eyes softened and lost focus as the lights within the theatre changed and re-emerged, gaudily yellow-green with an undertint of purple.

There was a gasp followed by a smattering of appreciative applause.

Then he glimpsed Jack (who was frightened he would be called Gershom by his 'uncle' and hence had kept his distance). Jack was sitting on top of the boxes of the opera company. They were taking up half of Milton Road, whence they had been unpacked hurriedly earlier in the evening. Jack was sitting on the very top of the pile of trunks, acting as night watchman.

But he was clearly sleepy. His head kept nodding, like a pod too heavy for its stalk. On seeing Samuel, however, he raised a hand to him in a victorious gesture, illustrating that he had neither fan nor posy.

'*O*h, if only, Barton, you had managed to be there. If *only* you could have heard Mademoiselle Hortense, whose voice is like the very nectar . . .'

Samuel did not precisely not listen. Rather he dimmed Toop's voice down into a dull drone, like a bluebottle banging against glass, with the same irritating effect. Samuel was reorganising his bolts of material according to colour. He was also, in-between times, serving the various women who came in, searching for some late and desperately needed addition to their opera-going costume.

'The very latest furbelow, madam, according to what I read in the latest papers from Paris, is a posy of fresh flowers. Nothing else can have that distinguished air of *je ne sais quoi.*'

Mr Barton shut his eyes and rubbed his fingers together, as if touching some fabric so fabulous as to need closed eyes to summon forth its glory.

He perversely enjoyed not making sales while under Toop's gaze.

It got worse.

Toop had taken to humming, then singing at a fast canter, in what Samuel could not help but admire as a quite reasonable church choir baritone:

> Things are seldom what they seem,
>
> Skimmed milk masquerades as cream,
>
> Highlows pass as patent leather,
>
> Jackdaws strut in peacock's feather,
>
> Very true, so they do
>
> Black sheep toil in every fold.

Toop seemed in some private heaven. When finally, after what seemed an aching eternity, it reached Samuel's lunch-break.

He could escape.

He had to try not to make his movement unseemly in its haste, but he was dying to get out the door. He pushed his arm deep down inside his jacket — his modest, shop assistant's jacket of navy serge, bought off the peg from within the store itself. He adjusted his spotted blue silk bowtie and placed his trusty straw hat on his head: not entirely in keeping with his costume but it signalled some final rebarbative eccentricity.

'Don't be back late, Barton. We're still running hot with customers.'

Very true, so they do . . .

Samuel cut up past the Masonic. Everywhere he went he could hear people whistling 'Things Are Seldom What They Seem'. Inside the Masonic, in an upstairs bedroom, he heard a girl with a high, thin voice attempting the tune. From another room came a later verse of the same song.

*B*efore him lay the incandescence of the sea. From inside the shop he had seen it was a beautiful day, by the blare of light burning through the striped canvas awnings. He was overdressed. He would be hot. But he must escape. He often went for walks along the shore. The old addiction continued, from the days when he and Madeleine had walked along together, even though it was he alone who now headed towards the sea.

But somebody was walking away from the shore. It was a stranger. Napier was sufficiently small and isolated for any newcomer to be irradiated with their novelty. This stranger was a gentleman of an unfortunate size. He was walking along, however, with the almost feminine delicacy peculiar to some overly large people. They came closer. Samuel could tell it was someone attached to the opera company. He was dressed a little too carelessly, in the flamboyant, easy style of a theatrical — neither so informal as to seem boorish nor so formal as to seem clerkish. They came closer still.

Samuel tipped his hat to the stranger, who was yet looking at him.

In that second, as the two men were about to pass, each man turned, simultaneously, both faces sharing the same look of shock mingled with a whole host — a history — of other feelings.

'*Fan! For heaven's sake!*'

'*Oh, Stell, it can't be. Oh, God. It can't be.*'

The two men clutched each other, hugged deep, hugged silent, and then simply held each other for a long, long moment. This clasp was death-insistent, the kind of clasp a mother might have with a dead son, with an intensity as if to awaken cold and long-dead flesh. Then this tightness lessened and grew warm, grew heated, and was slicked down, suddenly, by a rain of tears. Both men were weeping. In broad daylight. In a public street of Napier.

Samuel broke away first. He felt down desperately into his pocket and fetched up an old, dirty handkerchief. Both looked down at it and laughed.

'You always were a dirty slut,' said Stella, and he laughed. His laugh was wild, hard.

Samuel was aware of people looking. A housemaid on the upper balcony of the Masonic, airing a sheet, had paused, stood still as a statue. Yet some part of Samuel rebelled. He was overcome with a rash desire to flout all the old hesitancies, to end every uncertainty. He felt suddenly, and wildly, bold.

'Oh, darling, come on.'

Yet he could not stop himself, the machine that was Samuel Barton living in Napier and working at Towne & Neale, from lacing his arm through Stella's and pulling him — this is what it felt like — yanking him away from the public streets, the intensity of local gaze.

They had walked in silence for a while. It was as if Samuel were willing Stella away from the points of greatest danger.

Even as they had come apart from their hug, Stella — or Arthur as he now was — had intercepted Samuel's quick, haunted look around. Arthur understood. He understood, he thought, nearly everything.

He had quickly substituted 'Ernest' for 'Fanny', but this had led to another, deeper, more haunted look on his friend's *aged* face. (Samuel's face had grown thinner, yet more defined, as if its features now expressed his residual character. At the same time this definition had been overlaid with a whole drifting weather pattern of wrinkle lines. The antipodean sun had not been kind. He was tanned, like boot leather. But he was still so residually Ernest. A ghostly litmus of the lovely, brave and foolish Fan.)

'I am called Samuel here,' Fan had said quickly, looking over his shoulder, tears still running down his cheeks.

'Oh, darling,' murmured Stella. 'This is like a dream. This is *too* like a dream!'

They were walking towards the brilliance of the Bay — it was a radiant scythe of midday light glistening up into the air as vast waves unfurled on the shingle. In the far distance the white cliffs of Cape Kidnappers. And above, a dome of phosphorescent blue. It was all as vivid as a hallucination. The sea in the distance disappeared into a shimmering of salt haze.

Where to begin?

'So Samuel . . . *Samuel?* You always were fond of that moonstruck little tart,' allowed Arthur, now they were alone. 'Whatever happened to him?'

'Oh, I'm sure he's a happy papa who snores through plays and goes home to a nagging wife. I don't know. We lost touch.'

We had to.

Went unsaid.

The small town had dropped off behind them, like a leech. Only a row of rather poor-looking wooden houses — Arthur saw them as little more than shacks — lined the foreshore.

Samuel smiled. He could not stop smiling. Even through his tears. He turned to Arthur the full force of his past love.

'*But how are you? What are you doing here? How long are you here for? What have you been doing?*'

The words came tumbling out.

Arthur's fingers were feeling in his pockets.

'I say, Fan, steady on, old boy. Don't rush a fellow so.'

He seemed to be searching for something.

Samuel led him to a tree and they sat against its trunk, backs supported, legs outstretched — both like marionettes whose strings had suddenly, and unaccountably, been severed.

Samuel watched the plump white doves of Arthur's hands delve and thieve all over his person. It occurred to him Arthur was not dressed like a gentleman. His clothes seemed distinctly shabby, his fingers nicotine-stained. But his face shone with the radiance of memory.

'Oh, Fan, Fan, Fan,' Arthur moaned. 'If only I could tell you.'

He had just taken away from his lips a silver flask of conspicuous beauty. He had supped on it for quite a considerable moment — his eyes over the top of the flask looking back at Samuel, seeming to be divorced from his mouth and thus taking on a greater, more naked eloquence.

'Oh, darling, I needed that. The shock! The shock! It quite turns one!'

He offered the flask to Samuel.

Who underwent a convulsion of indecision. He wanted to say: I no longer drink. Not like that. But the shock had made him feel he needed some kind of tonic . . . and also, to a certain extent, drinking was what they had always had in common. It was the rootstock of their bliss. He hesitated only a moment longer, glanced deeper into Stella's eyes to see if he had noticed anything, then snatched the brandy.

He emptied the nullifying, awakening, putrefying, elucidating elixir into his innermost being. He gradually felt his being lurch, as a tree must do, when a great axe strikes against its base. He was not felled yet, however.

'Oh, Stell,' he murmured — almost moaned, and the two of them sat there, like tramps, like vagabonds, holding hands, on the beach at Napier, neither of them knowing quite where to start.

'You are late. Your pay will be docked.'

All the entrancements of the night before seemed to have evaporated from Toop's face. He gestured abruptly towards Barton's station — the wooden counter that Samuel had the uneasy sense of never having seen before. Indeed his whole life, his presence in Napier, had taken on a wild unreality. It was as if he were seeing his own life through Arthur's eyes — the disbelief in Arthur's eyes.

'You live *here*? For heaven's sake. *How long*?'

The words had come out before Arthur could stop them. Or perhaps he didn't want to stop them. Perhaps Arthur's confidence in his own world, his own way of life, was such that he never, for one moment, considered any alternative. But Samuel could not help but feel the unkind imputation that it was no life at all, to be living in Napier.

'Yes. I got washed up here . . .' Samuel had said, leaving unspoken a whole aching void of sentiment. 'I thought I should hole up for a while. And take my time in making my return.'

He thought of telling Stell about Linz and the lost jewel — how his hopes had turned to ash, how he had been forced to regroup — how he had had to arduously reconstruct a self. Yet now he felt himself losing control — rhapsodically losing control. Perhaps Stell's coming to Napier marked some new direction?

'Would you like to come to my house? Well, it is hardly a house at all, Arthur, as we would have once considered it . . . but if you would like . . . I would be most . . .'

Somehow their sentences, begun so warmly, with so much fondness, did not quite cohere. Coalesce.

It was as if the vast and silent changes in-between needed time to be expressed.

'I would like that, dear boy,' Arthur had said, a little too impatiently waiting for the flask to come back his way. And then, when he raised the flask and attempted to glug, Samuel had the unfortunate realisation he had swallowed the last of it. This brought about some little crisis of unpleasantness in Arthur: it was the smallest sensation, almost a vibration, but one that Samuel was sensitive to.

It was this, more than anything, that had precipitated their return to 'civilisation'. It had taken Samuel a moment to realise this. He had been running on about his life in Napier — his garden, the night skies. He did not talk about the Visitor. Some instinct told him to keep that treasure private. Only gradually did he realise Arthur was not actually listening. He was waiting. And when a silence yawned, elongated, then split wide open, allowing the roar of the surf to enter, the screech of gannets, a whole realisation engulfed Samuel's consciousness: *I am boring him. He wants to get away.*

It hurt.

But then Arthur, on standing up, seemed to recover his good humour. He pounded Samuel's back — Samuel noticed he had picked up a bluff comedy of male manners from somewhere.

'I'll tell all the others I've run into an old chum . . .'

'Be discreet,' Samuel said, grabbing hold of the pulpy meat of Arthur's arm — to the bone. 'For God's sake. I beg of you, Arthur.'

Arthur let out a rheumy, rumbling laugh that seemed to emanate from his capacious belly, which now promenaded in front of him, as if introducing to the world his ability to consume, eat and make merry in any and every circumstance, before his actual person — whoever or whatever that was — arrived.

'For God's sake, Ernest,' Arthur said dryly then, and not a little unpleasantly. 'What kind of idiot do you think I am?'

They had walked in silence back to the town. Both of them considering separately the implications — happy and otherwise — of their meeting.

They said their farewells before they came within sight of the Masonic.

'I am coming to *Der Freischütz*, on Monday night,' Samuel said.

'Come to the party afterwards . . .'

'You will come to my house, Arthur? We can talk then. In privacy.'

'You can always send me a note,' Arthur said, rather grandly. 'We're staying at some frightful dump. Golden Fleece, I think. A more correct term I have yet to hear.'

They were standing still, amid the blitz of antipodean light: the very air seemed to vibrate and break apart into glitteringly painful atoms. This same light made each of their faces into a brutal mask — of ageing, loss of youth.

Their eyes searched the other for some lost soul.

'*Au revoir, mon ami.*'

'*Au revoir*, dearest.'

They did not kiss.

A Pearl by Any Other Name

Samuel had been about to walk, in an elaborate three-sided square, back to the Emporium. He hoped this might walk off his drunkenness.

He also hoped to lose Arthur. Or rather, that he would be lost to Arthur.

He feared, terribly, Arthur seeing him behind the counter of a shop. It did not occur to him, in the shock of meeting, to ask exactly what Arthur was doing with the opera company. But he also wanted the strange hallucinatory sense to abate. He did not like inspecting his life in Napier with such intensity. He had never been to work drunk. He was obsessed with appearing normal in every way.

Yet like anyone drunk and trying to appear sober, he found the very act of walking an elaborate contortion, requiring extraordinary ambidextrous skill: walking a tightrope would be no more difficult.

He peered out of the corner of his eye at the women passing by. (The streets were full of out-of-towners: every shop was doing remarkable business, he quite separately noticed). He glanced down at his watch. He was late, he was late. Why had the extraordinary beauty of the day turned into something oppressive? The ghost that was Samuel Barton hurried back to the Emporium.

$\mathcal{H}$e passed the rest of the afternoon in an uneasy daze. The alcohol had unleashed in him a kind of rollercoaster ride of emotions: both high, to the point he considered resigning on the spot (Toop had never seemed so unendurable, nor his customers so stupid in the time they took to make the smallest, most unimportant decision); and low, when he felt a hammer blow of exhaustion descend and he wondered if he could actually lift one foot in front of the other. He wanted to lie down on the floorboards. He became dehydrated but Toop would not allow him away to have a glass of water, let alone a cup of tea.

'We are not an establishment that allows the staff the luxury of treating themselves as members of the public, sir.'

Things are seldom what they seem . . .

It was a nightmare. Samuel clock-watched until six o'clock. He mimicked himself with perfect precision, aware at the same time he was only acting as himself. He saw himself from the outside and he despised, suddenly, all he had attained — so painfully, so arduously — over the past eight years. It was as if some garden he had been tending had overnight become withered, barren, full of poisonous weeds.

Could he not escape?

Perhaps this was the hidden meaning of the opera company's presence in Napier? It was to rescue Samuel. He felt a terrible yearning, then, to simply take off his apron, to throw it on the floor at Toop's feet. To say to him, I am resigning. It would give him such pleasure to see the shock on Toop's face.

Black sheep toil in every fold . . .

Why had he been masquerading so long? Burying himself? For what reason? For whom? Surely it was time for him to take up his own life again.

All that glitters is not gold . . .

He longed to see Arthur. He longed, suddenly, with a terrible, overweening passion — one moreover born through all the painful intervening years — to dissolve the distance of time: in talk, in words, in laughter, in drunkenness maybe. Yes, he thought to himself as his fingers nimbly but furiously rewound the russet-red bobble-edging ($^1/_2$d a yard): he would get drunk. He would lower himself into the cauldron of anarchy; he would be eviscerated by all the dark forces. He would see if the barnacle of this impostor self would drop off. Perhaps — who knew? — a pearl might emerge.

$\mathcal{O}$n his way home, he detoured past the Golden Fleece and sent a note up to Arthur's room. 'Please come and see me tonight, when the show is over. I live at

No 15 Carlyle Street. It is modest but private. I shall wait up for you, my love. Please come, Arthur.'

He had hesitated long, his whole being focused, concentrating on the gradual gathering of the drip of black ink on the nib: it balanced there, ballooned there, threatened to fall, splatter and deface the note. *Who should he sign himself as?*

Fan? Ernest? Or Samuel.

This choice of selves suddenly seemed an enfilade of possibilities: fragrant, multiple, enriching. Why did he find it subtly humiliating that he could never be Ernest again? He could be Fan. He could be Fan. He would always be, in his innermost self, Fan — peering out through his eyelids, past his eyelashes. And as for being the impostor Samuel, he had made himself at home in the mask: he had made the mask, finally, so supple over time that it had grafted onto his skin — or was, perhaps, in the very final moment of grafting — when Arthur had appeared. When the ghost of Stella had appeared.

> Jackdaws strut in peacock's feather . . .

Samuel's pen, the nib so sharp as to be an arrow that might fly straight to the bullseye of Stella's heart, traced his truth, 'Yours forever and ever, amen! Fan.'

The frisky timbre, recalled over time, faint as an echo but powerful as a memory, seemed just right. He quickly folded the note, placed it in an envelope. (He had bought the best-quality notepaper he could find in the Emporium. 'Off writing love notes, are we, Barton?' said Toop, walking up behind him. 'Something like that,' Samuel had returned, voice flat, a millisecond away from mutiny.)

Now he was saying to the hotelier he had seen only this morning — so long ago as to be another life, 'I say, could you deliver this to a Mr Arthur Park, Mr Hunt?'

Hunt looked down at the envelope, then said the name over and over under his breath. (He had the happy look of a hotelier whose every room is occupied.)

He called out to a maidservant going upstairs, carrying a ewer of hot water.

'Park, Arthur Park. Is he part of the theatrical party?'

The maidservant craned around and looked Samuel up and down. She might have been seeing something else there, some nakedness.

'There's an Arthur Robertson. Not a Park. Not that I know of.'

The man in the black apron looked into the heart of Samuel's confusion.

'A plump-looking cove? A real fat chook of a fella?'

'That's him.'

'Would be tasty on a campfire,' Hunt said, sardonic smile on his lips. 'If a fella found himself in a tight spot.'

He laughed.

'He is an old friend from London days.'

The maidservant hissed at Samuel, 'Be quiet. Have you no consideration? The theatricals is resting. Don't you know anything? Theatricals', she said, turning around with great *élan*, 'have to rest in the afternoon and prepare for the nuptials happening later on in the night. They are just arising now.'

She carried the ewer of steaming water up the stairs as if it were a sacred vessel.

$\mathscr{N}$o lover could have prepared more carefully. Samuel had been profligate to the point that he had gone into the greengrocer's and taken, airily, as if charged with a higher purpose, the three oranges off the top shelf and placed them down on the wooden counter. This was so contrary to his normal pattern of scrimping that the greengrocer, a Chinese gentleman, grinned, and, seeming to empathise, nodded and raised the golden globes. 'You celebrate the play actors?'

Samuel felt uncertain: *was something written on his forehead?*

Or was it, rather, that the whole town had gone mad (the relief) at encountering make-believe?

It was clearly contagious.

Someone outside on the footpath went by whistling boisterously and perfectly in tune 'On an Ocean Blue'.

Samuel had nodded and scooped up the golden fruit. He hurried home, all the time assaulted, *insulted* by seeing everything through Arthur's caustic glance. He could not help it.

Carlyle Street had never looked more desolately empty. Just a day or two earlier Samuel had been congratulating himself on how the plane trees, just planted two years, already had a sapling pleasantness: how they were casting neat crinolines of shadow. He had touched the old blackberry hedge where Madeleine had lived, noted how it had gone wild, and how the new house-owners were in fact trying to dig it out. All the comfort he had taken in the fact that Napier was softening, growing more like a real town, was stripped from him.

He saw only dirt and dust and mud. He cringed at the fact that the footpath had run out half a mile ago. He saw, afresh, the rudeness of the tiny wooden cottages with their tin roofs. He felt oppressed.

Yet he also, in some other part of him, was delirious. The germ of his past had always lain dormant in him: as was common with all exiles and exotics, memory was often more powerful than what he actually saw. So the little cottage where he lived usually resembled (he liked to think) a dappled little *cottage orné* from the Regency period, covered with greenery and flowers in spring-flush: all was order and reproduction; it was beautiful.

How was it then that the cottage, as he came nearer, now appeared raw, transitory, the very image of poverty? His little marmalade cat sprinted to meet him, her tail erect, shimmering with pleasure. She rubbed against his legs in a private ecstasy of greeting. (He had bought some giblets for her — even in this current crisis he could not forget his favourites.)

His little cottage was nothing like the grandiloquent spaces Stell and Fan, in their high period, had known.

He slipped the key into the door. All the smells of his pretty little place — as he saw it normally — assailed him. (Wax, incense from the Chinese greengrocer, the last waft of some wallflowers.) For one second he embraced the sweetness that greets everybody on opening the door to the building known as home. This created an almost physical reaction in him: he softened, loosened, grew more into himself. He thought: *I do not care.* He hurried about opening windows. He fed the cat.

He placed the oranges on a deep green glazed plate. He sat down and gazed at them, his face growing more and more thoughtful.

*H*e heard the final crescendo of applause. He heard this in the peculiar silence of a provincial town anywhere in the world — as if all of them were attached to some universal principle of stillness. Samuel had listened to the ringingly rowdy, seemingly never-ending roar. This was followed by a swift descent into silence, the length of a song, then more applause, hungrier than the last. More silence. The length of a song. More applause. Long applause. Endless, a hunger of applause, a wishing-not-to-end applause, a sound tunnel that intimated that everyone within the cave of that pattering sound wished it could go on sufficiently long to deliver them in their ecstatic state to a supper room somewhere, or a room with a piano, or anywhere, really, where their state of bliss might continue for a moment, an hour, a minute, a few seconds longer.

The ache for enchantment seemed to reach out into the very air and pervade the starry heavens above Napier town that night.

Samuel left the door open. He had been standing outside, listening to the clop of horses' hooves, voices, departing footsteps. He knew it would take a considerable time for Arthur to appear. He went to a particularly obscure drawer. Under a weight of sheets he found a small, folded piece of newsprint. It had been folded, at some point, into the smallness of a postage stamp. With shaking hands, he unfolded and smoothed the paper. It was an engraving with the images of Fanny and Stella on it. He sometimes wondered why he had kept such a poor, almost nasty thing, yet there was almost some form of celebration in it — some memory. Some marker.

He looked now at the faces that had been given to Fan, to Stell. Stell was about to climb into the prison van. She seemed plunged into thought, her pretty face downcast. In the background a laughing plebeian, alongside a startled one. Fan's dress was raised above a cunning obscenity of lace and petticoats. She herself was looking back over her shoulder. As if she had just heard — was listening to the footsteps of Frederick as he ran away. She appeared distracted, yet almost over-elegant, with her thin waist, her tiny tapered fingers raising her skirts up to reveal the exaggerated elegance of her tight-buttoned boots. (There was a whole pornography of imagination involved in this image.)

In the background could be seen, just at the edge of the picture, a swell: a man-about-town in a top hat and regimental moustache. It could have been Freddie. Behind him another gent, this one in a Guardsman's bearskin hat. A woman, an actual woman, stood rather dowdily in front of the guardsman, her mouth formed into a perfect O of astonishment, a blankness awaiting enlightenment.

A knock.

'*Toodle-oo!*'

Fan rose in confusion.

Stell came in. Stella — that is, Arthur — his face still painted from the stage, entered. (Though, and this made him seem instantly foreign to Fan, as if she were seeing a visitor she had never met before — almost as if Fan were a prostitute quickly assessing and sizing up a new customer. Arthur had clearly played a man in *The Duchess of Gerolstein*: he had the faint imprint of a curled cork moustache above his lips, and his hair was slicked down with pomade.

'A mere sword carrier at your service, madam!' he cried out in a stentorian voice, loud enough to reach the back stalls. 'But one whose thrust is guaranteed to deliver — aha! — a maximum of pleasure.'

Samuel, in-between wincing and laughing, leapt up. They kissed each other on the cheek. A smudge of cork marked Samuel's cheek. He had lit a lamp and put it low on a table. He had thought to place a pink silk scarf around it. Arthur, suddenly seeming overlarge in Samuel's delicate surroundings, stood there, looking around. He had just placed down on the table a frosty bottle of champagne.

'Well, Fan,' he cried. 'Get up off your arse-warmer, old love, and go and fetch us some glasses.'

*T*he bottle was empty. Or rather had the smallest dribble of semi-warm champagne left at the bottom. Fan leant forward and poured it into Stell's glass.

They watched the dribble evaporate. They had been laughing until they cried. They had reached that moment of lovely silence between old friends. All around them, palpable, almost tangible, lay the ghosts of their past, yet they were not ghosts at that precise second — they were what was real. These beings — both older, one fatter, both visually males — were as if servants to those earlier beings, who had lived, it appeared to them now, so vividly, so wantonly, so unthinkingly bravely or stupidly, yet right within the quick of life.

Arthur had been telling Fan about life in the company. How they had travelled from Calcutta and other cities in India, through Batavia, then on to the distant cities of Australia.

'We had such a bad time in Calcutta, I can tell you. The heat and then the dysentery. We had a little mutiny there. Old Renwick, the buffo bass, was fiddling with the lead kid, a pert young thing if ever you saw one. So we had a right dust-up and half the company left and formed another company. Last heard of somewhere in darkest Borneo . . . We set off, by boat, for Batavia. Luggage left behind. Stolen. Got there with the clothes we stood up in. But the lovely people of Batavia . . . so glad to see some theatricals! God bless 'em. We had a benefit concert — well, two in a row. Slam, slam! Bought costumes, had some sets built and we were away again. It's all like that, Fan. As if you don't know.'

Fan had felt exhausted, said nothing.

'We've been on the road now for over four years . . . arriving in a town and straight into a performance. We sting the locals for all they're worth. Then once we've scooped up every spare farthing, we're off to the next town. It's a life, Fan. A life . . .'

Arthur, in one liquid move, had brought out his flask from an inner pocket and laid it on the table.

Samuel glanced down at it a second. He realised it was a statement: should he partake? He was already giddily, beautifully, perfectly drunk. He was coasting along in a golden sleigh over snow so soundless, and, on passing a bump that was imperceptible, he had been projected up into the starry sky: he was dazzled by all the light about him, the brilliance of the past, which had for him, at that moment, all the gorgeousness of limelight following him in perfect sync about the stage.

'Do you remember Eliza, little Eliza Clarke? The servant girl from Southampton Street?'

This was Arthur.

Samuel realised his tongue had thickened. He reached forward and touched Stell's pouch of a hand.

'As if I could forget.'

'I ran into her in Brisbane. It must be, oh . . . over two years ago. She was guiding along a great big strapping lad she'd met on the boat. Had married him. He plainly worshipped the ground she stood on. Told me she wasn't going into service any longer. "*Had enough of crooking my back for a lifetime, sir.*" She wasn't quite sure what to call me.'

'She was our Joan of Arc,' murmured Samuel softly. 'The Maid of Covent Garden.'

Arthur was not concentrating. It was as if Samuel's words had insufficient reality beside the vividness of his life on the road.

'And true enough, she sent a note to me down in Sydney. She's got the general store — and post office! — in some hell hole. Is making a good living. Her hubby, as she calls him, is already a farmer. "And if ever you was looking for a position, sir," she wrote, "I would do my best by you. Please rest assured."'

Arthur laughed fruitily.

'Looking for a position . . . Oh, darls. The only position I like is one she couldn't deliver.'

They both had a fit of the giggles: it was inane, it was perfect.

'Remember Billie, the fireman, and that backstage fuck, and the way he wanted to set me up in a cottage? . . . in a cottage! . . . '

Arthur was laughing, tears seeping out of the corners of his eyes, as if his interior were one vast damp swamp of unspent tears. He looked like a gorgeous laughing Buddha. He took another swig.

He began to sing a ditty about love in a cottage.

He stood up and noisily sang.

Then collapsed downwards. Inwardly tumbled.

'What about poor lost Freddie. Poor bastard.'

He raised the flask in toast. Swigged hard, swigged heavy.

He offered it to Samuel.

Samuel hesitated only a moment.

'Yes, here's to darling Freddie.'

'To poor old Fred.'

There was a coruscation of silence, the burning heat of memory. Then Samuel, as if to obliterate this, glugged deeper. He took, into himself, the fiery liquid. It burnt as it went down. He saw, behind his eyelids, phosphorescent stars. He felt a jagged lurch. He realised he would be hung over. But he also realised, eerily, at this second, he did not care.

He felt untouchable.

He felt he wanted to penetrate right to the end of the night.

He wanted, finally, to know.

'*S*tell, Stell, tell me now. Tell me.' He reached forward a little inaccurately and only belatedly touched Arthur on his sleeve. 'Tell me, love, what happened to you when we got out. Tell me.'

'My father paid for me to disappear.'

Arthur's face had grown serious. Mask-like. A kind of sadness weighed it down, turned flesh to a clay-like inertness. 'I went to Europe, I wandered around for a bit. Was a teacher briefly in Liège. I tried . . .' and here Arthur's gaze grew blurred. He appeared to be staring down at the table, at a small spot Samuel had never quite seen before, on the tablecloth.

What had he tried? (As if Samuel did not know: *to get back into life, to be an ordinary person, to live as anonymously as possible.*)

'I tried, oh, Fan, love, how I fucking well tried . . .'

Arthur's voice was bitter. His face lost in memory. He shrugged.

'I know . . .' Fan reached across the table, to touch him. Awaken him again. From the clammy clasp of their mutual past.

The fact was, they had lost touch with each other after the trial. After the trial, which had been held in the highest court in the land, before the Lord Chief Justice: the trial in which they had been found not guilty.

Not guilty.

But this was, as it were, a technical result that bore no relation to the ruin of reputation, to the wholesale public ransacking of the most intimate details of the lives of Fan and Stell, of Ernest and Arthur — not to mention their anatomy.

Their bodies, their lives, had been invaded, inspected, written about; they had become celebrities, but it was a thraldom of celebrity: it was a form of being placed in the public stocks. In the past they would have been pelted with bricks, rotten fruit, ordure; they might have died in the stocks: this happened. (Just as that audience whose cheers had been still ringing in the silence of the night could turn with the same intensity into killers.)

Fan and Stell were grateful afterwards they had been pelted only with words. But words in the end, if accurate enough, or sharp enough, or malicious enough, or delivered with enough hate, can wound, can puncture the aeration needed to give sustenance to a soul. In the end Fan and Stell had been driven out of London, out of England — by words. Words had pursued them right out of existence, until, indeed, those creatures known as *Fanny Clinton* and *Stella, Mrs Graham*, no longer, in fact, existed at all. And with the death of the words, so these wonderful, extraordinary contradictory characters, men acting as women, being women, had disappeared.

But Ernest Boulton and Arthur Park had been left behind. Sediment. Residue. Ghosts in their own lives. They had no desire to see each other, talk to each other, touch each other. Why should they? Had they not each spent a long night of infamy imprisoned with the other? They were, in truth, sick of the sight of each other. Each served only as a memory of all that had happened. Like a role so thoroughly explored on the stage, night after night, both wished only for a new, undiscovered role. For the freshness of a new identity.

They had left the courtroom together, then gone their separate ways. This had happened casually, yet in such a deliberate fashion as to seem formed to some pre-existing design.

Neither could help the other (though, ironically, they were the only two who knew specifically the reality each had lived through): the best they could do was part.

And this they had done, but on such a long circuitous route that it had finally brought them together: in a tiny room, in a cottage, in a small town practically unknown to the rest of the world, called Napier.

'*N*ow I've got a good berth, love. Keeping an eye on the profits. Investor's a friend of the family. Seems all right.'

Stell always was one for putting a brave face on it. Arthur sighed. Inspected a heavy leg. 'I sing a little bit. And get out on the boards whenever I can. Can't help meself, my dear old love.'

There was a minute, teetering pause.

'I say, Fan. Do you have anything to eat? I could eat a horse and the rider.'

Samuel brought out the supper: a chicken with sorrel stuffing in aspic jelly, fresh bread, a Derby cake, to be followed by the oranges. Samuel had been busy. Arthur seemed momentarily placated and settled in, a napkin around his neck, to the dismantling of the little feast.

Halfway into ripping off a leg he looked up at Samuel.

'But you. You look all right. You look as if you've found a cubbyhole.'

Samuel, pleasantly drunk, sentimentally maudlin, nodded and shook his head at the same time. He was standing, playing a maid to Arthur's gentleman.

'Do you still get into drag?'

Fan looked at him for a long moment, then slowly, very slowly nodded. His head motion was more like an oscillation than anything.

Arthur's face grew acute.

'Seeing someone?'

Samuel sat down. Or rather he collapsed onto the chair. He realised he almost had no will. He leant forward.

'Yes.'

'Well, tell!'

'No. Tell me first about the company. There must be some choice fellows.'

Arthur looked urbane. His lips were shiny from the grease. He grinned.

'A fella's never at a loss for something to eat, so to speak.' He went on eating, then his crafty little eyes moved back to Samuel. Noted the deep enigma of his silence. That it was not a haunted silence: it was a happy — dare one say, pregnant? — pause.

'*Et tu?*'

Samuel, on an impulse, leant forward and whispered. Who better to divulge his secrets to — or was it Secret — than someone who was visiting, was never likely to return? What better, safer repository than that?

Stell sat there with her hand over her mouth, eyebrows raised in a sunrise arch, murmuring: No! You baggage! You tart! Where did you meet him? He is . . . what? A *what*? And how big? I don't believe you. You're making that up. I want to meet him!'

And so they sat there, at their ease, giggling, and supping and tutting and fluting and faking and being real.

*B*efore he tottered off into the depth of a Napier night, Arthur turned back, for a moment, as if at the pulse of a spontaneous thought.

He captured Samuel's arm.

'Fan! What about this? You could join us! You could! *You could come away with us!* We need another dresser.'

Samuel pretended not to hear. He could not — afford — to make so much as a movement. But his eyes — he could not stop his eyes — from staring with almost forensic intensity into Arthur's.

Arthur nodded.

'Yes, darl, it's true. I'll talk to the manager toot sweet. And you know when we leave. It's two nights away. They hold the last boat back for us. Pack your bags, darl. On the quiet. Be prepared.'

They Toil Not

The following day was a Sunday. A day of rest and prayer. Nobody much moved in Napier, except those going off to church. And since the supporters of the temperance movement were by and large also the faithful, those who were walking brightly off to church had the doubly sanctimonious sense of being up and alert, of doing what was right, while the rest of the world slept in, hung over.

The opera company naturally was not expected to be alive at such an early hour. But they were paying their tithe later in the day with a public concert (a fund-raiser for the local fire brigade) in Clive Square, to be held at three p.m. sharp. It was a double trick: they garnered goodwill and publicised their voices.

Mr Julian Last, the tenor, would sing 'Consider the Lilies'. Mademoiselle Hortense would favour the public by singing 'He was Despised'.

The customary artillery practice of the Napier Volunteers would be moved to take place immediately after the concert, so it would appear that the concert itself would end in an astonishing hail of bullets. (The newspaper described this as 'Napier's Salute to Harmony'.)

Samuel awoke, feeling surprisingly refreshed. He was a little groggy from the grog, but he had not been brought low by it. Besides, he had this other whole incandescence: he might join the troupe. He might stitch Fanny back onto his persona.

He bathed slowly, dressed with care. What should he wear on a dawdle through Napier, through what could possibly soon be considered his past? He chose his most dandyish costume: a cream flannel summer suit, a sailor's tie and his trusty straw hat. (He had put a new ribbon around it: best-quality heavy Cambridge blue satin @ 1/6 per yard.)

He felt both pensive and curiously alert. A tourist in his own town.

He gazed upon the changes that had occurred in the time he had been in Napier — the gas lamps, increased pavement, new public baths, hospital on the Hill — and was unimpressed. He kept seeing the town through Arthur's saturnine gaze. It all looked rudimentary. Rude even. With its absurd and boastful signs: 'Awarded Second Order of Merit at the Melbourne Exhibition'; 'To-night! To-night! First Show of New Season's Goods at Cash Palace'; 'Harry Cohen Persists In Selling Goods At Reasonable Prices!'

After a little promenade he decided, on the spur of the moment, to look in on Arthur at the theatre. They would be rehearsing, probably. He would not take up much room.

Yet as he came closer to Milton Road a certain ambivalence tainted his enthusiasm. There was nobody so superfluous as an onlooker at the unmagical rites involved in a rehearsal. He knew this. But he longed to see Arthur again. He felt greedy for his company. Besides, he might soon be . . .

So he bumped up the dark corridor leading into the Theatre Royal. Because he had left a sunlit day, he was momentarily blinded. He held still.

Voices. A woman's voice. In the middle of a tirade.

'All I want, Harry, is to lie in bed one morning in a room I actually recognise. Where I don't have to wake up and see my suitcase sitting on top of a bloody wardrobe.'

Samuel tentatively peeled back one of the double doors.

'Where I can look out the window and know what bleeding country I'm in!'

Samuel seemed to have walked, unbidden, into a drama.

The singers, out of costume, were sitting down upon the stage. They all had a rather forlorn, downcast look. As if they had been sitting there a long time. Weathering a storm. Or waiting for it to abate.

Nobody looked up when Samuel slid in. Arthur was nowhere to be seen.

A musician absent-mindedly whirled his double bass.

'Listen, darl. Listen.'

This was the manager, and coincidentally, leader of the orchestra: he was Monsieur Henri Erreux, known among the cast as plain old Harry from Glebe Point Road, Sydney. But the woman on the stage, pacing up and down, would not listen.

It had the unfortunate air of a domestic taking place in public.

'I'm sick to death of the lot of it, Harry. I want a house. I want a garden. I want to . . . *grow roses!*'

The last was thrown out, almost as an unimaginable insult.

The termagant turned and threw at Samuel a brilliant, scalding look.

Samuel felt a strange sense of double vision.

He thought he recognised an earlier incarnation in the stout, almost bewhiskered beauty of Mademoiselle Hortense.

Samuel quickly thought back to the information about her in the newspaper. She was, supposedly, a distinguished singer hailing from an unnamed French opera company. She had allegedly been born in Provence.

He tightened his focus. Yes, if you took away a decade's damage he was sure of it. And added a kind of gloss burnished up by audience applause. Could it be . . . ?

Two words formed in Samuel's mind: Miss Louise . . .

She walked briskly past 'Monsieur Henri'.

'I'm finished! It's bloody over!'

Monsieur Henri — publicist, manager and conductor — stood on the stage and bellowed, hands on hips: 'You silly bitch, where do you think you're going exactly? You're croaking out your song in one hour flat in the local square.'

The termagant passed by Samuel, deleting him.

'See if I'm there! I'm buggered if I will be.'

She slammed the door. Hard.

A wan silence fell.

Monsieur Henri adjusted his vocal tone, as if only at this point glimpsing the unwilling audience.

'All right, everybody, a break for five minutes, then it's straight into the love duet.'

*S*amuel was in a predicament. He knew it was only sensible to leave the molten mademoiselle alone. She was nothing if not hysterical. Or rather, perhaps, professionally 'temperamental', as became a grande dame of the operatic stage. But Samuel also knew she was as likely to be outside, enjoying a cheroot, sunning her old hams and relaxing.

He went back up the corridor, preparing a floral feast of platitude and compliment. It usually worked. But on his way — and it was better to leave her to cool down — he passed the costume repository. A shrunken little woman was ironing away, humming to herself. In her own world. Happy. Samuel was obscured by a rack of clothes. But close to him, hanging on tapes attached to two stout galvanised nails, was an infanta's gown. All black velvet, cream silk, silver lace. Heavy petticoats. A note was pinned to it. 'The Duchess of G. Act Two. Sc 3.'

He could not help himself. He looked both ways. Nobody was around. He slipped the gown off its nails and held its great creaking implausibility up against himself.

He closed his eyes. He pulled all the camouflage of fabric about himself. He drank in the scent of powder, paint and sweat. He crushed his eyes shut. And he remembered.

'*What?*'

For a moment, Mademoiselle's French accent stampeded back to the flat assertive tone of a lass hailing from a Melbourne suburb.

'I beg your pardon, s'il vous plait,' she said a little too quickly, making sure this time her 'pardon' had the proper French intonation. At the same time she lowered her skirt down over her shins and looked at Samuel a little more closely. She was leaning against the weatherboards of the theatre, drinking in natural light.

Samuel had asked Mademoiselle if she had ever been to Napier before.

A haunted look had come over her face. Whatever she was on the boards, she was no actor in ordinary life. Indeed, a dusky flush had begun to mount from the dart of flesh by her breast and stain up her throat. Her deep blue eyes looked captured.

'Why do you ask me that?'

Her French accent had become appreciably thicker.

'Are you not, indeed, Miss Louise, who came to this town many years ago?'

Samuel's tone was as lightly spun as possible: a thin line of filigreed silver. Not threatening in any way. If possible, almost penitential. He took a step away from her.

'I should of got my parasol,' the prima donna murmured in an undertone, glancing about herself, as if she had misplaced it nearby. She showed signs of standing up. She was agitated.

He touched her lightly, lightly, on the arm. She shifted her arm with the brutality of a woman used to being pawed. Her eyes challenged his.

'What's it to you when you're at home, sonny Jim?'

'I ask only on account of a great friend of mine. A Mr Solomon Linz. I believe the lady I knew . . . was last seen aboard the boat on which the poor man disappeared.'

She said nothing. She seemed to suddenly not dare to move.

'I don't know nothing . . .' her voice seemed to speak, unbidden. 'I wasn't there. I was below decks . . .'

'I only ask because of the mystery about why he disappeared.'

A small cloud had covered the sun. Then it cleared away. There was a look of pain in her features. As of something unhealed. Still raw.

'I am being sunburnt,' she said, reassuming her French accent.

'Please,' Samuel begged. He longed to say to her: *I too am not who I say I am. I understand entirely all the exigencies involved in adopting a new identity. I do not even care for the jewel. I feel freed, if anything, by the loss of the jewel. I could become who I am. Whatever I am. But I would like to know, to solve the riddle . . .*

But the woman known as Mademoiselle Hortense had now gathered herself together. She threw away her cheroot, in a wide arch of sparks. Samuel was reminded, instantly, of Miss Louise's strong arms. She let out a most unmaidenly laugh, from the depth of her belly.

'Well, old rooster,' she declared in a strong and flat Australian voice, 'you got the wrong customer here. I don't know nothing about a Mister Blinz and I've never had the honour of meeting this "Miss Louise".'

With this, the 'French' mademoiselle removed herself indoors.

*H*e waited around for the singing. He wanted to look at Mademoiselle Hortense again. He had to make sure. There was an immense crowd in the square. (That is, the paddock that found itself at the end of Emerson Street. It was nothing for a cow to be found there, munching on the grass. It doubled as a fire-break for the wooden town.) But this afternoon, there was a rustling bustle. People, on the forlorn desert of a Christian Sunday, had been awarded the gift of something to do.

Samuel took a seat on a cast-iron bench at the very back of the crowd. He sat in the shade. He suddenly seemed to lack all energy. He felt mystified by this somersault in his feelings. He was aware of how combustible his feelings were. Disturbed. As if the pivot of his self had been shaken.

The singers were late arriving. Monsieur Henri apologised most fulsomely for Mademoiselle Hortense's absence. She was still getting over the seasickness that had struck her so lamentably on the voyage down from Thames. She sent a message, though, which was that she would ensure that her sterling performance in the following two nights' operas (which Monsieur Henri went on to name, adding the time of the performances, as well as ticket prices) would more than compensate. She also sent her warmest regards to her most faithful audience.

A rather lacklustre gentleman laboured through 'The Lilies of the Field'.

Then Mademoiselle Alice Tibbet, a second-string mezzo, sang 'He was Despised'. Her voice was surprisingly rich. It was powerful enough to override the chatterers near Samuel. (He had looked furiously at them but they, blasé colonials, had looked back at him and laughed, and gone on chattering — about the horse sale that had been timed to coincide with the opera arriving in Napier.)

Samuel, like a ghost, got up and pressed his body through the crowd.

> He was despised
>
> Rejected of men . . .

He pushed his way to the front, then became overcome with self-consciousness. Was there something written on his face? A plaint? People were looking at him as if they recognised something about him. Moved away, as if he were contagious.

> A man of sorrows
>
> Acquainted with grief . . .

Or was it that he was so moved by the power of the music, its gorgeous stately cadences, the sadness of the lyrics, that his face had formed into a rictus of remembrance: of grief itself?

> Rejected of men.

He felt so taut he could cry, at the slightest thing.

Solomon. Frederick.

His own life, perhaps.

The moment Mademoiselle Alice finished (to tepid applause, a satirical catcall: the locals were waiting for the real entertainment — artillery fire), Samuel pushed his way out of the crowd.

He became almost abrupt. In his desire. To escape. Get away. Be untouched. Mend in solitude.

Once he was in the open he found his shoes, of their own accord, walking in a harsh tattoo of sound right up Tennyson Street, around to Shakespeare Road, past the mouldy old barrels in the back yard of the Golden Fleece. He knocked on the wooden door, with its tiny slat that he had once known so well. This part of the hotel was obscured by wooden outbuildings. There was a thin-looking mongrel standing there, stationary, flies hovering over its pelt. Its tragic eyes, those of beaten dog, looked up at the strange palpitating individual. Tail wagging, then crestfallen, falling still.

Something flashed within Samuel. He could have been back, right back in the early days, when that little dog came running after him.

He knocked on the door like a man in a crisis.

Hunt pulled the slat aside, adjusted his gaze to the brightness outside. Then, when he saw Samuel Barton, there was the tiniest ricochet of a muscle on his cheek. It said: *You! You have not been to this place for more than five years!* But his face reformed to a granite stillness. He accepted everything — attached to coin.

Samuel asked for a bottle of brandy.

He paid for it in silence.

For a moment he felt Hunt's eyes pass over his face. The man's glance burnt.

'I . . . I'm in the mood to celebrate,' Samuel Barton said defiantly. 'I have received some good news.'

He placed the bottle inside his jacket, under the armpit, and walked back under the inquisitive gaze of various Napierites. Draped in church black.

He was sweating.

He made it back to his hovel, as he now saw it. He shut the door. He locked it. And he opened the bottle.

A Pair of
Kid Gloves

She could not decide whether to go that evening — whether to risk it. She had laid out her dress, the beautiful untouched gloves, the gorgeousness of kid, their limpid quality. She had fingered them, gazing down at the tiny stitches, the miniature pearl buttons. They were an exaggeration of what a woman's hand could be; they constrained, made elegant — a visualisation of containment.

Madeleine had accepted Samuel's dictum as to her dress. She would dress, she dreaded a little to accept, as a great lady, or at least a leading lady of Napier. The great swathes of café-au-lait silk, embroidered all over with tiny violets, winking with seeds of amethyst and seed pearls, lay out on a chair. Her daughter, Alice, had tiptoed in and touched it, almost with a fairy's hand.

'Oh, mother,' she had murmured (Madeleine reading her lips). The child had then lifted up the gloves, smelt them. Her wondering eyes returned to her mother.

'I am going to the opera,' Madeleine said to her, too loudly, sitting down before her glass. She looked within. She realised she would hear nothing at the opera, and wondered if this might not be too cruel a reminder of all that she had lost. Yet she carried in her mind almost a dictionary — no! an encyclopaedia — of sounds gathered up, almost too feverishly, in her maidenly youth. She knew *Der Freischütz* from her London days; she had hummed, annoyingly, because it was so cloying, 'The Bridesmaid's Song'. She did so now, experimentally. Only to see, in the glassy mirror, her child twist over her shoulder, her face at first alarmed, then settling into an impulsive, uncheckable giggle.

Was that to be her lot? To be laughed at? The child, though, with instinctive courtesy, came towards her, brushed against her shoulder, and leant up and kissed her on the cheek.

'What is an opera, Mummy?'

'It is when people tell stories through song.'

'What is the story?'

Madeleine hesitated for a moment. What was the story?

'It is about a man . . . making a pact with the Devil.'

'Why?'

'Because he wants to win his sweetheart. He is a marksman and he can't shoot straight. The Devil will provide him with magic bullets, which have a price.'

'What price?'

The child's eyes had grown wide.

'The Devil will keep one or two bullets for himself. He will kill whomever he wants.'

There was a long pause. Madeleine had had to make a quick judgement about whether she had said too much. For a child's mind.

'Can I come too?'

'No, child.'

'But all the other children are going.'

Madeleine sighed.

'Not to this. This is not for children,' she said, leaning down and kissing the beautiful clean smell of the child's hair. Alice looked unnervingly like her own mother: a miniaturised version.

'I hate you,' Alice said, experimentally.

Her mother smiled. The child ran out. She had heard something.

Madeleine returned to her dressing. It was now six o'clock. She would need the help of Mrs Risington, who was Methodist enough to hate the theatre. Perhaps she should try to dress alone? What jewels? She went to the box she had earlier taken out of the safe. And opened it.

Within, nestled on oyster-grey velvet, was a rope of old family pearls, a glittering amethyst, almost gaudily set around turquoise, flecked with topaz and tourmaline — a mediaevalised piece of artwork, all wrought and overwrought. (A wedding gift from Leyland.) She searched deeper. There was her mother's only piece of valuable jewellery: a wheat sheath set in old diamonds — Georgian diamonds, before they were so faceted and cut. She could wear this in her hair.

For one second she thought of her mother, and seemed to feel her: missed her absence so keenly, even as she touched something her mother had owned. She placed the jewel in her hair, which was losing its colour, she noted, becoming less and less of itself, as if she risked fading away.

But what was this? There was some movement behind her. It was the two boys running down the stairs, two at a time. They were yelling. Even she could hear that. Now Alice ran by. She looked as if she was screaming. The children were fighting again . . .

But no. Madeleine got up and looked out her bedroom window. There, down below, was Mr Leyland, climbing down from his buggy. He eased his crotch, bent his legs and looked with satisfaction all around his spread. The children had come flying out but a sudden shyness brought them to a halt. The boys lined up. Alice hung behind them, peering around the corner of an arm.

Madeleine felt her heart constrict. Some kind of darkness entered her vision. She tried to keep breathing: *I will go to the opera.*

It was almost as if some sixth sense had brought him back from the farm, some foreknowledge that she was spending money, was luxuriating in 'self-indulgence', as he saw it (as he saw all music, actually: if Madeleine was deaf, he was tone deaf, immutable before the Muse).

He glanced up now, at her window. His dark face was glinting, obsidian.

Brownlee ran into her room.

'Wake up, Mum. Dad's home.'

*M*rs Linz was waiting. Samuel was late for their appointed meeting. She had been waiting now for over forty minutes. She had heard he had not turned up at work that day. (Jack had told her — he was a genial spy on all that happened in the town.) She had thought of sending around a note, inquiring whether he was ill, but she was too busy with her boarders. The house was still full. Finally she had dressed late, putting on the new cloak the Scandinavian giant had given her. This had happened earlier in the evening, in a lull of utter exhaustion.

It was just before he left. He had asked if he might speak to her privately. Creaked into her room. She was prepared: she thought he might ask for a loan.

Instead he stood there, water dripping off his hair, face raw from a fresh shave, awkward as a beau. He had virtually flung the cardboard box at her.

Mumbling: *Mr Barton.*

She was under the apprehension Samuel had bought it, sent it by this — cavalier.

She was aware of the man's raw bobbing Adam's apple as she unwrapped it — first snipping the string, then pulling back, carefully (she would reuse it), the tissue paper, to reveal the contents of the oblong cardboard box. She had drunk in the smell of newness. How beautiful it was: how lovely with promise. It was many years, she reflected, since she had had such a gala present — not since she had lived in Krakow. She took her time, all the while wondering why the great lunk of a lad was standing there, flushes sweeping up and down his face to the point where he looked crucified. He was fiddling with his tie, his starchy collar, energetically thrusting his great digit in.

'Please, sit down,' she murmured, hardly aware of him. While pulling open the box. Gershom had come in. Zeroing in, as any child would, on excitement. There, among the sheaths of tissue paper, lay a sky-blue cloak. Its lining was equally exquisite: a sharp and brilliant red. It rustled, like something living. She had pulled the cloak out of the box and found herself standing.

She was blushing. The giant had risen to his feet. Gershom was crying, 'Mum, you look so beautiful, beautiful, beautiful.' As if picking up something in the atmosphere he began whirling round and round, on the spot.

Mrs Linz said, trying it on experimentally — she longed in that second for the consecration of a mirror, 'Oh, that Mr Samuel. A man of exquisite taste. But he shouldn't have . . . he really shouldn't.'

At which the big lug stammered, in a voice of genuine pain and protestation, 'But Mrs Linz, madam, it is I, me, this man standing before you, as naked as he was born, expressing however with difficulty his adoration . . .'

It seemed to be a heavily rehearsed speech, perhaps borrowing something of the florid excess of the two operas the man had seen while in Napier (*HMS Pinafore* and *The Duchess of Gerolstein*).

She could not help smiling. And blushing. Actually feeling on her cheek such an unaccustomed tender feel. It was as if, within her body, some other feeling, long dormant, was being awoken. But her hands, her worn hands, were taking the cloak off. The impropriety of it all overcame her.

'Ask your grandmother to come here immediately,' she said to Gershom in Yiddish. He looked at her, took some sense of urgency from her tone. He hung about for a moment, though. 'Oh, Mum,' he murmured, 'please wear the cloak to the opera tonight. I would be so . . . proud,' he picked finally the delectation of that adjective from all the adjectives he knew in the world.

She made a shooing gesture away, and held the cloak distant from her body.

The poor man sank back into a chair.

Mrs Linz, with great dignity, sat down. The cloak lay beside her on a kitchen chair. She could not help straying out a hand to settle it: it must not crush.

He attempted to speak — she dreaded what further protestations and avowals were coming. She felt her whole being effervesce at the same time. She felt as if tendrils were opening and closing through every pore. For this reason she sat with her eyes downcast, but furiously blushing.

This of course made her the very picture of beauty for the poor lad.

Finally Gershom's grandmother, grumbling as she came, entered the room. She wore a floor-length apron, her hair was covered in a scarf, and whereas ten years ago she had appeared ancient, a crone, now she appeared shrunken into almost a defiance of old age: she was even more herself, more fearsome.

'What's this? What's this?' she hissed.

The poor boy stood up. Alarmed.

'Mother,' said Mrs Linz. She found herself at sea. 'This kind gent here . . . ' she indicated the man who gazed out the door, looking for all the world as if he wanted one thing only: to escape. 'This kind gent here has given me this . . . '

As if it were the last gesture possible, Mrs Linz pointed to the sky-blue cloak.

Everything held still for a moment.

Out of the window could be heard, down on the beach, a particularly large wave crash down onto the shingle, then hiss in, in a prickling fizzling fan of foam . . . then it retreated.

Mrs Linz senior advanced towards the cloak. It could have been a dangerous animal, a goose that would turn nasty. But instead Mrs Linz did something strange: she turned around, glanced into her daughter-in-law's face with sharp perception — her old eyes themselves seemed to glitter, briefly catch flame — as if she remembered her own womanliness — its needs. She pulled the cloak up. And held it open.

'You must wear . . . '

'Yes, Mum, please do, Mum, I would be so proud, Mum . . . '

The Danish gentleman had arisen. He suddenly looked immensely relieved, and proud.

'If I could. If I can. Return,' he said. 'If I may return. At some later stage. Please, Madame, Mrs Linz . . . '

But this was too much for Mrs Linz senior, whose customary scowl returned almost of an instant. She turned to him, as if she saw, instantly, he was the goose she might like to fatten, then capture and pluck, but first she must get some exercise out of him: so, grinning a little to herself quite wickedly, she shooed the poor man away.

This had happened at half past six. 'The Danish gentleman', as he became known, had only fifteen minutes to get to the train station. He had run all the way. Mrs Linz had retired in confusion. Jack had gone off to hawk the remaining fans; he also had a tray of the day's freshly made posies.

Mrs Linz was exhausted. It was as if, at that moment, she realised all that she had had to do, ever since Solomon had disappeared — all she had had to give up. Not only the steadying hand of that maddening man, but also the caresses, the bodily warmth and yes, all the love-making, which she could return to only in her mind, and then only with trepidation, unsure whether it was sinful to do so. Yet in the end she gloried in the memory, since she realised — or assumed — that was all she had, would ever have.

But now . . .

She sat there, as tired as if she had arrived at the end of a journey she had been completely unaware she was on — until that moment, when it seemed the journey might have lurched to a stop.

She was aware, looking around the little room, with its piano and the strange, stiff little oil painting from her parents, that the room had become . . . a waiting room. As if she were sitting, poised, in a railway station. She did not mind this seclusion. She did not mind these moments now, as she sat there, enwrapped in the gorgeousness of sky blue (a blue she instinctively knew Samuel had taken from the Danish lad's eyes — the same paleness as cornflowers when they fade). Her hands tentatively stroked the material, then, knowing herself to be alone, knowing herself to be unobserved, knowing herself to be at a key moment in her life, she laid the pads of her fingers, the flesh of her whole palm flat against the shimmering fabric. Closing her eyes, she let her hand feel and fall, and fondle, what she sensed could almost be a metaphor for flesh.

'Oh, but Mrs Linz!'

Samuel was standing at the door, looking in.

'The picture . . . the very picture . . .'

He seemed at a loss for words. Was pale. Very pale. He looked as if he had been sick. But for once he was beautifully dressed, in some almost antique-looking costume of tails and white tie. She smelt mothballs. But he looked a fetching gent.

'Samuel, you are all right?'

'Yes, yes. A temporary . . . indisposition, brought on by . . . over-excitement.'

He let out one of his strange laughs. She did not quite understand, though she sensed him to be disturbed.

'Are you sure you are well enough to . . .'

'I would not miss it for anything on earth.'

There was a passion in his voice that reassured her. Then he said a strange single word — almost plaintive.

'Please.'

She rose, the material all about her shimmering and making that lovely almost hissing sound of sliding moiré silk. She went to the mantel. She had made Samuel a posy for his buttonhole: saved him an exquisite little spray of lily-of-the-valley, surrounded by parma violets.

He laughed. 'I'm not sure, Mrs Linz, if I qualify as "a violet, blushing unseen".'

She looked at him, across the chasm of those who do not share, completely, a language. She noted that he was sweating. Yet it was not hot. Out the window the day had glimmered down to the beautiful blueness of evening. It was a still night — another still night — as if all our bewitched characters had gathered at a special moment, when anything might happen.

'May I have some water, madam?'

He was treating her in an exaggeratedly deferential manner. She recognised the manners from her youth. This was one reason she liked Samuel. And also for the conversation she could have. Especially about young Gershom.

'I want him to have Solomon's faith — my faith,' she had said to him at one of their private meetings. He had come to her place on a Sunday, and she played him some Schumann, then they had a courtly afternoon tea, Mrs Linz senior acting as a monosyllabic maid. Almost curtsying.

He had nodded his head.

'It is not easy here, in Napier,' Mrs Linz had said. 'Solomon, of course . . .' and she left a filigreed silence.

Samuel did not know quite what to say.

'But Gershom is getting to the age,' Mrs Linz took up again, 'where it is more and more important.'

Samuel nodded. It occurred to him, glaringly, he was not in a position to provide moral education to a young gentleman — especially a young Jewish boy.

'I would like to send him to Auckland. Or Wellington. I have been in correspondence with a friend of Solomon's, a rabbi . . . He has been instructing Gershom through letters. Of course we keep to the dietary laws,' she said impatiently, 'but at times — you understand? I feel like a barbarian living in a wilderness? I feel . . . detached from my own God. At times it feels to me . . . dangerous.'

There was a delicate pause.

'You understand?'

Samuel had sighed, shot out his leg, changed the crease on his trousers.

'I understand the feeling of living in a wilderness. Almost. But sometimes I feel as if the world I left behind was an equal, or a different kind of, wilderness.'

She considered this. And thought of the pogroms. Her face became wan.

'I understand what you are saying,' she said, 'but it is dangerous — *dangerous* — to become detached from what sustains, what is your lifeblood — what is you.'

Samuel looked lost in thought.

Then he shook himself as if coming awake.

'At times one must detach oneself from the past — for survival.'

She looked at him, had the sudden sense there was a depth, a pain in his life that she did not understand. Oh, she sensed there must have been some scandal, some unpleasantness, but the entire country, from Cape to Bluff, was full of Europeans who had come to escape unpleasantness in various forms — be it monetary, or some mysterious other. She understood that. But . . .

'I do not want my *Jack*,' she consciously used the name, 'to grow up to be a barbarian. An uncivilised being. Such as I see . . . I see . . .'

She made a gesture towards the window. Out there they heard some laddish chorus shouted from footpath to footpath: . . . *sold his wife for a pair of shoes.*

They did not speak as the sound grew louder under the windows.

'Jack will never be a barbarian,' he said softly, when the noise had abated. 'He is Solomon's son, and added to that, you are his mother.'

She bowed gracefully from the waist at what she perceived to be a compliment: but she had decided that for his own good Jack must be sent away from her. Jack must be sent, at least, to Wellington or Auckland; and perhaps in time, she would follow, if she could.

But now . . . but now, this evening . . .

She pulled the cloak about her.

'You look . . .' Samuel said, offering her his arm. Old Mrs Linz had dragged her slippers scuffling along the floor into the room. Was standing critically to the side, a one-person crowd. She nodded as they passed.

'So pretty,' Mrs Linz Snr muttered. It could have been a reprimand.

'You look . . .' Samuel murmured to Mrs Linz as they walked along outside. 'Different. I cannot put my finger on it. But you look . . . younger somehow. More carefree.'

His arm was courteously crooked under hers, and she sent through the gorgeousness of fabric a frisson, an almost bodily discharge of nervous electricity.

Samuel turned around and gazed into her eyes.

She modestly looked down.

'It is the excitement of the opera,' she murmured.

Entrances and Exits

Toop stood by the door of the Opera House, in a queue. This was a bad moment. He saw Barton passing by.

Toop had, on his arm, his own lady wife, who was wearing something respectable and brown. She bobbed into a curtsy, but was restrained from sinking too low by Toop's wooden arm. He was outraged at seeing his employee out and about. He said nothing except a hissed, 'I shall expect from you tomorrow, Barton, *a full explanation.*'

For not only had Barton not been into work that morning, but no note had been sent. And here he was flagrantly showing his disregard for all the conventions by appearing as a gentleman.

This outraged some democratic sentiment in Toop's already over-tightened breast — he was wearing the suit he had got married in, but his Betsy had fed him too well: it bit mercilessly under the arms and laid across his broad back a kind of perpetual claw of tension.

Toop felt a kind of bewilderment. Seeing Samuel dressed as he was, he understood something that had always been missing. Samuel wore his clothes

— even his antique, mothball-smelling tails — as if they were a second skin. He appeared careless, graceful, even (and here Toop crushed his lashes down, as if seeking to lower a curtain on such obscenity) — *beautiful.* Could a man be beautiful? He knew he could; he knew he could. This only made it worse.

But.

'*It is not right,*' he muttered under his breath, as Barton swept grandly past. (Those who had paid twelve shillings for the dress circle were admitted fifteen minutes before the performance began. Everyone else had to wait.)

'What is not right, dear?' his wife had asked in a semi-abstracted voice. She herself was blitzed by the beauty of the blue cloak that little Jewish woman was wearing.

Toop was almost beside himself: *why could his wife not see?*

'He is my assistant, for heaven's sake! What sort of example do you think that sets that we . . . that he . . .'

'He must have paid the twelve shillings, dear.' Mrs Toop could not keep a certain tartness, even an airy sense of victory, from pervading her voice. She shook her brown poplin edged with citrus velvet and examined the topaz brooch upon her breast.

At this point a pesky little child, a boyling, thrust a cardboard box under Toop's nose.

'Sir, would you care to buy your sweetheart a sign of your intentions?'

The little tyke had the lingo down pat. Toop, almost despite himself, found he was impressed.

'A mere threepence, sir, can make the lovely lady happy.'

Mrs Toop tittered, as did the crowd around them.

'Go on, Toop,' said a rough voice behind them. 'Spend threepence and make your lady happy.'

Flushing now, and looking as if a thorn were being drawn from a particularly tender part of his flesh, Mr Toop delved deep into his pocket and drew out the requisite coin.

It was Mrs Toop's turn to blush. Her work-worn hands — wearing the little amethyst and pearl ring her swain had bought so long ago, on the day Samuel had brought the ruby earring to Mr Linz — hovered over the tray, as if trying to sense, by emanation alone, which one was best: the little cabbage rose, or the artful spray of freesia. Both were scented, and in the coming soup of smells, either would do good service.

*M*rs Linz arranged herself to best advantage. She had slipped the cloak aside and left it, most unwillingly, in the cloakroom (a green velvet curtain, attached to what looked suspiciously like a broom handle).

'Shall I?' she asked in a suddenly timid voice. She was wearing, beneath the cloak, an old-fashioned plaid dress edged with maroon satin — a gown she had worn around Napier to every occasion of note. (She saw around her a confusing fusillade of new costumes on every woman in the dress circle.)

Samuel had taken the cloak from her, masterfully. This is how she conceived it. He had flicked it out, so for one moment there was a beautiful shower of blueness. Then he had trembled it closed so the scarlet, like the inner lips of some gorgeous flower, disclosed itself. Everyone had watched.

For this one evening he was a man of the world. A regular swell. It was as if some latent being was reasserting itself: and the long absence made its return sweeter, more joyful. He was still sweating, however, she noticed. And he looked so pale. He might still have a headache?

They had taken their seats on the balcony. (Their seats at least had backs. The cheaper seats, costing three shillings, were actually backless pews removed from St John's Church.)

Ada was surrounded on every side by the *bon ton* of Napier — in fact of the Hawke's Bay province. People had travelled on horseback eighty, ninety miles to be there. Extra trains had been laid on, and the dress circle was almost besieged by every person of note: barristers, land barons, bank managers, tradespeople of the superior sort. Samuel looked about for Madeleine. There was one seat empty towards the end of their row. (He and Mrs Linz were sitting towards the left of the front row circle.)

Mrs Linz admired the fern and palm decorations inside the Opera House. An entire forest of nikau palms seemed to have been stripped to create, inside the tongue-and-groove interior, a sort of chapel to Nature. Or was it Nature saluting Art? It could have been a tableau.

There was that sappy, just-cut greenery smell. Samuel was reminded, painfully, of Palm Sundays as a child.

Outside they could hear the pomp of the Napier Spit Brass Band playing a quickstep, 'Thy Voice is Near'. The Napier Volunteer Fire Brigade were also outside with their beautifully polished machine, in case the technicals got out of hand in a wooden hall.

The air was almost delirious with excitement.

Samuel leant out and nodded towards Dr Cogswell. He was no longer the lithe and handsome young gentleman of several years ago: he had expanded with his consequence and transformed into the sum total of his appetites. He was rubicund and heavily bewhiskered, as if hair tentacled up his unseen body and burst out, victoriously, all over his face. (He dressed his facial hair, like his hero, President Lincoln.)

Dr Cogswell unctuously saluted Samuel, but in such a way as to indicate that the very slightest acknowledgement from himself equalled probably half an hour's feverish negotiation with someone of lesser importance. At the same time, it was incumbent upon himself never to pass up the possibility of a vote. (He was campaigning for the lagoon to be drained, and for Napier to create a wharf of some substance, so it could become a proper working port.)

He had a generously papal air.

Dr Cogswell's somewhat hungry stare turned and flickered along to Samuel's female companion. He looked away but Mrs Cogswell, seeking to follow her husband's glance (such was her uneasy life: she was always treading two steps behind him, taking the wrong route, jumping to the wrong conclusion) stared with almost open-mouthed astonishment at the sight of Mrs Linz in their midst.

Of all the cheek.

She ruffled the navy blue silk around her shoulders. Had Mr Barton deliberately betrayed her? Had he purposely selected this dark silk to obscure her? Cogswell had not so much as glanced at her when she came into the room, resplendent (actually painfully shy, like a girl of sixteen off to her first dance). She had had to ask him, and, in asking him, destroy any hope, any illusion: *'What do you think?'*

This had led to one of their spats (the children erupting into a brawl out in the hall, as if in syncopation). *'How am I meant to know what you think if you don't say so, you stupid woman?'* She had cried. Her eyes still stung. He had become contrite: she was, after all, the daughter of Mercer, owner of the Aerated Drink Factory and, if truth be told, Cogswell might never have become mayor without the extravagant dispersal of free lemonade on that extremely hot day during the drought year in which he was elected . . .

Now they sat there, one beside the other, the dark penumbra of their argument hovering over their heads.

'Fancy that little creature being brought among us by Mr Barton,' she said, as if trying to think of conversation. 'Whatever can he be thinking of?'

It was important that they at least appear as a harmonious couple since they were, in theory, the leading husband and wife of the town.

Cogswell let out one of his characteristic '*hahs!*', almost an expletive of a laugh, a destructive burst of sound. 'Your *Mr Barton* . . .' He was about to say something contemptuous but Mrs Cogswell did a most uncharacteristic thing — she who always feared to touch him on her own initiative. She reached out and squeezed his ample thigh.

'Dear,' she said. Daringly. 'Hush. It is about to begin.'

*M*rs Linz beside Samuel had let out a sharp sigh when the curtain went up. It was like a body-sigh, of deep and utter longing.

The audience held still for a moment, then burst into applause.

Samuel looked critically at the backdrop he had seen Mr Kemp painting. He knew everyone in Napier was so sick of the existing backdrops — all four of them (the quaint cottage, the gaunt castle, the bridge on fire, the storm-tossed sea) — that to see a new backdrop was as good as foreign travel. He felt the plunge into absorption; looking along the row of profiles he sensed the hunger — the longing — for illusion. (A row of open mouths, stilled eyes.)

They might have been breathing in unison.

The atmospheric music of the overture began with soft incoming violins, lulling and distant horns, as a scrim descended — it was of a magic forest, glittering all over with tinsel and foil. Immediately there was a change in the tint of the limelight, so the interposing wall seemed pale as a dawn. The audience *ahhhhed*. Mrs Linz beside him burrowed into her chair. Between the backdrop and the scrim a puff of smoke crept across the floor, bubbling and rising, diffusing and providing its own softening illusion.

The strings poured in, adding intensity to the scene, rising to a climax, and Samuel — Samuel felt his skin go into goose-bumps. He lost the sense of where he was: the ferns nailed on the ceiling, the window sliding up, so now a boy — it was Jack! — had swung himself up onto the ledge, was looking in. Someone near the boy went '*hushhhhh!*' with tenderness, as if asking him only not to break an illusion.

Amid the smell of the chemicals used to create the limelight effects — sulphur, arsenic — Samuel felt his whole being explode out into space, so he seemed surrounded on all sides by the vividness of the music, its pulse, its driving energy. At the same time the whole construction of his being — the Samuelness of Samuel — fell off him, brittle as clay.

He lulled back into his seat, his arm accidentally brushing Mrs Linz's sleeve. Without either of them looking at the other, each adjusted themselves so they occupied an untouched — untouchable — space.

Mrs Linz felt the breath in her body fall away: she could have been dying, except she was — she knew it — living. She was occupying her own life in a glorious consciousness of the present.

He glanced at her, she smiled at him; their eyes spoke to each other so powerfully at this moment, they might have been farewelling . . . something.

They might have murmured '*Solomon*', except the musical instruments rose into a powerful crescendo, and Samuel and Mrs Linz, separately, found they were staring down at the stage intently.

A gun had just gone off.

'*B*ut I have paid! I have paid! I have paid!'

This was Madeleine to her husband. He was sitting with his back to her, in his study. He was looking at invoices, studying them with a gravity that seemed to indicate that the entire financial future of the Leyland dynasty depended upon the rising price of chaff.

Madeleine was walking up and down. She had taken off her evening clothes: it would have been too provocative to risk appearing in silk and jewels.

Of course he could not hear. She was even uncertain of the sound of her own voice. He did not turn around. She gazed at the back of his head. She wondered if she actively hated him, or was it only that she hated this part of him? As is common in all marriages, she wondered if she could only change that one part of him — that brackish, dark, considering, realist eye: the one that always assessed everything according to what it could purchase.

If only she could change that, he would actually be a living human being. Yet he had no ear for music. He despised the theatre as the locus of the shabby, the mean, the profligate. He did not see its point. He certainly did not approve of his wife — his wife being, supremely, Mrs Leyland, rather than the woman known as Madeleine — frequenting such a low place. She might have been going to a saloon, or the public bar down at the Golden Fleece.

Yet if he was as passionate in his dislike, she was as convinced in her advocacy.

There was nothing to keep her there that particular evening. That is, there might be a chance he would walk into her sitting room and sit down beside her. He might even lift her hand and hold it for a while. But was she to sit — like a dog? Waiting for its master?

She did not approve. The intelligent woman within herself did not approve. But she also was aware she was dealing with something more, something darker:

the ego of a male. She knew the tenderness of her husband's self regard: that it was intimately tied up with his security in having her as his dependable wife, the mother of his children. She saw him as quite a different man to the one nearly everyone in Napier knew. (When he had first approached her, at the beginning of her deafness, she had looked forward, so much, to sitting beside him, reading him George Eliot and discussing literature. She had had a whole idea, based on her London life, of what married life might be. Instead he had bought the land two days by horse away from Napier, had built a plain house in the middle of nowhere, taken her there, and isolated her. How hard, how rude, how raw their honeymoon had been. How like two strangers rubbing into each other's private hurts. She accepted the rutting — she was a realist — but even his tenderness was awkward, truth to tell.)

She was sure she did not love him, but as a woman of forty, she was not sure if love was actually a possibility with a man like Leyland. He had not once spoken to her of love in their 'courtship' — a matter of weeks, of conveyancing as much as romance. He had spoken instead of trust, need, will-power, abnegation.

This was the sum total of his romance: his raw neediness, his total dependence on her — in one sense it was a gift, and a precious gift of one human to another; but on another level it was a form of debt, and one that she could never repay.

'But the money is paid over! I have paid the twelve shillings!'

He had isolated the two words — *twelve* — *shillings* — as if they should both inspect the heinous nature of such extravagance.

She wanted to say: out of my own money. But here she entered a more difficult terrain, as she was unsure precisely what was her own money. Her mother had come to live with them in her dotage. Her few sticks of furniture (so quickly faded in the harsh light, veneers lifting, borer attacking any cheap interior wood) had been sold, and the money, theoretically, was her own. But didn't she owe it to Mr Leyland for giving her mother a place to rest her weary and increasingly confused head?

'The horses are exhausted. You have no way of getting down there.'

She left a little silence here. She had heard this. He had turned around and shouted it.

She understood what this meant. She said to him, 'I will not use the horse. I will walk if need be.'

She had gone upstairs and, with trembling fingers, dressed.

All her enjoyment, the lightness of her being had evaporated. Instead she felt a kind of leaden determination.

As she came down the stairs the entire house had sunk into an ominous silence. She did not need hearing to sense this: it was a kind of physical dread.

She had dressed even more boldly than she had intended: she had both the diamond spray in her hair, and her mother's pearls. Perhaps the argument had given her cheeks colour too. She descended the stairs, rustling, fast.

He came out of his study and stood by the door.

'I shall walk. You do not need to worry about your horse.'

He followed behind her.

'You will not walk. Mrs Leyland does not walk. Not dressed like that. Unless you want to be mistaken for a jay. Besides, it will be over by the time you get there. Stupid woman.'

This last was said as a form of tenderness. She was looking at his lips. He had on his face a naked expression — he might have looked like that as a boy, she realised, when something was being taken away from him, some favourite game he utterly loved. Marbles. He was being naked with her. Humble almost. Pleading.

Do not leave me. Please.

She went towards the door.

She pulled the door back.

She would not be imprisoned.

The buggy was outside waiting.

The groom held a whip in his hand.

Leyland had ordered it for her.

She turned back to say something to him.

But he was gone.

Who Comes?

Madeleine had come in late. The Opera House was submerged in a communal dream.

> Soar softly, softly,
>
> Gentle song of mine,
>
> Into the sky's starry circle . . .

Madeleine had been hit by a wall of heat as she climbed the stairs. Seated on each step, even though there was no view of the stage, was a statue of a dreaming person, head leaning against the wooden walls, a half smile formed on lips. (They were students from Te Aute, the Maori school.) Mademoiselle's clear high tones, strong in the middle and lower notes, and distinctive and clear in the upper range, were bathing the hall in a radiance of sound. As Madeleine tiptoed past, each statue came awake and glanced at her, strangely smiling. It might have been some seance she had come to.

> Everything has long since gone to rest
>
> Dear heart, why do you tarry?
>
> Though my ear listens eagerly
>
> It is only the fir tree tops stir . . .

She came out onto the level of the circle: she was submerged in the murk of the hall. A gloaming of gas-lights burnt overhead, and a flicker of white revealed people fanning themselves with libretti. Most people had that intent stillness of people concentrating all their senses in the rapt act of listening.

Down on the stage — and because she had arrived late the force of theatrical illusion struck her more powerfully if anything — was an antechamber adorned with stag's antlers. A maiden in white, Agathe, was standing on a balcony cut into the back of the set, the doors disclosing a further backdrop, which was of a star-drenched night: this effect was particularly successful, little pinpricks of light dazzling against a brilliant azure.

Agathe, a rather too plump lady, was dressed somewhat improbably as a maiden.

She spun around, as if hearing Madeleine's entrance.

> But wait, do my ears deceive me?
>
> That sounds like footsteps!
>
> There from out of the pines,
>
> Someone is coming!
>
> It is he! It is he!
>
> Let love's flag wave!

Agathe began waving a long white silk scarf, leaning out the window. The kerchief rippled in an unseen breeze.

Madeleine had the slightly queasy sense of arriving at a prearranged moment. A face turned to her, or rather a mask of enchantment detached itself from the dark and formed into the human face of Samuel, who, coming to consciousness, smiled a strange cat's smile of recognition. The luxuriance of the singing and music rose around her. Of course she could not hear, but everything around her — from the little boy leaning his head back against the window, seemingly asleep but actually watching intently every movement on the stage, to the row of faces along which she glanced (she had quietly sat down on the seat at the end of the row) — everything seemed so still, so poised, waiting for something to happen.

*T*he lights sank back, the curtain rose.

There was a tree trunk blasted by a lightning strike in the centre of the stage. It illuminated a dark and Gothic clearing in a forest.

But already the music, underneath, was thieving in. Was pouring in its note of unease, of lifting, hair by hair, every filament on the flesh of each person trapped in the hall.

On a gnarled branch an owl sat, with fiery round eyes. One eye blinked. The other trees rustled into life: they were atwitter with an anxiety of ravens, rooks, strange night-birds.

Caspar, a huntsman dressed in tight green hose and doublet, was making a circle with stones.

In the centre lay a skull, lit from within with a demonic purplish light.

Nearby, a severed wing of an eagle, a casting ladle, a bullet-mould.

The ominous music fingered out, subtle as a poisoned mist creeping along the ground. The violins shimmied, summoning up a liturgical chant of some unearthly singers. But just as the voices settled down to their plaint, others rose up, wailing, wailing.

In the distance a midnight bell sounded. At its final toll the huntsman, Caspar, pulled out his huntsman's knife and plunged it right into the skull.

> Samiel! Samiel! Appear!
>
> By the wizard's skull,
>
> Samiel! Samiel! Appear!

Samuel sat forward on his seat. He was hunched forward, his toes clenched tight, his heels digging into the side of the chair. Hands covered his face. To anyone looking at him he might have appeared like the Michelangelo figure gazing through his fingers at the rising waters of hell. But Samuel was rapt, was in the full force of his enchantment:

> You know that my term has almost expired . . .

He had, initially, been analytical about the stagecraft: that is, with his practised eye and ear — a faculty once trained, never quite lost — he noted the occasionally wobbly note from the soprano, and the tenor whose top notes were quite flat. In these loops of disbelief Samuel considered how they had contrived the stage: the moon was an oil lantern, with a circle cut out of dense black card. As was the owl's peeping eye: attached to a string on a pulley, which in turn was attached to a rivet on one of the wings. A stage mechanic was operating it.

> I am bringing you a new sacrifice . . .

Unbeknown to him as he sat there, Samuel lifted up out of his body and appeared behind the wings: he saw the thick, almost tar-blackened ropes holding up the drops; the tubs of limelight chemicals. Two chorus women waited for their cue, listless and seemingly hardly present, while another singer stood dressed in clinging scarlet tights: Samiel — the Devil — poised to enter.

On cue a mechanic exploded a bomb of ash, lighting it from behind with a red glass: it looked like roiling fire. And the Devil, who was attached by wires, appeared to shoot through the air, somersault, then land on his feet amid the eddying smoke.

Swiftly a mechanic had removed the red glass shade. A green light now shone out, eerily. A scrim soundlessly descended and all the animals' eyes began to glow. The light concealed within the log had had its cover taken off: a fierce purple light flickered away, propelled by a tiny windmill rotating with the heat.

> Ha! Fearsomely yawns
>
> The gloomy abyss: what horror!
>
> My eyes seem to be gazing into
>
> A slough of Hell!

Madeleine leant forward. She had instantly begun to sweat, like everyone in the hall. The dreadful scene below was playing itself out. Caspar had invoked the Devil: he would exchange a living sacrifice in order to obtain some magic bullets. He had implicated Max, the simpleton (as Madeleine always saw him — the man who couldn't shoot — an unfortunate if ever she saw one). Max was played by a meaty-looking man, a little too old for the part. His face was heavy with paint. But there was something about the brio with which he was carrying his part: the excitement, the hunger of the audience was contagious.

Caspar, dressed in huntsman's green, was more agile. Madeleine sensed that Caspar's voice might have been more compelling. He believed in his ability to enchant.

She fanned herself with the libretto and gazed along the row of faces.

This is my world, she thought. There was Cogswell, having eased himself so he sat with his legs wide apart, gazing down slightly open-mouthed: she glimpsed him as he might have been as a credulous boy, trying to decide on whether to invest a hard-earned penny (or cent, in his case). His bulbous eyes moist, he was trying to weigh up the bargain Caspar was driving with the Devil. His wife's face had crumpled in as if she were living through a toothache: she hardly seemed to be present. She had shrunk into the catacomb of her lustrous blue silks, which had the unfortunate aspect of heightening the blotchy unevenness of her colour; yet, even as she sat there, a worrying hand rose up and rearranged the neckline of her gown, pulling it downwards. She glanced for a second at her husband.

But he was not noticing.

Further along, the little Jewish woman, Mrs Linz, was seated as far back as possible in her seat, but she appeared to be gazing down an immense distance: was she looking back to Europe? Was she remembering other opera houses where she might have heard this music? Her face seemed mobile, alive — lit by something more than the strangely torpid colourings from the stage.

Had the music altered? Everyone in the row seemed to plunge into a further depth of concentration. Mrs Cogswell lifted up her right hand and began gnawing on the quick of her ring finger. Cogswell himself was gazing down, a flit of lust animating him.

Madeleine glanced down to the stage.

Max was pointing and there, on a distant craggery of rocks (lit from behind, with an eerie fountain-play of sparkling light), was a veiled woman's figure.

Samuel leant forward. He had the eerie sense he recognised . . . He tightened the focus of his eyes. Yes, he was sure of it. That ghostly feminine figure, a little too bulky for the role, was none other than Arthur Park.

> What appears there
>
> Is my mother's ghost!
>
> Thus she lay in her coffin,
>
> Thus she rests in her grave!
>
> She implores me with a warning glance!
>
> She motions me back!

A drenching happiness overcame Samuel. He wanted to yell out loud. He glanced quickly along the row. Only one person was conscious: Madeleine. Their eyes met, and a smile flitted over her face. It was a smile of such effulgence that, for one second, Samuel halted on the precipice of a thought: was she so unhappy? Was she, who was so removed from his life now, so bereft in her new life that this moment counted as . . . everything?

Their gaze held: he returned her smile — they could have been lovers. But there was something else in their smiles: a recognition of the distance between them — not only of the seats in-between them but on a larger scale: in their changing lives. He could never be her child. She could never be his lover.

> Ridiculous fancies! Ha! Ha! Ha!

Samuel broke the glance. He looked to the left. To Mrs Linz — Ada — sitting right beside him.

Ada seemed to be weeping. Or rather, her eyes were so moist that her entire being had become molten — with memory? She was far away. She was thinking about when Solomon had first introduced himself to her, apologetic, constantly touching his dark hair, as if he sought to tidy away the grease and dirt and poverty of his past. Her eyes were wide open but she was hardly there in that little hall in Napier. Hardly breathing.

> Hush! Every moment is precious . . .
>
> Watch what I am throwing in,
>
> So that you learn the art . . .

Caspar was casting the magic spell.

Samuel was aware of the shallowness of his own breathing. Sweat was running off him in rivulets. He was also gloriously, suddenly, ecstatically happy. *This is my world!* It didn't matter that it was happening in a tiny wooden hall, tin-roofed and creaking, with odd bits of mismatched carpet in the passage ways to deaden footsteps; that there was a salty lagoon out there into which people still flung dead cats; or that a barefoot boy sat balanced on a window. Inside here, inside this hall, was a universal world of enchantment.

It was as if all stages were but echoes of the one universal stage.

He felt his blood sing. A curious, intense and utter sense of ecstasy overcame him: he was home.

> Protect us, you who watch in the dark!
>
> Stay by me throughout the night
>
> Until the spell is completed!
>
> Samiel! Samiel! Appear!

Down on the stage the dreadful incantation began. The crucible began to glow.

Someone, a man in the audience down below, actually groaned out loud. Immediately other voices hushed him.

Wafts of green smoke rose towards the sky. Caspar's face became a ghastly mask. The bows of the violins were the only motion in the audience as they shimmied. The music tentatively fingered forward. He poured another bullet. An explosion of blue fire this time. The music lifted onto another level of intensity. Unconsciously everyone in the theatre leant forward in their seats.

The third bullet was poured.

The music was driving everyone, was pushing them forward into a strange psychological state so that each person sitting there felt their mouth go dry, their skin crawl: some people actually felt the backs of their necks tighten, their shoulders became sore with the sheer effort involved in not standing up, crying out, pushing along the rows, running out of the theatre. At the same time they realised they could not move. They were entrapped. They were as much creatures of this scene, that music, as Caspar himself. The music, remorseless now, physical as a powerful wave, rode into their ears. Caspar had poured the fourth bullet! And just as their ears were enslaved, so were their eyes: forest birds began to flitter all across the stage. A black boar burst out from the wings, screeching as it went, bringing along in its wake the most terrible roar of wind.

A woman in the audience, remembering the great flood out at Clive, groaned with terror. Offstage, bullwhips were cracked; there was the thunder of horses' hooves; and at this point of frenzy, when the audience was in a state of subdued hysteria and panic, four vast flaming wheels lumbered onto the stage, sparks flying out in every direction — *fire!*

The audience gasped in a delirium of excitement — would the hall catch fire? Wasn't that gunpowder they could smell? Might this be the moment of all their deaths? This apotheosis of fear — delicious, horrible fear, of extinction — passed through the hall with a swoon of an almost sexual excitement.

What was that sound?

There was a weird, disembodied booming sound, like the cry of a demented underworld.

> Over hill and dale,
>
> Through gorge and ravine,
>
> Through dew and clouds,
>
> Gale and darkness,
>
> Through cave, swamp and chasm,
>
> Through fire, earth, water and air!

Caspar poured the sixth magic bullet.

A clap of thunder resounded inside the hall.

And it was at this point, in a masterstroke of the theatre, the whole building began to shake.

The windows in their sills rattled.

The walls themselves began to undulate.

Was it an earthquake? Or an effect of the Royal English and Italian Opera Company? (Should everyone rise and rush out of the building? Or would this prove that you were a fool?)

What to do?

Caspar himself upon the stage was walking about, looking frightened.

He was gazing up at the roof.

The chandelier in the centre of the hall began to make eerie, almost drunken motions, moving around in a slow, never-ending, pendulous swing. Dust was falling from the ceiling . . .

A child was crying. Shrieking. With terror. But the mother on whose shoulder the child lay could only pat it, almost abstractedly. She could only pull the babe down onto her breast, she could only hug the child to herself in some fierce, almost absent-minded grip — because the mother's emotions were themselves so distraught. She was panting.

The extraordinary scene on the stage — no, in the hall itself, for the drama had projected itself off the stage and engulfed the hall so that there was, in these violent, intense moments, a complete unity: she could only try to keep the babe alive while she herself lived through the beauty of her terror.

For the Devil had appeared. At this precise moment of chaos the Devil had appeared in the Theatre Royal, Milton Road, Napier.

He was wearing scarlet and he had appeared in a puff of scarlet smoke from out of a tree trunk. He was advancing towards the very front of the stage. He was looking at everyone in the audience and he was screaming at the top of his voice, in a tone that was visceral with hatred, with a lust to destroy: 'HERE I AM!'

The lights dimmed.

There was a complete lack of sound.

This silence continued for what seemed an unendurable time, until finally someone awoke and the first sound of a hand percussing on a palm cracked out. And, as if another dreamer had been summoned awake, so another clack sounded, and then, swiftly, almost like a hailstorm striking a tin roof, other people began clapping and soon the interior of the Theatre Royal, in Milton Road, Napier, resounded to the most ringing acclamation: men yelled, women screamed, babies shrieked, hats were thrown up. The entire production came to a halt.

The applause would not die.

Nobody had ever seen anything like it.

They had got the chandelier overhead to swing!

They had mimicked an earthquake.

A theatre troupe in Napier had defied Nature itself.

The applause would not die. The applause would not die. Nothing would sate the audience but that, first, the strange lumpish ghost of Max's mother must appear (a great swoon of a curtsy, too pert by half). A man's face peered out from under the flaxen wig. More uproar from the audience. A note of hilarity suddenly introduced itself — the sheer relief of laughter. People began to laugh themselves hoarse. The lights were raised. Agathe came out, in maidenly form, curtsied; Max bounded on, face wreathed in smiles — he was in love with this audience. Caspar, more saturnine, a courtly exaggeration of a bow, and then finally — the audience went mad and would not stop cheering and clapping and stamping their feet — the Devil himself somersaulted out onto the stage, attached to wires.

It was a triumph.

The King of the Cannibal Isles

Ada Linz stood at the scrummage by the cloak counter. *Der Freischütz* was over. At last. The audience had threatened, in the end, not to leave. It had taken Mademoiselle Hortense herself to come out and almost admonish them. She had announced that she understood that there had been an earthquake that evening in Napier, yet she could vouchsafe that no earthquake could ever equal the affection that the people of Napier had shown to the Royal English and Italian Opera Company that evening. She herself in all her born days . . .

She then sang 'Soar Softly, Softly, Gentle Song of Mine' and at its end walked off the stage with such determination even the rudest yokel got the message that any further applause would be pushing matters beyond even the most distant encapsulation of what manners might be. Unwillingly, grumbling a little, yet their faces filled with that peculiar enlivening quality that comes from a good evening at the theatre, the audience set about making their way home.

Yet immediately the clapping had stopped, the ordinary boorish level of behaviour returned. It was almost as if people wanted to return to prosaic life as a relief. To offset the exaggerated emotions of the theatre.

This is what Mrs Linz thought as she flattened herself against a wall away from the swill of excited chatterers . . .

'It even beat the shrunken New Guinea chief they had in that big preserving jar in the visiting circus . . .'

'What a lark of a quake!'

They liked, in short, a good few hours' release, but the thought of this going on any longer actually frightened them.

So men scratched themselves in parts of their anatomy that had been pushed painfully together; women looked and noticed one another's décolletage; some assessed who exactly was leaving with whom; little protective social groupings were formed, almost as barricades, to exclude those people who were not invited to further festivities. Mrs Linz sighted that peculiar little man with the florid hairdo who worked with Samuel. His wife was holding his arm — they looked so sweet, so alone, so much as if they longed only to be invited somewhere.

Where were they all going? Was there a supper room opening late? Or were there one or two select houses in Napier where the merriment would continue?

Samuel at last had Mrs Linz's cloak. Unfortunately it had been crushed up against a hundred other garments; it suddenly seemed to Mrs Linz a little too strident in its blueness. But as Samuel held it out for her (he had fluffed it up quickly so the moiré came to life, glinted and welcomed her) she slid into its gorgeous scarlet interior, and felt its cool embrace. She shivered as it touched the naked skin on the insides of her arms.

'Shall I walk you home?'

There was a note in Samuel's voice she could not quite decipher. He looked pale, as if determined. He seemed hardly to be with her. He seemed in some other place. As if an extraordinary excitement burnt beneath his skin. His eyes looked glazed.

She had a feeling she did not know him.

'I can find my own way home, Samuel,' she smiled at him. 'I have not lived in Napier all these years not to know my own way home.'

'No,' he said, 'that is impossible. Of course I'll walk you home.'

But she still had a feeling he was not being truthful. She sensed that every fibre of his being wished to stay behind. It was his ghost she was talking to.

She laid her hand on his sleeve.

'No, Samuel. I would like to walk alone.'

He looked over at her. He had not seemed, quite, to hear. All around them the good townsfolk of Napier — of Hastings, of all the little towns in the province

— were dispersing. It was amazing how quickly it happened. There was Mrs Leyland, waiting for her buggy. She was standing alone. The diamond spray in her hair glittered.

She came forward. She was smiling. Mrs Linz, who thought of Madeleine Leyland as a rather formidable woman, looked at her in wonder. Yet perhaps it was the special enchantment of this night that strangers would speak to stranger — as friends. New friends.

'Oh, Samuel, Samuel!'

Mrs Leyland was crying. She was actually crying. This so feminine moment in Madeleine affected Mrs Linz. Swiftly she felt within her cloak and located the tiny scent-drenched handkerchief she had placed in an inner pocket for just such an occasion (imagining it might be herself).

Madeleine took the handkerchief, wept into it, murmured, 'So silly. So absolutely silly. I'm sorry. So sorry.' And went on weeping. Samuel and Mrs Linz exchanged a smiling glance. Samuel seemed to have swiftly occupied his body again: this was the peculiar fission of his relationship with Madeleine. Mrs Linz, not a little jealous, recognised this. He reached out a hand and tentatively touched Madeleine's shoulder.

She gave one giant hoot! into the handkerchief and, looking directly at Mrs Linz, murmured, 'I must apologise. Oh. Your kerchief. If I could return it. Later. If I could call . . .'

Mrs Linz nodded.

'But of course.'

Madeleine turned then to Samuel. Mrs Linz thought perhaps she had been infected by the opera. Her turn was so dramatic.

'Samuel,' Madeleine said to him, reaching out in her turn to touch him. 'The most curious thing on earth has happened.'

'Yes?'

'My hearing . . . I can hear. My hearing has *returned*.'

She laughed then, a delicious canter of a laugh.

'It happened during the singing. There was the shot . . . the shot, you know, towards the end of the piece? Something happened. I could hear.'

Samuel looked at her. He did not know precisely what to say.

'Something broke. Something cleared. I can hear, Samuel. I can hear!'

'*D*id you happen to think of . . . Solomon during the performance?'

Mrs Linz had asked this of Samuel tentatively just before they parted. They hardly ever spoke of the tragic disappearance any longer. They had talked of it so intensively at the time — he had listened for so long — it was as if, by now, it was all unsaid, and in being unsaid, was somehow spoken.

Mrs Linz thought she glimpsed something in Samuel's face, but he said nothing.

'I felt his shadow tonight,' she said simply.

Mrs Linz had gone.

'I have the protection of my beautiful cloak,' she had said firmly to Samuel at the last. 'Nobody would think of harming me in this.'

She had gathered it around her shoulders and walked away. He had stood there, in Tennyson Street, walking her dimple in and out of the gas-light. There were couples walking along, arm in arm, as if it were already a summer's night. She would be safe.

As if sensing him waiting, she turned at a certain point, and waved. This was a lovely moment.

He waved back.

*S*amuel had bounded backstage. He pushed his way in, past the locals who had gathered tentatively. (There was a cluster of lads, the red points of their cheroots lighting up the dark like cats' eyes poised to pounce, the moment the backstage door opened.) They shifted aside unwillingly for this insignificant little man. Who walked in, as of right.

Under the stage was a riot of undressing. Kerosene lamps hung low from nails bent over, attached to rafters. Doors were open off a tiny passage and he passed by a woman squatting over a kerosene can, piddling ecstatically. She smiled at him as he passed.

'Helloah!' he called. 'I'm looking for Arthur! Arthur Robertson, who doubles as a ghost. A female ghost!'

He waded through the world of fantasy: of spears lining up against the wall, discarded armour flung on the floor, racks of costumes reeking of body odour and sea spray; half-naked women, their breasts lulling out, were standing about smoking. One drank from an upturned bottle of brandy. Another combed her hair. Some had their stage makeup off, which gave their faces a chaste nakedness; others stood about, revelling in their whorish make-believe.

'Who are you? What are you doing here?'

It was Monsieur Henri.

Samuel smiled: nothing could go wrong this evening. *He was home, he was home.* This little happy unstopping pulse, like a second hand ticking on a watch that might never now wind down — sent its message through his whole being.

'I am —'

Arthur came towards him, still dressed as a female ghost, complete with padded breasts, bushy moustache and men's trousers.

'This is —' he called.

He opened his arms wide (he had suspenders looped off his shoulders, his shirt unbuttoned, revealing, behind false bubs, a sweat-slicked chest of feathery greying hair). Arthur had all the exhilaration that follows a winning performance. He kissed Samuel resoundingly — theatrically — on either cheek. Then he turned over his shoulder, yelling to the others pushing around the dimly lit, reeking corridor.

'Ladies and gentlemen, we have here one of the great actors of the stage in London. It was my great honour to work with Mr . . . (for a moment his tongue seemed to falter, as if it might of its own accord leap into the groove of the wrong word) . . . *Mr Samuel Barton.* When I was a mere neophyte in the dramatic arts I had the honour — the honour, ladies and gents — of accompanying this here *Mr Barton* on the stage and I can tell you . . .'

There was a polite, if faintly uninterested, pattering of applause. Yet Samuel felt included. The exhausted actors and singers brushed past, some smiling, others completely blank in expression.

Arthur moved in for a second histrionic stage embrace, which yet managed to be quite sincere.

'Yes, dearest Fan,' Stell whispered moistly in his ear, 'be at ease. Your secret is safe with us forever.'

*T*he party afterwards was extraordinary. Long after the night, even the most debauched theatrical among them recalled the evening with a special smile. Perhaps the quake had loosened some extravagance of spirit: the fact was every human was celebrating the fact they were alive.

They had all gone back, *en cavalcade,* to the Golden Fleece. The place was almost asleep by the time they arrived but no sooner had they got up into their rooms and decided one room should be designated for the party, than outside, on the street, could be heard the somewhat inaccurately rendered musical tones of the Napier Spit Brass Band: that is, those members who had imbibed enough to go home, climb in windows, grab their precious musical instruments and reassemble outside the hotel on Shakespeare Road.

They played a tipsy version of 'The King of the Cannibal Isles.'

One by one the hotel lights went on. It was no use. It was one of those nights when one might as well give in.

Mr Hunt appeared in a somewhat magnificent dressing gown and moustache-waxer and begged to inform Mr Henri Erreux that the saloon of the hotel would be placed at the disposal of the company. (He earnestly hoped, however, that the following afternoon Mademoiselle Hortense would favour his patrons with a rendition of her immortal 'I'm a Simple Peasant Maid' from *The Rose of Castille*, standing on the crook of the stairs, if she so pleased.)

The gas-lights were burning. 'Monsieur Henri' and Susan, a buxom member of the chorus, were finishing a somewhat maudlin rendition of 'Who'll Buy My Pretty Flowers?', to general catcalls, laughter and whistles. One of the boy singers, a tender youth of fourteen, was outside vomiting. Mademoiselle Hortense was standing, gloriously naked, in front of Mademoiselle Alice: they had got into the pantry of the Golden Fleece and divested themselves of their wrappings. They were covering each other in flour from head to foot, laughing and drunken, guzzling on a magnum of champagne: they had become two gorgeously powdered pink arabesques.

Arthur and Samuel, Arthur and Ernest, Fan and Stell were talking together, in quiet voices, about 'Mademoiselle'. Samuel had been explaining about the jewel and Solomon's disappearance.

'Perhaps there are mysteries that . . . don't have an answer,' said Samuel finally, shrugging. 'I'm not even sure it is her.'

Arthur glanced into Samuel's face.

'Well, you know the theatre. It's always been a lost and found. More lost than found, really . . .'

He looked at Samuel.

A moment's silence.

'You are coming, ain't you?'

Samuel smiled.

Arthur sighed.

'Darling, you've seen what I do now,' Arthur went on. 'I was, it's true, sent out to keep an eye on the receipts. But, well, you know, Fan, how a girl likes to have a good time, and well, you know . . .' Arthur laughed dryly. 'Let's face it. I'm just a dirty old bitch who loves fucking.'

Samuel blinked a little and looked into the face of his old friend. There was some sort of honesty here. Arthur looked back at him through the ruins of his face. He shrugged eloquently. 'I have my tot,' he raised the silver flask, 'I have my . . .

moments with the boys. I'm often on call, darls; you wouldn't believe it. And as you see, I still grace the stage with my ineffable presence . . . '

Arthur took a sip, a deep sip this time, and had the grace to laugh. It was a big silent belly laugh.

He reached forward and grabbed Samuel's arm.

'Come with us, darls. Come away. You don't belong here.' Then, as if diagnosing some subliminal pulse in Samuel's face, he added, 'Even though I can see it is a sweet little place and the people are gorgeous, absolutely one hundred per cent gorgeous, and I've seen some extremely well set-up lads on the streets around here, some real Achilles. What is it, d'you think, that gives them such nice big thighs . . . is it rugger?'

There was a pause. Arthur took another swig. Then offered it.

'I know you said you're not drinking . . .'

'I was sick as a dog.'

Arthur still held it out.

'Hair of the dog. Hair of the dog.'

Samuel took the flask and laid it to his lips. He raised it. But as he did so, he glimpsed the fact that Arthur was turning over his shoulder, looking over at Monsieur Henri and Susan, who were executing a highly suggestive can-can. Samuel stoppered the flask with his tongue. Even so, the rawness of the spirits bit into his system. He felt his head grow lighter.

In turning back, Arthur's face seemed to move into the light. Samuel looked at him fondly.

He had the distinct feeling that Arthur's face was, in one sense, all he could rely on as part of the known world of his past: it was something which, in its fundamentals, had not changed, whereas so much else had. It was familiar, and as such it was deeply comforting. It represented the past, or more particularly, the whole sordid, difficult, semi-triumphant reversal of Samuel's past — the disaster of the trial. The very fact that they were together now was part of this same victory, to do with survival, with surviving a past disaster.

Yet Arthur's face (and his own) had aged. Appetites were laid across it: partly disfiguring, partly skewering the native elements into the pendulous, the flabby. Arthur was getting older. Red veins were quite perceptible on either side of his nose. Greying hair was starting to invade his tonsure. But even beneath all this, or rather through it, and in defiance of it, was the same lively, unstoppable spirit. Yet what was their future? Wasn't it a fact they shared a past rather than a future?

As if he sensed Samuel's thoughts, a flicker of a smile animated Arthur's face.

Samuel wanted to embrace him, so he did.

'Oh, darling,' he said, and he wept. Arthur was weeping too. Suddenly both of them were heaving with emotion.

'Oh, Stella, who would ever have thunk . . . *who?*'

It was later still. Monsieur Henri had discovered his wife powdered from head to foot with flour (certain points of her anatomy glowing and ruddy) in bed with Madame Alice. They were in Mr Last's bedroom (Mr Last watching raptly). A blazing argument had ensued in the second-floor corridors, with language that was definitely not fit to print. Madame Alice, ejected, had become maudlin. She was standing on the stairs, singing and supping directly from a gin bottle. The boy singer still lay outside weeping quietly amid the ladder ferns.

Arthur and Samuel had retired to Arthur's room. But on opening the door of what Samuel glimpsed as a narrow room — the kind of room a second maid might live in — they saw a pair of energetically thrusting hirsute buttocks, while beneath lay the tranquil face of Susan, chorus member, enjoying a pensive cigarette.

Arthur pushed the door open a little wider and turned around to Samuel, his face a little lupine.

He winked lewdly.

Arthur flagrantly went in.

It was one of the local boys from the Spit Band, who had been waiting around the stage door. He had followed them back to the hotel, climbed the balcony. From here the trajectory of his adventure need not be followed.

'Look at our little local hero, what huff and puff he brings to his play,' Arthur tut-tutted.

The boy's face was flushed: intent, yet faintly bewildered by his audience. He did not know whether to stop, yet he was so far gone in his lunging pleasure — the sheer athletics of his romp — that there was no real question about what would win. So he kept up his rapt momentum, even adding to it a few exhibitionist thrusts, as if to illustrate to the appreciative gentlemen the secure degree to which he was attached to the member of the chorus.

'Darls,' Arthur said to the girl in an unperturbed voice, 'when you've finished being right royally rogered, fuck off to your own room so I can have my bed.'

She blew up at him a concentric fluff of smoke, which effectively said *bugger off.*

Samuel and Arthur retired to the stairwell.

Out of various rooms could be heard the enchantments and disenchantments, the enchaining and unchaining of the unquiet urges of the flesh.

They looked at each other in eloquent silence. And laughed.

This last laugh was loveliest and longest.

They laughed and laughed.

Until they grew into a cave of silence.

Then Arthur took Ernest's hand and began to sing. His voice crackled, hoarse.

> My pretty Jane, my dearest Jane,
>
> Ah, never, never look so shy,
>
> But meet me, meet me in the ev'ning,
>
> While the bloom is on the rye . . .

'You haven't forgotten, have you, love? When we were on top of the world, up in that lovely balloon? Before it all happened?'

> The spring is waning fast, my love,
>
> The corn is on the ear,
>
> The summer nights are coming, love,
>
> The moon shines bright and clear!
>
> Then pretty Jane . . .

He held Samuel at an arm's length.

> . . . My dearest Jane,
>
> Ah, never look so shy,
>
> But meet me, meet in the ev'ning . . .

(He gathered Samuel in, pulled him into himself.)

> While the bloom is on the rye . . .

They laughed. And kissed.

'You'll come away, won't you?' Arthur whispered. 'You will come.'

Arthur radiantly smiled at Samuel. Winked.

He offered Samuel his flask.

Samuel took it, raised it to his lips and tipped it back.

But it was empty.

'*We*'re off!'

Samuel was wandering home. It was four o'clock in the morning. He knew he was due back at work in a few hours at the Emporium, if he was going to continue his Napier life. He knew that if he did not turn up (and eat humble pie, as the saying went) he could kiss his job goodbye (as the saying also went).

But the last words of Arthur, so murmurous, so confidential, kept echoing in his inner ear.

'Well, darls, it's like this. We finish our last performance of *La Somnabula* at 10.35 p.m. Do our customary fifteen maximum curtain calls. Mademoiselle does her encore to intimate to the adoring public they should bugger off, then we're on the boat out of here. Within an hour. Everything is packed in advance, waiting for us, apart from the set from that night. That's struck immediately, behind the lowered curtain. While the clapping is still going on. Once we're aboard we're off . . . *We're off. We're off.* So you need to join us by midnight. All right?'

Arthur had left here a quivering emanation of silence. He had arched his eyebrows. His pulpy lips had formed a tremulous smile.

We're off, we're off, we're off — its lovely sibilance echoed in Samuel's ear.

Yet as Samuel walked, so he looked about the sleeping town. It had plunged into the deepest point of its nightly slumber. The quake, he could see, had brought down one or two chimneys.

A single brick stood expressively in the middle of the road, surrounded by a corona of crumbling plaster.

But apart from this, the Royal English and Italian Opera Company seemed to have passed through Napier without changing anything fundamental. Or had it? Hadn't it, in fact, revolutionised his entire being? He knew now where his home was: and it was, of course, in all the intoxications of the theatre. This was when he was most viscerally alive. This other being walking home now, inside his clothes, was a kind of impostor. Even his name was unreal.

Wasn't it?

He thought of the reality of life on the road (his footsteps sounding, so loud in the early morning stillness). Arthur had told him, laughing until tears had leaked out of the corner of his eyes, about their arrival in Napier. Being kept out in the slipstream for thirteen hours, the whole troupe seasick, suffering nausea from the ordure of the pigs and sheep miserably grouped on deck. Yet they had managed to pull together a convincing enough *Pinafore* within hours.

Arthur had shot his legs out, gazed down. 'It's a life, when you get used to it,' he said modestly. Suddenly he was exhausted. He had stood up, grey as a ghost, and said, 'Listen, darls, I'll just die if I don't crawl this moment off to bed. I'll see you later tonight. After the show? That's a promise?'

They had embraced quickly, lightly, in that fleeting way of people who expect, within a few hours, to meet.

Samuel detoured so he walked past his place of employ. Past his past. He gazed in through the dark plate-glass window. The earthquake had rearranged the window display: a tottering mass of pickle jars had collapsed and come to rest against the window. One had broken and a dark puddle, a lake, was slowly spreading out, down the crêpe paper, heading towards a broken shard of a teacup. Samuel's first instinct was to get in there: to clean up, to restore order. He was surprised at his proprietorial urge. He laid his face against the glass. It was cold. Chill. It calmed him curiously. He realised his skin was burning. His breath fanned out across the glass: in the crepuscular light he traced his initials — no, his name.

Fanny Clinton was 'ere

He webbed the words on glass with his fingertip, but already the name was fading, the mist was flittering away the words — his proclamation had gone. Only a faintly dirty smudge lay there, in the fine mist of dust from the quake . . .

He peered within. It looked as if nothing fundamental had been broken: the skylight, showing the first paleness of night turning to dawn, had not come down; the brick walls had stayed in place; but further back the shelves of the men's department had disgorged their contents in one swift throw — as violent as a fling of dice from a cup — onto the oiled wooden floor.

Samuel wondered how his own department fared. Had the women's dummies hopped across the floor? Undergone their own mad, enchanted dance? He could not see.

He placed his hand against the glass, peering in. On closer inspection he could not actually make out the lineaments of anything — everything had been subtly altered. All was changed. Bolts of black material had fallen out and merged, mucked up, with the pale greys . . . It was as if whatever current of energy had emanated from within the molten core of the earth had, that evening, issued forth such a chain of repercussions, over so wide an area and into so many lives, that one was a change to the immutable order of everything within Towne & Neale's Napier Emporium.

He sighed.

Couldn't he get in there?

He took his hand away from the glass. There, in ghostly apparition, was a model of his face. The enigma of the words — Fan . . . 'ere — was chalkily present still. He reached forward — both good citizen and person hiding something — and brushed the shapes into a murk.

He turned away.

*H*e wandered back homewards. Down Emerson. So still. (He wandered down the very middle of the road: living in a small town made him marvellously proprietorial.)

Moment by moment, light was increasing in density; second by second it was as if some brilliantly raw sun had risen, rinsed in the purest waters of Antarctica, magnificent in its truthfulness of colour and the intensity of its scrutiny. Shadows were leaping long, hitting wood, scurfing up weatherboards in a percussive bang; the gilt on St John's cross was glistening now, was afire; the first rooster of Napier made its cockcall.

What was everyone dreaming?

Was the entire town listening in their slumber to the songs they had heard? Each person selecting for themselves the role they might like to play — or in a nightmare be condemned to play? Max, the man who cannot shoot; Caspar, in league with the Devil; Agathe, the brightly oblivious maid; her cousin, mocking, knowledgeable; or the Devil himself, so saturnine, so attractively physical as played by Mr Last, filling his tights with such conspicuous concupiscence.

And then, Samuel thought to himself, there was the hermit, who came on the stage at the very end of the opera. This improbable, sacred creature, listened to humbly by everyone: an oracle of course. The Hermit of the Forest.

This was not him. Could never be him.

He retraced his steps, homeward. Yet as he went, little by little the night was slipping away its gorgeous canopy so that his world — the world he had been living in for the past eight years, the town that had given him refuge — rose into the first fingerings of morning light.

His mind went back to Madeleine Perrett. It was early on in their acquaintance, when they were still circling round each other. They had halted, one day, outside Towne & Neale. It was early spring, when clouds of dust were caught on every breeze. Mosquitoes and fleas were rampant. The townsfolk were struck down with sore throats, colds and fevers. Madeleine and Samuel alone seemed excepted.

A new shipment of goods had arrived and was being unpacked, from a dray, outside Towne & Neale's front doors. She and Samuel had been discussing the immortality of the soul. (Samuel had been mute.) Madeleine was agitated. She had thrust her umbrella towards the vision before them.

'Is that all we are here, Samuel?' she had cried. 'No more than one case of Tartaric Acid, one case Coleman's Blue? One ton of figs, five tons of hoop-iron? Thirty drums of raw linseed oil? Nothing more? Always trapped in the inert. The purely material?'

446

So many years later, Samuel sifted through his soul to see if he disagreed.

He found himself listening. For so long all he could do was ache for the great roar and bustle of London streets. He had longed to be back in what he saw as his real life: the world of plate glass and gas-light, of department stores, hotels, banks, exhibition halls, docks, warehouses — in the beautiful din of London.

He had taken to walking along the Napier seashore immersed in the roar of waves: this was the real core of Samuel and Madeleine's communion: both of them had listened raptly to the beat of the ocean waves down onto shingle, and they sought to absolve the loneliness of their souls by hearing within it the roar of the great city.

It only lit their isolation more startlingly. But now the silences, or absences, had a different tune. His soul had become attuned to the great matt of silence, which comes from living in so isolated a part of the globe. He was, almost unknowingly, soothed by it.

Everything looked suddenly, and almost appallingly, beautiful.

It is true that on a still morning, in clear light, most things can appear annunciatory; but this morning this quality seemed particularly potent.

Samuel walked on.

But wait, who was this?

A very old man, bent as a question mark, was going from door to door. He was mumbling to himself. He was ghost-like, dun-coloured and faded.

It was Old Tom, doing his rounds.

He did not know, as Samuel did, that he was no longer officially Napier's night watchman. But, as if the termination of his duties were immaterial (or pertained to the daytime), so in the darkest hour before dawn he awakened, pulled on his old greasy frock-coat (the silk now tattered, run almost into feathers), he took up his lantern (still unlit, the wick saved for emergencies) and, unbidden, he did his rounds.

Samuel's compassion flickered for the old fellow.

Old Tom came closer, closer. He mumbled before the padlocks of the Venice Saloon door, shaking them, clanking them: testing them.

And now he came towards Samuel, not precisely looking at him — Old Tom was now so bent he could not stand up straight. It was more like one animal sensing another.

'Good morning, sir,' he said in a light, reedy voice — a voice that seemed to float far away from his age, his old bones. He lifted his gaze: a pale bleached blue stare for a moment glanced over Samuel.

'You are of good spirit?'

'I am, Old Tom.'

The old man paused, nodded, and seemed to be about to go on. But something nagged at him. Kept him there.

He raised in his hand the lightless lamp.

'Did you know, sir, that I fired a gun at the funeral of the great Napoleon?'

'I did, sir. I heard tell of it.'

The old man nodded, as if in agreement.

'What was he like?' Samuel asked, of a sudden.

There was a long pause. The old man was about to go on with his rounds.

'Who, sir?'

For a second Samuel gazed down into the old man's eyes. There was both a residual crafty look, of an old dodger and survivor, and beyond (or around it, or even in its depths), a deeper blankness: a kind of eternal silence into which eventually the human form itself would pass.

'Who, sir, indeed,' Samuel murmured, his eyes watering. He reached forward and impulsively patted the old man's greasy shoulder.

'Be of good cheer, sir,' said the old man, turning. 'We on St Helena here, sir, have every reason to be happy.'

He moved on, to rattle and pull on the next padlock.

The tide was running. The tide was running fast, and out. It was near to midnight.

Captain Bush was eager for *The Silver Cloud* to get under way. The theatricals, unwilling to be parted from the rapturous farewells on the wharf, were being rowed out to the schooner. There had been singing; there had been a brass band playing.

Mademoiselle Hortense had had to ride in an open carriage from Milton Road to the port, preceded by the Napier Spit Brass Band. They were themselves preceded by the young blades of Napier in their dashing Volunteers' blue and scarlet uniforms, bayonets glittering and flashing.

It had become a competition to see how many bouquets could be thrown into Mademoiselle Hortense's open carriage. She was wearing every jewel she possessed — including, if one had looked particularly closely, one piece in the shape of a fly. She wore this boldly, wantonly, placed on her breast where, in another person, their heart might be.

She acknowledged most gracefully the adoration of the crowds.

On arrival at the port she had curtsied low, waved, curtsied again, then stepped aboard the boat in which she would be rowed out to the ship.

The crowd had pressed forward, roared its approval.

*A*rthur was waiting.

There was one final boat to come.

He had scanned the crowds, searching for his friend. He had prepared certain members of the cast. These lucky individuals were looking forward to meeting this (confidentially acknowledged) legend. 'You wouldn't recognise the poor love. She's been masquerading as a clerk, I think. Timid. Wretched as a mouse. Living on the smell of an oily rag. But we'll rescue her! We will.' Arthur had prepared a feast and party, once they were all aboard. He had laid aside frocks, going so far as to talk Mademoiselle Hortense into allowing Samuel — or rather Fan — to wear the Duchess of Gerolstein's grandest ballgown.

And now, as the last boat was rowed out to the ship, Arthur hung over the side. There was a fresh wind rising. The captain was pacing about, flexing his fingers. All over the deck the opera company trunks were being stowed. The rowboat came alongside. Arthur peered down. He could see there were four people aboard, one of whom could be Fan.

The captain called out that the moment the last passenger was on the rope ladder, he would sound the bell.

Already Arthur could hear the spume and foam of the sea at the ship's bow. It was tugging, tugging.

Could it be Fan?

Let it be Fan.

Up the rope first came a very drunken Caspar.

'Never have I seen such a totally wonderful, *maaaaarrrvellous* audience. I have half a mind, half a mind — hic! — to stay in Napier.'

He was pulled, animate as a sack of spuds, over the side and onto the deck.

He was followed by a similarly intoxicated parcel — Max.

The third person aboard was the Devil.

In the light coruscation of fireworks going off from the shore — the ship's bell had sounded, the ship began to slip away — Arthur looked down and saw that the fourth person was not Samuel at all: it was the beautiful young man he had last seen, in athletic performance, on his very own bed. He was now dressed in sailor's clothes: he was commanding the little vessel back to land.

*W*hat had delayed Samuel?

It was something as discreet as his weekly appointment.

The Visitor had come.

Samuel was to tell him he was leaving.

He had packed.

The Visitor said nothing but presented himself, his full physical magnificence, to Samuel. Samuel knew to say nothing but there was for a moment a long appreciation, of delectation. With his hands, as if he were a sculptor moulding, he let himself touch the Visitor. He glimpsed, as he did so, the man's eyelashes. They were moist. Lip found lip. From here there was the long rapture, the isolation within the moment.

Perhaps if the Devil had looked in the window he might have seen two men engaged in something sordid. It might have been a death struggle, but this was its trick: it was the other half — the beautiful half — of two men engaged in physical contest. The splayed thighs, the open panting mouths, the attempts to subjugate, to triumph — even, at moments, to humiliate: all this was here, too, in the iridescent ideogram: but what the two men were engaged in was that perpetual search which enlivens human nature: which is to end time, to seek for one moment to stand upon the brilliance of a moment — to live purely within the second, and only within the second.

It was impossible of course, this search. Even within the second, Samuel found himself both watching and remembering. He was selecting what he would remember and storing it for whatever lay ahead: loss of physicality, loss of self perhaps. Disappearance from his Napier life. He glanced at the clock. He still had time.

But this was richness now, this was bounty and beauty, this was everything to him: and it was nothing too. It was a truly ridiculous rite — laughable, obscene and childish. A tear slid his face. And soon enough — too soon! — it was over.

It was over, and Samuel realised it was already too late.

*I*t was through the gift of literature that Samuel Barton met his true friend. Madeleine Perrett had begged Samuel to contribute to a Penny Reading for her favourite charity. The Readings, she explained, were popular with *all classes*. Samuel agreed, to this extent, to lend his voice: he would read from *Bleak House*, choosing as his scene the immortal and touching moments when Esther reveals that she has lost her beauty to smallpox.

So it was that the lovely loops and tendrils of language reached out and attached themselves almost organically — without the listener being aware of it — to the enigma that was Samuel.

Among the audience, towards the back, were a visiting Danish forestry worker who believed he was at a Temperance meeting; a Maori worker for the Napier Gas & Pipe Company; and a sailor who worked the East Coast.

Samuel's reading had been poignantly delivered. In fact he had brought to his performance the consummate intensity of an actor who intuits the essence — the iridescent shape — of a possible other being.

People had wept. Miss Perrett had adorned herself almost ostentatiously with a pair of deeply reddened eyes. Many people had simply got up at the end of the Reading and, like ghosts, walked from the hall.

That special silence descended.

And bloomed.

The loveliest gift of all was the Visitor. Who had presented himself, unspeaking, silent, waiting at the back of the crowd that had crushed around little Mr Barton. He and this silent man had exchanged an (at first) questioning look, which had changed (on second glance) into a questing look, which had softened, melted and became finally (on the third exchanged glance) a frank admission that one was waiting for the other.

Perhaps all their lives.

With luck, they might even grow old together.

We Escort You to Games and Dancing

*T*oop had hardly a moment to chafe Samuel. Indeed, on seeing him come through the door exactly on time, and without more than a pale 'Good morning, sir' putting on his apron and digging into the hard work involved in cleaning up after the 'quake, Toop's carefully prepared insult — *Well, a comedown from the dress circle, no doubt* — died on his lips.

Toop seemed to glimpse something in his own soul then that he did not quite like. Barton had gone into his own section, and stood there silently. This moment had lasted longer than would be considered normal so Toop called out to him, 'Still in a dream from the other night? Wasn't it wonderful?'

And he began — this was truly terrible when Toop thought back on it, lying in bed that night — he began singing, with his lovely light baritone, almost the voice of a lyric tenor, floating high and soft, 'The Bridesmaid's Song'.

> We entwine your bridal wreath
> With violet blue silk;
> We escort you to games and dancing,
> To happiness and wedding bliss!

> Beautiful green, beautiful green bridal wreath!
>
> Violet blue silk! Violet blue silk!

Why not 'The Hunting Song'? he excoriated himself later that night. Or 'The Drinking Song'? So much more suitable. But the simple fact was that it was 'The Bridesmaid's Song' that had burst from his lips.

The other shop assistants had been startled; then one, the little woman who worked in the shoe department and who prided herself on her gentility, went towards a new piano, raised the lid — this was strictly forbidden — blew the powdered mortar off the ivory and ran her fingers across the keys in a tentative caress.

> Beautiful green, beautiful green bridal wreath!
>
> Violet blue silk! Violet blue silk!

Toop had not stopped. It was as if whatever was within him had to come out.

They all began, then, to sing. And clean up the Emporium. Return it, as far as possible, to rights.

(Later the *Daily Telegraph* would print an encouraging — nay boosterish — piece about the singing heard on the street outside Towne & Neale and how it displayed the pluck of the British spirit . . .)

Yet Toop noticed after a while the one person not singing was Samuel Barton. Perhaps he had no voice? Poor thing, he thought. As he laboured.

Yet just when Toop's spirit had run dry, just when all the emollient in his voice had gone — *Violet blue silk! Violet blue silk!* — he was surprised to hear behind him a new voice: a voice that sounded rusty from lack of use.

It was faint, uncertain — tentative as to tone, as well as power. But it was, unmistakably, a mezzo-soprano.

Gradually the voice took on authority.

It was a woman's gorgeous voice.

> Beautiful green, beautiful green bridal wreath!
>
> Violet blue silk! Violet blue silk!

Other voices fell away.

The voice grew stronger — found its pitch, its clarity of tone.

The voice bewitched. It was full, clear, resonant and sweet to a quite remarkable degree.

Toop turned. He walked behind the cast-iron frame on which was enthroned the elaborately florid cash register. He turned the corner and there was Mr Samuel Barton, covered in dust from head to foot, barely recognisable in his dirty apron, not even stopping but rapturously, it seemed — *Violet blue silk! Violet blue silk!*

— stacking the bolts of material back on the shelves, according to their exact tincture and shade: and he was singing.

The End

Historical Note

*I*ridescence is, frankly, an imagining. But it is based on a very real nineteenth century British scandal, which occurred in May 1870. The case was so explosive that it introduced a new meaning to a word in the English language: *drag*.

A little more than one century later, in 1974, I studied the scandal as part of my doctoral studies in social history at the University of Warwick, England. Ironically I decided to stop my university studies in order to become a writer of fiction. In some senses then, *Iridescence* is part of my life come full circle.

The repercussions of Boulton and Park being arrested at the Strand Theatre in 1870 were far-reaching. The case started out as seemingly an amusing frolic. Within British Theatre, there was a long-standing tradition of gender reversal which seemed to underlie the amusement with which the case was initially treated. But swiftly the case became a nationwide moral panic, exploding into newspaper reports, editorials, debates about what could be printed in newspapers, limericks, jokes, steel engravings, line drawings, carte-de-visite photography and eventually into the sexual imagination of the period — as pornography.

As the *Saturday Review* put it, 'The loathsome disclosures of the trial, given in disgusting detail, made the charge a national scandal.'

Boulton and Park became contemporary celebrities whose infamy lasted long in the English imagination. In a pseudo-scientific book on 'sexology' at the turn of the twentieth century, they turned up as transvestite prostitutes working on

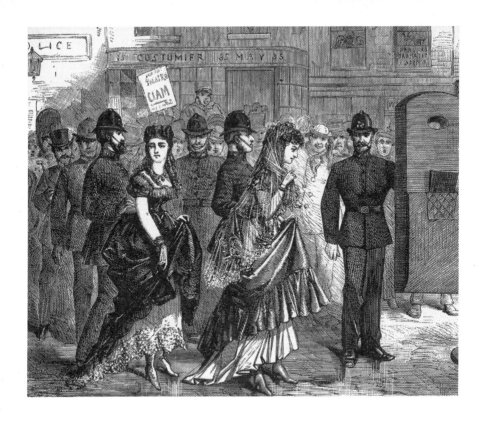

the streets of Lisbon. They also re-emerged in pornography, more than thirteen years after the scandal, in *The Sins of the Cities of the Plain, or The Recollections of a Mary-Anne, with Short Essays on Sodomy and Tribadism*, a short excerpt of which I reproduce in the novel.

In 1974 I did an extensive study of the case, using contemporary broadsheet newspapers from the *Times* to the working-class newspapers, like *Reynolds News* and the *Illustrated Police News*. Part of the dynamism of the case came from the way Boulton and Park could be used to illustrate political theories: they represented a morally bankrupt leisured class, for working-class papers. For the broadsheets, they were worrying symptoms of decline in an imperial nation at its zenith.

The case, in some senses, paralleled but preceded that later defining moment in British culture, the Oscar Wilde case of 1895. The parallels were that Wilde and Boulton and Park had all existed in the semi-protective world of the theatre — a world of make-believe which allowed, and even celebrated, a degree of sexual ambiguity. In both cases, they came to grief when they took this freedom off the stage and into life. But one could argue that Boulton and Park, and Oscar Wilde, were exponents of a lifestyle that would become commonplace in the next century. They were unwitting pioneers. Dare I say it, but the entire case of Boulton and Park really did illustrate the importance of being Ernest.

*S*ome details: for reasons of euphony, I swapped round the drag names of Boulton (known as Stella of the Strand) and Park (known as Fanny). I could not forgo the delight of a drag heroine called 'Fanny'. For similar reasons I appropriated Park's Christian name (Frederick) for Clinton. Ernest Boulton, Frederick Park and Lord Arthur Clinton were very real characters. Clinton was, indeed, the third son of the fifth Duke of Newcastle, an MP for Newark. He also fought, with distinction, at the Siege of Lucknow.

Boulton and Park's case was finally heard, after an inordinate delay, a full year after their arrest, in May 1871. By this time much of the steam had gone out of the case. The Boulton and Park families obtained legal counsel of the most illustrious sort, allegedly costing more than 3000 guineas. A decision was handed down in startlingly quick time: fifty-three minutes. A contemporary wit, using a fittingly theatrical image, described the scenario as 'The Power of Gold: An Entire Operetta in Five Minutes Flat'. It was written by 'Mr Whitewash'.

The first hearing had taken place in May 1870, in the lowly magistrate's court in Bow Street. The second was held before the Lord Chief Justice and according to the *Daily Telegraph* — 'was elevated to the dignity of a state trial'. Between the two, a much larger event had occurred which shifted people's understanding of the world. The French had been defeated at Sedan by the Germans. The map of Europe had been swiftly rewritten. The glittering and corrupt French Second Empire was over. Various newspapers tried to ally the Boulton and Park case to the French defeat: it illustrated a decadence at the heart of the British establishment. As the *Irish Times* said in an editorial headed 'English Rottenness': 'England has fallen from its supreme position: externally it is the systematic and ruthless plunderer of the weaker nations on earth. Internally its upper classes have led lives which disregard fundamental principles . . . England is slowly and surely losing power in both moral and military regards.' With sepulchral grandeur it added: 'The future historians of the Decline and Fall of the British Empire will disclose this case to the wondering and horrified gaze of posterity.

'Yet the second hearing of the case had none of the heat of the first. It still attracted crowds, but the numbers had much diminished. Newspaper coverage was extensive but seemed to have no traction. Of course by this time Lord Arthur Clinton was dead ('from exhaustion, resulting from scarlet fever, aggravated by anxiety' according to *Burke's Peerage*. He had not surrendered on his arrest. He died within a matter of weeks of a warrant being issued for his arrest.)

In the event, the defence had the authority of an illustrious medical specialist, Dr Le Gros Clark, Examiner of Surgeons to the Royal College of Physicians. His testimony outweighed the unauthorised investigation of a simple police surgeon: the damaging evidence of anal dilation, which had so caught the sexual imagination of the Victorians, was translated into the innocent by-product of heat. It illustrated, partly, how little was known about homosexuality, let alone transvestism which is not necessarily synonymous with homosexuality at all. Servants disappeared, and when they were brought back, their evidence had shifted considerably from their earlier testimony. Frederick Park bulked up and grew a moustache. Mrs Boulton gave testimony that her son had been given, from childhood, to harmless play-acting as a girl. Mr Park testified that he gave his son large sums to live on: his son had no need to live as a homosexual prostitute.

Boulton and Park were speedily found not guilty. But the implications of the case were so disturbing that Boulton and Park's reputations were forever after ruined. They had been placed in 'that moral pillory', as the *Daily Telegraph* intoned, 'from which there is no escape'.

A hastily scribbled pencil note I found in the archives says it all. Dated 17 May 1871, the note is from the Metropolitan Police Commissioner to the Home Secretary and concerns the warrants of arrest for Boulton and Park's friends (who were seen as part of a wider 'conspiracy to entice people into buggery'): 'Were the warrants for arrest to continue to be in force or be set aside?' asked the Police Commissioner.

The answer from the Home Office was: 'I should hardly think they would, but whether or no, I think there is no occasion to give any directions as to the warrants other than that it should be — confidentially — not to execute them. I think it would be just and, with that end in view, the parties should keep out of the way for a bit'.

My imagining is that Boulton 'kept out of the way for a bit' by holing up in Napier, a small New Zealand town.

The rest is fantasy.

Sources

$\mathcal{T}$he plays Boulton and Park acted in were *A Morning Call*, written by Charles Dance and *The Hunchback* by James Sheridan Knowles. (Julia was a role first created by the inestimable Fanny Kemble in 1823.) The songs Boulton sings, 'Fading Away' and 'The Bloom is On the Rye' were written by Sir H.R. Bishop and Anne Fricker, respectively. *Der Freischütz* of course is by Carl Maria von Weber. I used Henry Mayhew as one source for information about nineteenth-century London. I spent many enjoyable hours at the British Library and the Alexander Turnbull Library in Wellington. Jenny Horne gave me valuable help concerning nineteenth-century plantings in Napier, and Adrienne Simpson information on opera in colonial New Zealand. All mistakes however are my own. I also have to thank the Randell Cottage Residency in Wellington, which gave me the freedom and spark to start off this story.